D1521967

WATERGATE AMENDMENT

A Novel

JOHN FITZGERALD

Dedicated

Pammy Sue!
My Children
Erin, Sean and Kiernan
My Grand Children

&

To Mary
Who held the light.

PROLOGUE

President Nixon sat staring fixedly into the camera. He knew what he was about to say, but could not comprehend how it all came about. The technician finished a whispered countdown, "Four, three, two, one," and pointed his finger at the camera. "Good evening, my fellow Americans. I am addressing you from the Oval Office. On thirty-seven other occasions, I've spoken to you from this office, where so many decisions have been made that shaped the history of this nation. Tonight, I wish to discuss another situation that will have an effect on our nation, and me as president. I shall resign from the office of the presidency effective noon tomorrow...."

He mustered all the strength and discipline he could as he labored on through the prepared phrases, remembering not to display clenched fists or his forced smiles. His real thoughts were on how this all happened. On his last election, he carried forty-nine out of fifty states. How could everyone turn against him? How could he be brought to such a humiliating end of his public life?

He'd never find out.

PREFACE

It was a warm summer day as Father Mulrooney drove through the rolling farmlands of upstate New York. The fields were a lush green, as it had been a wet spring and warm summer. The black and white Guernsey cows looked content, grazing in the open pastures, some under shaded trees. This time of the year he enjoyed being a priest; summers afforded him a lot of free time. He could play golf when he wanted and fish the many streams and lakes in his parish. He had a long list of invitations from his parishioners to use cottages or boats. He enjoyed this casual, leisurely lifestyle. However, he did take on the responsibility of visiting the Farview Hospital for the Criminally Insane, the local state mental hospital. It was an interesting, but temporary assignment, just for three summer months. He took over this summer post as Hospital Chaplin for Father Horan, who was off studying in Rome.

This was the third visit Father Mulrooney was to make to Farview. After entering the large facility, he had to go through a security check just like any other visitor. It was not so much a concern

with smuggling in contraband, but rather innocent items that could be used as weapons or help
in fabricating tools. Father noticed that he was always checked when he went into the hospital, but
never checked when he left.

After completing his security check he remarked to the guard, "You gentlemen always
check me on the way in, but not on the way out. I
guess you're more concerned with things appearing than disappearing."

"Well, Father," said the smiling guard, "it's
that most visitors don't understand that what
they bring in could cause problems. As an example: a gift of a regular belt to you is fine. But to
certain patients it could be a means of suicide, or
they could strangle someone with it. Even some
types of magazines can cause certain patients
problems." He then smiled at the priest and added, "So we just make sure we understand what
is going in for everyone's safety, and the patients
well-being, Father."

"I understand, Officer Labinski," Father
Mulrooney said. "One of the patients gave me a
present. It was a Kleenex box holder made out of
playing cards. It was quite an interesting piece of
artwork."

"Oh, you must have gotten that from Jude
Thaddeus," said the guard. "He's an interesting
one. Been here longer than me, and that's been
many years now. He just sits by himself and
plays chess all day. I heard him babble one time
about some big chess game in the 1800s in Berlin.

Anderssen versus Dufresne, I think. He kept saying it was the greatest grand masters match of all time."

The guard paused, thinking for a few moments. "He must have done something horrible; don't know what it was. His file is locked away deep in the vaults. They have to keep him on heavy medication."

Father Mulrooney said, "I didn't have the box checked when I left; I just took it for granted that it was okay."

"That's fine, Father. You might say it's like food," the guard said in an exaggerated Irish brogue. "We're more concerned about what's going in than we are about what's coming out." Both men laughed.

Father Mulrooney made the rounds of the hospital. In the early afternoon he celebrated Mass in the small chapel. Some patients and a few staff members attended the service. Afterward, Father Mulrooney noticed one patient who remained at the rear of the chapel, and recognized that it was Jude Thaddeus. He was holding another tissue box.

Father Mulrooney smiled at him while walking slowly up the aisle to greet his summer parishioner. "Hello Jude. How are you today?"

Jude sat in the pew, slumped over, clutching his prized tissue box. He lifted his head; his eyes clear and hopeful. "Father, can you hear my confession?"

"Yes, Jude. if you like I'm free now, ," Father Mulrooney said.

"I don't want to go into the confessional. I think it's bugged," Jude said, pointing at the two small closet-sized rooms used for confession. "I want to sit in the middle pew, in the center of the chapel."

"That's fine Jude," Father said in a kind voice, as he waved his hand in the direction of the center of the chapel. The two men walked slowly and sat down, both facing the altar.

"Bless me Father for I have sinned." Jude spoke in a low but determined voice. "Now this is an official confession. Upon your sacred vow to the Catholic Church and God, you can't disclose to anyone what I am about to tell you."

"In confession, it's between you, me, and God alone. What is said here remains here. Jude, I took a vow of obedience to the sacraments. I'm obligated with my life and soul to keep that vow," Father Mulrooney said with compassion and authority, but he was thinking, *perhaps he will confess his terrible crime*.

"Father," Jude cleared his throat. "I have little time between medications, and they're probably looking for me now, so I must be quick." He then handed the box to Father Mulrooney. "I made you another tissue box. It looks like the first one. I had to make the first one to make sure it got out undetected. This one has the first ten sheets clean and on the remaining tissues I've painstakingly written a manuscript. Do with it what you can. It's my story, and that's why I'm here."

The rear door of the chapel suddenly opened, and standing there in white uniforms were two large male nurses. "Jude, we've been looking for you," said one of the men. The nurses walked quickly down the aisle.

"I'm hearing confession," Father Mulrooney said flatly.

Jude stood up, looking directly at the priest and said softly, "I'm finished telling my sins, Father. If they ask I only talked about chess." He then walked like a robot toward the two nurses. "In Berlin 1852, Anderssen put on the greatest exhibition of precise devastation. He crushed chess's Grand Master Dufresne with a record of subtle moves."

The large male nurses latched onto his arms and started escorting Jude down the hall. He was still talking loudly. "Anderssen would crush Spassky, Smyslov, or Larsen. And I could crush Anderssen."

As Father Mulrooney witnessed this sorrowful event, he was saddened that such a brilliant young man had lost his mind because of his obsession with the game of chess. Later that day Father Mulrooney left the hospital. He walked out holding the tissue box Jude had given him and no one took notice. He carried it back to the rectory, hurried up to his bedroom, and in the privacy of the room, he lifted off the top tissues. He was surprised to see the neatly printed words written quite legibly on delicate tissue. *It must have taken Jude years to complete this work.* That very evening, he started to transcribe the tissue writings to type. This book is a result of that work. This is Jude's story.

CHAPTER 1

Pocantico Hills was a beautiful estate in the lush green Hudson Valley of New York. The grounds were groomed to perfection on this warm spring day. The trees were filled with leaves, and flowers were everywhere. Jude seemed in a trance as he looked out the limousine window as they slowly drove up the mile long driveway. This would be the day Jude had planned and dreamed about. He was being courted by one of the richest, most powerful men in the world, Governor Nelson Rockefeller. Jude was confident he would make the right impression. His college professor from Harvard, Henry Kissinger, was sponsoring him for this rare introduction.

Dr. Kissinger had his own thoughts as he stared out the window without speaking. He had made many visits to this estate, but this trip was somewhat different. He was introducing a real maverick to Governor Rockefeller. Jude Thaddeus was a genius all right, but he was raised in an orphanage. Jude had no family or background to feel comfortable with. His appearance was quite common, although his jet-black wavy hair blended well with his dark almond eyes. He had a Roman look with chiseled features. He stood almost six feet tall, not muscular, but trim. The girls were attracted to him like moths to a light. However, he had kept his distance from any long-lasting relationships. Dr. Kissinger liked him, respected his intellect, and the fact that he was quite mature for his age. He was a loner and a planner.

Kissinger reflected on his own background: escaping from Nazi Germany in 1938, coming to America without money, and how the Rockefeller Foundation helped support him. Henry worked in the army's counter-intelligence service during World War II. That's when he worked very closely with Nelson Rockefeller. Both were members of the OSS, which later became the CIA. Those were good times, and Nelson had helped Henry to get a scholarship to Harvard. Kissinger studied the world of politics and power. He and Nelson would work very closely, so they could make this world a better place if they had control.

When their limousine reached the main house, a doorman was waiting to escort both Jude and Dr. Kissinger. The three walked quietly down the impressive hallway. The walls were adorned with an original and expensive art collection. The white and black marble floors glistened, reflecting the abundant flowers on the various tables. Before Jude realized it, he was entering the Governor's study.

Governor Rockefeller rose from behind the enormous desk, showing his guests the famous "toothy smile." Extending a hand to Kissinger, he said, "So nice to see you again, Henry."

Kissinger said something pleasant in return; his marked German accent was an odd contrast with Rockefeller's raspy, nasally New York voice. Kissinger continued, "Governor, I would like you to meet the young gentleman we discussed, Jude Thaddeus." Kissinger put an arm around Jude's shoulders. "Jude, it gives me great pleasure to introduce you to a very good friend of mine, Governor Nelson Rockefeller."

Jude jerked his eyes away from a series of pictures showing Rockefeller greeting notable world leaders, politicians, and celebrities, and gripped the Governor's extended hand. Managing a stiff smile, nervous but confident, he said, "It's a great pleasure to meet you, sir. I have studied you and what you have accomplished. It's a remarkable record."

The Governor's smile became broader, showing most of his large, square teeth. "I've heard a great deal about you. I'm pleased to meet you too, Jude."

Jude reflected for a moment basking in the warmth of his host's greeting. Rockefeller managed to sound as if he were interested in his meeting with Jude. Or was it because Dr. Kissinger had arranged the meeting? Rockefeller didn't have any idea, yet, of just how interesting this meeting would be.

While Jude was trying to decide whether or not to sit without being invited, Governor Rockefeller went over to the elaborate, cupboard-topped bar against the sidewall. His back to them, he asked, "Would you like a glass of Sherry, grown and fermented right here on Pocono Hills? I can assure you this is the finest white Sherry outside of Spain."

Mildly lecturing, professor to student, Kissinger told Jude, "This is perhaps one of the finest Sherry's in the world. The Governor takes great pride in his vintage wines."

Jude said, "I'd appreciate the chance to taste vintage Sherry." He wished they'd get these preliminaries over with so he could tell Rockefeller the opportunity he was prepared to offer him for the right price - ten million dollars.

Jude sat down when Kissinger did, in the big leather chairs facing the large ornate desk. Rockefeller handed his guests their glasses and took his place in the even bigger, throne-like chair behind the desk.

After ceremonially tasting the wine, the Governor looked directly at Jude and he remarked, "The secrets of making great wine are in the selection of the grapes and the timing of the harvest. Doctor Kissinger has told me you're one of the brightest students he's met at Harvard and you possess some unique talents."

"He has a very unique ability to see things others miss and he has the highest intellectual mind of any student I have encountered," said Kissinger.

"Yes," Jude agreed calmly, and looked the Governor directly in the eyes. "Thank you Dr. Kissinger, I believe you're correct."

As if a little annoyed by Jude's objective assessment, the Governor said, "If you're so intelligent, why don't your Harvard grades reflect it?"

Kissinger put in, "I didn't say he was the best student I have encountered - only the most intelligent."

Jude said nothing, watching Rockefeller, who was again attending to his Sherry. After a minute, Jude said, "I have the brains and ability to get higher grades than anyone who ever attended Harvard. But why should I? I'd be conspicuous, and that's not what I want. I prefer to be noticed only when I want to be. I don't have any interest in being famous - at Harvard or anyplace else. I want to be wealthy. A straight four-point-0 won't get me that. There's an old saying, 'A student's work for B students that manage companies that are owned by C students.' Being inconspicuous and making things happen is the best way... for those of us, not already in the political or business arena," Jude added, pointedly looking around at the expensive knickknacks decorating the Governor's study.

"Only money and power can buy invisibility," remarked the Governor dryly. "Unless you're broke and stay broke. Then it's easy to be invisible. However, I trust you seek money and power. Just how are you going to achieve such a lofty goal? And please be brief."

"From you, Governor Rockefeller," said Jude bluntly and firmly. The Governor smiled, but was not amused. He had just acknowledged the end of the preliminaries. Jude went on, "I can attain my goal by helping you to attain your life-long goal... the goal you have been seeking all of your adult life. The goal you have been planning for, working for, and campaigning for. You see I understand your main drive in life is to be president of the United States, and my plan is to make you the president of the United States."

"The presidency?" The Governor laughed out loud and shook his head, though still not amused. He turned and looked at Dr. Kissinger and then turned his stare to Jude. He continued his criticisms. "I didn't invite you up here to discuss political matters or my ambitions. I don't care how smart you think you are, or that others think about you. You're just a kid, a senior in college, even if it is Harvard." The Governor rose from his desk and started walking towards the large bookshelves on the far wall. He stared at the books and the many pictures as if thinking as he walked slowly. Now with more emotion in his voice, he said, "I am the governor of the most powerful state in the Union. I have more money than my children and their heirs will be able to spend. I have more business and political power than anyone you know or know about. I can make or break millionaires with the stroke of a pen. I have enough political power to make a call to the White House...it doesn't matter who is there...and they will listen to me."

Jude sat motionless as did Dr. Kissinger. Rockefeller took a sip of his Sherry and said, "You may be a bright kid...Doctor Kissinger thinks so. And I was willing to meet with you to see if you're the kind of person that could fit into our organization. I pay top dollar for key people. In fact, I think enough of Henry's opinion that I was willing to double the best offer you had. You will make more money working for me than you would with any other job you will ever have. I know we can find a spot for you, and you will have a bright future with us." He paused for a moment, and then in a low voice, said, "Now, let's not start off with you trying to sell me the Brooklyn Bridge. Hell, I almost own it now. I am not interested in chasing distant clouds at my age."

"It's not the Brooklyn Bridge or clouds, sir," Jude responded steadily. "It's the presidency, and it's not chasing, it's achieving."

"Now, Jude..." Kissinger broke in anxiously in a high-pitched voice. He then fell silent at a slight gesture from Rockefeller.

"All right kid, I'm listening," Rockefeller said with a serious look on his face.

"I'm not interested in being invisible because I'm part of your organization, or any other organization where everybody stays anonymous for a salary. I intend to make my fortune by manipulating people and events. I'll only be paid if I deliver." Jude paused for a moment and then continued, "I will deliver. I am good at chess." Annoyed at having slipped into false modesty, Jude corrected himself. "Hell I'm better than good, I'm excellent at chess! I've taught some international masters, and I've beaten them all at one time or another. It was me who trained and coached and laid the game plan of Bobby Fisher to beat the Russian."

Rockefeller nodded, still willing to listen a little longer. "You remained under the radar screen, you might say," he suggested

"Precisely chess, like life, involves maneuvering players and their interactions and circumstances. Chess is a game of knowing when and where to move and how to make your opponent move for your advantage. A chess player learns how to be patient, how to bide time, how to see an opponent's strengths and weaknesses, and how to take advantage of both. He learns how to set up promising situations and how to take advantage of other's mistakes. If I'd wanted my picture in chess magazines for a month, the major papers for a day, I would have taken the title from that fat Russian and walked away with a couple hundred thousand dollars. I believe that's cheap notoriety. Instead, I decided to take charge and ensure that for the first time in history, a young American would be the World Chess Champion. My price for this service was that if a verified representative came to ask about it, Bobby Fisher would admit that his win was due to my influence. He will also admit that I've beaten him in unofficial matches in the last two years. Governor, you are welcome to send a representative to verify this information."

Rockefeller's playing-along look had faded. His face was now perfectly blank...no expression at all. After a few minutes thought, he remarked, "It's a little hard to see where you'd fit in. If you have a campaign plan for an election, forget it. So far I have spent thirty million dollars and have gotten one electoral vote for it. I'm not going to spend anymore, so forget about getting rich on my campaign treasury. I guess it's just the Brooklyn Bridge, after all. I already have a few fast talking people that have many ideas and plans. I don't need any more. And certainly not one with delusions of second-hand grandeur."

Dr. Kissinger set his glass down carefully on a low table between the chairs. It made a little click. "Governor, I wasn't forewarned about Jude's proposition. But, it occurs to me that I've seen him play chess. He plays with uncanny determination and I don't recall ever seeing him lose."

" Rockefeller and Kissinger traded a long, expressionless look. Then Rockefeller turned, looking directly at Jude with piercing eyes, holding his glass in one hand like a pointer. "Just for the sake of discussion, then, what game or strategy do you have in mind, Jude?" he asked in a smooth, questioning manner.

Jude's lips turned up slightly forming a devil-
ish smile, with eyes of confident determination he
asked, in a soft voice, "Have you ever heard of a
chess player by the name of Frank Marshall?"

Both Rockefeller and Kissinger again glanced
into each other's eyes seeking some indication for
response. Both men mumbled no, they hadn't.

Jude waited till there was silence, and then began to speak as if he were lecturing the two adults
in the room. Jude continued speaking in an infor-
mative pleasant voice saying, "Frank Marshall
was a brilliant chess tactician and a champion
player and was the U.S. Chess Champion from
1909 till 1936. He became famous for his unique
strategy he termed 'The Swindle'. The swindle
strategy is not even taught today, because it is so
difficult to pull off. But Marshall was proud of
this ploy he developed, even wrote a book on the
subject. Marshall's Chess Swindles. Bear in mind
gentlemen, in the game of chess a swindle is a
ruse by which one player tricks his opponent into
not realizing the real strategy. Utilizing this tactic,
one employs a hidden agenda with the freedom
to implement undetected movements cloaked by
obvious but plain faulted moves. Utilizing this
psychological method he can create confusion and
other subtleties as means of controlling the board.
He can direct the opponent into pitfalls and other
areas for his own benefit which will result in victory. In this game plan our player appears to be in
a total loss position, or in this case with no chance
of success, then in faint incomprehensible moves,

he eliminates his unaware opponent. The end result of this victory is achieving our goal with the Governor becoming President Rockefeller."

Rockefeller and Kissinger traded a long, expressionless look. Then Rockefeller turned, looking directly at Jude with finely tuned eyes, holding his glass in one hand like a indicator. "Just for the sake of discussion, then, what game or strategy do you have in mind, Jude?" he asked in a smooth, questioning manner.

"I'd like to have another meeting with you in two weeks, Governor." Jude spoke as a clever salesperson closing in on a deal, only to make sure the customer was worthy of the product. "At that time, I'll have prepared for your consideration a complete game plan that will put you in the White House...as president."

The Governor smiled, looking back toward Kissinger. "I appreciate your bringing this young man so I could meet him, Henry. But you know my schedule's going to be busy for quite a while. I believe the best way to handle this would be for Jude to meet with Jack Chandler. Jack's knowledgeable about our plans and our resources. He can put Jude in the picture."

Kissinger's grunt was noncommittal. Jude wasn't sure if he was being given an opportunity to prove himself or shoved off on some subordinate. He felt uncertain until the Governor spoke again quickly.

"Jack will report to me, and if your plan makes sense to him, he'll have the authority to approve the plan and make all the arrangements. He is a key member of my inner circle. He has access to power and influence like no one you have ever met." The Governor paused for a moment longer, then said, "As to your fee, Jude...if Jack approves and we can accomplish the goal, you will be paid your ten million dollars."

"I appreciate that, sir," said Jude, thinking that at least Rockefeller hadn't choked when Jude stated the price tag, and that he was being taken seriously. He was to get a hearing - a real hearing. All he had to hope for now was that this Chandler didn't turn out to be the deal-killer type. Jude was aware that many powerful people would have on their staff those appointed to keep them out of trouble. Their job was to hear proposals and then politely and effectively say no thanks.

As if reading his mind, Rockefeller added, "Jack's a capable man with my complete trust. Top of his class in law school - Yale." Rockefeller again showed his toothy smile. "He's in *Who's Who*, if you want to look him up - he is not the anonymous type, that's not his style. But he is effective."

"Your confidence in him is all I need, sir," Jude said quickly. "I look forward to meeting Mr. Chandler. Perhaps Doctor Kissinger can contact him and let him know how to reach me."

The Governor smiled and walked over to both men, offering his hand first to Kissinger and then to Jude. "I'm afraid I have another meeting now. But this certainly has been interesting.

I appreciate your bringing him up here, Henry." He then turned, looking directly into Jude's eyes, saying, "Jude, we'll be in touch. I hope you have a comfortable trip back. Goodnight and thank you again for coming."

As they left the office, a tall man in a gray pinstriped suit, an aide or secretary perhaps, approached them. He fell into step with them as they moved down the corridor and remarked, "Your car is waiting." Then he handed each of them an envelope. "This is from the Governor, for your time. I trust you'll have a pleasant journey home, Mr. Thaddeus. Always nice to see you again, Doctor Kissinger."

Jude waited to open the envelope until they were safely on the private plane. While Kissinger was in the restroom, Jude quietly tore the envelope open. His eyes grew large, for this was the first time he had ever seen a thousand dollar bill. His envelope contained three of them. He folded them carefully but kept them in his hand, thinking. When Dr. Kissinger returned, Jude said, "The envelopes must have gotten mixed up. Mine had three thousand dollars in it." He opened his hand to expose the cash, looking for a response from Henry.

Kissinger smiled and shook his head. "No mistake. The Governor is a very generous man. He compensates me far more than a couple of thousand dollars, for time spent on his behalf. If money is what you want, he has it, and will pay handsomely for what he wants. I will say he watches his money. He doesn't give money to bums on street corners and he doesn't remain rich by wasting time or money." Dr. Kissinger then paused for a minute looking out the small window, and then slowly spoke in a formal direct voice. "Jude, I was a little embarrassed in front of the Governor, and disappointed in you for not telling me of your intention of laying out this plan of yours. I think now is a good time to explain it to me."

"If the Governor is interested, I'm sure he'll tell you all about it," said Jude in a light cheery voice. "If he isn't, well, the plan is designed for him alone. Without him there is no plan, and no use discussing it."

"All right Jude, keep it to yourself for the time being," Dr. Kissinger said, as if thinking of it himself. He then turned to the side to prepare for a comfortable nap.

Two weeks later Jude was on a plane to New York City. He was picked up at JFK Airport in a long limousine. Jude was surprised that the driver had recognized him as soon as he cleared his baggage. He was driven without any preamble to a tall nondescript office building in midtown Manhattan. Jude was escorted through a busy first floor reception area, then up a private elevator. On the forty-seventh floor, the elevator doors opened to a large office space. There was a receptionist sitting behind a large dark wooden desk. She was beautiful, well dressed and well groomed. With a bright smile, and eyebrows raised, she said, "Good morning, sir. Will you follow me please?" She walked like a model, every movement smooth. They walked down a narrow hallway to a large conference room. She entered first, directing Jude to the large conference table. "Is there anything I can get for you? Coffee, juice, or any other drink you may wish?"

Jude said, "No thank you," and as he spoke he noticed a man sitting at the far end of the table. He was dressed like a Wall Street lawyer; thousand-dollar suit, razor cut hair, in good shape, with a leathery tan face.

The stranger rose to introduce himself. "Good morning. I'm John Chandler. It's nice to meet you, Jude."

Jude spoke warmly. "Good morning, Mr. Chandler. I didn't notice your name on the directory. Are you one of the junior partners?" He said this knowing it would put Mr. Chandler off-guard.

"You are quite observant, Jude." He now paused gathering his thoughts and emotions.

"No, I am not a junior partner, nor am I listed with this firm. This is just one of the many offices I might be found in on any given day."

Chandler picked up his attaché case and set it upon the table. He opened it slowly and took out a yellow legal pad, placing it on the table. He began right away. "The Governor said you had a novel proposition and asked me to look into it for him. I understand you have a plan that is quite interesting to him."

Jude pointed at the attaché case. "Are you recording this conversation?"

Chandler responded quickly, "Why do you ask?"

"I hope it is being recorded because I want no inaccuracies in what I am about to tell you."

"You can rest assured there will be no inaccuracies. I made a career on not making mistakes."

"Well, then let's begin," Jude said. "In a nutshell, I have a plan to make Governor Rockefeller president of the United States."

"Oh please, don't tell me you have a scheme to get the Governor elected president," Chandler said almost in despair.

"I didn't say I would get the Governor elected president, I said I have a plan to make him president," Jude said.

"Is there a difference?" Chandler asked quickly.

"Yes, a big difference," Jude said flatly. "One is possible. The other is not."

"As everybody says, it's a great country. Anybody can grow up and be elected president, theoretically of course. As you're surely aware, the Governor has poured millions into past campaigns without even managing to get the party's nomination. He's accepted that the time is not right and the opposition's too strong for him to pour more money, effort, and time into another doomed attempt. Quite frankly he's not up to it. So then, Jude, what is your plan to make him president, a revolution?"

Fleetingly, Jude wondered if the man would even blink if Jude said yes to a revolution. He held his temper, but did say, "A revolution is too impractical; too difficult to control. Who can predict the outcome?" Jude said with a sigh.

"Well, Jude, I am pleased your plan doesn't include a revolution, but what is it all about?" Chandler's tone was serious.

"It will take an amendment to the Constitution. That, in turn, will require a lot of money, a lot of maneuvering, financing of various campaigns, perhaps many favors called in. It will require a great deal of control and influence in the oil industry. I know, it sounds rather convoluted, but the goal can be accomplished. For Governor Rockefeller to be president, he must be appointed to the office."

Chandler made a notation on his pad. "Well, that's a new approach, at least. An amendment to the Constitution, hmmm, precisely what sort of amendment were you considering?"

"An amendment that would change the Constitution and enable an un-elected person to be appointed president." Jude spoke as though he had thought of every detail in depth.

"I gathered that," said Chandler, equally as patient. "But we live in a democracy, Jude. I think you would have a better chance with a revolution."

Jude felt his anger rising, but kept his voice cold. "Since the assassination of President Kennedy, do you realize who is next in line, if anything happens to L.B.J.?"

Chandler thought a moment. "The Speaker of the House, McCormack."

"You're correct, Mr. Chandler." Jude continued speaking in a matter-of-fact attitude. "Speaker of the House of Representatives. There is no vice president, and there will not be one until the next election. Mr. McCormick is the oldest member of the House. A Republican with a bad heart is one heartbeat away from being president. Just the thought of having a Republican fill his shoes is enough for L.B.J. to stay alive and have legislation enacted so he could appoint his own vice president. The amendment would be the vehicle Governor Rockefeller would need to become vice president...by appointment."

"And then president?" Chandler asked.

"In due time, that's the goal," Jude said quietly.

"There are those who claim that Kennedy's death was...arranged."

"I wouldn't know," said Jude firmly. "I suppose it's possible. Many things are possible given sufficient desire and means and planning."

"An amendment," said Chandler, and made another notation. "Yes, that is a novel approach. What level of financing are you estimating?"

This was the moment Jude was waiting for. Chandler was convinced enough to inquire about the money. If he was comfortable with the plan, the money part should be easy.

"First, twenty million dollars. Seed money. To be disbursed by an intermediary of the Governor's choosing, for his protection and control, and for my security. This money will be needed to influence elections and people. Second, all the political influence the Governor can muster to push the approval of the amendment. Third, authority to speak in the Governor's name to his people involved in the oil industry here and abroad, to direct and coordinate their actions. This may seem unrelated, but it is not."

"This sounds like a major campaign," remarked Chandler, as though he were thinking of the military, not the political kind. "The Governor is no longer a young man. Time is also a consideration."

"It won't happen overnight," Jude admitted. "My current estimate is five years, maximum. I'll adjust the estimate as we proceed. The Governor will know, from time to time, where we stand."

"The Governor would require that in any case," Chandler said abstractly, making another notation on his pad. "The figure of ten million was mentioned, I understand. Is that included in the twenty--?"

"No. That ten million is my payment upon completion, and it is separate."

"Honoring Murphy's Law, what if things don't go as you plan?" Chandler asked.

Jude had thought through all the contingencies. "If the Governor becomes vice president, and dies before becoming president, my payment is five million. If, through my actions, he has the opportunity of becoming president and should decline, either because of health, or for any other reason, my payment would be seven million."

"That's not exactly what I meant. What if you fail in your plan?"

Jude spoke with cool determination. "If the office of president is not made available to the Governor, through my actions, within seven years, I will be his servant in any capacity he chooses for the rest of my life."

Chandler smiled, slowly, like an absentminded shark. He put his legal pad away and shut the case, snapping each latch with his thumb.

"Well?" demanded Jude sharply.

"Someone may be getting in touch with you soon," said Chandler. "It may even be me if the Governor is interested. If you'd like, stay in the city for a few days. See the sights before going back."

"I have final exams," Jude blurted.

"Oh, I don't think you need concern yourself about that," Chandler responded blandly, rising. "It's your future that's most important, and that's what I am looking at.

"There's a suite I sometimes use at the Plaza Hilton. I won't be needing it this trip." He slid a key along the table's polished surface. "I think you'll find everything you'll need. Or call room service. There will be some cash under the pillow for your expenses. Enjoy yourself."

"Thank you," Jude said. "I will."

Jude smiled to himself. Chandler and the Governor just moved the first pawn. They were now committed.

CHAPTER 2

Jude's New York office came complete with the lavish furnishings a major executive would require. There was a large foyer, complete with reception desk and expensive furniture, to impress visitors. Sylvia was the receptionist, attractive and friendly, but not inquisitive. She spent most of her time learning Spanish with a micro-recorder and tiny headphones lost in her elaborate hairdo. Her dream was to travel to Spain and drink red wine in the famous cellar *Tapas Bars* of Madrid. She wanted to attend Mass in the Cathedral of La Giralda, in Seville, and to pray at the same altar of "Our Lady of Antiqua," as Columbus did before he sailed off to the New World. She concentrated on that and other dreams to fill her days.

Valerie was Jude's personal secretary with her own well-furnished office. She was a true professional with little small talk and no office whispers.

The conference room was slightly smaller than a bowling alley, with a large polished table to match the expensive leather chairs. Jude's private office had all the perks of power and money. There was a private bathroom, complete with shower, and private elevator to a private entrance. He required state-of-the-art communication systems, with six separate phone lines, three video recorders and monitors. Jude had his own secure phone with scrambling capabilities. The office complex was impressive but not gaudy. Everything was in good taste, which meant expensive taste - just as a successful Wall Street brokerage maker should be.

On paper, Jude managed a large hedge fund that was restricted to certified investors. This would limit his visibility but not diminish his appearance of power. All could be arranged with private untraceable money.

The intercom buzzed. Jude touched the toggle and Valerie, his secretary, announced the visitor. "Miss Gala Dufante to see you, sir." Jude smiled. The chessboard was set; he was ready to proceed. He also smiled because he knew the visitor very well and she was destined to be a key player in his strategic game.

She walked into the room like a model, her head held high, holding her purse in her arms like a baby. She was beautiful to look at, early twenties, light brown hair with a touch of blond sprinkled in for interest. Her hair was elaborately groomed, falling in waves. The clothes fit her like they were designed for her body. She wore a beige wool suit that was hemmed just right to display her long, long legs...every inch gorgeous.

As Jude stood, she came right around the desk and embraced him, just closely enough, then stood back holding his hands, looking him in the eyes as if he were a long lost friend.

"Gala," he said, clearing his throat. "How nice to see you again. You look better than I remember. And that's saying something."

She was the highest priced call girl he'd ever heard of, let alone met. She looked like what she was: a Vassar graduate who'd made it good.

"Jude," she said warmly, "this is a splendid place. I always had confidence in you, but I had no idea you were in the city. I was surprised to hear from you after all this time. Glad, of course, but surprised. What's the occasion?"

He invited her to sit, and pushed the ashtray nearer when she took out a cigarette from a case that was probably platinum. She paused a moment, then snapped a lighter and smiled brightly at him, showing several thousand dollars' worth of effective dental work. Jude sat on the corner of the desk and said, "I'm not going to beat around the bush." Her mouth twitched slightly, as though he'd said something amusing, and then she was giving him her full attention again. He went on, "I know you're a smart, beautiful girl. Remember in our younger days at school, both of us orphans on scholarships, we both wanted to make a lot of money after we graduated. It seems you have started already."

"You're not far behind me," Gala replied, looking appreciatively at the first-class reproduction of a Picasso behind the desk and the genuine hand-loomed Persian carpet covering nearly all the floor. "I live well," she added with a self-deprecating smile. "Perhaps someday I'll tire of variety and become the mistress of a prominent podiatrist. And someday he'll get divorced, and I'll be left with all his money. Mrs. Podiatrist's widow. Someday."

"How would you like to make two thousand dollars a week for an indefinite time, beginning today," Jude asked in a mildly excited voice.

She breathed a little smoke and tapped her cigarette on the ashtray. "I don't murder people, dear, and I don't do sex starved perverts."

Jude said hastily, "Nothing like that. Just form an intimate relationship with a powerful, attractive man for an extended period of time. You will make yourself useful in every way possible, so he won't even think of doing without you. His company will pay you handsomely, and I will pay you a healthy salary. In addition, you will receive a bonus of a million dollars when the assignment is completed."

"I believe," said Gala, "I'm a little tired of variety already. Is he a podiatrist? And I can see that you're up and coming in your profession, whatever it may be. If the money is real let me know who and when."

Jude slapped an envelope onto the desk. "Here's your first month's pay. Go to the bank on the first floor and see if it's real." Jude smiled and added, "Explain to the teller that you have twenty or thirty of these checks and ask if they're worth anything. I'll give you eight minutes to cash your check and be back in my office ready to go."

She picked up the envelope. "Make it fifteen, I don't like to be rushed doing something I enjoy." As she swept out the door, Jude chuckled to himself. "She's the piece, 'the queen.'"

She was back eleven minutes later, Jude was sure, for he had timed her. She came brushing through the door without waiting to be announced and resumed her seat, pushing a wisp of her hair off one shoulder. "I'm impressed and ready for duty sir," she said in a jetty manner. "Who is this wonderful man I'm to seduce?"

"Well Gala, your assignment will begin this way. You will go over to the Pepsi Cola Company headquarters at Rockefeller Center and ask for Jack Wilkinson. He'll handle your job status."

She surveyed both perfectly manicured hands. "I don't see myself capping bottles, somehow. Why not just introduce me to the gentleman and let me handle it from there. Is Mr. Wilkinson my pigeon?"

"God no! He couldn't afford it, even if his heart would stand it. No, you're going to have an affair with a former Vice President of the United States. He's not going to pick up some broad in a bar, or on a plane..."

"I've seen," began Gala dubiously.

"Never mind what you've seen. The target is the target."

"The target is the target," Gala repeated dutifully. "I'm sure this will be interesting. I'm sure he will be delightful."

"Delightful enough to have been elected, anyhow," Jude said matter-of-factly.

"Who could ask for more?" Gala said with a smirk.

"You're to be his secretary, become his friend and, as soon as you can tactfully manage it, his lover. Your responsibility is to befriend and bed him."

"What about Mrs. Vice President?" Gala inquired.

"You were chosen, Gala, for your many talents, one of which is your ability to have an affair with him and become the wife's best friend also." Jude spoke as if he had trained Gala for this task.

"Well, I guess I shall have two dear friends in the near future." Gala paused. "We'll be the best of friends. I do have contacts throughout New York and Washington; I'll make sure they are on the 'A' list, in both towns. I can even help her choose the right clothes."

"Pick her clothes later. Handle it any way you want, so long as you're there when I need you." She raised her brows and showed the slightest twitch of a smile, and this time Jude knew she was laughing at him. "Not for that," he disclaimed. "But there will be times when I want you to influence him to do something, go somewhere, say something. And I need to know what's happening...regular reports. I'll see that you always have a direct line to me. We're embarking on a project that will take years. I trust you're willing to spend that much time to make that much money."

"I learned a long time ago, you gain nothing without sacrifice." She added, "Neither of us is eighteen anymore, dear Jude. Old executives are all handsome. But old hookers are just old hookers. I always had a feeling that someday I'd be dealing with you for money. Too bad it couldn't be for love." She gazed at him wide-eyed, until he had to laugh. She was, he thought with satisfaction, very, very good. While he sat thinking, she spoke up. "I don't know the scam, but I have confidence in... shall I say, in your eye for opportunities? I always have. So, I'll go to the Pepsi Cola Company and apply for the job of executive secretary to - what did you say his name was?"

Jude smiled and spoke quietly, "Richard Milhouse Nixon."

The following day, Gala sat in the office of Frank Wilkinson, a thoroughly uninteresting middle-aged man with a bad cold. Gala kept her gloves on while shaking hands. He didn't seem to notice. She made it her business to notice things like that. Eventually, after the usual pleasantries, he said, "This is a very important position. I hope you can handle it. Looking over your resume and background, I believe we are lucky to find someone of your caliber." He then sat for a moment, not wanting to give away anymore of his enthusiasm. Then he said, "It seems you're just what the doctor ordered."

Gala only smiled, sure that whatever references Jude had supplied would be impeccable and impressive. She hadn't bothered to study them too closely. If she'd been required to supply verification, Jude would have briefed her. The meeting went as well as could be expected. Mr. Wilkinson was putting on a front that he was considering all the information before making up his mind.

"Please understand that the man you'll be working for is not only one of our top executives, but a former vice president of the United States. He's in charge of the company's public relations, and we are an international company. So Mr. Nixon's position requires a great deal of travel and work. I assume you're prepared to handle this?"

"I believe so," said Gala firmly. "I'm seldom unprepared."

"Fine, fine," burbled Wilkinson and sneezed into a big handkerchief. Then he escorted her to the office of Richard Nixon.

Nixon was a man with a permanent five o'clock shadow, a longish sloping nose, crisp dark hair, and a gloomy, scowling expression that instantly became a cordial smile when he saw Gala.

Gala reached out her hand and smiled. "Good morning Mr. Vice President. It's nice to meet you."

Her formal demeanor and pleasant smile startled Nixon. *This girl has class*, he thought to himself. Then he said, "How nice to meet you. I'm
sorry, ah, your name is Gala?" he said as if he had
never heard it before. Gala was pleased; he was
flustered.

Nixon then expressed in an apologetic manner, "I must apologize for my cluttered desk. I'm
in the process of arranging a trip to France."

"I'll be glad to help you with tasks like that,
Mr. Nixon. I am familiar with travel arrangements on the Continent. I was a great admirer of
yours while you were vice president. I particularly enjoyed the way you handled foreign affairs,
and I will never forget how you outwitted Nikita
Khrushchev at the World's Fair confrontation.
Not many vice presidents took the opportunity
for such decisive action. They generally get lost in
the president's shadow, so to speak."

Nixon looked pleased. "I appreciate the compliment very much. After my defeat in California,
compliments are a rarity. I must say after reviewing your credentials, I was greatly impressed: Top
of your class at Vassar; correspondent for Ladies'
World, covering the U.N.; a freelance newswom-
an with international experience. I must say you
may not find this position as prestigious as what
you're leaving."

"There was excitement, true - but really, the
work was difficult, demanding, lonely, and
thankless. Men often seemed to feel hostile and
threatened by a professional woman, and women

were jealous of any success. I had my fill of trying to make it to the top of the heap. For what? I'd rather have stable work with a large company like this; regular paychecks, familiar faces to say good morning to everyday. I want to work hard, enjoy my job, and have friends again."

Nixon took her arm and urged her to sit down. The frown was gone, and he looked and felt comfortable. There was a loud sneeze by Mr. Wilkinson, who immediately excused himself and left the office, leaving Nixon and Gala alone. Nixon settled behind his desk, saying, "It's similar to the political life that I left behind, Miss Defante. I had a few friends, and there's a lot of envy, resentment, by some people, and at the end...only criticism. We may have a lot in common. I believe we can work well together."

"I'm looking forward to it Mr. Nixon," Gala said sincerely.

Returning to his office, Wilkinson placed a call. When the ringing stopped, he said, "This is Wilkinson. Your client made a nice impression and has the job."

The young voice at the other end said, "Very good. Your cashier's check will arrive at your home before five today." The phone clicked, and then went silent.

Wilkinson scrubbed at his nose and wondered if he'd ever find out what that'd been about.

Nixon was saying, "I trust Mr. Wilkinson has already told you the terms of employment, benefits, and so on? The base salary is twenty-five thousand per year plus a bonus if you and I are successful at increasing the product's territory and worldwide sales of Pepsi Cola. I hope you realize travel will be extensive, and there will be times when you and I will travel alone." He paused, uncomfortably, apparently waiting for a reaction. Gala just gazed at him as though she couldn't think of anything worth commenting on. Eventually Nixon blurted, "Miss Dufante - Gala...my wife Pat and I are happily married. I don't cheat on her. I apologize for being blunt, but I want matters understood before any, ah, any misunderstandings could arise. I'd initially felt the job as my assistant could, and perhaps should, be handled by a man. But you have a god-father somewhere, and you were highly, highly recommended..."

Gala waited for a few seconds then spoke in a serious voice. "Mr. Nixon, I understand the rigors of achieving certain goals and lifestyles. I can assure you I am mature enough to handle our relationship in a professional manner. And, yes, I have some godfathers. While at Vassar, I spent many vacations and holidays with classmates whose families were the rich, famous, and power-ful. I am still friends with them. I think some still watch out for me."

Nixon met her eyes, produced something like a smile, and seemed a fraction less tense.

"Hmmm. Well connected. Of course. If I tend to be suspicious of public opinion, it's because

I've had some sore lessons in that area. It's appearances I'm chiefly concerned about."

"Of course," Gala said quickly. "Perhaps I could meet Mrs. Nixon so we could get her feeling about your new assistant. I'm sure she will have some suggestions on how appearances can best be managed."

"That's a wonderful idea. We'll have lunch together." He was positively beaming. "Pat's a wonderful woman, and a good judge of character. I'm sure you'll get along famously."

"I'm looking forward to meeting her," Gala declared. "As I said, I've been wishing I could greet familiar faces everyday. Hers would surely be one of them."

"That's great. That's the way I like things - up front," Nixon said as he rubbed his hands. "I've always felt that the people you work with have to know their job, and the family. They also have to be loyal and know where they stand at all times."

"Exactly my feeling, Mr. Nixon."

Nixon suddenly looked at his watch. "Oh my God, its lunchtime already. Let's go. The cafeteria food is awful, but fortunately we have the executive dining room...much better...nicer atmosphere."

As they walked toward the elevator, Nixon said, "I'm leaving for Paris on Friday. Pat, my wife, will be joining me also. We'll be gone for about two weeks. Will that be any problem, since you'll be coming too? The short notice, I mean?"

Gala considered for a moment. "No. But I wonder... have you been to Paris since you left office?"

Nixon tilted his head, puzzled. "No, come to think of it, I haven't. Why do you ask?"

"Where are you planning to stay?" Gala asked.

"They booked us into the Paris Hilton. I've stayed there before and was treated royally."

"But then you were the vice president of the United States. Now they'll treat you like a typical traveling businessman. Believe me...I know. May I suggest the Continental? It is in the heart of Paris. It is a first-class hotel. It has the same style as the Ritz, but not the phony trappings. The food is great, and they have the right class of guests. It's the place in Paris to be seen, respectfully."

Nixon stood thoughtfully before the elevator. "Well, I'll surely look into whether we can change our arrangements on such short notice..."

"Please," Gala said. "I can handle the short notice change, if you like. I can make the arrangements to ensure that you and Mrs. Nixon have a comfortable visit."

"Do you speak French?" Nixon asked with a delightful look on his face.

"Oui, monsieur," Gala said. "And they all speak English, though most Parisians refuse to acknowledge English, for they believe it dilutes their culture." She looked at her watch, and then said, "Let me see what I can do about the arrangements. I will join you and Mrs. Nixon in a little while."

"Leave the arrangements until later. I would like you to meet Mrs. Nixon," he said.

"It'll only take a couple of quick calls and then I will join you in a few moments," she said, taking control. She turned and started back down the hall.

Nixon called after her, "Can you find your way?"

"If I can't, I'm sure I can find someone who'll direct me."

"I'm sure you can," agreed Nixon, and entered the elevator with a wave.

Gala didn't bother with overseas operators. She called Jude direct at the number he'd given her. When he answered she said, "This is Gala Dufante calling on behalf of Mr. Richard Nixon of Pepsi Cola. There's been an error in his travel arrangements to Paris next week. He's been booked into the Paris Hilton. I am changing the schedule to more appropriate lodgings for Mr. and Mrs. Nixon. They would like to stay at the Paris Inter-Continental Hotel." She paused for a moment, and then said, "It may be difficult to get rooms there, but I trust you can handle it."

There was silence for a few seconds while Jude thought and just breathed into the phone. "I'm sure it can be arranged. Will you be accompanying Mr. Nixon?"

"It will be a party of three: Mr. Nixon and Mrs. Nixon, and myself. We'll need flight arrangements, travel to and from the airports, with a suitable car and driver during the Nixon's stay, and any other simple perks you may come up with. When the details are complete, I can be reached here to finalize everything at my new office, Pepsi Cola, Rockefeller Center."

"I have the number," Jude said. "I'll call to confirm within an hour."

"Make it two," Gala responded, and then remembered to add please. "I'm lunching with the Nixon's and won't be free until then."

In a joyful pleased voice, Jude said, "Two it will be, Gala. Very, very good."

Gala sighed and then reflected that Jude was precisely where he ought to be...where he wanted to be... behind the scenes. Jude was demonstrating so far that he had a lot of money, and he was skilled at using it. They were just getting the thing into operation, after all. So far this was turning into an interesting career change. Gala had no idea where it was leading to, but she was not paid to think. When the music played, she danced.

$\sim\!\smile\!\sim$

At the airport, Mr. and Mrs. Nixon seemed surprised to be received by an airline official who directed the handling of the baggage and escorted them all to a private lounge. The room was private. It was not an airline clubroom, but a private VIP lounge. It was small and nicely furnished, with a well-stocked and attended bar, a table of hors d'euvres, fruit basket, TV set, and a desk with phone. Gala surveyed the room critically, turning as the Nixon's entered the room.

Mrs. Nixon spoke first with a large smile. "Miss Dufante, do we owe this special treatment to a result of your efforts?"

Gala, knowing she was being appreciated, said, "Well, this is part of my job. If I can help make this trip more pleasant, I will enjoy my job even more. I have a lot of connections, and I like to use them," Gala said. "I believe my responsibility is to see that Mr. Nixon is free to concentrate on business with as few annoyances as possible." Gala then picked up a plate of fresh cut fruit offering it to both Nixon's.

"Richard," Mrs. Nixon said to her husband, "you've found a treasure. Does she have a sister for me?" She then looked at the fresh strawberries covered with chocolate. "Well...just one before the trip."

Nixon grinned. He had a look of happiness. "Shall we have a little champagne to start our trip?" he asked in a loud voice.

There was adequate service at Orly Airport, and the Continental was even better than Gala had expected...thanks, she conjectured, to Jude's connections, whoever they might be. But she decided that the mysterious connections had passed this first test with good marks...and so had she.

During the day, she concentrated on learning the routines and protocols of business meetings, learning what was required and making sure it was provided beforehand, and ready at need.

Then, when things seemed to be running smoothly, there was time to help Pat Nixon enjoy herself touring, shopping, and entertaining. Everything was harmonious. Gala did nothing but work and offer undemanding, friendly company. She had the ability to be there when needed and to exit graciously and inconspicuously at the proper time. Soon the three were on a first-name basis. Gala was careful not to be too friendly, remaining pleasant at all times but never overly familiar, solidifying an amicable but thoroughly professional relationship. The meetings proceeded uneventfully, except for the occasional interruptions of press coverage. Nixon's public relations activities on behalf of Pepsi Cola had increased interest to the news media. He was being spotlighted in the news more and more as a pleasant goodwill ambassador. A role he visibly enjoyed.

CHAPTER 3

At 11:30 in the morning, President Lyndon Johnson was sitting on a couch in the Oval Office leafing through newspapers to see how he and his policies were being talked and written about. He had a clipping service that collected items from the domestic and foreign press, but his habit of looking himself, begun during his many years in Congress, was too hard to break. He was of the opinion that the more people that read your name in the papers, the better off you'd be at election time. He often said, "It makes people back home think, if they see your name, you're hard at work spending their damn money."

The intercom on the desk buzzed. "Mr. President, Mr. Tallsand is here for your eleven thirty appointment."

Stuffing the papers into something like a pile, Johnson said, "Send him on in, then." He mumbled under his breath, "Of all the money pushers. Well, he is at least a Texan."

William C. Tallsand was a registered lobbyist for the American Oil Company Association. His experience dealing with congressmen and White House personnel spanned decades. He dressed in a style that Johnson, a native Texan, sometimes called "Wall Street Wrangler." Everything was custom-made with enough fancy stitching to hold together two tents, and Anaconda handmade boots. But Johnson had known Tallsand a long time and mostly liked him. He greeted him in the middle of the room and, with the habitual affection of a lifelong politician, shook hands and wrapped one arm over Tallsand's shoulder as part of a ritual, steering him to a place on the couch.

Johnson said, "Billy, how in the hell are you, you old rattlesnake skinner?"

Tallsand, who'd likely never been closer to a rattlesnake than a zoo or a stockholders' meeting, took the familiar joking amiably. "Well enough, Mr. President, if the damp in the sinkhole doesn't carry me off."

"Potomac fever. It's the price we all pay. They say it goes back to an old Indian curse, when this whole area was a swamp. Sometimes I think it still is," Johnson said, as he rubbed his sore leg. "And forget that bullshit...my name's still Lyndon. When we're both retired, not so very far along now, I'll really take you hunting rattlers. There'll be no Mr. President bullshit then, so I might as well get used to it."

"Polls bad again?" rejoined Tallsand, acutely and sympathetically.

"Oh hell, they are like the humidity in springtime - up one day, down the next," Johnson said slowly.

"Like the stock market," said Tallsand, and they shared a chuckle.

"I'm wondering, Lyndon, do you still keep that Kentucky bourbon around?" He went on to say, "That's the real reason I came over here today."

The President looked around as if to see if anyone was looking or listening, then said softly, "That doctor doesn't know I have it. He thinks it's bad for the heart. If he had this job, he'd realize there's nothing good for the heart but a little relaxation."

Retrieving the bottle from its hiding place in his bottom desk drawer, Johnson poured about two fingers into a couple glasses with the Presidential seal.

Reaching with a nod of thanks, Tallsand remarked, "This is the best bourbon in the country." Then sipping it slowly, he enjoyed the smell.

"You better think so. It's free. You're a lobbyist...you know free is always the best there is. This no-label stuff...a fellow back in the hills cooks it up for me, and somehow the Alcohol, Tax, and

Firearms boys never manage to shut him down. It
pays to have friends in high places."

"That's a fact," rejoined Tallsand pleasantly.

"Would I lie to a taxpayer?" After a sip,
Johnson went on quietly, "I want to say how sorry
I was to hear about your Mary-Sue. She was one
fine lady. I know you understand that she passed
right after the assassination, and at that time the
office dropping in on me, it was weeks before I
could trade words with my own family..."

Tallsand interrupted. "I completely understand. And it was very kind of Lady Bird to come
to the funeral. We all appreciated that."

Johnson said nothing, just sipped idly at his
drink and listened. No matter how it was sliced,
the subject of his own death was on his mind. But
there wasn't much he could do about that. All in
the good Lord's time.

"There's one other factor," Tallsand continued.
"Those damn polls. As we sit here with our drinks
in hand, things look pretty sour. With Vietnam
raging and all the demonstrations it's rough.
And you don't even have a vice president to help
you. You have to wait until you get reelected before you can choose your own vice president. If
anything happens to you before the election, the
Republican Speaker of the House will become
president. As an incumbent, he'd have a great
shot at keeping the office. Hell Lyndon, you don't
have a vice president to help you campaign for the
next election." Tallsand paused for a moment and
continued, "Mr. President, the people I represent,

like things to flow smoothly, and with some kind of control. Both in oil and government."

Johnson didn't like thinking about death, but he was aware of the importance of his, and his position of leader of the Government and leader of his own political party. He also liked the idea of playing kingmaker. The next vice president would be solely of his choosing. He could demand what he wanted.

"Well, I'd just as soon not see the speaker warming that chair myself," Johnson said quietly. He knew from experience, how many ambitious politicians had the taste for the office and the power. He also knew Tallsand was not just speaking for himself. That for him to suggest something, meant it was already in the minds of some powerful people.

"It's worth talking about this vice president vacancy situation. I will talk about it with a few people and get some ideas."

"I appreciate it Mr. President. It could make your life a little easier to have a vice president, to help with the workload." Tallsand, standing up, added, "The American people should have the right to know that the party of the President will be represented throughout his term and there would be a continuity of policies."

"Bill, I'll look into it. There must be something we can do. I don't recollect ever having anybody bring this particular point up before." Johnson paused for a moment, knowing Tallsand knew more than he was casually talking about. He also knew it was important to find out quickly from other sources and other viewpoints. "What are the drawbacks if we look into this idea?"

Tallsand answered, "If something isn't done quickly, perhaps the Republican Speaker of the House being president."

"With nobody to sit on him...keep him in line," commented Johnson, and both men laughed. "You may like it Bill, but not me."

Johnson gulped his last mouthful of bourbon. "Aha... that's a pause that refreshes." He stood up and walked toward Tallsand. "Bill, I sure do appreciate you coming over. Friendly faces are a rarity around here. Make it soon. Next time try to make it at night. Want to get back the eighty bucks you took from me in that last poker game on Air Force One."

They walked to the door slowly, shook hands, and exchanged a few parting words, then Tallsand left. Johnson wandered back to his desk, thinking that Tallsand had shunted a good lot of money his way in the last campaign, and could be expected to do the same again. Keying the intercom, he told his secretary to locate his legislative coordinator, Chuck Dawson, and get him in before lunch. He'd get Dawson checking over the idea Tallsand had brought up to see what kind of legislation would be needed to bring it about.

Having received his presidential instructions, Dawson reported back two days later. Dawson was always uneasy in the Oval Office. He sat waiting for the President to finish his phone call. When the President finished his call Chuck opened his briefcase. He took out a large folder and handed it to the President. "This is what we came up with so far, Mr. President."

"I don't have time to read it all, Chuck. Just give me a verbal read."

"Well Mr. President," Chuck drew in his breath. "The legal staff has checked laws and precedents, such as exist at this time. We concluded that for a president to appoint a vice president, there is nothing on the books. The Constitution is clear about succession. Any change would require a Constitutional amendment. And that, as you know, will take some time."

"Then we better start now," rejoined Johnson curtly. He'd been thinking about the matter, reviewing the increasingly unfavorable polls. He made up his mind to push this idea for all it was worth. "It's just good for the country and party politics. Continuity of leadership. We'll get bipartisan support on it if we handle things right. After all, it'd work the same if a damn Republican were in, maybe a hundred years from now."

Johnson smiled and, obediently, Dawson smiled, too. Pushing the memo into a pile of unread correspondence, Johnson added, "If someone is going to be remembered for patching that hole, it's going to be me. You'll see to it. Whatever help you need just let me know."

"Yes, Mr. President, right away. We will start working on the amendment."

CHAPTER 4

Jude was enjoying his new lifestyle. Although he didn't think of himself as being pretentious, he liked to impress people who had known him in what he sometimes called his "white sock" days in college and before. Supposedly, his brokerage concern had connections to a large British investment firm. Allegedly he monitored the market and noted promising developments before they became public knowledge. And, surprisingly enough, tips did come his way - cryptic phone messages and unsigned mail. The latter generally delivered by courier. These tips he dutifully relayed to the London office and what happened to them thereafter he neither knew nor cared. He never was particularly interested in corporate espionage. He did purchase notable shares of 144 stocks in various companies. This would give him a noticeable paper trail...useful to demonstrate a flow of income, and in keeping clean with the Security & Exchange Commission. For outward appearance, all he had to do was manage the New York office and collect gigantic commissions.

His image was footloose and fancy-free. Everything seemed to be going well with nobody visibly looking over his shoulder. His decisions were his alone, and he had a large bank account with which to play.

He was relaxing at his desk, reading the Wall Street Journal, which he was coming to find more interesting than he'd expected, when his secretary buzzed to inform him he had a personal call. She said, "The caller wouldn't identify himself. He just said it was personal."

Running through a mental list of possibilities, Jude picked up the phone. "This is Jude Thaddeus."

"Hello, Mr. Thaddeus," responded a voice he thought he recognized as Chandler, Rockefeller's button-down bagman. "I suppose you've been expecting to hear from me?"

"Maybe," said Jude cautiously. "Tell me why I should be expecting a call."

"Not on a phone line, we'll talk in private. I'll be at the Mayflower in Washington tomorrow night. I trust you will be able make a trip down. We'll visit then. You'll find a room reserved in your name. Expect to stay three days. As soon as you've checked in, come to room one two four.

Travel light. There's no need to commit any of our projects to writing. Any questions?"

Jude was about to ask some questions, but calmly said, "I'll be there tomorrow night." Jude then heard a click as the phone went dead.

Jude decided to ride the Amtrak high-speed rails to Washington. He liked the first-class cabin and feeling of travel, riding in a train. From the window he could see the country at work, congested cities, and the farmland in-between. All the way to Washington he was nervous, checking his watch every few minutes. He was afraid that the Governor had done an audit of all the money Jude had spent on his firm, which, after all was only a front, with only a vague connection to the project. In his mind he reviewed all the arguments of why a carved rosewood desk and a dozen Early American antique matching chairs were a basic necessity of a creditable brokerage office along with artwork, and highly paid personnel. But it does take money to 'make friends and influence people.'

As he entered the hotel lobby, he noticed how crowded it was. He had been here before, but this time it was during the election season. As soon as he mentioned his name he was whisked to his room with the head bellman. It was a large, expensive suite. He felt he was still in good standing. Jude tipped the bellman a $20, looked around for a few moments, and then went directly to room 124. Jude knocked on the door twice, softly.

The door opened quickly. Chandler stood
in the doorway, a big smile on his face. He was
dressed casually in his long sleeved white shirt,
opened at the top, with the sleeves rolled up halfway. He had a drink in one hand and extended
the other to shake hands with Jude.

"Jude, it's good to see you again," Chandler
said in a somewhat loud voice, another indication
of his having had a few drinks already. "Come in.
I've wanted to talk to you for some time. How
was your trip?"

Jude walked in rather anxiously, and said,
"The train ride was quite enjoyable." In his heart,
he was concerned about this meeting.

"Good. Would you like a drink, to settle you
down?" Chandler asked.

"I'll have what you're drinking," Jude said
quickly.

"Scotch it is," Chandler said as he walked to
the bar. "I'll freshen mine while I am here." They
both sat at the bar. Setting down the glasses,
Chandler came directly to business. "Jude, it's
time for a progress report. There'll be nothing in
writing - not now, not ever. We'll just keep it verbal, it's safer that way. The Governor has charged
me to look after his interests and this plan. Now...
can you tell me what you have accomplished, beyond some lavish interior decorating and interesting business relationships?"

Jude began one of his prepared defenses of
the rosewood desk, but to his surprise and relief, Chandler waved him to silence, remarking,

"That's of no interest to us. I meant that only as a pleasantry. The Governor has authorized you with Zebra rating and number - virtually unlimited credit, and access to a world of connections." He paused for a moment and then continued. "There's no question of itemizing every piddling expense. We have complete trust in you. I assumed you understood that."

"I appreciate the governor's confidence," Jude said, and took a healthy gulp of his drink.

"The governor's opinion is that you couldn't steal enough to make you happy. Your profile strongly indicates that you're a task-oriented person. We believe you are quite intent in achieving this goal. That's what makes you tick. I am merely here to find what's been accomplished so far, and if we can help in any way."

"Well, we're on schedule," Jude said confidently. "I have the most viable of the presidential candidates lined up. I have a trunk line directly into his innermost circle. I mean close...right to his thoughts and actions. More importantly, I've initiated the process of a Constitutional amendment necessary to accomplish our objective. This amendment has the full and active support of the incumbent President. And he is pushing it hard."

"Who is your candidate?" Chandler asked as he picked up his drink.

"The former Vice President of the United States, Richard Nixon," Jude said, the boast in his voice was implicit.

Chandler looked startled, and Jude smiled a little to himself. Chandler then took a gulp of his drink, and exclaimed, "My God, why did you choose him? He couldn't get elected when he ran the last time, and that's with Eisenhower's endorsement. Then he made a fool of himself when he ran for governor, and couldn't even get elected in his home state."

"True enough," agreed Jude quite comfortably. "But that presidential election was the closest in history. Many of those who voted for him that time will vote for him again. And this time he won't be running against Jack Kennedy. But what's more important is that, to get elected, he'll need us. I have chosen him because we can control him. He will want to get elected, but the only way he can is with our help. We can dictate terms - in particular, which people will be on his staff. And I'll manipulate that staff to do what we want done. So he's our man. As I have mentioned earlier, I have someone in place very close to him. The rest will come, in time." He looked to Chandler, who only nodded for him to continue, his expression neutral.

Jude went on. "The key to the plan is the Constitutional amendment. As I said, Johnson has taken it as a personal objective. He's lining up support for this amendment on a bipartisan basis, treating it as a popular measure to reestablish his influence with Congress. And that's been strained lately."

"The war or the Great Society?" asked Chandler with a sneer.

"Probably both, and more," Jude said. Then added, "I do expect the amendment to be formally proposed before the end of the year without much hoopla or opposition."

Chandler was silent for a moment, looking off toward a wall as if formulating what he'd be reporting to Rockefeller. At length he said, "What's the next move?"

"To divide the Democratic Party after the next presidential election. Nobody can beat Johnson this election. He will use the martyred Kennedy for all it's worth. We will use the time to our advantage."

Jude paused for a moment. "You realize it's going to take a decent amount of time to run the amendment through the necessary state legislators before it can be enacted into law. I mean two-thirds of the states, 34 in all, must approve the amendment. The trick is to keep it moving, but under the political radarscope. It can't be done over a weekend, but I am confident we will get it through in the prescribed time."

Jude took another sip of his drink, then said, "In the meantime, Johnson will finish out this term and be re-elected. He'll have for his running mate who he believes to be an unbeatable vice president to step into the office when he retires. While we're waiting for the amendment to pass, I'll start the necessary moves to produce a third party formed from a branch of the Democratic

Party in the south, thus ensuring the Republican carrying the north. The end result will be our candidate elected president."

"Nixon," commented Chandler.

"Nixon it is," agreed Jude.

"Interesting," remarked Chandler neutrally, but didn't put forward any further objections to Nixon. "We have certain contacts among the southern Democrats, as you no doubt know. I can arrange their service."

"We need powerful, amenable people with well-placed influence," replied Jude coolly. "And we need Nixon's running mate. And this running mate must be a politician we can control, someone when we say step aside, he will step aside smartly."

"We have a stable full of such candidates that would fit the bill." Chandler said thoughtfully. He then continued as if thinking aloud saying shrewdly, "Standard Oil has a lot of refineries and other interests in Maryland. Oh Yes, I have a very good candidate in mind... And we've done business with him already."

"Now Jude, it's very important that any contact we have should be indirect. The governor wants no direct involvement. If you need me for anything, call your Zebra number, give the month and day of your call, and specify Code C. I'll be in touch within hours."

The Zebra system was proving invaluable...for more than just money. Jude had only needed to specify Nixon should be offered a job with world travel in some appropriate organization. Within a week, Nixon had been made Public Relations Manager with Pepsi Cola. Zebra had also given him access to William Tallsand.

He was now confident enough to ask,

"Why three days?"

Chandler blinked, then made the connection. "Very simple, really. I'll be leaving early tomorrow morning. I prefer not to have our stays here visibly coincide. I'd suggest you spend some time sightseeing. Enjoy the city. Get a feel for the layout. Visit some investors; meet some colleagues. You may want to backslap a few politicians for practice. It could be a useful pretext, later."

"Very good suggestions. I'll make use of the time." He then looked at Chandler. "Is there anything you would like to know, or that I should know?"

"No, Jude. This meeting is complete." Then with a little laughter in his voice, he added, "Just make us proud, boy."

Jude smiled. He was beginning to like Chandler.

CHAPTER 5

J ude's prediction proved accurate. Lyndon Johnson ran for a term of his own and carried with him the most powerful Democratic Senator, Hubert Humphrey, as Vice President. Humphrey, the happy warrior, was a favored potential presidential candidate in his own right. Politicians on both sides of the political aisle and the American people seemed to like Humphrey. If LBJ chose not to run in the subsequent election, Humphrey certainly could control the party and win the nomination. It was time for Jude to put his "southern strategy" into motion.

Jude and John Chandler were traveling on one of the Governor's private jets for a meeting with the newly elected Governor of Arkansas. For the first time in ninety-four years a republican would be the occupant of the Governor's mansion in Little Rock. To many in the south the new

Governor might be considered a 'carpetbagger.' He was born and raised in New York, a member of wealthy northern family. A Yale man and his brother was also a Governor.

The newly elected Governor of Arkansas was Winthrop Rockefeller the younger brother of Nelson. As a conservative southern leader he was considered the most powerful politician south of the Mason-Dixon Line. It was going to be a tough sale to get this new leader of the fledging Republican Party to carry out such an audacious move. To convince the Governor of Alabama, George Wallace, to betray his political base, the Democratic Party. And then convince Wallace to run for the Presidency, as an independent candidate. If anyone could do it, Winthrop Rockefeller could. He was a nonconformist and rebellious by nature, tough and smooth.

Jude knew the family bonds of the Rockefellers were close, but Winthrop, was his own man. He was the tallest member of the Rockefeller family, towering six feet three inches with a husky two hundred pound frame. In his youth he dropped out of college and joined the Army even before the United States entered the Second World War.

"How soon do we land?' Jude asked staring out the small window.

"We should be landing in a few minutes." John paused for a minute. Then he added as if thinking out loud. "We'll be landing at our new Mena Airport. We just spent a ton of money putting in concrete runways and instrument landing systems."

"You built a airport just for the convenience of Winthrop?" Jude asked.

"We don't spend that kind of money for convenience Jude. The Mena airport project is a sound financial investment and we have plans for it." Chandler said as he started to stare out the window. Then added softly, "Although it was chosen because it is close to Petit Jean Mountain. That's where Winthrop bought thousands of acres of good grassing land and built 'Winrock Farms'. He takes pride putting the "WR" brand on some of the best cattle in the world, his famous pure-bred Santa Gertrudis."

John Chandler turned slowly glancing over toward Jude asking slowly "So tell me Jude, how are things going so far," As if he wanted to change the subject.

"Well, to tell you the truth, we're at a very precarious spot. What we do next is a very important move. This meeting is critical for our plan to run smoothly. It's like moving the queen for the first time on the chessboard. The rest of the strategy and movements will be determined by what we can accomplish here." Jude said thoughtfully.

"Jude you surprise me. I was under the impression you had a guaranteed plan. Every move laid out well in advance, every detail weighed, measured and dissected." Chandler paused for a moment, he then took on a serious tone adding, looking directly at Jude for a response. "You're spending a lot of money. If you have any doubts, now's the time to let me know?"

"Let me tell you John. I don't have any doubts. I have the entire sequence of events laid out perfectly in my mind. You know I can't put anything in writing so I keep it all in my head. Just like in chess, every conceivable move is considered and countered with three alternatives for each. No one else knows how these isolated moves and events will lead. I know the finial objective, or as I prefer to call it, check mate. No one can know what I'm doing and how I'm doing it. But I'll fill you in on a few points. On this trip we're going to be making a big move; it'll be a powerful and delicate maneuver so it must be well executed.

Jude paused for a moment then added, "If I looked concerned I am. Look what I have to accomplish here. I have to bribe one of the wealthiest men in the world and now the most influential republican in the south to do something against his nature. Which is to convince the most powerful politician in the South to leave the Democratic political machine forming a new independent Party to run for White House? These are powerful men, there're not going to go do something of this magnitude on a suggestion. But they must be convinced to do it. The entire strategy is to get Nixon elected, and he can't get elected in a two man race of him and Humphrey. So we are here to find us a third candidate to pull votes from the Democrats. If we can pull this maneuver off, I am confident the rest of the plan will be just moving players around the chessboard. And that's what I am good at."

"Very interesting Jude." Chandler said as he sipped his coffee. "You know, I've worked for the Rockefeller family for a long time. I'm a very loyal and trusted member of the inter-circle. I've been involved in a lot of deals throughout the years. I've made a lot of money using my talents and skills. Met all kinds of charlatan schemers and hustlers, and a couple of good solid business people. But you're the first one I've ever met that's making his mark in life as an anonymous chess player."

"Well, I haven't made my mark as yet. So to set the game in motion I'll need the help of Winthrop Rockefeller. Can you fill me in a little more about this black sheep of the family? Any hints that might help in dealing with him." Jude asked warmly like a freshman in college seeking advice from his guidance Counseler.

"Hmmm," Chandler said while thinking of what to say. "Winthrop Rockefeller, Nelson calls him big Rock from Little Rock. He's a real gregarious character, out-going, fun loving type, likes people, and gets along with almost everyone. He's a real personable guy and knows what he wants. In public he's very shy and clumsy, a terrible stump campaigner. He doesn't travel with an entourage; usually he has only one or two people around him. But he is independent in every sense of the word. As a young kid, he dropped out of Yale and worked in the oil fields as a roustabout.

He drinks a lot even though Arkansas is a dry state. He once told me the bootleggers keep the state dry. They get their customers to go out and vote against changing the liquor laws. He smokes three packs of cigarettes a day. With all that smoking his teeth are in very poor shape, in fact they are yellow. Not like the signature smile of Nelson."

Chandler took a cigarette out of the pack on the table. After lighting it up, he starred at the smoke he was exhaling. "You know he was quite a war hero, Purple Heart Bronze Star with clusters. He joined the army as a private and worked his way up through the ranks. At the end of the Second World War he was a full colonel. After the War he went back to New York, tried for a while, but just didn't fit in. He had a close friend he met in the Army by the name of Frank Newell. Frank was from Arkansas always boasting about how beautiful it was. One day Winthrop went down to visit him. Fell in love with Arkansas. Bought a big ranch and moved in. Made his home there. Some locals call him a hillbilly billionaire. Although he is mild mannered, he's a real determined fighter. He got elected governor, with only eleven percent of the voters considered republican. He's respected and well liked. When Martin Luther King was assassinated, he stood on the Capitol steps arm in arm with mourners singing. "We Shall Overcome" He wants the south to change, and he's doing whatever he can to bring that about."

"I trust he gets along well with Nelson," Jude asked.

Chandler thought for a moment. Then replied, "Winthrop didn't fit in the mold of the New York City Rockefellers. Even as a child he seemed always to be the odd man out. But he always respected the family and Nelson in peculiar. I believe he'll do whatever is reasonable for the family and Nelson. Bear in mind Jude, that the Rockefellers through the Foundation and other means have pumped a lot of money into the economy of Arkansas, not counting all the money we spent on his last election. It cost plenty. So I believe we'll have the attention of the newly elected Governor."

Chandler took a deep draw on his cigarette, and then added "Jude I'm sure you will be able to get Winthrop on board, but it will cost you plenty. He is a Rockefeller. Anything he does requires a compensation package, usually quite expensive."

The engines of the Gulf Stream II whined as the luxury jet touched down then rolled to a smooth stop at the far end of the runway. As the door opened the two passengers slowly stepped down a short stair well. Standing alone off to the side of the private hanger was a tall man dressed casually in a beige slacks and western style jacket wearing cowboy boots and a big Stetson ten-gallon hat. Jude could tell in an instant it was Winthrop Rockefeller. He looked as he had been described waving his hand in a welcoming motion, a broad smile highlighting his tarnished yellow teeth.

"Over here John", Winthrop was yelling, making sure he was noticed as if he were the head of a delegation.

The exchange of warm greetings between John Chandler and Winthrop seemed to lighten the atmosphere. Jude was pleased with his introduction to the Governor of Arkansas. Winthrop extended his large hand, and peering into Jude's eyes said loudly, "Welcome to God's country, young feller. I know you're going to enjoy your visit here."

"Thank you Governor It's a distinct pleasure to meet you Sir. And I appreciate you taking the time from your busy schedule to see us." Jude said showing deference toward his host.

"Thank you Jude. I may be a Governor, but when John Chandler says he's coming down for a talk, well, I make time to see him." Winthrop said with a fresh smile. "I even had my new vehicle all set up for a private ride to the ranch.

"What's that Governor?" Chandler asked as they walked toward the odd looking motor vehicle.

"Oh you mean my 'Texas Cadillac'. That's my new Chevy Suburban over there." Winthrop pointed to a sparkling shinny large size black four door sport utility vehicle. It was an impressive looking automobile, dark tinted windows, large off road tires with chrome rims. Even the suspension system set the vehicle apart. The hood ornament was a sterling silver sculptured bull. At a glance one could tell it was a custom built vehicle.

Winthrop jumped into the driver's seat grabbing the wheel with both hands as he made himself comfortable. "I just picked up my new toy last week. I thought it would fun to use it and drive up to the ranch, just the three of us. That way we can talk in private without being interrupted. And I know John Chandler well enough to know that most of his talking is very private."

"We do have some interesting subjects to discuss with you Governor. And a ride through the country is just fine with me." Chandler said as they pulled out of the parking lot.

"I couldn't ask for better accommodations, this is some truck. Was this car made just for you Governor?" Jude asked.

"Yes it was Jude. It has a four hundred fifty-horse power engine. The windows are bullet proof and the body is skinned over armor plating. The tires can do sixty miles an hour completely deflated. It's designed to float if we end up in a river or lake. It has lot extras. Not counting the eight track stereo system, the four captain's chairs. And most important my custom built-in bars. I prefer the one up here next to me. But there's a bar in the back seat for your pleasure Jude." Winthrop said as he had one hand on the wheel and with the other pulled out the cigarette lighter from the dashboard. As he was lighting his latest cigarette he yelled out, "In those bars, there's beer or whatever you want to drink. John, would you get me a 'Rolling Rock'. That's the little green bottle of beer."

Chandler lifted the top of the console made into a front bar between the front seats, taking out a bottle of green beer, opened it, and handed it to Winthrop.

Jude sitting in the back rummaged through the rear bar looking for something to drink. He thought for a moment. Saying to himself, while in Rome, do as the Romans do. So he opened a beer and took a small sip. Then he said cautiously. "I'm glad this vehicle is secure. Because what we'll be talking about is very important and must be kept completely secret."

Winthrop seemed a little taken back. He turned over at Chandler saying "I'm surprised, John, you usually do the talking."

"Jude is working directly for Nelson. But he reports directly to me Governor. This project is very important to your brother." Chandler paused for a moment letting the message sink in. "I'm assisting wherever I can. Jude's been given the authority to make sure this project works. So I'll let him do his own talking."

"Well Jude, we've got about an hour's drive before we get to Petit Jean Mountain. So why don't you tell me all about what my dear brother wants?" Winthrop paused for a moment then added, "For someone who has everything, he sometimes comes up with the damnedest requests. I should have known he wanted something for the help he has given us down here. So tell me young man what does the powerful Governor of New York want from me. He's never been shy about

asking for anything himself. So why did he chose
you to do the asking?"

Jude cleared his throat and speaking clearly
said, "To be quite frank with you Governor, he
is asking you to intercede on a very sensitive
and discrete mission. He wants you to convince
Alabama's Governor George Wallace to run in
the next Presidential campaign as a third party
candidate."

"When I said the damnedest requests, that
was like saying the great Mississippi is a little
stream." Winthrop was clearly shocked. He understood that if Nelson Rockefeller wanted this to
happen, it probably would.

"How in the hell am I, as a newly elected governor, a Republican to boot, going to convince
the strongest politician in the South to desert his
party and go out tilting at windmills?" Winthrop
started to shake his head, as he grew more upset. As he continued, his voice rose to a higher
level. "George Wallace is the embodiment of the
Democratic Party. And that Party rules the South
with every political job and office holder from the
Governor's Mansion to local dogcatcher. George
Wallace is more than a governor, he is the pinna-
cle of powering the South."

"I agree with you, Governor. George Wallace
is the most powerful politician in the South. He's
already used his high office to run for president.
In '64 he did quite well in the Democratic primaries in Wisconsin and Indiana where he got over
thirty percent of the votes and almost forty-five

percent in Maryland. He would have done a lot better if LBJ hadn't put the screws to him," Jude said in a confident voice.

"You said it Jude. He ran in the Democratic primaries. That's where his power is. I can't see him walking away from his party," Rockefeller said scornfully.

"I've studied George Wallace. I know what makes him tick." Jude responded quickly. "He's a fighter. In his younger days he was a Golden Gloves Boxing Champ. And In the political ring he's a fighter as well. Remember he stood alone in the doorway at the University of Alabama facing down the power of the United States Government. He likes the image of the little guy fighting against big government. He is well aware that it was his own northern controlled Democratic party that screwed him in 64."

Jude paused as if getting his second wind. "You're right about one thing Governor. Wallace is no Don Quixote from La Mancha. He won't go out and do battle with a windmill. But he will fight for his own beliefs and his own best interest. And if he believes he can muster real financial and political support, I'm sure Governor George Wallace will play the role as the little guy taking on the power of black robes of the liberal courts and what he calls the duplicate interests of both the Democratic and Republican Parties."

Winthrop took a large swig of his beer as he kept one hand on the wheel and both eyes on the road ahead. He cocked his head and in a loud voice said, "Now who am I suppose to be, Sancho the servant trying to convince Don Quixote, or Wallace to ditch his Party with all its power and influence and run for Presidency as an independent. Come to think of it, battling with windmills makes more sense."

Jude was ready with a quick response. "Governor you're in the mists of changing the south. You're the first Republican Governor to be elected in the Deep South since the civil war. It wasn't a fluke. You're the harbinger of things to come. But look at how much it cost, even the Rockefellers can't afford to buy all the states. We need a different strategy for the other states. We both know down here many people are still fighting the civil war. There's no way they will ever vote Republican. But if a third party can be introduced, with the right financial and organizational backing we could form a new political force. George Wallace has a large powerful following. He just might be the fighter we need to help put an end to the democrat one party system."

"Why is my dear brother Nelson so interested in eliminating the Democrat Party in the South?" Winthrop asked.

"He's not necessarily trying to eliminate the Democrat Party. But it is our desire to have George Wallace run as an independent candidate for the Presidency. And that may in turn create the possibility for a strong third party to emerge," Jude said with a cool voice.

"So, Nelson sent you and Chandler down here to help develop a new political landscape." Winthrop paused for a moment, then with a chuckle in his voice continued. "Why is there a little voice in the back of my head telling me there's something in this deal for Nelson?"

Winthrop again paused, and slowly turned toward Jude. "So tell me Jude, why does the Republican governor of New York want the Democrat governor of Alabama to run as an independent?"

"I can give two answers," Jude said slowly. "The first being for practical and obvious reasons. States rights. Knocking down the good old boy system that has plagued the South. Eliminating the one party system. A new party would reveal a new independent South with all the opportunities and economic benefits. And I'm sure we can come up with a few other good reasons to support Governor Wallace. But the second answer to your question and the real reason is, because Nelson wants this done. He has his own political objective. We believe there's only one person that can convince George Wallace to run. And that's you, governor. And your brother is requesting your help in this matter. You're family, and I might add he expects your support."

"He wants my support, what good is that? May I remind you all that I am the only elected Republican governor in the South? At the last governors' conference, I was as welcome as a skunk at a lawn social. These politicians down here treat me like a Baptist minister at the Vatican. I have almost no political influence outside of Arkansas, not to mention, that I have to concentrate on doing my job and getting re-elected myself," Winthrop said as he seemed to be thinking things out. His voice lowered as he began to mumble, "I will do what I can, but I just can't see how we can possibly pull this thing off."

"That's where we come in, Governor," Jude said as if he were waiting for the cue. "We can build your image as the new renaissance leader of the South. We are going to have a powerful public relations campaign highlighting positive changes taking place in this developing southern economic heaven. I've already arranged to have your picture on the cover of 'Time Magazine', along with a well-written article praising all of the wonderful things you are doing for the great state of Arkansas. As a result of this, and a few other behind-the-scenes maneuvers, you're the next chairman of the Southern Governors' Association. With all this positive coverage you will be a shoe in for re-election and the new darling of Southern politics."

"Sounds like Brother Nelson's making me a deal I can't refuse," Winthrop said without conviction.

"I would rather say your brother is seeking your assistance in this delicate matter and he is willing to make it worth your while," Jude said. After taking a swig from his bottle, Jude continued. "In addition to what we already are committed to, Nelson has agreed to finance the construction of that model school you wanted in Morilton. He also has agreed to finance the fine arts center in Little Rock, and of course the Rockefeller Foundation will increase scholarship funding in Arkansas and Alabama. So you can see, Governor, the compensation package is well worth the effort."

"All right, I'm on board. Now how am I going to convince George Wallace to run for president?" The Governor said looking over at Chandler. "John, will you make me a vodka and tonic with a squeeze of lime, if you please."

"First of all, Governor, you won't have to convince George Wallace to run for president. He's already intoxicated on the wine of presidential ambition. All you need to do is show him the advantages of running as an independent candidate," Jude said in a voice of growing strength.

"What advantages?" Winthrop's voice was elevated and a little surly. The booze was having some effect on his speech.

"He'll have advantages that no other candidate will have in the next election. The unofficial support of the Rockefeller organization for one, which in itself will have a monumental effect. He'll have the financial support other candidates only dream of. We will strongly help finance his campaign and he'll have behind the curtain support from the governor of New York, which has the power of an earthquake."

"You talk a good game, Jude, and I might even believe you myself. When we get to the ranch we're going to have to make a phone call to Governor Wallace," Winthrop said while sipping his vodka tonic with one hand as he steadily drove through the rolling countryside. "I've known George for quite a while. We had one hell of a time at the sixty-two Sugar Bowl. But those damn Rebels of Alabama beat our Razor Backs by a touchdown. At least I think they beat us. Anyway, it was a hell of a party afterward. I was so upset at that game I tried to recruit Bear Bryant to coach the University of Arkansas. You know, he was born in Arkansas in a little place called Moro Bottom. We offered him the moon to get him back, but he turned us down flat. Just goes to show yah money can't buy everybody," Winthrop said as he waited for a response.

Jude said nothing.

"How much of a drive do we have?" John Chandler asked.

"We should be at Winrock in a little while. When we get there I want to show you boys the pride of the South, our herd of purebred Santa Gertrudis cattle. Their color is quite distinctive, a white face with a reddish cherry hide. A nice docile animal, specialty bred with deep muscular form that produces the highest quality of beef. Yes sir, the line dates way back to the King Ranch of Texas. We're now building up our herd and soon we'll have the best beef cattle in the world. Yep, when we Rockefellers do something we do it with world class," Winthrop said with reflective pride.

"How big is your ranch, Governor?" Jude asked.

"Winrock Farms are almost thirty-five thousand acres of the prettiest land in America. But it's rather small in comparison with the ranches Nelson owns in South America. He has a few ranches that cover over a million acres. For some reason he likes life and some of the women south of the equator."

The trio drove up the private driveway to the main home nestled in the base of the rolling hills. The design of the mansion was simple but elegant. Four large white pillars held up the sizeable porch roof that ran the full length of the front of the mansion. As the vehicle stopped, out ran a butler to open the driver's door. A short conversation took place.

Governor Rockefeller started escorting Jude and Chandler up the sidewalk toward the front entrance. "Well boys, let's take a walk down to my private office. We'll have a drink and I'll make a call to my good friend, the governor of Alabama."

In a few short minutes the three were sitting in the study, a very large brightly colored open room with two bars. One very long well-stocked bar was off to the side of the entrance, and the second bar was at the far end of the room near the exit door to the patio. Winthrop sat in a large-winged chair; Jude and Chandler sat on the large couch opposite the glass coffee table. All had fresh drinks in hand.

"Governor Wallace, thank you for taking this call on such short notice. I appreciate it," Winthrop said with a newly acquired southern drawl. "I have you on a squawk box because I'd like to introduce you to a few Yankees that came down here for a visit."

The speakerphone came to life. "I'm always happy to meet some damn Yankees. As long as they're not wearing black robes. It's those northern judges I don't cotton to. You boys aren't judges now, are you?" George Wallace said in a whimsical joking voice.

Both Jude and Chandler answered in unison, "No, we're not judges, Governor."

"I can assure you George, John Chandler and Jude Thaddeus are anything but judges," Winthrop said jokingly. "They both work for my brother Nelson. And they're down here on some political business and they would like to bounce some ideas off you." Winthrop's voice became more serious.

"Good afternoon, Governor Wallace," Jude said leaning toward the phone as if he were closer to it he would sound better. "My name is Jude Thaddeus and it's a pleasure to speak with you, sir. I'm doing some political consulting projects for the governor of New York, Nelson Rockefeller. You may not know it, but he's a big fan of yours."

"Why thank you, Mr. Thaddeus. It warms my heart to know I'm liked in high places. Now, is that the reason you all called?" Wallace spoke in a light sarcastic tone.

"No, Governor, the reason we called you is because we know you have a strong following not only in the South, but across the country as well. We noticed how strong you did in the democratic primaries in sixty-four. In northern states you did exceptionally well receiving almost forty-five percent of the votes in one state. You could have done much better if President Johnson hadn't put the screws to you."

"No argument from me so far, Mr. Thaddeus." There was a silent pause on the speakerphone and then it came alive again. "Now, are you looking to offer me your services as a political consultant? If so, I can tell you right up front. Down South here, we may be proud, but we sure ain't rich. And we sure ain't in the same financial league as the Rockefellers. No offense Winthrop."

"No offense taken, George," Winthrop said as he toasted his vodka and tonic.

"Governor, I'm not offering my services directly, but I'm working with a group of influential people that share many of the viewpoints and values you stand for. There are a lot of Americans who believe as you do. I've seen the polling data. You have a strong political voice that should be heard. But under the present political scheme, you're just a lonely voice crying in the wilderness," Jude said sincerely.

"I'm hardly a lonely voice in the wilderness. I am the governor of the great state of Alabama and I too have seen some of that polling data my-self. Now if you're trying to move this old mule in a certain direction, you may want to try a little sweet-talking, plain and simple, without Madison Avenue's confetti and streamers. Do you under-stand where I'm coming from?" Wallace said.

"I understand, Governor," Jude said clearing his throat. "Let me start by saying the last election may have been the death rattle of the Republican Party. Barry Goldwater led the Republicans to near destruction. After that debacle of a cam-paign, a lot of people were disillusioned and now there's growing grassroots support for a new political party. A party built on fundamental American beliefs. I've heard some of your cam-paign speeches, Governor. I heard you complain that both the Democrat and Republican Parties have become too powerful and the common man can't even tell the difference between either one. We both know, Governor, even though you have a national political following, you'll always be the Southern bastard child of the Democrat Party. Oh yeah, they'll slap you on the back and thank you for all the votes you can deliver, but they won't accept you in the inner circle where the real pow-er is. Nor will they ever give you the opportunity for national attention."

Governor Wallace broke in with a southern drawl. "I hear what you're saying, Mr. Thaddeus. And I might even agree with you on some of your points. But what are you asking me to do, join your Republican Party?"

"I'm not asking you to join the Republican Party, Governor." Jude paused for a moment then added, "I'm asking you to be the leader of a new political party, the American Independent Party."

"Now boys, I thought it was interesting of you to ask me about a third party. Quite frankly, I may not agree with everything that's happening with my Democrat Party, but I'm a loyal party member. My whole family and almost everyone else I know are Democrats. I can't see myself leaving my party for some startup organization with a couple of pipe dreamers telling me what a good idea it is."

"I can assure you, Governor, we're not a couple of pipe dreamers trying to drum up business by creating a new political party," Jude said as his voice picked up steam. "There's a need for another party; there's an opportunity now to take the bull by the horns and make this possibility a reality. And your leadership would be the keystone building block to get this new party organized and ready to elect our kind of people."

"As I've already said boys, I'm a loyal party man. I've worked my way up in the Democrat Party. I know we have some problems and we'll try to work them out. But I believe my future is to remain in the Democrat Party," Wallace said as if he was waiting for a rebuff.

"Governor, let's talk about the future of the South," Jude was quick to respond. "Bob Dylan's a popular hippie song writer with a new catchy tune 'The Times they are a changing.' Believe me Governor, times are a changing, but not like the way that hippie's yodeling about. I'm talking about the industrial changes that will shift the manufacturing center of this country. The rust belt states in the north are in deep trouble. They're being hampered by the high cost of labor and increasing union rules. Their production facilities are outdated with growing environmental barriers preventing them to build new plants. I tell you Governor, Ray Charles can see what's about to happen. The big industries are going to move south, to a more favorable labor pool, with lower energy costs, with more suitable weather...a smoother social understanding of businesses. For this to work properly the political atmosphere must be suitable. We need the right people in public office to help in this transition. How do we get these people? We realize that the Republican Party is cursed in the South and has been for over a hundred years, so they won't have any political influence. And the Democratic Party in the South is too powerful, and quite frankly, Governor, its corrupt and not likely to welcome changes. We believe now is the time to start a new political party that's free from generations of family-controlled politicians. Like you, Governor, we want a party that represents the interests of the people. We would like you to consider leading this party. And this is not just as a regional party we're talking about, but as a national organized party with a shot at making big changes from rural America to the White House."

"I should have known, when a Rockefeller became my new neighbor, changes would be coming," Governor Wallace said thoughtfully.

"I told you George, stick with me and I'll make you rich and powerful," Winthrop yelled toward the speakerphone with a laugh.

"Mr. Thaddeus, you're sure talking about a lot of big changes." Wallace paused for a moment then slowly spoke in his southern drawl. "Yah know, down here some folk say that talk is kind of cheap."

"I can assure you, Governor; I can put a lot of money where my mouth is. It took a lot to defeat six-term Governor Orval Faubus, but Winthrop did it. In addition to money we can marshal the talented people necessary to set up and operate a national political organization to win elections. We know what needs to be done and how to do it," Jude said confidently.

"Governor Rockefeller," Wallace was yelling in his phone. "Now, I'm beginning to understand just how you got elected with only eleven percent registered Republicans. With enough money, the right people, and a good organization, that's a pretty good receipt to win elections."

"Don't forget about all my fine barbecues, it also cost a lot of good prime steaks for me to get elected," Winthrop said jokingly in response.

"Governor Wallace, I'm here representing Governor Winthrop Rockefeller of Arkansas, and I am speaking unofficially for his brother Governor Nelson Rockefeller of New York. As you know both men have tremendous political clout and a great deal of influence with the New York based news media that's headquartered near Rockefeller Center. And there's more, a lot more that will be used to help elect the next president of the United States," Jude said in a cold tone. All was quiet.

"We would like you to consider being our candidate for president of the United States. I can assure you, that you will have the support of the Rockefellers and all that goes with the name; including money, organization, and influence."

"With all the money organization and influence why doesn't Nelson run for the presidency himself? Hell, everyone knows he wants the job so badly he can taste it," Wallace said sarcastically.

"Nelson has made a lot of political enemies inside the party and they carry grudges for a long time. As I said earlier the Republican Party is in complete disarray. Whoever gets the Republican nomination will lose in the general election. And let's face it, the growing industrial power is being shifted to the South and that's where the new political force will come from. We know you're popular in the South and you proved in sixty-four that you attracted a lot of voters in the North. We believe the time is right and the people are ready for a third party with fresh viable candidates. It's important to the new South and it's important to the country as well."

"I'll bet you're a Harvard man, aren't you Mr. Thaddeus?" Wallace said with a humorous southern drawl.

"Yes Governor, I paarked the caar in the yaard at Haavaard. But I know the real world as well. And I think you do also," Jude said quietly.

"Well, I must say you boys give me a lot to think about. I'll be meeting with my brother later this evening. He's my personal political advisor ya know. He has a good feel for which way the wind is blowing. I'll fill him in on our conversation; it's always helpful to get an outside opinion, if you know what I mean," Governor Wallace said smoothly.

"I enjoyed our conversation, Governor," Jude said and then added, "I'll be leaving later tonight. I'm going back to the land of bright lights and tall buildings. I'll keep in touch through Winthrop. Please let us know your intentions. We have a great opportunity to rearrange the major players on the political chess board."

"You might be right, Mr. Thaddeus; you give me a lot to ponder. Good night Winthrop, good night boys, I'll be in touch soon." There was the sound of a click as the speakerphone went dead.

"Well Jude, what do you think?" Chandler asked.

Jude looked across the room toward Winthrop saying, "Governor, I expect George Wallace to be on the phone by noon tomorrow. Not first thing in the morning because he wants to show a little stature. But just as we are talking now, he's talking to his brother, the political consultant. I'd bet those boys are laughing up their sleeves about how George hoodwinked a couple of Yankees to finance his campaign. Incidentally, we will funnel the money through his brother who knows how to hide it. And John, we want to add a extra couple hundred thousand dollars in cash in a slush fund for his brother to play with."

"I can handle that. But why the slush fund for Brother Gerald Wallace?" Chandler asked, with a confused look in his face.

"Because we don't want George Wallace to run for president again in seventy-two. This slush fund will be our insurance that he won't run. All we have to do is produce receipts of a lot of cash that went to the Wallace brothers, which can be interpreted as bribes. Thus we will remove that piece from the chess board," Jude said with a smile.

"What is to be my role in this grand scheme?" Winthrop injected as he made himself another drink.

"If I'm correct, Wallace will want to know more about what he can expect from you and Nelson. All you have to tell him is that you will support him openly. That will show him a divided party and help you in the South anyway. Tell him that Nelson will help quietly, but effectively behind the scenes, and that's significant. He'll get all the money he needs and the organization and a lot of one-eyed winks from prominent Republicans. He has to believe we have the money and the know-how to get him elected. Our staff will control the direction of the campaign. All he has to do is accept our offer to lead the ticket of the American Independent Party," Jude said confidently.

Four days later, on Thursday morning, Jude was leafing through the society pages of the New York Times when a phone in his private office rang. He recognized the ring; it was his coded phone. He had a special phone that could be used only after a four number code was dialed, thus eliminating anyone answering by mistake or intent. Hastily, he grabbed his keys and quickly opened the door, wondering who was calling this early. "Hello?" he said.

"Good morning, Mr. Thaddeus, this is John Chandler." He spoke in an enthusiastic, cheerful voice. "I just heard from our southern friend. I understand that Governor Wallace was ecstatic at our proposal. He had been trying to get something started on his own, but didn't have the capital. With the silent assistance of the Brothers Rockefeller he's decided to form a third party and run for the presidency."

"That's good news. The Bishop is in play and ready to be moved?" Jude asked quietly.

"Yes he is, Jude," Chandler said with a little hesitation in his voice. "But, just one thing."

Jude hated to hear that "just one thing" bullshit. It was the phrase he heard most often that killed deals.

"A little clarification. I've been thinking about our discussion before that meeting with Winthrop, setting up the campaign. I appreciate that it's crucial for Wallace to carry the Southern states, but why not some Northern ones as well? In sixty-four he did great in the primaries up north, I mean Michigan, Ohio, and Maryland. It seems we could go after those Republican states as well... hit both Republican and Democrat states. It gives him a better chance."

Jude bit his lip. He briefly wondered how John Chandler would react if he replied, *"Because, you idiot, we want Wallace to take votes only from the Democrats, but not enough for him to win. Wallace is the spoiler, not the victor. His role is to get our guy elected."*

He kept his cool. There was no need for Chandler to know about every part of the larger plan...only what he needed to know about his involvement.

"The money is there for Wallace to campaign hard in the Southern states and some selected Northern states. We need him to concentrate on the states where we can guarantee certain electoral votes, and they are in the South. We're going to spend a lot of time and money on Nixon campaigning the rest of the states where we may have our best chance against Humphrey."

He paused for a moment then added, "The Wallace strategy is campaign hard against Humphrey, and anyway that's who Wallace needs to attack. Let Wallace's people think Nixon

is a has-been with little appeal. Wallace won't get
Nixon voters anyway. The candidate they need to
beat is Humphrey. If they can attract Humphrey
voters, Wallace has a chance. That's our Southern
strategy. We expect the Wallace campaign to follow that game plan. And assure Governor Wallace
that this plan is in his best interest. And the money will follow this formula." Jude spoke in a voice
of unquestionable authority.

"Of course, Jude. It sounds like a good, work-
able plan. I'll keep a low-key profile with the interested parties," said Chandler. He had been in
Washington long enough to know how to take orders smartly where money was involved.

"One other thing," Jude said with almost
humor in his voice. "What is the status of the
amendment?"

"So far, twenty-eight states have ratified it. It's
going as planned, unnoticed and unreported in
the news. In fact, my friends at the White House
expect it to be enacted by the end of the year."

Jude answered quietly, "To quote Franklin D.
Roosevelt, in politics, nothing happens by accident. If it happens, you can bet it was planned
that way'."

Jude hung up gleefully.

CHAPTER 6

For several months, the Nixon's traveled internationally, promoting Pepsi. Sales were increasing; his connections and prestige were paying off. In Russia, Nixon began working a deal to trade Pepsi for vodka. This was less bizarre than one would suppose. Considering the Russian ruble was not worth much as currency, Nixon came up with the idea: product for product. This would increase profits for Pepsi, being the only licensed dealer of quality Russian vodka. This was one of the first large commercial trade agreements between the U.S. and the Soviet Union.

Throughout these travels, the former Vice President was treated with respect by both press and governmental representatives. He was considered as a traveling business statesman. Many doors were opened to him. It seemed as if an

invisible force was helping him to become a business success. He was discreet. He refrained from
criticizing either America's treaty commitments
or the political problems peculiar to whatever
country was his current host. He went so far as to
support the policies of the Democratic President,
Johnson. As a result, politicians back in the states
spoke more kindly of him, seeing no harm in
such an unofficial roving goodwill ambassador-
ship. His travels were helping American business
and didn't cost the taxpayers a dime. The common wisdom was that Nixon's political career
had been finished by his famous farewell speech
to the press in California, the "You won't have
Richard Nixon to kick around anymore." Even
the American presses, Nixon's longtime adversaries, were reasonably civil, just reporting where
he was and what dignitaries he'd met with. To the
press he was like a single large summer cloud,
visible but not threatening.

All seemed to be going well for the former Vice
President. His family often traveled with him,
and Pat was a gracious diplomat in her own right.
With the added help from Gala, Pat's wardrobe
discreetly became designer quality. Gala worked
with her on subtle ways of European etiquette.
These and a few other introductions helped Gala
to cement a bond with the Nixon family.

As for Gala, she too was enjoying her job. She
found Nixon easy to work with and he was quite
appreciative of how well she was doing. Pat Nixon

was unvaryingly cordial. Even the Nixon daughters made it plain that they liked and respected Gala. She maintained her tastefully luxurious apartment in New York. She dated discreetly. No money changed hands, and her dates were often under fifty and sometimes even unmarried. Overall, she lived the life of a hard-working high-powered executive secretary...not unlike many in the big city. The only drawback was that Gala hadn't yet been able to cajole Jude into explaining why she should be earning a thousand dollars a week for performing a normal job.

Gala was unpacking from one of her most recent trips when the phone rang. She was hoping it was one of Jude's infrequent phone calls. Without greeting, his voice said, "It's me. I'd like to meet you at that favorite little bar down in the Village in about an hour. Can you manage that?"

"How delightful!" Gala responded. "I'll be glad to see you again." Pushing her suitcase aside, she wondered if there'd be time to shower and change first. She thought about asking Jude for a few extra minutes, but she decided to just take her time and be fashionably late. "Let's think for a moment. Yes, I know the bar, and I'll see you there. Ciao."

When she reached the noisy, fern-burning bar called Iggy's, she found Jude looking at his watch, but he made no comment while she slid into the booth opposite him. Then, as if he'd been practicing it, he announced, "Gala, you look better every time I see you. Your new career does something for you."

"Why thank you, Jude." Gala smiled, considering the time well spent, after all. "I see you so seldom; sometimes I think maybe you have forgotten about me. But then I check my Swiss account and find the deposits. It's so reassuring knowing you do care."

"Trust me," Jude said in a quick voice. "I care about what you are doing, and I'm aware of what you are doing. All the reports I get say you're doing a great job, just as I thought you would." He paused for a moment and added, "So I have no doubts you'll handle the next phase of our project with the same expertise."

Gala sipped experimentally at the pre-ordered beer, now warm, withholding comment a moment while she thought. "Ah yes, the seduction phase," she said with a chuckle in her voice. "I have done some groundwork...good relationship with him and his family. Now I use my charm for the closing in part. When should I spring my irresistible trap?"

"Tomorrow would be all right," said Jude, with no hint of a smile. But when Gala coughed a little laugh, Jude did smile as if waiting to hear the joke.

"Why don't I call him right now and ask to meet him in the backseat of my car?" Gala said in a joking voice. Then she spoke in a cooler tone. "You know he's the original family man. In town, he's at the office or home...and either Pat or the daughters travel with us. I will need a little time to set it up."

"Pat Nixon has her favorite charity obligation in two weeks. Tomorrow, Nixon will get an invitation to a four-day bottle manufacturing convention in Denver. It's a local franchise-holders meeting also. He'll have to attend. And he'll be asked to speak on his around-the-world goodwill trip. But there'll also be impromptu meetings with local politicos, business people, that sort of thing. Nixon will need you to be hostess for him, set up the catering, and so forth. Pat won't be available until the weekend, and he'll have to get there on Wednesday night or Thursday morning. That will give you two nights, maybe three without the wife and kiddies around. I trust you can manage to take the ball over the goal line." Jude patted her hand.

"It's going to take some doing," Gala said dubiously, then added with a smile, "But rest assured he'll score." Both laughed.

"I am confident you'll succeed. Use your best judgment. If it isn't right, let's not jeopardize our position. I can always arrange another trip."

"Yes, I'm sure you can," said Gala as she slowly sipped again at the flat beer. She smiled at Jude and said, "Well, I will give it my best college try. And the next time we're together, perhaps you could order something other than draft beer. We are no longer in college. We are in the real world now." She then looked into Jude's eyes. "In this real world how is our real plan coming along?"

"In time...Gala...In time you'll know more. But for now, just keep up the good work."

⌒

Burning Tree Country Club was one of Washington's most exclusive and expensive golf clubs. It takes more than just money to be nominated for membership, but money is still a major prerequisite. There were some politicians with seniority who were members, along with many lobbyists who paid the bills for the seniority members. William Tallsand was such a member, and played each weekend...usually with a different partner or politician. This week he had the manager of Standard Oil's Baltimore refinery, Bruce Donlan, for a guest, along with Spiro Agnew, a Baltimore County Executive. The fourth member was Jack Fehan, president of Ever Green Development Company, a large developer of shopping centers and office buildings. The four players completed their game early in the afternoon that Sunday, then adjourned to the Grill for drinks and a sandwich. It was also a time to pay off the bets and to listen to stories of the "near perfect/ if only" shots. They grew a little noisier, speaking louder as the drinks took effect. The waiter, a young man, clean-looking, with a lot of energy, delivered another round of drinks.

"To the best shot of the day: Bruce Donlan's birdie on the twelfth hole," Bill Tallsand yelled.

"He saved me forty bucks with that eighteen-foot putt."

"Sounds like a hell of a putt," the waiter said as he put down the drinks.

"It *was* a hell of a putt," Tallsand said in a slurred voice. "Waiter, you seem to know golf. May I ask your name?"

"Bill Moylan, sir," the waiter answered quickly, as he started picking up dirty glasses.

"Fifty bucks if you can answer my question on golf!" Tallsand said loudly, waving his hand at the waiter. "Where does the name golf come from? Fifty bucks is yours if you're right." Everyone look perplexed, not wanting to yell the answer even if they knew.

"Gentlemen Only - Ladies Forbidden. They say it was written at St. Andrews in Scotland," he said loudly.

"That's it! Here's a fifty dollar bill." Tallsand gladly handed the money to the happy waiter. They laughed and drank some more.

"There's another debt that has to be paid today," Tallsand said, looking at Jack Fehan. "Did you bring it with you, Jack?"

Jack Fehan bent over to his gym bag and ruffled through his dirty socks and underwear looking for an envelope. "I have it right here." He picked it up, handed it to the waiter and said, "Would you hand this over to Mr. Agnew, the distinguished gentleman on the far side of the table?"

The waiter walked around the table and handed the envelope to Agnew, who looked somewhat startled. "What's this for?" he asked with a blank look on his face.

"That land we purchased four years ago over in Silver Spring. Well, the deal closed three weeks ago. It's going to be a large shopping center. Your share is fifty thousand, and that's the check." Jack then looked at Tallsand as if for approval, then added, "That's the reason you were invited here today. We thought we could win it back." They all laughed. It was a fun afternoon. Although Agnew didn't remember the details of the agreement, a few more drinks and all was well with the world.

On the flight to Denver in the small hours of Thursday morning, Nixon chatted wistfully to Gala about the days when he had Air Force II at his disposal, and all the service and personnel that went along with it. By contrast, he found the company Lear Jet cramped and noisy. After a few scotches, he added with a tired smile, "Well anyway, this is better than working for a living." He sat back and spoke again. "Sometimes I think of how close I came to becoming a sports writer."

As usual, Gala had efficiently smoothed their arrival. A waiting limousine zipped them through the dark, snow-shadowed hill to the Sheraton Hotel on the outskirts of the city. Two bellhops pounced on the suitcases and Nixon followed them toward the elevator while Gala took care of the formalities of registering.

When she rejoined Nixon a few minutes later, he was exploring the twentieth floor suite, pulling back drapes to peer at the barely-visible loom of the mountains. He commented, "All this space seems so large for just one person."

"Well sir, Mrs. Nixon will be joining you here on Friday night. Remember, we are hosting a reception this evening in this very suite and you will need space for the meetings beforehand." Gala looked around visualizing a large group of people talking and drinking. "All things considered, this large suite may just fit the bill. It doesn't take too many people to fill this room, and some are important people." She walked over to the large bar that ran along most of the side of the living room. "And you never know just who will show up...your popularity is growing, so we do want to make friends and influence people."

She then walked behind the bar, looking to ensure that it was well stocked. Satisfied, she asked, "Can I make you a drink? It's been long day."

"Mountain time. It's still last night on my watch." He glanced over at a large dark window. "Or is it the other way around?"

"It's an hour earlier than California time," suggested Gala.

"Okay, I'll have one scotch with a little water. But I will not drink alone," he said with a warm command.

"Ah, yes," Gala said as she proceeded to make the drinks. "Johnny Walker Black, on the rocks, with a splash of water." She made sure the bar had his favorite scotch. She then handed him his drink and lifted hers in a toast. "To California time."

"To the great state of California." He then took a large gulp. "What time is our reception tonight?"

"It starts at six thirty. Plenty of time for you to rest while I see to the final arrangements. And I promise this room will be cleared by nine tonight."

"If you can, you're a better man than I, Gunga Din." He laughed as if the scotch was having some effect. "Give politicians and news people free booze and they will stay till dawn or until the booze runs out."

Gala laughed, "I agree, but I am like a nor'easter subtle but powerful. I'll be able to move them out like the sand dunes of the Jersey shore."

"These are westerners...cowboy types. They may be a challenge, but again, you handled all those folks in Hong Kong quite well. So, I trust you can handle them also." He then finished his drink. "I'm tired. We don't have anything scheduled in the morning, so I'll sleep in." Then he added as an afterthought, "Ah, yes...I'll be doing some paperwork in the morning, so only disturb me if you need to do so. I'll be sleeping." Both laughed again.

Gala responded, "I'll be up early in the morning. I have to make the final arrangements, and oh yes, the changes on the notes for your talk tomorrow night."

"You get the proper rest," Nixon said leveling a finger at her.

"You're very kind, and so thoughtful," she said warmly.

"I mean it," he said with a smile.

Punctually at six, Gala knocked at Nixon's door. He opened it in shirtsleeves, his tie half-knotted. Knowing how he disliked being seen without a suit jacket and everything complete, Gala went at once to tidy the sofa where his speech was still laid out, expecting him to go right back to the bedroom. She said, "The bartender and maid are due in ten minutes along with the hors d'oeuvres. So excuse me while I get ready for them." She straightened, gathering the typed sheets of papers into a neat sheaf, and was surprised to find him still standing by the open door. She raised her brows inquiringly.

"Was it just three hours ago I saw you leave here in a sweater and slacks, with a scarf around your head?" Nixon asked. "You can change things so rapidly."

Gala brushed lightly at the side darts of her carefully chosen white evening gown, and then lifted fingers to touch her freshly styled hair, lying loose on her shoulders like spun silk. "No, that was the day costume for work and play." As she revealed her complete wardrobe and figure she said, "This is my evening costume for work and play."

"Well, I think the day costume and the evening costume are both..." He paused for a moment, seeming a little frustrated, then patted his own hair. "No, I don't mean... well, you look very pretty in either outfit."

"Please, I have to..." she gestured with the papers, turning aside as if flustered, and straightened a couch pillow.

Taking the hint, Nixon shut the hall door and went off to finish dressing. But Gala was pleased, having created exactly the impression she intended for the evening. Demure but flustered... that was the way she wanted it. The old, old briar patch game. She hummed softly as she pulled the drapes closed against the snow-stark vista and hid a used glass in the kitchenette cabinet.

The help and food carts arrived promptly, and Gala supervised the placement of the trays and bartender's final preparations. At six thirty the first guest arrived, followed within minutes by a half dozen more. By seven, crossing the room required careful planning. Big-brimmed hats were becoming a hazard and, as predicted, men were looking vaguely around for places to put those big hats down. Gala collected the hats and relayed them to safety in one of the side bedrooms. Passing near the group gathered around Nixon, Gala heard somebody asking the standard questions of whether he'd ever run for public office again. In private conversation he'd say, 'I'm enjoying life too much to run for public office. I enjoy private life. Why, even the press is kind to me once in a while. I think they like me working for someone other than the people.' The comment got the usual laugh. But in his heart he had to admit, he doubted it. A two-time loser had no chance of being elected to the only office he'd consider - the presidency.

The decibel level and the temperature seemed to be rising satisfactorily. The bartender was busy. There were bursts of general laughter around Nixon.

Things seemed to be going well, and among friendly faces Nixon seemed to be abandoning formality. He was loosening up a little. Sliding past, Gala saw to it he never held an empty glass for long.

As she was collecting a glass from a guest, she heard Nixon's voice mutter just behind her, "I think this will be a late night."

With a gleam in her eye, as if to frown, she replied, "Just wait...I feel a north-eastern breeze."

At ten minutes to nine, Gala tapped on a glass until she had most people's attention. "Ladies and gentlemen, thank you all for coming this evening. And thank you for your goodwill. The Pepsi Cola Company has taken the liberty of making dinner reservations for all of you tonight at the famed Cattleman's Club. You're all invited. Your reservations are for nine thirty and there are limousines downstairs which will take you to and from the club. Unfortunately, prior commitments prevent Mr. Nixon from attending. On behalf of the Pepsi Cola Company, it's been our pleasure to share this evening with you. We hope the Cattleman's Club will live up to its outstanding reputation for fine food and outstanding atmosphere. Thank you all for coming and goodnight."

The noise level went up at least a factor of three. Gala got close enough to the maid to hiss, "Hats." While Gala helped guests locate coats and scarves, the maid passed the headgear to its owners as they milled toward the outer door. There was a crowd around Nixon for several minutes, people offering thanks and good wishes. But finally the tide really turned as the last hat was claimed.

As the maid and bartender started collecting trays, Gala brushed her hands briskly together. Meeting Nixon's amused eyes, she remarked smugly, "They're all gone, and no sand left on the beach."

"Miraculous!" he commended her. "I was sure this would go past midnight and end up in a political brawl. However did you pull off a mass invitation to the Cattleman's Club? Forest Lawn has a shorter waiting list. I recall that Rockefeller sold it, but I didn't think it was Pepsi that bought it."

"Pepsi didn't buy it," Gala settled on the arm of a chair sighing cheerfully. "A friend of a friend bought it, so I arranged a little business for them and saved you from a political brawl."

"Until tonight nobody could have convinced me that this ex-politician had as many friends or this kind of business clout."

"Watch out - you'll start thinking of potential campaign contributions, shaking hands, then the rubber chicken circuit. And then where's your private life?"

The bartender came to ask if there'd be anything else. Gala pointed to the table by the hall door, responding, "In the drawer there's an envelope for you and another for Marie. Thanks so much, and goodnight." Turning back to Nixon, who'd dropped down to the couch, she added, "You could have eaten at the Cattleman's Club, too. But you seemed tired. You still could, actually, and give them all a happy surprise, if you'd like."

"No, your guess was right. I'd rather order up something from room service." He started to look over to the bar and said, "I noticed a menu here somewhere."

Before Nixon could think of where to look, Gala had the menu in her hand, handing it to him. "For your convenience, sir," Gala said with a smile.

"You must be beat after all you did today," said Nixon with concern in his voice.

"Night gnome showing wear and tear is she?" Gala asked with the least quirk of a smile.

"No, I didn't mean, not at all. Gala, I hate eating alone. Will you join me here?"

"That's a wonderful idea. With this convention, everything's jammed. And I've never liked eating alone either."

"Then it's settled. We will eat here tonight," he then added, "quietly." He handed the menu to Gala saying, "You do everything so well, would you order dinner and I'll make a few fresh drinks?"

"Another wonderful idea." Gala commented happily.

Gala made the call for dinner. She had already arranged with the hotel chef to have fresh Romaine lettuce, Roquefort blue cheese, raw eggs, and Russian anchovies on hand. These were essential for the classic Caesar Salad Gala was to make tableside. The main course was to be the chef's famous Chateaubriand, with golden western potatoes. The dessert was Crème Brulee, with fresh crushed vanilla and Cuban brown sugar melted on top. She requested two bottles of French Bordeaux, 1956. This meal was to be special.

"Well you did it again, Gala," Nixon said as he took a sip of his after dinner Napoleon Brandy.

"I did what?" Gala asked softly.

"You created another wonderful evening for me. That was the best hotel meal I have ever had. I doubt if it was standard room service," Nixon said. "You have a way of making travel smoother and life much more pleasant."

The radio played soft music while they continued consuming the after dinner drinks. They talked about many topics such as family. He told her of his Quaker mother and her spendthrift ways, and of his ancestor Joseph Milhouse who crossed the Delaware with George Washington. They spoke of the world in general; of different places of interest both had seen. The conversation developed into a pleasant sensation of drifting into a melancholy mood. Nixon set his glass down, remarking, "That's one of my favorite

songs. Sad but beautiful - The Tennessee Waltz."
He sat listening for a moment. Then, in a soft
voice, just above a whisper, he said, "Would you
like to dance?"

"I'd be honored, Mr. Vice President," Gala replied, drifting to her feet as he took her hand.

As they danced, his clasp was at first soft and
tentative, but eventually his hold became more
assured. Her eyes were almost shut, to not im-
pede his looking at her. She hummed along with
the music. She felt his hand lift to the back of
her neck, stroking her hair. When the announcer's voice came on, announcing the song, she
and Nixon stood apart, uncertain. Her eyes still
downcast, Gala murmured, "Oh that was nice.
That was very nice. I wonder…"

He moved forward and gently kissed her.
Then again and again. Gala didn't return to her
room that night, or the following morning. When
she finally persuaded Nixon, during the afternoon, that he really had to go over his speech
again before the evening's presentation, he put on
his formal appearance, as if to return to business.
And gradually, without anything being said, she
transformed again into the efficient personal assistant: friendly, but no more than friendly, letting the details of the conference separate them
as though it were inevitable. On Friday evening,
when the limousine delivered Pat Nixon to the
lobby, Nixon greeted his wife warmly, and Gala
and Pat exchanged the usual light embrace and

everything was almost as it had been before. Almost...

Less than five minutes after Gala returned to her apartment that Sunday night, her phone rang. Groping for it, she heard Jude's brisk voice inquiring, "Well, do we have soup yet?"

"Well you might say we have mixed the ingredients," Gala quipped.

"Same place in the Village?"

"Jude, it's nearly midnight..."

"They don't close till two, I checked." Jude then hung up.

Gala splashed cold water on her face, reapplied her makeup, and ran a brush through her hair. As an afterthought, she made an obscene gesture at the dark window.

He was having her watched. With that timing, she was certain of it. Or maybe the apartment was bugged so she added a few choice words. A thousand dollars a week didn't seem nearly enough at that moment. Then she tugged at her coat and phoned the doorman to flag a cab.

Sunday nights were quiet even in Greenwich Village. Iggy's was not crowded and the noise level and music were lower. Jude sat at a corner table facing the entrance door, waiting for someone. Gala walked in with her head held high and a smile on her lips. Although tired and a little disheveled, she still looked beautiful. Jude sat anxiously, wanting to get the scoop.

Gala spotted him and walked directly to his table. "I'm not drinking beer tonight," she said in a voice to be reckoned with.

"Kendall Jackson Chardonnay," Jude said, as he slid a glass of white wine in her direction. "I haven't forgotten. So please sit down and tell me all about your adventures."

Gala slowly sat down looking directly at Jude with almost contempt for him, ordering her out on a night like this. "It will take more than a glass of wine to win my good graces." She began to chuckle and added, "Of course, you pay me for my good graces."

The conversation went on about the Thursday night encounter. In their in-depth conversations, Nixon told her how close he had been to Jack Kennedy; that Kennedy had given him money for his first Senate campaign. She went on to say how intimate they had become, and how as adults they realized it was merely a sexual encounter. She assured Jude that their working relationship would remain intact, and that she and Nixon had a good understanding. He was a decent family man, she was a career executive assistant, and they could help each other and work well together. They were professionals. She spoke with a sense of achievement, recovering her usual animation.

"Excellent. I knew you'd manage it with flying colors!" said Jude with a voice warm with enthusiasm. "Now, tell me, would he run for the right office if he had the chance?"

"Like an old race horse that hears a bell. He'd be off and running," Gala said without hesitation. "Well, let me rephrase that. He would, but it would have to be a big office, I mean really big." She then looked startled. "Is this part of your plan? Just what is happening, I mean are you priming him to run again?" She paused as Jude looked around to the empty booths nearby as if he expected them to be crammed with spies. "You certainly didn't need to spend all that cash on me to get him to run. All you had to do was ask him twice."

"You are doing your assignment just fine, Gala," Jude said coolly. "Stay close to him. We want him to want you around for a long time."

"He's the true blue type. We must take into consideration that he may want to get rid of me, just for appearance sake." She paused taking another sip of her wine. "Especially if he is thinking of running for office. And by the way, what big office are you planning for him?"

"I'm sure you are in good standing now. We want to keep it that way," said Jude. "I'll be meeting with him in a few days. For the record, you and I have known each other since our college days. From a distance, we knew some of the same people; visited some of the same hangouts, right?"

Gala nodded her head. She was getting tired now, and she yawned as delicately as possible.

Jude spoke again. "I understand that you want to know more about what's happening. After my meeting next week, you will see a few more tiles in the mosaic."

Jude seemed to lighten up smiling saying in a jovial mystical manner, "You'll find the future quite interesting. As Vladimir Nabokov used to put it, chess is the game of the Gods, because of the infinite possibilities."

Gala stared intensely at Jude, and in a forceful whisper said, "What office, Jude?"

Jude smiled saying, "You'll see a few more tiles in the mosaic appear."

CHAPTER 7

Jude was becoming accustomed to some of the better ways of life in the Big Apple. Due to his business activities and contacts he was able to join the more exclusive private clubs. However, his favorite haunt was the Jockey Club. The Grill consisted of a large bar area decorated in impressive dark wood paneling. A man's drinking habitat, it was frequented by many famous authors and politicians. This restaurant was open to the public, and was considered an "in" place to be seen, and a decent place to impress clients. If you were known there, you could be known anywhere. There were areas that were semi-private alcoves, where busy businessmen could talk, more-or-less in private...assuming sophisticated snooping gear wasn't employed.

When Jude arrived, he went directly to the table he had selected earlier in the week. He tipped the formally dressed maitre d' a twenty-dollar bill, with instructions to escort his guest, Richard Nixon, to his table. Jude sat quietly sipping his glass of water. He would not have any alcoholic drink alone. He glanced sourly at his watch until Nixon arrived, almost twenty minutes late. When he saw Nixon being escorted through the dining room, Jude stood up to greet him. But the popular Nixon turned aside, here and there, exchanging greetings with other diners and, in general, behaving as though he owned the place. Finally Nixon shook the hand of the maitre d' and said, "Thank you Charles. It's always a pleasure to see you." Jude noticed Nixon slipping him a twenty, also.

Jude extended his hand, saying, "Good afternoon, Mr. Vice President. It's a pleasure to meet you. I'm Jude Thaddeus."

"Jude, it's my pleasure to meet you. It is a beautiful day outside. I love New York in this kind of weather," replied Nixon while being seated by Charles, whose raised hand summoned a waiter. The waiter was prompt to ask if they cared for anything from the bar. Nixon smiled at the waiter and the waiter spoke first. "Your usual cocktail, Mr. Vice President?" Nixon smiled even more broadly and remarked, "Yes, thank you, Ivor. And will you join me for a drink, Jude?"

"Yes, I will. May I ask what you are having?" Jude asked quickly.

"I'm having a dry martini, up, made with Bombay Gin, with one olive," Nixon replied.

Then looking again at the waiter, "Isn't that right, Ivor?"

"That would be fine for me also," said Jude, winning the good will of Nixon.

There was idle talk about the weather, living in New York, and recent football games until their lunch came. There was less idle, but still general talk about politics, and the political arena. After their coffee cups had been refilled, Jude judged the time appropriate to speak more directly.

Jude sipped his coffee slowly. "It's obvious that you enjoyed being in the political arena, and others remember you quite fondly." Putting down his coffee he continued, "It makes me wonder whether you'd consider getting back into politics?"

"No. I enjoy my private life too much," Nixon said with a confident smile. "There's half the work, half the heartache, none of the public criticism, and four times the money."

"I'm sorry to hear that you're so content. Because I, and many substantial followers, believe you can be elected the next president of the United States."

Nixon was a great poker player. He didn't blink an eye. He just shook his head, commenting, "Johnson can't be beaten. No matter how unpopular Vietnam is, we are still involved in a war, and the American people won't change horses in the middle of a muddy, even though bloody, stream. Add to that his so-called War on Poverty.

He'll be one of the most popular presidents in this century."

"My sources, which are quite reliable, are convinced Johnson won't be running again," Jude said softly.

With a frowning stare, straight from the Alger Hiss investigation days, Nixon snapped,

"I haven't heard a word about any such thing. Why is he setting up his staff for the primaries?"

"Your involvement with politics has been somewhat restricted in recent years. I assure you, on good information, Johnson is finished. It's personal."

After a moment's thought, Nixon lifted a dismissive hand. "A distinction without a difference. With Humphrey as vice president, nobody else has a chance. George Washington couldn't beat him in the primaries, and the Democrats control Congress and the White House. Lyndon Johnson's coattail will cast a long shadow." He paused, took a sip of coffee, and spoke again. "Believe me, I have spent a lot of years in the arena of politics, as you call it. One thing it taught me was to be realistic."

"Johnson's coattails may not stretch as far as people think. The war is creating serious ill feelings in this country. Electing Humphrey means no change of policy. Humphrey is a big talker and spender. The country can't afford him. That's why there are people of influence who are serious about supporting a strong candidate to win the next election." Jude paused, looking causally around the restaurant, then continued, "There has been some serious discussion on this matter. And the upshot of it was that I was asked to meet with, and find out your opinion, and to ask, quite bluntly, with the proper support, would you be our candidate for president of the United States?"

Nixon sat for a few moments thinking, then said, "When Henry Kissinger suggested we have lunch together, even though I had never heard of you, I thought it was for a significant reason. I take it this is not the idle talk of a young upstart." He paused and spoke again. "Before I could seriously consider, I would be interested in knowing who the influential people are that you speak of, and how serious is their commitment?"

"I'm sorry. I'm not at liberty to say. However, I can say that the man in the governor's mansion in Albany is prepared to give you his support. The next president will have to carry the state of New York in order to win." Jude waited a minute for that to sink in, and then went on moderately. "We realize that if the Republicans are to win, we'll have to present a united front. With the governor of New York behind you, you're off to a good start. With Rockefeller's help you can carry New York, and with your base in California you might just carry it. With those two states in your camp, you stand a good shot." Jude watched Nixon's face to see any emotion. He saw none. He continued. "To show you that there is widespread support from many sources, I've brought an initial contribution for your campaign chest." He lay on the table a blank check written to the as-yet non-existent Nixon Election Fund. The amount was one million dollars.

Nixon picked up the check, looking at it front and back, as if resisting the impulse to hold it up to the light like a suspect twenty-dollar bill. Then he laid it on the tablecloth. "I accept that as a demonstration of serious intentions. But it surprises me in more ways than one. The governor and I have been political enemies nearly all my political life. I think it's odd to choose me. I understand he is running himself. And frankly, I'd say that right now he stands a better chance of being elected than I do."

Jude hadn't expected either the insight or the directness. "I understand Governor Rockefeller has recently made new political assessments. Quite frankly he is not finding fertile political base outside New York. Among other considerations are his age and health. He doesn't feel up to another primary like in sixty-four. In fact, he's looking toward retirement. For him, the next best thing would be influencing the party platform and the choice of candidate. He believes you have the greatest chance of winning. You're a fighter; you'll go back in the ring. Last time you had forty-nine percent of the popular vote. This time, with the right support, you'll win."

Nixon sat quietly, taking in as much as he could. "If I choose to run, it will be with the political backing and the financial support of Governor Rockefeller. As I have said, I know him well enough to know that he isn't interested in supporting me because he likes my viewpoint." He then looked directly into Jude's eyes. "What does he want for his support?"

"The Governor, too, is a realist," Jude quickly assured him. "He can't be president, but he can help elect the next president. For that he wants to have a voice of influence. He'll want some of his people in key positions in the new administration. I'm sure there are some friends whom he would like to make ambassadors, and such. He would like to have your personal ear on key legislation, but nothing binding." Jude paused, looking for effect, then continued. "There is one particular position that the Governor has requested to be filled with his recommendation: and that is your running mate. He wants his close friend and loyal supporter, the Governor of Maryland, Spiro Agnew. Their friendship goes back some time. In fact, in the last campaign, Agnew headed up the Rockefeller for President Committee."

"To name a vice president - that's a considerable piece of the pie he's asking for."

"Yes, but the rest of the pie is yours, and you can eat it at the White House. You'll have to determine how crucial the role of vice president would be in your presidency," Jude said blandly, certain that the role of vice president was like choosing a spare tire. You need one, but hope you never have to use it.

"What he wants seems reasonable," Nixon said, and then added, "This check is only seed money, you know."

"When you give me your favorable decision, I will deposit an additional four million in your campaign fund. That will cover startup costs, gathering a campaign organization, and making yourself available as a speaker. You can help local Republicans get elected, thus creating some political obligations. However, you needn't declare right away. Keep under the political radarscope. Your position with Pepsi Cola's already given you considerable visibility."

"An undeclared candidate can get away with a lot of things. Making allies without too much compromise." He paused for a moment, gazing across the room. "Hence, they are slower to take up arms. And a prince may more easily win them and hold them." He smiled and added, "So wrote Machiavelli."

Jude said to himself, *Fiat accompli. It's a done deal.* However, he wanted Nixon to confirm his intentions. "Time is a major concern. When can we expect your decision?"

"Oh, I've made my decision," Nixon said quickly, "but I'll have to discuss this with my wife and daughters. And I want to talk to some colleagues to see what they think. I'm more than interested. Yes, very interested. Agnew, did you say? Don't know the man."

"Please remember, Mr. Vice President," Jude became serious again, "what we discussed here today is of a very confidential nature. You understand?"

"I understand completely. I will be back in touch with you in a few days. You'll have my decision then."

Jude passed him his embossed business card. Nixon studied it closely and put it away, almost as carefully as the million-dollar check from Jude. Nixon then said in a casual voice, "But if you need me, feel free to call my office at any time. I understand you know my personal assistant, Gala Dufante?" Belying the tone, Nixon was looking at Jude for a reaction.

"Dufante? It's an unusual name, but I don't seem to place it." Jude's voice was slow and careful.

"College...she said she knew you from her college days. I believe she went to Vassar," Nixon said.

"Gala Dufante. Yes, I do remember her. I think she was an archeology major. Quite a pretty girl and very smart as I recall. How long has she been with you?"

"Just a short time. You're right. She is attractive, and very bright. Quite an asset to any organization."

"I only wish I had known she was available. I would have scooped her up before you had a chance. Please give her my best, and tell her I hope to see her soon," Jude said.

Jude's being openly envious of Nixon's assistant seemed to reassure Nixon of her reputation and loyalty. Both men shook hands and expressed their delight with the lunch, and agreed to be in contact within days. Both were inwardly quite happy as they left the restaurant.

But Jude heard far earlier than the expected few days. Gala called the following evening to report. She told Jude that Nixon came back to the office after their lunch very enthused, and as an afterthought, had said to her, "Jude sends his best regards." Soon afterward, he went home early. Then Nixon had cancelled all his appointments and spent the whole day on the phone. There was a fluttering of calls throughout the day with some very interesting people. He spoke to his wife off-and-on all day, and with his daughters who were obviously excited. He was happy and planning.

Incidentally, all Nixon's hints that Gala might be happier at some other job had stopped abruptly. Much organizing would need to be done. She'd been asked to become a founding member of the unofficial Nixon for President Team.

"So, Jude," Gala said in summarizing the conversation, "you may expect a call tomorrow, early in the morning. He is as excited as a high school cheerleader on Prom night."

"Very good, Gala," Jude said as if thinking aloud, then added, "Pin and the fork, a classic move on the chess board. Two separate strategies and both control the moves of the opponent."

CHAPTER 8

The following spring of 1968, demonstrations increased in numbers and intensity, as did American military troop strength in Vietnam. Almost all of the colleges were hot beds for strikes and upheaval. There was unrest in the black community, with riots in many large cities. Most politicians were looking for cover and a means of getting re-elected. President Johnson's own party was turning against him; Bobby Kennedy was making gestures toward seeking the presidential nomination.

At last, due to a bad heart condition and pressure from his family, the party, and certain lobbyists, chief among them Bill Tallsand, Lyndon Johnson informed a stunned country that he had decided to not seek, nor accept re-election to the presidency.

Events thereafter fell out pretty much as Jude had predicted. Through a carefully orchestrated ground-swell movement, Nixon captured the Republican nomination, to the surprise of many. Almost as surprising, he named the little-known Governor of Maryland, Spiro T. Agnew, as his running mate. Rockefeller loyalists found it easy to support a Nixon-Agnew ticket, and the campaign was underway.

The campaign of 1968 was tough. Nixon and Humphrey fought long and hard. However, the presence of the third party candidate, George Wallace, shattered what marginal unity Democrats could have mustered even in the best of times. Humphrey needed those southern states. But the well-financed organization of George Wallace not only took electoral votes in key southern states, but also drew a large number of votes in northern states who would have gone to Humphrey. The Democrats held both the House of Representatives and the Senate with large majorities. Vice President Humphrey was very popular; he came within one percent of Nixon in popular votes. It was an election result no one would have predicted, except for Jude. The stealthy victory belonged to the enthusiast who planned the plan and celebrated in solitude.

As soon as the results were certain, Jude put in a call on the secure line for a meeting the following morning with Jack Chandler. Jude had been keeping in phone contact with Rockefeller's man every week or so during the campaign. It went well, but it cost more money than expected. It was the results which were important anyway. Now there would be additional requirements for the plan to go forward. These would have an effect on more than politics alone. Jude wanted this meeting with Chandler to use his sensitive persuasion.

It was a cold rainy morning as Jude jumped out of the cab. The doorman greeted him and said, "Welcome to the Ritz." Jude smiled and went directly to the private suite Chandler maintained at the New York Ritz.

Jude was escorted into the suite by the butler. As he walked into the living room, lavishly decorated in the style of early American, he expected a band to be playing, with heaps of congratulations. Instead he met a cool Chandler. He was standing rigid, with a cigarette in hand, nattily dressed in a dark blue pinstriped suit, white shirt, and a bright yellow power tie. "Congratulations on the election results. However, this election was very expensive...cost us over twenty million dollars."

"Thank you, Jack, for your overwhelming appreciation," Jude said in an irritated voice. "We got our man elected. Sure it was expensive. Remember, we had to finance two campaigns, and Wallace needed more money than we originally thought. His electoral votes and the votes he took from Humphrey were worth every dime. If we didn't spend that money, Humphrey would be president. And that I couldn't afford." Jude walked over to the sofa and flopped down as if to demonstrate that he was in control and wanted to be comfortable. Jude started to think...perhaps Chandler was whining because Jude's plans had been so spectacularly successful. Chandler had been somewhat skeptical in going along with the plan. Not really believing, but acting as a reluctant agent for Rockefeller.

"I'm going to have some coffee. Would you like some, Jude?" Chandler asked as he walked across the room. He turned and smiled at Jude as if with restrained hospitality.

"Yes, I would, thank you," Jude said getting up and walking toward the table. "I'll make my own. I am somewhat fussy." As Jude walked over, he was thinking about Chandler. Perhaps he realizes I'm not one of the many hustlers Rockefeller has run into over the years, flimflamming him out of money with scams. So far this plan has worked like a Swiss watch. Maybe he doesn't like being summoned to an early meeting with a new player, half his age. He's been with the governor for a long time. He may be afraid of the power I have demonstrated. Maybe he's afraid of what lies ahead. Whatever his concerns are, one thing is for sure, he now knows I'm for real.

Both men walked to the dining area and sat at a small table. "This table is an original Shaker," Jude said, then added, "one can tell by the hinges on the drop leaves."

"Yes, it is, Jude. You have a good eye for antique furniture, and a great mind, shall we say, for other things." Jack, sitting across the table from Jude, put his coffee cup down. While looking at

Jude, he said, "Well, Jude...we spent a lot of money, and the governor has not complained." He paused. Then in a joking way, said, "Although he did say, 'A few million here and a few million there...pretty soon it could add up to some real money.'" Chandler's mood seemed to improve with his coffee. Jude thought that perhaps he had some booze in it.

"Jack, as I said earlier, the money was well spent. We're on target. Phase one is complete. Our man is on the way to the White House, with our team. The twenty-fifth Amendment to the Constitution has been ratified by the states and is now law." Jude was gaining back his enthusiasm. "We've accomplished a lot. Yes we spent a lot, but the governor will get the money back many times over with the oil profits he's going to realize in a very short time...when we initiate our next phase."

"Oil? What phase is that? Nobody ever mentioned oil. What's oil got do with it?" Chandler asked, seemingly startled. Then he continued, "There's nothing new in oil. There's no way to get a price up to increase profits. Don't you think we've been trying? The Rockefellers made all their money in oil. At one time we controlled eighty percent of the world's oil; we are still the largest organization in the industry. But look at the retail outlets. They're all cutting prices, trying for a bigger slice. And the independents are the worst of all. The oil supply is increasing and prices are decreasing. Everybody's trying to get into the oil business. That's the basic theory of marketplace economics."

"Marketplace economics is determined by two major factors: supply as well as demand. I can assure you that the twenty million spent so far will be peanuts for what his return will be, as a side benefit of our plan. And it is all for the better that it will seem a mere side effect. Neither Rockefeller nor even Nixon will be seen as directly responsible. To accomplish this side distraction, we will need the considerable services of our most powerful agent in the Middle East - which, by no coincidence, is where most of the world's oil comes from." Jude thought for a moment and asked before Chandler could speak, "By the way, Jack, do you know who is the largest purchaser of oil from the Middle East?"

"Standard Oil is," Chandler said quickly.

Jude smiled, saying, "You're right, Jack. And Standard is owned by...?" Jude bent his head in a jovial manner, pointing to Chandler. Both men chuckled. Jude continued to speak. "The western countries are hooked on oil. In this country, there's a limit to what any individual company can charge for domestically produced oil. The cost is rising all the time. So it's simple to buy abroad on the international market, although it's fragmented and chaotic. But with the right players, it can be controlled. And we will be the beneficiaries."

"I'm still listening," Chandler said, appearing to be in deep thought.

"In the chaotic international oil market, the Arab states, which are the largest producers, are trying to under-cut and out-produce one another. They're desperate for hard cash currency. Now all we have to do is educate them and organize them." Jude hunched closer to Chandler, saying, "Bear with me, Jack. You have read how John D. Rockefeller became a monopoly. Well, one of his tricks was with the railroads. As an example, he would go to the local railroad company and ask, "How much is it to ship a carload of oil from Pittsburgh to Philadelphia?" Well, the railroad person would say, "Seventy-five dollars." John D. would say, "Okay. I am going to ship one hundred cars, and I will pay seventy-seven, but only if you charge my competitors one hundred dollars per carload." The railroad went along making more money, and thus eliminating his competition. The government finally made such practices illegal. They called it restraint of trade. Well, I hope to work a similar operation. Look... Standard is the largest buyer of Arab oil. Hell, Standard Oil developed the majority of fields over there. We can deploy our agent to the area. Our agent will say to Abdul, "Who is your biggest customer? Abdul will reply, "Why, you are Mr. Standard," and then we ask, "How much do we pay now for a barrel of oil?" Abdul will reply, "Three dollars a barrel, if we can get it." Then we say, "Standard will buy all the oil you can pump for ten dollars a barrel. But we will only buy from an Arab recognized organization we set up; and you must sell to everyone else at twelve dollars a barrel."

"A little far-fetched, isn't it Jude? We're having a hard time selling what oil we have. Making a deal with our suppliers to raise prices seems foolish. As you said earlier, it's marketplace economics. If we can control the supply, we will control the demand. And in doing so, Mr. Rockefeller will enhance his fortune immeasurably."

Jude was quick with his response. "If our organization controls sixty percent of the oil being shipped to the U.S., and suddenly we stop shipments, at the right political time, it will cause havoc like nothing in American history. There will be long lines of cars waiting for gas at any price. There may be gas rationing; there will be a public outcry exceeding any Vietnam War protests; and this will be an issue that will touch everybody, not just the college demonstrators. In the middle of this confusion and upheaval, hardly anyone will notice the change of personnel in the Oval Office."

Chandler just sat as if stunned. Eventually, he commented, "I hadn't realized you were entertaining a plan quite that ambitious."

"That's part of the plan I will be working on next. Of course there is a lot to be done behind the scenes. That reminds me, Doctor Kissinger will be of immense help." Jude breathed in a large gulp of air as if to swell up his chest. "I may need his services for the next few years."

"In what capacity?" Chandler asked meekly.

"Secretary of State. The suggestion will reach Nixon from several quarters, including the press. Considering his public distaste for Nixon, the press will love and respect him as being independent and there is no visible link to the Governor."

"Interesting...Nixon and Kissinger working together. In nineteen sixty, Kissinger actually cried when Nixon got the nomination over Rockefeller. He has never liked or trusted Nixon. What, pray tell, will be his real mission for the new president?" Chandler asked quietly.

"He will become the architect of American foreign policy, in time. However, at first, he will be a global trouble-shooter. And Nixon will need all the help he can get. Because of Kissinger's Harvard academic background, the press will applaud his movements. All his deeds will be considered brilliant. If we play our cards well, he just might get a Nobel Peace Prize in the process. Gradually he will grow in stature and influence to become America's most powerful Secretary of State." Jude paused, smiling. "Having had Doctor Kissinger as a professor in college, I can see his relishing in this job. The travel, prestige, women. Yes, he will be very happy for the next few years. And he'll take comfort, knowing that he'll be preparing the Oval Office for his pedagogue, Governor Rockefeller."

CHAPTER 9

Some weeks later, there was another conversation, which was to be of considerable later significance. It was held in the President-Elect transition office.

John Mitchell, having headed the campaign, was a member of Nixon's transition team, preparing for the change in administration. He handled many of the inauguration festivities. He worked for Rockefeller to raise bonds to build the new state buildings in Albany, called the Marble Monuments. Now, he reported to Nixon on progress and various other recommendations.

Mitchell was a distinguished New York corporate lawyer who'd been Nixon's law partner in an earlier time. Mitchell had a long, lugubrious face that made him look like a cross between a bloodhound and a character called the Deacon in the *Pogo* comic strip. Quite a bit older than Nixon, he was overweight and almost bald, but he still looked physically tough. That was appropriate, since he was strongly recommended by interested parties to be the next Attorney General.

"Well," Mitchell was commenting, "we've finished with the furniture, carpets, and drapes in both the public and private quarters. The new phones are something special. The TVs will be installed tomorrow. Even the light switches are being replaced. Just about everything that belonged to the Democrats is gone now, and will stay gone for at least eight years, I hope. Maybe longer." Both men laughed.

The President-Elect leaned back in his chair. "That sounds fine, John. I want everything taken out. We will create our own image."

"There's one other thing I think we should discuss, Dick," Mitchell said. "Johnson has a recording system all over the White House. It's in the Oval Office, Air Force One, and other places. He even has the phone lines tapped."

"I want that recording system removed," Nixon said smartly. "President Johnson told me about it on my first inspection visit after the election. He told me Kennedy's people originally installed it. But, when Johnson became President of course he liked the system. Johnson wanted it so he could have the proof of what any of the congressmen said after a few drinks, when their guard was down. That's when he would like to 'strong arm' them into doing things his way."

"Probably Bobby's idea," Mitchell comment-ed sourly. He'd never made a secret of his low opinion of the former Attorney General. He'd often refer to him as "a carpetbagger," referring to Robert Kennedy's nominal New York residen-cy that allowed him to run for Senate as a New Yorker. "The Kennedy's were snoopers. The stuff Bobby got on Martin Luther King would melt the phone." Mitchell had a habit of burying his head when he was in deep thought, and that's what he looked like when he began to speak again. "Dick, there may be some merit to having a recording system of your own put in, say only in the Oval Office and the conference room at Camp David. When you have a private conversation with a world leader, you can't sit there like some bushy-haired young lawyer taking notes on a yellow legal pad. With a voice activated system, there'd be no notes, no witnesses, but an accurate record of every conversation. I think that would be of great historical use. You know we have a lot of campaign money left over. The committee could purchase a modern system as a gift to you. Then when you left, you could take the whole system with you, tapes and all, for your memoirs and your presidential library."

"It certainly would be valuable to have a pri-vate recording system. Especially when I sit down to write my memoirs." Nixon seemed in deep thought. "What about the legality of campaign funds being used to buy something like this?"

"As Attorney General, off-hand I'd say no, there should be no problem. The committee would gift it to you, and you would depreciate it over the years to zero." Mitchell then added, "When your term is up, you leave the White House, and you'll take your personal items with you. This will be one of them."

"It sounds good to me, John. Do you have any system in mind?" Nixon asked.

"There have been a lot of developments in the technology since the Kennedy's put that system in. The new voice-activated system works great. No buttons or switches, and now they come with long tapes that will record all day, if necessary. In fact, we had a system put in our offices in Rockefeller Center. We had a conference room outfitted with one. It worked great. I'll see if I can get the same company that did our office. They do very good work, and they work very discreetly." Mitchell paused, smiled and said, "This will be a very private system. The fewer people who know about it, the better."

"I may not even tell Pat." Both men laughed.

CHAPTER 10

The Hawthorn Inn was one of those few, quaint little out-in-the-country restaurants, which at one time was a large colonial farmhouse. The exterior had a postcard quality one would expect to see in historical New England. The Inn had been standing for over two hundred years. The interior had been preserved with Early American furnishings. It was located on the famous Concord Pike near Cambridge, not far from Harvard. It was a nice quiet place to have lunch, famous for its lobster salad sandwich. Jude chose the site, knowing it was one of Dr. Kissinger's favorite haunts. Jude arrived early to choose the table, to ensure that they would have privacy, and to mildly demonstrate that he was in control of his former university professor.

After the pleasantries of their greeting, they began to discuss the reason for this lunch meeting.

Kissinger maintained, civilly but firmly, that he was concerned about his ability to get along with the Nixon people. They had a real distrust for him, and he had no personal relationship with Nixon. His joining a new administration, and having only a behind-the-scenes presence, meant he had little influence or power. And he felt that the Nixon people would keep it that way.

"I'm only taking this position for the Governor," Kissinger said in his heavy German accent. "I don't trust Nixon or his people. Once they have me in a third rate job in the State Department, they will forget all about me." He then lifted his glass of water, sipping it loudly.

"We will change all that, Herr Doctor. In the words of Patrick Henry, 'A convert's argument is always heartfelt.'" Jude smiled. "And your conversion will be historic."

"Now Professor," Jude said as he picked at his shrimp cocktail, "how would you like to be awarded the Nobel Peace Prize?" Jude took a bite of his shrimp. "If that happens, no one will forget about you."

Kissinger laughed, a sudden Teutonic bark. "I've seen members of the academic community receive such an honor, and I thought...maybe someday. But in American Government service, not a chance." He thought for a moment, and then added, "I'm almost afraid to ask what prompts such a question. I'm waiting to be surprised."

"It's Vietnam," Jude said in a low determined voice. Both men fell silent, as a serious matter was about to be discussed. "I have a plan for you to consider. With your skill, and with Nixon's clout, you could settle the war over there. We need Nixon to win another term. He can't if this war continues, and with this plan we can ensure his election."

"As I said, I am surprised - novel and certainly ambitious. You realize, Jude, that there's been fighting over there since nineteen thirty-eight. The Japanese, the French, and now the Americans, all have been bogged down there. Doctor Ellsberg and I did extensive research on Southeast Asia. We even wrote a paper for the Pentagon." He dragged out each word as he spoke, as if they were back in class. "We've had advisors there since Truman's time. The first American killed there was in nineteen forty-five: Captain Dewey. His uncle ran for president in nineteen forty-eight, almost beating Truman. No administration has been successful handling the problem. But I am, nevertheless, still willing to listen." Kissinger realized Jude was no longer just a young student idealist, but a world-class mover, and he had already demonstrated his ability to make things happen.

"Vietnam can be resolved."

"What do you mean resolved, Jude? America wants victory, they don't want another Korea, with our troops still there twenty years later." Kissinger was sounding like a college professor again...lecturing.

"I said resolved. It can be settled with a plan. It will take some hard work, but it can be accomplished... with your effort and Nixon's blessing."

"Go on," Kissinger said, now listening attentively.

"North Vietnam has a reason to want a settlement that would let America save face. Ho Chi Minh saw how we rebuilt our adversaries after the Second World War. After the war we treated our enemies with favor and ignored our allies. Japan and Germany received billions of dollars in aid and reinvestments. They now are economic giants. Our allies didn't fare as well. Russia received hardly anything. And we gave England, our strongest supporter, nothing. Now, England is practically broke, with little power. We need to make a proposal with great discretion. I believe that the North Vietnamese would be willing to consider allowing the U.S. to disengage for the right compensation. It would be a carrot and stick approach. The stick would be to inform the North Vietnamese that we will mine the harbor of Hai Phong, and begin a large scale bombing campaign, using B-52s to destroy the present and future industrial capacity of the country, and bomb every major road and bridge in North Vietnam. We would destroy the water and irrigation systems that make the land arable, and food production would come to a standstill. Our goal would be not to conquer North Vietnam; we would have no plans to invade it. No, our plan would be to force the north to turn to China for its continued support. That would make North Vietnam a ward of the Chinese."

Jude looked at Kissinger to see if he were still following. Kissinger seemed intrigued with Jude's presentation.

Jude continued. "They're allies now, but the Chinese and Vietnamese are natural enemies. You talk about thirty years of fighting, well just look at that region. They have had to fight the Chinese invaders for over a thousand years. They know that China would like to annex them, just as they did Tibet."

Kissinger, having finished his lunch, was sitting up

Straight and alert. It was his turn to speak. "I must say that's quite a stick, Jude."

"It's more of a club than a stick I assure you, they'll know the difference, Doctor Kissinger," Jude said with a chuckle in his voice.

"Just in case they don't fear our bombing capabilities, we would inform them of our intention to invite the Nationalist Chinese Army from Taiwan to join with us in South Vietnam to fight Communists. This would give the Nationalists a foothold on the mainland, which, in turn, would trigger the Mainland Chinese to send troops to North Vietnam, from which they would never leave. North Vietnam could be the host country for a battle between the two Chinese Armies. I think that would send fears up Ho Ch Minh's beard. It's a real threat that they would have to take seriously, and it's a threat we could deliver on, in whole or in part."

"That's quite a stick. After listening to that, I don't know if we need a carrot," Kissinger said slowly with his gravelly German accent. "But let's look further into your plan to resolve a settlement."

"We would want their assurance not to interfere with a plan we will call Vietnamization. This will allow their troops already there to remain in place. And we will want them to cease action against American troops as we begin a phased withdrawal of all U.S. troops, according to a fixed timetable, leaving the fighting entirely to the South Vietnamese, who, unfortunately, will collapse in a short time. But we will be long gone by then. Now the carrot: In return, the United States would supply aid comparable to that extended after the Second World War. We will supply big money, technical personnel, and economic support. They will have the captured military hardware we sent there. In a short time they will be a giant force in their neck of the woods."

"Very interesting, Jude," Kissinger said as if he were on "Laugh-In."

Jude continued. "It will have to be presented to all parties with a great deal of diplomacy; but first to the north. They are the ones we can't control. We need them to sign on. We'll give them the choice. If they cooperate with us they can be politically and economically independent, with our substantial blessing. Or, they look upward to a rain of bombs not yet seen by mankind, and then play host to the Chinese occupation forces."

"Why should they believe that we would carry out such a plan? They know the opposition to the war in this country," Kissinger said slowly.

"Because they're facing a new administration and that is an unknown quantity to them. Your job is to convince them that Nixon is a political animal who would do this, and more, to get re-elected, and that he has the support of many 'Hawks' in Congress who have been quiet so far. So he's prepared to do one or the other."

"As I expected, a novel proposal. I'm not aware of anything like this being discussed by any party who's involved in the war. This is a new and unorthodox way of looking at the alternatives." He paused, picking up a small piece of lobster that had fallen out of his sandwich. "It's worth further consideration. South Vietnam will have to do what we tell them. Hmmm. It just may work."

"If it does work, the man responsible for resolving the Vietnam Conflict would be certain to be a prime candidate for the Nobel Peace Prize." Jude looked to see what kind of reaction, if any, came from Kissinger. He went on. "This can't be a firm promise, of course, but we have an excellent chance of using our contacts within the nominating committee. If successful, I can promise you a rapid ascension in influence and prestige at the State Department. And, Doctor Kissinger, you may very well be America's first foreign-born Secretary of State."

"I see there's a large carrot for me, also." He lit his first cigarette, and slowly exhaled the smoke, watching it disappear while almost in a trance.

"Yes, there'll be lots of carrots. You're going to be in a very important position, at a very opportune time. It is designed so. When this happens your position will be of inestimable value - to both the Nation as a whole, and to a certain mutual acquaintance."

"I was looking forward to this luncheon today, and it was delightful. But I must admit that you gave me more food for thought than I consumed at the table. Yes, these could be very interesting times ahead."

"Yes, Doctor Kissinger," Jude said smiling. "Spoken like an intellectual diplomat."

Kissinger smiled in return.

The inauguration in 1969 was on a cold January afternoon; it was an occasion of great cordiality. The festivities went off without a hitch, considering all the protesters in the area. However, the military wasn't there just for the parade. In his inaugural speech, President Nixon declared, "I ask you to share with me today the majesty of this moment. In the orderly transfer of power, we celebrate the unity that keeps us free. For the first time, because the people of the world want peace, and the leaders of the world are afraid of war, the times are on the side of peace. We have found ourselves rich in goods, but ragged in spirit, reaching with magnificent precision for the moon, but falling into raucous discord on earth. I know that peace does not come through wishing for it - that there is no substitute for days and even years of patient and prolonged diplomacy. After a period of confrontation, we are entering an era of negotiation.

"I have taken an oath today in the presence of God and my countrymen to uphold and defend the Constitution of the United States. To that oath I now add this sacred commitment: I shall consecrate my office, my energies, and all the wisdom I can summon, to the cause of peace among nations."

His speech was applauded with more than ceremonial politeness. People were hoping for a change in foreign policy. Nixon was pleased with both the tone of the speech and how favorably it had been received. The presses had advanced copies and were mildly appreciative of it.

Following the ceremony and the public celebration there was a private reception in the upstairs living area of the White House. This was an exclusive gathering for only top aides, very close friends, and family. "Close friends" were defined as those who had contributed at least a million dollars to Nixon's campaign. The guest list numbered just over twenty-five. All were gathered in the freshly refurbished living quarters with the

First Family. Nixon made his first public entrance as President, beaming widely, shaking hands in a two-handed clasp as he met each person. He circulated, saying a few words to each of the guests, until he noticed Nelson Rockefeller in a corner, apparently studying one of the presidential portraits.

Nixon walked slowly over to him, remarking, "Good afternoon, Governor. I hope you are enjoying yourself."

"Yes, I am. Thank you, Mr. President," Rockefeller said warmly.

"You're a well-known connoisseur of fine art, Governor. May I ask your opinion of this portrait of Andrew Jackson? 'Old Hickory'?"

Holding his glass of champagne up toward the painting, in his characteristically raspy voice, he replied, "Old Hickory was one of my favorite Presidents. By the way, do you have a large block of cheese downstairs?" They both laughed, referring to the inaugural party Jackson hosted, which included a two-ton block of cheese. The inaugural reception of 1829 was a riotous affair with tubs of spiked punch for the thousands that attended. Jackson even needed protection against being crushed to death.

"No large blocks of cheese, Governor," Nixon jokingly said. "Jackson was a Democrat."

Rockefeller continued to stare at the painting. "It's a Velome, and it's very good. Jon Velome only painted six portraits, and I'm happy to say I have five of them in my collection."

"You remind me that I'm only the tenant here, but as such I can enjoy the many treasures of this magnificent house." Nixon was a little uncomfortable and tried not to show it. "Old Money," and those it represented, like Rockefeller, ran a sharp twinge up the back of Nixon. He never felt comfortable around these "blue-blooded" or "country club" Republicans. They seemed to sense that he came from a working class family, no matter what office he held. To them he was considered hired help. "If the painting were mine, I'd give it you as a gift, to complete your collection, if only a token of my very real appreciation and gratitude."

"You worked very hard; your campaign was well organized. I'm happy to have been of help in bringing about your well-deserved election. I thought you did an excellent job on the inaugural address. I hate to give speeches; I have to memorize them. I have dyslexia so notes turn into chicken scratches the minute I get behind a podium." He took a sip of his champagne, turned and started to walk slowly toward Nixon. "I do look forward to seeing what progress your new administration will make on some of those issues you spotlighted this afternoon."

Nixon glanced around to make sure that his other guests were being well taken care of. His wife was chatting animatedly, and Gala was applying her usual, elegant charm a few yards away. Looking at her, Nixon wondered how he ever could have contemplated doing without her. Turning back to Rockefeller, he put an arm over the Governor's shoulder and proposed. "Come on with me before anyone spots us." Before Rockefeller could comment, Nixon pushed against the wall, which swung open without a sound. "The Secret Service just showed it to me earlier this evening."

They ducked into a narrow paneled passageway, with steps that led to the lower floors. Rockefeller remarked, "I thought these things were only in *Abbott and Costello* movies."

"It's a private passageway to the Oval Office," Nixon said in a whispered voice. "Top secret. Ike never even mentioned it to me."

"Quite a short-cut. In the old castles they had passage ways like these for the servants." Then Rocky chuckled and added, "And for the royalty who wished to fool around." observed Rockefeller, sounding lazily amused as he followed Nixon through the dimly lit passage.

"Not this one." Nixon said seriously. "The Secret Service monitors this all the time."

Nixon opened the hidden doorway to the Oval Office standing aside to let Rockefeller through, the Governor offered no further mildly jeering comments, but just stood, soberly regarding the huge desk and symbols of Office: flag and presidential Seal; the vista of Capitol lights glittering beyond the windows. This was the office of the president of the United States. Both men stood silently for a moment. It seemed surreal.

Nixon remarked in a low voice, "This is the first time I have entered this office privately as

President. It's quite a feeling to think of the men who worked here and the history made in this room."

"I can only imagine," Rockefeller said quietly, in deep thought.

"The first time I was here, Truman was President. To me, this has always been Ike's office. I had great respect for that man. In a way, it's better to win the way I did, instead of inheriting the office, had Ike suffered one more heart attack." Nixon thought for a moment, and then added, "Yes, it's better to win the office outright, in my own way. Not just because I was Ike's Vice President."

"I wonder if Johnson ever felt comfortable here," Nelson asked. "After the tragedy of President Kennedy; having to deal with his brother Bobby as his Attorney General, and then having to put up with Teddy in Senate. I don't think Lyndon ever got over the thunderous reception Bobby Kennedy received at the sixty-four Democratic Convention in Atlantic City. Between the war and the ghosts, I don't think he was ever comfortable here."

Nixon didn't go to the desk, but took one of the leather covered guest chairs. Still looking around him, Rockefeller sat in another.

Nixon commented, "So far, each time I have been in this office, there were a host of people here, so I haven't been able to visit with the ghosts. At least none have appeared yet. Some claim Lincoln still walks through the place, still worrying about the Civil War. Maybe he uses that very passage we just came down. Of course he died in that tiny little house across from Fords' theater. Perhaps his spirit came home that night and has remained."

"I don't believe in those things," remarked Rockefeller quietly, testing the drink he still held. "But a place like this puts one in awe...with the intense sense of history. And decisions made here breed legends. It's only natural to visualize the historic players in this room."

"Governor, I wanted some time to talk with you privately," Nixon said suddenly, feeling he was blurting. "I just want you to know how much I appreciate your complete support in this election. Not only the financial help, but the unseen support that was critical. I realized how much you helped even if no one else did."

Nixon wanted to say more about the subtle but important help; favorable elite New York based news coverage, powerful contacts, competent staff appearing from nowhere to fill sudden vacancies, prime television advertising time being offered at substantial discounts, favorable interviews, key New York (not normally Republican) ad agencies, and other things Nixon couldn't trace directly to Rockefeller. But he felt that Rocky had put out the word, and it was done. "And may I say one thing? I don't forget friends. Whatever prudent help I can give, it's yours for the asking. You want someone appointed, it will be done. And, in fact, we have already appointed some of your people, all good quality men. I just wanted to say privately that while I am President, you will always have my ear."

Rockefeller again showed his wide, meaningless smile, and in his raspy voice said, "Mr. President, I am pleased you were elected. And yes, I did whatever I could. In fact, I did a little more than usual. But I felt it important that you were elected. I believe you'll do a good job as president and party leader. I have gathered, through the years, contacts with top-notch people. From time-to-time I may recommend some for your administration."

Nixon was quick to point out, "We have already added Doctor Kissinger to our State Department I know he has been on your advisory staff for years. He brings with him many international academic connections." He stumbled in his words a little, saying something he didn't quite believe. "I am grateful to have him with us. I'm sure he will make his mark."

"Professor Kissinger is one of the brightest people I have ever met," Rocky said with enthusiasm. "He has a grasp of international history and understanding. He's been on the Council of Foreign Relations since nineteen fifty-five. He's his own man...somewhat of a renegade. But give him free reign and he'll perform feats."

"I know you have great interest in world affairs. In fact, I believe yours is the only state with a Foreign Relations office." Nixon then asked, "Governor, I'd like you to consider being the next Secretary of State. You and Doctor Kissinger would make quite a team."

"Thank you Mr. President, but I have a full-time job running the State of New York. I'd like to keep doing that as long as the people keep electing me. And to tell you the truth, retirement isn't in the too distant future."

Nixon was pleased with the meeting. He had conveyed his special 'thank you' to Rocky, and he found out that Rockefeller wasn't trying to upstage him by taking Secretary of State with his protégé, Kissinger. But, there remained one question Nixon wanted answered.

"Well, I appreciate the people you have recommended." He thought for a moment and continued asking almost as an afterthought. "I met a young man early in the campaign. From what I understand, he is connected with one of your companies or foundations. His name is Jude Thaddeus. Precisely, what is his job?"

"Hmmm. Thaddeus?" Rocky was stalling for time. He had to be somewhat truthful. "Yes, I know the name. I believe he is with an investment group. Of course, there are many young, bright people working for us. Our organization gets a little unwieldy at times. I honestly don't quite know what they all do."

"He seems to know Doctor Kissinger," Nixon said.

"That's where I heard the name. Doctor Kissinger introduced me to him quite some time ago. He's a Harvard man. And if Henry took interest in him, he must be bright. It's difficult to find top-notch people. I believe in home-growing them. We do recruit from the best of schools. After we recruit and hire them, it may take a long time to find what they're good at. Occasionally one stands out, and he is a keeper, but most don't. One of our managers calls them cannon fodder. We only keep a small percentage of any given group." Rockefeller gave a blank look at Nixon and asked, "Are you thinking of stealing him from us?"

"No, not at all," Nixon denied with unexpected forcefulness. "It's just that he was chosen for... that is...he seemed to carry a lot of trust, especially in money matters...and in some confidential matters. I wondered what his actual work was. After all, it was from him that I first learned of your interest in my campaign. And it was through him, and what he brought to the table that I decided to run."

Rockefeller spoke in an authorial raspy voice. "Well, Mr. President all seemed to go satisfactorily. You're the President, Doctor Kissinger is at the State Department, and the Republican Party is happy. Now, if you can perform that magic trick that opens the passageway, I'm sure your other guests want to add their congratulations, too."

Obscurely frustrated, Nixon felt for the hidden latch. He didn't get the straight answer from Rocky regarding Jude, or the set of patronage requests. But it didn't matter now. This was his office, presidential seal and all. Nixon turned one

more time to look at the Oval Office, and then followed Rockefeller back through the passageway.
*Hmm, maybe Ike was right about Rockefeller, he would
hire brains instead of using his own.*

⁓

The new administration got off to a slow but
steady start. Kissinger accepted the post of
Under-Secretary of State. His work was low-
key and went unnoticed. Two new and close
friends of the President were controlling the new
administration. Nixon had complete trust in
Erlichman and Haldeman, who had responsibility
for all presidential legislation, foreign affairs,
and domestic relations. The President could not
have asked for more zealous assistance. The two
men neither smoked nor drank; and during the
inauguration festivities, both were very closely
watching who was drinking too much, talking
too much, partying too much, and gawking at
women too much. Nixon intended to run a "tight
ship," and this initial surveillance was a sign
of things to come. His own affair with Gala, of
course, continued, but was kept exceedingly
secretive. For his part, Nixon told no one. They
were so discreet, that even the Secret Service had
no idea. Mrs. Nixon and Gala continued as warm
friends. Gala screened invitations for the new First
Lady. She made sure, in her recommendations,
that the invitations accepted were always to the
advantage of the First Lady. Gala knew who was

using whom in the Beltway circle. Gala only chose the "correct" affairs for Mrs. Nixon to attend: the ones where she would not only be noticed, but respected by both the "blue-bloods" and the "wanna-bees."

Pat Nixon seemed greatly impressed with the social calendar Gala was able to arrange. The First Daughters benefited from Gala's influence, appearing on the A-list of the Washington social register. Invitations were being sent to this First Lady, the caliber of which hadn't been extended since the royal days of the Roosevelt's. The "old money" matriarchs were jostling each other for invitations to White House Teas, formerly quite routine affairs. It was increasingly evident that Gala, in her own self-effacing way, had powerful connections, and was using them to benefit the Nixon's. They were appropriately appreciative and grateful. Pat Nixon treated Gala almost as an adopted daughter. It was a close mutual friendship.

Gala was also careful to get along with the White House staff and Nixon's intimate circle, never pushing her authority or boasting of her connections. She made no attempt to extend her influence beyond the First Family's social life. For all appearances, she was Mrs. Nixon's personal assistant, who worked also with the President. Keeping this profile, she was not considered a serious threat by any of the new administration's real or would-be power seekers.

It was a good time for Nixon. He was being personally accepted as a first-rate politician, and saw potential for enhancing his reputation by becoming a first-rate international statesman. He wanted to change the image of his kitchen-Wshouting match with Nikita Khrushchev, and of his being intimidated by rioters in South America. The most obvious way to achieve international respect was to end America's longest war, Vietnam. The war was a quagmire, bogging down the American military and sapping American prestige and strength. If he could end the war with honor, then he would be considered a first-class world leader.

Negotiations seemed to be deadlocked. The new administration had discussions on both intensifying the war and decreasing America's involvement, but no satisfactory plan of action had yet been formulated. In a conversation with Haldeman and Erlichman, Nixon said, "By God, I made a campaign promise to end this war, but we have more troops there now than when I took office. Did you see the papers? They're calling this war Nixon's war. I want action on this, and I want it started now!"

It was an apparently casual remark from Gala that started him thinking about Kissinger, whom Gala had encountered for the first time at a reception for a visiting dignitary. Gala commented that such a charming, accomplished professor was wasted in Washington and ought to be out charming America's enemies. Nixon's reply was somewhat surly. He didn't like Gala's praising another man's abilities in his presence, and Gala teased him about his boyish, petty jealousy. The subject was carelessly dropped. But Nixon found himself reviewing the idea of Kissinger's becoming active in foreign policy. He was a man with international experience who was also an academic egghead. The press would like that. All things considered, if he were given an active role and failed, well, he'd had his chance. Nixon could feel more comfortable in ignoring him thereafter. And considering the situation in Vietnam, other notable diplomats had no success so far, but a low-level agent like Kissinger could work covertly and allow the North Vietnamese to negotiate out of the view of the press.

A few days later, Kissinger was sitting in the Oval Office alone with the President. The President's staff cleared a half hour meeting with Dr. Kissinger. No one took much notice of this meeting. Rockefeller's protégé, a low-level guy in the State Department, probably was in for a photo op to show the folks at Harvard he was important. Kissinger himself had no idea why he was there. He had learned earlier in life to enjoy the unknown. This was their first private meeting. Kissinger thought Nixon was quite confident in his new job. He was soft-spoken with a determined attitude.

Nixon sat behind the large, dark, ornate desk which had once belonged to Eisenhower. Dr. Kissinger sat in front alone, like a college freshman seeking admittance. Nixon was starring for a few moments at Henry and wondering what it was that made him so attractive to so many women. It certainly couldn't be his looks or personality, it must be his snobbish self-assurance; his noted professional career...whatever? Nixon then cleared his mind as they got onto official business.

They reviewed the current situation, agreeing the existing peace initiatives were getting nowhere. "Too many voices speaking, each with his own solution," Nixon stated harshly. "Too many bureaucrats giving one set of signals, while too many generals give another. It's confusing. And the news media is giving all the attention to the demonstrators. The presence of TV cameras is like throwing gasoline on their so-called peacenik fires. No wonder the Commies think they can win. They're united and we're confused."

Nixon leaned back in his chair in a relaxed posture, and stared at the ceiling, then continued. "I'm visualizing something more concise: one voice...mine, as President...speaking with authority." Kissinger merely looked attentive. After a moment Nixon went on. "Doctor Kissinger, I'd like you to accept the position of Special Advisor to the President. You'd report directly to me, outside of the 'proper channels' in State."

Kissinger cleared his throat, and then asked in his low German-accented voice, "Mr. President, what would my duties be as Special Advisor?"

"You will be my personal representative in settling this war in Vietnam. I believe too much has been said and done in public to have any effect in ending this war. We need absolute private diplomacy. I think you're the man to take this responsibility."

"I agree with your notion of private diplomacy, Mr. President." He thought for a moment and added, "You can be assured, Mr. President, that I will represent your voice and your views as clearly and forcefully as I am able."

"As Special Adviser, you will hold the title of Minister without Portfolio: a roving commission. That will give you the diplomatic authority to do what's necessary, and keep a low profile," Nixon said matter-of-factly.

"Mr. President," Kissinger said again in his slow manner, "if I accept this position, I must have your absolute support and authority to act on your behalf. I must have easy access to you at all times, and our communications must remain conventional until it's completed." He looked at Nixon for a reaction. There wasn't any.

He continued. "I know in the past we have not agreed on everything. If we disagree on anything, we must do so in private. Neither of us can criticize the other in public. I must have freedom of movement and speech. I know this sounds like quite a demand list, but the course we are going to follow requires complete confidence. I've seen negotiations collapse because one party is waiting for instructions from headquarters. Opportune timing is essential. I will do everything in my power to end this dreadful war. But I, in turn, must be able to rely on your influence and your support at all times. If that's satisfactory, I'll formulate a written policy for discussion. I can have it on your desk Monday morning."

"Fine, Doctor Kissinger." Nixon stood and shook his hand. "We understand each other. I agree with your proposal, and you have my support and confidence. I pray we succeed." The men exchanged the handshake neglected by mutual consent when Kissinger had come in. Nixon was pleased with the appointment, although he didn't completely trust him.

Kissinger was even more pleased. He now had a free reign to travel the world; the power to impress people; and the opportunity to implement Jude's Stick and Carrot Settlement Plan.

CHAPTER 11

The time had come when Jude was ready to set his moneymaking operation into play. It would be a two-sided campaign. The first goal was to distract the American public at a time of his choosing. The second goal was to make good on his promise to recoup the thirty million dollar expenditure Rockefeller had fronted so far.

He requested a meeting with Jack Chandler at the Americana Hotel, a convenient meeting place they'd used before. At first Jude detested the place. It had a reputation for attracting a certain class of clientele, and was known as a fun house for sexual proclivity. It was a hotel that catered to hot romances, special anniversaries, and prostitution. The ground floor and the bar were salted with hookers scanning the patrons with predatory eyes. The security was something else, with two-way mirrors and bugged rooms.

Jude changed his mind after Jack informed him that the hotel was owned by one of their organizations. It was a handy place for gathering information and to entertain and intimidate certain people. The accommodations were perfect for clandestine meetings. It had an underground private entrance; one could get in without detection. The secure entrance had a private elevator to service only certain floors. The suites on the invulnerable floors were quite secure. They checked for listening devices on a daily basis. The walls were lead-lined, and the windows were specially designed to prevent any electronic snooping through voice vibrations on glass. It was now Jude's favorite meeting spot.

The meeting was scheduled for three-thirty in the afternoon. This was a good time to hold a meeting. Police shifts were changing, the stock market was near closing, and most people were still at work. Jude was first to arrive. He went to the secure floor, and then to the private suite that was off-limits to anyone other than Chandler. Jude walked in, went over to the bar, and poured a large tonic on ice for himself. In the refrigerator he found fresh lemon, squeezed it into the glass, placed it on top, and relaxed.

Chandler arrived a short time later. He carried an attaché case that seemed rather heavy. He greeted Jude, while setting the case on the coffee table. He opened the case, revealing an attached electrical cord, which he plugged into a wall outlet. "It's my new toy, Jude. It's a portable scrambler, and it is state-of-the-art. With this, no one can record or listen to our conversation. When we've finished you can take it with you. I suggest, for security reasons, that you use it."

With the scrambler hooked up, both men sat in comfortable wing chairs, ready for the big meeting. Chandler appeared to be in a good mood, and spoke first. "First off, I'd like a drink. Yours looks good...maybe I'll a have the same." He got up and walked over to the bar.

"Straight tonic on the rocks with a twist of lemon," Jude yelled out.

"That's like gas without octane," Chandler said quickly. "What do you call it?"

"I call it keeping sober," said Jude jokingly. "I learned a long time ago, the only drink people don't question is tonic with lemon or lime. Everyone thinks it contains gin or vodka, so they leave me alone. And it's a tasty drink."

"Just the same, I'm going to put gin in mine."

Chandler finished making his drink, walked back to his seat, and said, "Speak to me, Jude. You wanted this meeting, so let's start talking."

"Oil is the reason for this meeting," Jude said loudly. "I need to get in touch with our agent in the Middle East who is responsible for purchasing the oil. It's very important. I'd like to meet him face to face."

"That would be Dennis Porkenhime. You'll have to track him down and go there to meet him."

"I'd like him to come to the States for our meeting," Jude said flexing his growing sense of power.

"No, he doesn't work that way," Chandler smiled wryly. "If that seems odd, consider that even the Governor has never met him directly. Since our Mr. Porkenhime has made profits for us in the hundreds of millions of dollars, the Governor is content to allow him his quirks. I suggest you do the same. I've met him. He is quite a delightful chap."

"Is he the only one I can deal with? I just don't want to be out of New York right now," Jude said in a concerned voice.

"Well, it depends on what you're expecting to accomplish. Dennis is the most influential and knowledgeable man in the area," Chandler said.

"I want someone in intimate influence with the royal families in the Middle East. Someone who is trusted and who knows how to get their attention."

"No –non-Arab is really trusted in those quarters," Chandler said quickly.

Jude took a deep breath, and then said mildly, "Jack, you're not being very helpful."

"Sorry," Chandler said indifferently. "I can't make recommendations until I have adequate information."

"I want someone who can orchestrate a program to establish an oil cartel in the Middle East. This will help control both international oil supplies and, as a result, the price of oil on the world market." Jude didn't like spelling out his plans to any third party, but had decided, with enforced patience, that in this instance it was necessary.

"That's Porkenhime. He claims to be British, but nobody knows for sure, actually. He first turned up as an advisor to the Saudis during the Second World War, a personal friend of that notorious Thomas Edward Lawrence, known as Lawrence of Arabia."

"I recently read his book, The Seven Pillars," Jude interrupted. "Sir Lawrence certainly painted an interesting picture of the way the Arab neighborhood was set up."

"Well, because of Porkenhime's relationship with Lawrence, he could open a lot of doors, or tents in this case. He knows all the kings, sheiks, and political leaders in the region. And he has remained in their good graces, which is a marvel in itself, for better than twenty-five years...an amazing feat. The Governor has come to rely on him implicitly, not only in oil matters, but other things as well. In the Middle East, he's our go-to man. Do you want me to set up a meeting?"

"Yes by all means," Jude replied quickly. "Sounds like an interesting character."

"I'll have him contact you next week and you can take it from there. Please be polite to our Mr. Porkenhime; he's a rather complex type person who doesn't necessarily trust, or like, too many Americans." Chandler took a long sip of his drink. "He's kept his thumb in an unspeakable tangle of local feuds, coups, disputes, and some discreet assassinations. Through wars and feuds and construction problems he's kept our oil flowing. We would be very unhappy if anything were done to jeopardize his position."

Jude translated that as meaning Rockefeller valued this guy over anyone else in the organization. Seems like Porkenhime was the trainer of the Golden Goose. "He sounds like a man I'd really like to meet. I will make myself available to meet him when and where he likes."

"Jude," Chandler said with a jovial, loud voice, "you're in for a treat...and good luck."

"Good luck is often with the one who doesn't include it in his plans," Jude said quietly.

~~~

"You have an overseas call, Mr. Thaddeus," came his secretary's voice over the intercom. "A Mr. Edwin Trotter, I believe. He's kind of hard to understand."

Jude couldn't place the name, but picked up his receiver saying, "Hello, this is Jude Thaddeus."

There was an instant's pause while the radio-type overseas call transmitted his voice through the considerable static. Then a voice broke through on the other end. "Trotter here. Can you understand me all right?" Without waiting for a reply, he continued. "Our mutual friend the Rooster tells me you're interested in visiting the Continent, and suggested that I might make the arrangements." The voice was brisk and British. "Be a pleasure to set things up for you at this end, sir." Then there was more static.

While Jude was still trying to figure out what was meant by "Rooster," the British voice continued. "I say, do you hear me all right, chap? Lots of noise on the line."

"Yes," Jude said hastily, yelling in the phone and hoping he sounded better. "I can hear you. I'd appreciate it if you would handle all the arrangements." Surely, this had to be Porkenhime's man.

"Old Chanticleer said you'd be in a bit of a rush to get off. Will departure Friday a week do?" the static-laden voice asked.

Jude yelled into the phone, "Yes, that would be fine."

"Your passport in order, all the pokes of needles from the medical buffons?"

"Yes," Jude yelled again, "everything is in order. I can leave at any time. Do you have my address?"

"Yes, I have your address, Bub." The voice was still difficult to hear. "Well done...okay... consider it complete. I'll post the necessary tickets, travel documents, and directions right away. You should have them no later than Monday. Anything in particular you need set up on this end?"

"Nothing I can think of," Jude yelled again. "Just looking forward to a pleasant holiday."

The voice chuckled with static noise. "Think I can guarantee an interesting one, if nothing more. Have a nice day. We'll take care of you. Cheerio."

The line went dead and Jude was left to wonder, "Where on earth am I going?"

A few days later a packet arrived by courier. Inside were a dozen travel flyers on the Swiss Alps, together with a round-trip first-class airline ticket to Geneva, Switzerland. It contained guaranteed reservations in his name at the Hotel Simi. "Looks like I'm going to see the Matterhorn first-hand." Checking the envelope, he found a handwritten note.

I'll welcome you personally at the hotel bar on your arrival date, at 9:45 P.M. That should give you enough time to dust off the snow and relax. Please, sit at the bar and order an American drink, like a shot and beer. Many thanks, E. Trotter.

Jude thought it rather cloak and dagger stuff, but then again this was cloak and dagger stuff.

Jude walked slowly to the bar, which was rather small as bars go, with only a dozen stools. It had a clean appearance, decorated with light colored Danish wood. He was nervous; this reminded him of his youth, going into a bar with a fake ID. He sat quietly at the bar, looking up at the shelves containing bottles of whiskey and beer from around the world. The bartender came right over, and with a broken accent asked if he wanted a drink. "I'd like Heineken draft beer and a shot of Southern Comfort on the side," Jude said in a low voice, not wanting to be noticed.

No sooner had the drinks been set down, than a loud voice from behind Jude declared, "You must be a Yank to order a drink like that. Am I right? A shot and a beer - you must be from Pennsylvania."

As the stranger approached and took a seat next to Jude at the bar, Jude turned to see a red-faced man with bright blue eyes, a gray walrus mustache, and gray hair cut close. He was slightly overweight, but looked physically fit. He was wearing a gaudy Scandinavian sweater, on which several files of orange reindeer seemed to be jumping in all directions.

"Reminds me of home," was all Jude could think to say.

Porkenhime settled in comfortably on the next stool and then slapped him heartily on the shoulder. "Thirty-odd years ago, I was involved in an anthracite coal project, near Scranton, Pennsylvania. That anthracite is the hardest coal in the world and burns the hottest. Perhaps that's why they drank shots and beers, as mouthwash. I guess you needed something to take away the taste of coal dust from those mines." He got the bartender's attention saying, "I'll have the same here, mate." He then turned again to Jude saying, "I've met a lot of Yanks since, but they don't fancy the good old Pennsylvania Polka drink. They are now into cocktails. Dreadful muck, cocktails, rots out your tum in no time. So, I figure only Yanks from Pennsylvania like this particular mix. Believe I'll order another of the same, for old time's sake."

Beaming companionably, Porkenhime drank just enough of the beer to pour the whiskey into the larger glass, and then downed the mixture in two hearty gulps. "Dennis Porkenhime, here," he said, wiping his moustache with a forefinger. "Pleasure to share the bar with you, Mr.?"

"Jude Thaddeus. Can I buy you a drink? Anyone who has eaten Pennsylvania coal dust deserves one," Jude said happily.

"Why thank you, yank. I'll have one if you'll join me," Dennis said loudly.

"God, no! Dreadful stuff, actually. It's a wonderful thing for reminiscing, but one's the limit for me. However, I will have a Bombay Gin on the rocks with a twist of lemon. Kind to the tum, my old mom used to say, as she finished the bottle." Both men laughed.

Jude ordered the preferred drinks and listened while Porkenhime launched into an increasingly surreal discussion of the merits of alcohol and the preferences of his old mum. Their voices and laughter rose slightly. "Well then, I will tell you where the term cocktail comes from," Dennis said to Jude. "In Ireland, years ago, most race horses were thoroughbreds, but sometimes someone would enter a horse in a race that wasn't a pure thoroughbred. Well sir, they would break the tail and cock it up in the air to show it was a mixed breed. So those betting money would know it wasn't a purebred, but a mixture. Well, for those at the track who mixed their whiskey with water or soda, the drink was called a cocktail."

Jude was trying to enjoy the entertainment, although Dennis was pushing his stories to the boring point. To a casual observer they looked like traveling barflies who enjoyed each other's stories. Porkenhime sat up intently and said suddenly, "Of course, you're here to ski, it's the only other thing to do in this winter wonderland."

Worried, Jude said, "Actually, I haven't brought..."

"It's all laid out by management," Dennis said in a sober voice. "Just call the front desk and give your height and shoe size; they'll take care of the rest. By eight in the morning the slopes will be clear, nice and quiet. It's a nice place for a chat, the Intermediate slope...very nice. It's called "Torches on Poles," or something of the sort. Very scenic. You will like it, I'm sure."

"Tomorrow morning would..." Jude was attempting to say.

"Oh, jolly good. I must go now. Keeping the nose to the grindstone, don't ya know," Dennis said as he stood up. He was bright-eyed and cheerful, and plainly enjoyed Jude's company. This is one American he did like... so far.

"You seem to know the slopes and the bars around here," Jude said patting him on the shoulder. "Perhaps I'll see you in the morning." Jude also sensed having found someone whom he liked. It would be interesting to see if Porkenhime was as sharp as Jude was led to believe. After all, he seemed to drink quite a bit. Jude didn't trust anyone who drank too much.

"Good-o, so pleasant to meet you, Mr. Thannythingus," Dennis said in a tipsy voice.

"The pleasure is all mine, Mr. Porkmine." Jude's voice showed signs of intoxication. He was confident that he had made a good impression on his bishop. Jude was in control of his actions and his chess strategy.

⁓

As Porkenhime had predicted, the waiting area for the chairlift was deserted. Jude thought, *No wonder! It was freezing, with a sharp wind coming off the moonlet peaks*. Every minute or two, the chairs swung by empty, and rose on the all-but-invisible cable toward the first of the towers. Jude buried his gloved hands deeper in the pockets of the rented ski jacket, balancing the rented skis and poles upright. He had skied a little in college, but that was just to meet some babes.

"Ah, there you are, lad," called Porkenhime coming from the inner room carrying only poles. His skis were on his feet. He pushed Jude into position as the next chair reared, then shoved him onto the seat and let the chair's lift pull him neatly off the wooden floor.

"How do you feel this morning?" Jude said implying a hangover.

"I'm just fine. Oh, you are suspect of my drinking," he smiled. "I had been in the bar earlier in the day and tipped the bartender quite heavily to give me drinks that had very little or no alcohol content. The drinking was for visual effect."

As the chairs lifted above the cold, clear, deep, snow-covered valley, both men relaxed while looking down at the few, unhurried skiers. As they reached the first tower, Porkenhime said, "This is the most private place I could find, on short notice, for us to meet." The cheerfulness was suddenly absent, the voice a flat growl.

Jude looked at the white expanse of snow in the valley, some hundred feet below his dangling feet. "This is not the most comfortable place, but I'll get through it all right." He remembered that he had to placate Porkenhime.

"I don't fancy skiing at my age," Porkenhime remarked, "but this place is ideal for certain meetings of a private nature. Our associate is a partner in the hotel, so we know who is who...and the who's are quite interesting. I have a very sensitive position. Some people are aware of my oil involvement, but I trust they don't know to what depth. So I must be careful." He paused, looking around the valley, then added, "At the hotel, there are three Russkies, two Yanks, and six Arabs that may be interested in me. And they do hate this weather and location. They are all so clever," he chuckled, "you would never suspect them, except that the Russian KGBs have an odor about them, and drink too much vodka. If they ski, they try to out-do the Americans, which usually results in a Russian wearing a cast, hoping to get autographs. The Yanks of the CIA come in with the most expensive equipment, the best clothes, unlimited expenses, all in their early thirties and in good physical shape, pretending to be business people. The Arab info-seekers are the cream of the crop. They pretend to love skiing and cold weather...as much as dogs love cats; and they are very poor actors. Other than the humor of watching the gang of goofs, I enjoy this extrusion because of the snow and cold weather. There are no cars allowed in the village of Zermatt; everyone must take the train. So people must travel light. The eavesdropping equipment they sneak in their luggage won't work in these conditions. And, with the bulky bundle of clothing, pictures aren't as effective. Plus, the view of the Matterhorn is mesmerizing. That's why I chose this place."

"You, of course, are not conspicuous. No one would have recognized that reindeer sweater you had on last night," Jude said jokingly with a small amount of sarcasm.

"Entirely different thing, don't you know? I'm not Intelligence, hard to get a fix on me. And we British, we're a clever lot...been in the business for centuries. The empire didn't control the world by subscription, as some would have you believe." He paused then asked, "I'm sacrificing two extra days in Paris, freezing my arse off up here. I know it's important, so what is it, Jude?"

Before he could answer, the chairlift reached the turnaround point, and deposited the two men in the snow. Dennis skied off to the side, turned, and came back to Jude who was off to the other side struggling with his equipment. It had been a long time since Jude was on the slopes. He still was not in his skis when Dennis arrived. "Can I be of any assistance, my good fellow?" Dennis asked. "There's a bench in the shelter over to the side trail, just about thirty meters."

"I'll be fine. Let me get situated and I'll meet you there." Jude gathered up his thoughts on the best way to present his plan on short notice, and under difficult weather conditions. He swooped over as if he were on the ski patrol. He had command of the snow and his skis. He kicked off the skis and walked to the small shelter, which contained only a bench. Dennis was already there. Jude sat next to him and said, "You're being asked to implement a plan from the highest authority that will have a drastic effect on the oil industry."

"What is this plan and what is my proposed role?" Dennis asked coldly.

"We want you to have your suppliers form an organization to boost the cost of oil, and reduce production, and establish an oil embargo on the United States." Jude's words came out as if he were asking for the hand of the only daughter of a grumpy old man.

"Never happen. Can't see any of them joining together," Porkenhime said without any doubt. "Each Emir and Sheik hates the Sultan across the next dune. You can't travel directly from one country to the other. If you think your Hatfield's and McCoy's feuded. Hell, they're all Hatfield's or McCoy's in the Arabian Desert and feuding is their sacred honor. The only thing they hate more than each other are the infidels. And America is the land of them."

"That's what I'm depending on," Jude said. "The western industrial world of the infidels gets eighty percent of its oil from the countries bordering the Persian Gulf. May I ask, who is the largest single purchaser of their oil?"

"Single? Standard Oil, I suppose." He thought for a moment. "Various consortiums buy a lot, but the largest single commercial purchaser is Standard Oil."

"That's what I understand," Jude said. "And how much do we pay per barrel of oil?"

"Well, it depends. I can make special buys, but the general market is three dollars a barrel," Dennis said.

"Yes, but what if we were to offer to buy the same amount of oil as we do now and pay twelve dollars a barrel?" Jude asked intently.

"You'd go broke, quite quick. You couldn't handle all the oil they could pump at that price," Dennis quickly replied.

"Suppose we help them form an organization to help limit their production and maintain the price. I mean, an organization that will be recognized by America's Secretary of State."

"It's doubtful those desert rats would agree on anything. When it comes to the mighty dollar they want theirs now, not in the Paradise reserved for the Faithful. At this time, they're pumping every drop they can, and prospecting for more," Dennis said with a humorous tone.

Jude was talking like a used car salesman trying to get his point across. "But they could get more money for less oil, and make their oil reserves last longer. They could form a union of oil-producing countries to set production rates and the selling price of oil. They need to be persuaded that it would be in their best interest, individually and collectively, to slow down production, forcing prices up. This is the way organized unions work in the rest of the world. The way John D. Rockefeller, who founded Standard Oil, did. In his railroad monopoly days, his rule was roll at my price, make more money, and limit the competition. It's the modern thing to do."

"It's the modern thing to do," echoed Porkenhime, sounding thoughtful. "They're all hell bent on being modern, that's a fact. As long as that doesn't mean giving up absolute bloody autocratic power, their religion, or any of their two hundred-some wives..."

"We," Jude said loudly, "as the largest purchasers of oil, will support their efforts and pay twelve dollars a barrel for their oil. And they are to charge our competitors thirteen dollars a barrel. This should make the sheiks very happy, making a lot more money for pumping less oil, and keeping more of their natural reserves." Jude calmed down somewhat and added, "Timing is very important, though. I want this cartel to come into being soon after the next U.S. Presidential election."

"You expect me to set in motion a complete revolution in the Middle East oil industry, and you want me to keep to your schedule? I've been in the area for nearly thirty years, and all that time I haven't even attempted anything like this. Things are tough enough now just to keep the oil flowing."

Jude realized Porkenhime's support was essential, and he could not force him to do anything. He had to convince Dennis it was in his own best interest to support his plan. "Dennis, you make a commission on all oil you buy for us. If we raise the price of oil, your commission will increase automatically, and your suppliers will be happy because they will be getting more money per barrel." Jude paused for a moment, looking around, to ensure that no one was aware of their conversation. "This arrangement is part of a scheduled strategy for Nelson of New York, to achieve a life-long goal. Your participation will play a key role in helping him achieve that goal. Now, can I count on that support?"

"It won't be a walk in the park," Dennis said as if thinking out loud. "To get this mob to agree to anything is a tough maneuver, and getting them to act is even more difficult."

"Dennis, I'm told that you have connections back to Lawrence of Arabia, is that true?"

"Yes it is. Very few people knew that Lieutenant Lawrence was married. He was, for a short time, to my aunt, Molly Bryant. Family is important to the Arabs, you see. I do have a certain rapport with the royals. And, there is no Caucasian who is respected like Lawrence. He was one of them, and he liberated them from six hundred years of the Ottoman Empire." Dennis stood up, strapped on his skis, and looked over at Jude, saying, "I owe Nelson a lot, but that's another story. You can count on me Yank. I'll get the job done."

"I know you will," Jude said putting on his own skis. "Shall we hit the trails?"

"I suggest we now separate. I have a plane out at midnight. We can settle the details later." Seeing Jude's perplexed face, he added, "Don't worry lad. If you break something, the Russians will sign your cast." They laughed for a short time and bid each other farewell, and skied on separate trails.

C H A P T E R **12**

As the months passed, Nixon became known internationally as a shrewd and effective chief executive with a particular flair for foreign policy. He moved ahead with decisive diplomatic strength. His policies opened new doors that were previously closed. Throughout the world, America's friends and adversaries alike respected his stewardship and the development of policy. But his domestic image stayed much the same. He was still regarded as a poor loser who'd finally won by sheer persistence, taking ruthless revenge on his enemies whenever it was possible and expedient. Those enemies continued to dislike and distrust both Nixon personally, and anyone that was a member of his administration. The New York-based media certainly maintained the negative image for more than one valid reason. First, it sold newspapers. Second, it was good for TV ratings. All three major networks were located within a mile of Rockefeller Center. The New York City metropolitan influence had subtle, yet pervasive influence on the nation's foremost electronic reporters and commentators. The key media personalities were often seen at the same social events.

The Nixon administration took, in stride, most of the opposition's journalism, occasionally objecting to some specific story or report, but this was the exception rather than the rule.

One area, which the news media seemed to neglect, was the office of the Vice President. It didn't seem fair that Agnew should continue to enjoy a sense of anonymity, "Spiro Who?" However, other members of the administration were besieged with critical press coverage.

Some of Nixon's staff suggested that the Vice President should share some of the limelight, or more accurately deflect some of the negative press coverage directed at the President. The VP could also attack critics without much political capital being depleted.

Nixon was of the same opinion, and passed the view to the Vice President, who agreed. Agnew began a widely publicized counter attack, lambasting the press as elitist, inaccurate, and self-serving. After the administration passed the halfway point, rumors began to circulate that Agnew was going to be dropped as Nixon's running mate. Perhaps by no coincidence, Agnew became even more visible and vocal, attracting considerable news coverage. Not only did he become a highly visible public figure in his own right, but he did also attract the negative coverage that otherwise would have been focused on the President. Agnew was frequently invited to address the boards of large corporations and even stockholders' meetings. He was a rising symbol of those who had money and those working for money. Agnew was his own man, and he was becoming better known and respected. In the time of Vietnam demonstrations and other disturbances, a bumper sticker began to gain popularity: "Spiro is my Hero."

As the election grew nearer, the two candidates were growing in popularity. Agnew's new image of Mr. Clean had a good impact on the public and would ensure his name on the ticket.

The Russian Tea Room was one of New York's landmark restaurants. It was located on Fifty-seventh Street near the Rockefeller Center. It was one of the places where Dr. Kissinger liked to be seen. And he insisted on having his and Jude's next meeting there. The meeting was scheduled for one P.M. and Jude made his entrance to the main floor at one fifteen. He knew Kissinger would be angrily waiting at his private booth on the third floor. Jude wanted him to know who was in control.

Jude went directly up to the third floor; he knew it was a unique place. Its décor was bright red and gold, and gave an impression of a Christmas atmosphere all year. The ballroom was decorated in gold, glass, and brass with etched mirrors of cavorting Russian bears. There were imperial bronze chandeliers and a magnificent stained glass ceiling. Dr. Kissinger had his private booth in the far corner. Jude went directly to it.

"The traffic is terrible and getting worse all the time," Jude said in a cold voice as he arrived.

Kissinger took a quick look at his watch and said, "If you were still in my class, your blatant tardiness would be taken into consideration when grading."

"Well Doctor, we're not in a classroom anymore; it's the real world and we have important things to go over."

Kissinger picked up the menu to show Jude that he, too, had things on his mind.

The waiter was at the booth in an instant taking the drink order. Both men had believed their time was valuable, so they wasted little time on small talk. As soon as the drinks were delivered Jude spoke first. "Doctor Kissinger, some time ago you and a colleague named Doctor Ellsberg worked on a research project for the Pentagon. In fact, you wrote a rather lengthy report on how America immersed itself in Southeast Asia. That material would be interesting reading now, especially since Vietnam is in almost every headline.

But, as we know, that material is considered classified. I have a very important request of you."

"What is it you want me to do, Jude?" Kissinger said in his low-accented voice.

"I want you to contact Doctor Ellsberg and let him know that you want him to release some of the information in that classified report. Pitch to him that the American people have a right to know how we got into that mess. I don't want this released all at one time. He'll have to dribble out the material to certain newspapers, a few days apart. If we're lucky, we can keep it in the headlines and prolong the story. He may catch flack over this, but he doesn't have much to lose. He has fallen out of favor with a certain clique, due to his getting a divorce, and his career is at an end. I think he'll cooperate." Jude paused for a moment, then picked up where he left off. "Now Doctor Kissinger, while this information is being released, you are to be raising hell about this secret information leaking to the press and weakening the prestige of the United States of America."

Kissinger took a sip of his drink, stared up at the stained glass ceiling and said, "The material is old stuff now anyway, but releasing classified material from the Pentagon would be interesting. New York's Gray Lady would fight the Washington Post to see who could print this secret information first." Kissinger seemed to enjoy the intrigue.

"Remember, it's important," Jude said. "The information must be leaked to the newspapers slowly, a little at a time. This will start the action for a major play. I'll try to move one play in advance to clear the path for the other pieces."

⁓

Jude was reading a dossier on a young lawyer named John Dean: Law degree from Georgetown University in 1965. After graduation, he joined a Washington, D.C. law firm, but was fired the following year in a conflict-of-interest dispute with one of the firm's partners. It seemed he liked to brag about his non-existent connections, and he went so far as to claim authority he did not have. Jude thought, *Hmmm. He's the kind of weasel ordered up from Central Casting. Smart enough to finish law school at Georgetown, pass the bar, and get accepted into a firm; this proves that he's clever, ambitious, and greedy. He had draft deferments through college; that proves that he's spineless. And then, as an intern, to get into a pissing contest with one of the legal partners proves that he has no commonsense. He may be just what the doctor ordered; the right pawn for the right mission.* He'd have Mitchell put Dean in a minor position for now. He will be quite convenient in the near and troubled future.

He laid the file down relishing his find, when Sylvia resignedly announced an anonymous long distance call. She knew such calls were not unusual. Everyone knew he was successful, but no one seemed to know what he did. She was still his secretary, still working on her plan to visit Spain someday. It seemed the more successful one appeared, the more we were impressed. As Mark Twain said, "Clothes make the man. Naked people have little influence on society."

When Jude picked up the phone, a gruff mystifying voice said,"Read the Washington Post tonight. On Page three, column four, you'll notice brilliant chess move...Nxf3." The phone line went dead. Jude knew the play meant a knight move to the square f3. A subtle but decisive move, his plan was running like a Swiss watch.

Jude looked at his watch: it was five-fifteen. He had a dinner date at six with a fashionable model he had just recently met. He picked up a copy of the Washington Post in the lobby. He tried to read it in the cab, but New York traffic made that impossible. He arrived at the restaurant with the paper clutched under his arm and asked for his table immediately.

Jude sat nervously as his table, as he unfolded the newspaper he carried securely under his arm. He laid the paper on the table neatly so he could read the specified section. His eyes widened with excitement as he read about the signing of the 25th Amendment. On page three column four, there was a brief announcement of a fact of very little interest to the general public, but of immense importance to Jude. It may have looked like a rock to everyone else, but to Jude it was an uncut, unpolished diamond in the rough.

The newspaper announced that an amendment had been ratified by the requisite number of states, and approved by voice votes in both houses of Congress, and was signed by the President. The Twenty-fifth Amendment was now law. "Section 1. In case of the removal of the President from office, or of his death or resignation, the Vice President shall become President."

The ceremony was held in the East Room of the White House. Jude noted the date, February 27, 1967. Jude's emotion swelled with pleasure as he read, 'in attendance for the signing was the Amendment, Senate sponsor New York's Senator Kenneth Keating and the House sponsor, New York City, tenth district Representative Emanuel Celler. Both were New Yorkers, befriended and supported by the Rockefellers.

This underreported monumental move was the key to Jude's strategy. The event went off with little notice and no glitches. Jude had already set in motion his critical antiwar PR program, calculated to plummet Johnson's popularity thus helping to persuade Johnson not to seek reelection. Jude was confident, as he made a mental note to himself to convey to Tallsand, that Johnson should not seek and will not accept the nomination of his party for another term as president. Thus the election goes to Nixon.

Jude thought for a moment reflecting on a chess move, 23...Qg3, a great move in chess. So underrated, but so powerful.

He was the only one in the restaurant who didn't notice when his date arrived. She glided across the floor in a classic gray custom designed outfit catching everyone's attention. She was an 11 on a scale of 10. But Jude didn't notice her at first, he was engulfed reading and rereading the brief report on page three. When he looked up, he was so happy and excited. She thought she was the reason for his high spirits. He was on the top of the world right now and thought what he had just read should have been set to music. He was with a beautiful woman and tonight was a time for celebration.

Jude followed his escort down the dimly lit hallway of the private club thinking it must be the dark, expensive walnut paneling that made everything so shaded. The only light was reflected from the individually lit paintings on the walls. He found himself smiling, thinking that if the walls could talk, they'd have interesting things to say. All the important financial giants of New York City were members.

The escort silently led Jude to a door and opened it. It was a small dining room with a table set for two. At the table, reading the latest newspaper, sat the Attorney General of the United States.

"Mr. Attorney General, it's so nice of you to take the time to see me, sir." They shook hands although John Mitchell didn't get up. Jude sat in the vacant chair.

"Welcome to my little hideaway," John said in a friendly voice. Whenever I'm in the city, I like to come to this place. No one bothers me here-- clients, media people, and even, or maybe I should say especially, family isn't allowed to reach me. I reserve this room for special meetings with note- worthy people, like you, Mr. Thaddeus."

"Thank you, Mr. Mitchell, for the compliment and the invitation," Jude said as he readied his talents for his next move.

Mitchell had already ordered lunch: London broil, thinly cut, rare with hollandaise sauce, and buttered mashed potatoes. The lunch was brought in, and they ate, chatting of politics and related matters. Eventually Jude brought up the real business of the meeting.

"You've done a very good job getting the right people close to Nixon," Jude said as he started the conversation.

"John Erlichman was one of Rockefeller's peo- ple. Nelson felt he had a chance to beat Nixon in the nineteen sixty primaries. So we put John in as a spy in the Nixon camp. The Nixon people hired Bob Haldeman to spy on Rockefeller," Mitchell laughed. "Well, Rocky met him in South Dakota and hired him on the spot. He's been our guy ever since."

"Mr. Mitchell, from this point on, we're in a client-counsel relationship," Jude said in a sober voice. He then slid Mitchell a five-dollar bill across the table. "That's your retainer; we're official.

First, let me ask, do you clearly understand who I am representing directly?"

Without comment, Mitchell nodded solemnly. He seemed to understand and accept everything.

Jude continued. "Mine is perhaps the most sensitive position Governor Rockefeller has ever authorized. I'm involved in an undertaking that boggles the mind. You will be a key player in this enterprise. As in the past, the Governor will compensate you handsomely for your efforts. I know we can count on you. However, it will mean sacrifices."

"Over the years, I've tried to be a loyal and useful counsel to the Governor. I hope he considers me so," Mitchell said in a very low voice.

"I wouldn't be here if he didn't. He values both your help and your friendship. He knows you will do what is asked." Jude paused, looking at Mitchell for reaction. "I've recently spoken to the President. He is planning to ask you to head up his re-election committee. We want you to accept, even though it will mean resigning as Attorney General. And it will mean more sacrifices than that. I'll be honest with you; this may be tough. You'll be asked to do certain things that may seem foolish, illegal, immoral - even un-American. It may mean you will personally have to make unprecedented sacrifices. The Governor regrets this possibility, but it's unavoidable. He's confident that, given your cooperation in past situations, he can rely on you completely."

Jude knew, but did not mention, that some of those past situations involved Mitchell's private family affairs that wouldn't bear legal or public scrutiny. He was sure that thought would cross Mitchell's mind without his having to mention it. Rockefeller is a powerful friend and he kept all the evidence.

Mitchell's waxy complexion looked even paler. "The chickens are coming home to roost," Mitchell said in such a low voice Jude could hardly hear him. Then he added, "To quote Albert Einstein, 'With fame I become more and more stupid, which of course is a very common phenomenon'."

"No need to look at it that way. He wouldn't ask you if it weren't essential. You'll have his gratitude, which you can expect to be expressed in quite concrete ways."

Mitchell sighed, looking slightly uplifted, trying to put a positive face on. "Of course. What do you want me to do?"

"There's a man named E. Howard Hunt I want you to employ for a top security role. He's been a CIA operative, which will make him very useful; plus he is a natural for what we need. We'll want him to recruit some special agents to help carry off an unusual project. Another man that now works for the committee is G. Gordon Liddy. He's a former FBI agent, a red meat man, and from what I hear, quite a character: tough, loyal, and has good connections. And both these guys are leaders that can be depended upon."

"I know Hunt. He is steady as a rock. Liddy, I believe, was once a prosecutor upstate. Both are smart and good at what they do," Mitchell said quietly.

"There's another one we want. His name is Alex Griffin and he's a New York cop. I think you have worked with him in the past. An interesting fellow. It seems he wanted to get some mobsters off the street, so with a little vigilante activity on his part, he bumped off a mob boss and started a gang war among rival mob families. He was successful thinning out the mob and getting a few thrown in jail. He is a man that can make things happen. I'm sure you can cajole him into joining the team. We wouldn't want any information to get out on his involvement in mob deaths. He'd be dead in hours."

"Griffin has always shown himself to be a reliable and resourceful individual. I'm sure he will be with us."

"Good," said Jude with a take-control attitude. "I want him to quit the NYPD and be ready for new employment, at a substantial raise in pay, effective immediately."

"Yes, I will arrange that." Mitchell was taking orders like a waiter at lunchtime.

"As chairman of the President's re-election committee, you'll have certain financial responsibilities, which will include funding certain questionable operations. You should handle this in a rather sloppy way, so that a second-rate reporter, once alerted, will have no trouble detecting shady pay-offs. You'll be receiving a lot of cash in hundred dollar bills. I want that money traceable to the committee; it will be used for special intelligence gathering operations. Keep yourself distantly clean. Try to keep Nixon in the dark about these special projects. He won't bother you much; he still remembers nineteen forty-eight, how Dewey lost because everyone sat on their hands at the end, and that cost him the election. He also remembers in nineteen sixty, when he lost to Kennedy by sixty thousand votes, between Daley voting the dead in Chicago, and the missing votes in Texas with Landslide Lyndon. He knows you have great influence and money people in the Big Apple...especially with the TV networks headquartered here." After a breath Jude continued. "I will work directly with Griffin; take the lead for him. Stay close to the President. Maintain your friendship with him and remain his chief legal adviser." Jude pulled from his pocket a note. "Before you resign as Attorney General, I want you to choose a good investigating lawyer and get income tax information on Jack Fehan, President of Ever Green Development Company. There will be something to find, regarding a payment ostensibly for refurbishing Mr. Agnew's office. Start the investigation, get the data needed for indictment, but keep the lid on it until after the election. It must not break before the election.

"Oh yes, one other thing," Jude said almost as an afterthought. "There's a young hippy lawyer working in justice, by the name of John Dean. I'd like to have Haldeman take him under his wing for a while. I have a unique assignment for the imposing lightweight counselor; I believe he will work out just fine."

Mitchell's head lifted up with a look of concern. "I've seen him once or twice at meetings. He's a new brash attorney with more image than substance. His main concern is looks and women. You sure he's your man? He's not the type you can depend on, if you know what I mean," John said in a somber voice.

"'For everything there is a season, a time to plant, and a time to pluck up what is planted.' Ecclesiastes," Jude said as if to lecture.

"Well, I believe I understand my task and responsibilities quite clearly," Mitchell said with a certain glum dignity, as he laid aside the menu. "I don't believe I'll have dessert, after all."

"I think I will," said Jude. If the Attorney General lost his appetite, Jude found that the conversation had increased his own.

CHAPTER **13**

Thursday was a bright sunny morning, a good opportunity for an enjoyable drive from the Big Apple to Cape May, New Jersey. The trip was a pleasant experience for Jude. It afforded him time to be alone, to think, and relax as he drove down the Garden State Parkway. Numerous miles of the parkway were beautiful, lined on both sides with the famous Jersey pines. Driving through the rich farmland planted with tomatoes, blueberries, cranberries, sweet corn, and various other garden plants, he understood how the state got its nickname, "The Garden State," and why Campbell's Food chose to make their soups in south Jersey, near the farms. The drive down the parkway would be a pleasant journey if it weren't interrupted by a tollbooth every few miles, resulting in slower traffic and unhappy motorists. He resented the fact of paying thirty-five cents every few miles for the privilege of driving slowly.

The destination of this next meeting was the Lobster House. It was a quaint seafood restaurant sitting on a fisherman's wharf in scenic Cape May, at the southern tip of New Jersey. Built over 100 years ago, it remained a working fishing wharf, unloading and selling fish fresh from the ocean, or the Chesapeake Bay. The restaurant and bar were added a few decades ago, with a spectacular view of Cape May's harbor full of expensive pleasure boats of all fashions and designs. This famous eating habitat was brought to Jude's attention due to its reputation of supplying the freshest raw bar on the east coast. It was also known for authentic turtle soup, served with house cream cheese and Spanish Sherry. The food and ambiance were well worth the time and effort. Jude arrived early: he wanted to be in position when Officer Griffin arrived.

He entered the long bar just off the main dining room. The smell of the salt water and iced fresh fish permeated the restaurant. The bar area was a very large dark paneled room accented with an assortment of sea going paraphernalia. It was designed in a maritime motif with large paintings of three mastered sailing ships on white-capped tumultuous seas. The bar was very long with over 20 bar stools. Behind the bar, the shelves were loaded with bottles of liquor. Also on the shelves were impressive large models of actual sea vessels. Jude chose a bar stool at the end so he could watch the boats in the harbor and also to keep an eye on all the vehicle traffic entering the parking lot. The weather had changed and a light drizzle of rain began to fall.

Jude noticed a blue Ford sedan with a New York license plate pull into the parking lot. The car seemed to have a lot of mileage and was in need of a washing. Jude looked and wondered as it parked a few dozen yards away. The man who got out looked as if he'd had a long drive: his hair was messy, his clothes were disheveled, and he appeared to have seen nearly as much hard usage as his car. He walked toward the entrance, looking in all directions, scoping out the area. When he arrived at the front entrance he took the cigarette from his mouth, threw it on the ground, squashed it with his foot, then strolled in.

He put a fresh cigarette in his hand as he made his way down the bar. Just in front of Jude, he put it in his mouth asking, "Do you have a match?"

Jude picked up a book of matches from the bar. "Certainly, Officer Griffin. My pleasure."

Griffin lit the cigarette and sat on the bar stool looking over Jude's shoulder, glancing at the harbor and the small boats gliding by. "Well, I'm here. Now what?"

At that moment, the young attractive barmaid interrupted, asking, "Would you gentlemen like a drink?"

Jude spoke first. "I would like a tonic, with a twist of lime."

Griffin seemed as if he wanted to make a statement of sorts. "It's getting cold and rainy out there. I'd like a Southern Comfort Manhattan, up, with a twist of lemon."

The barmaid said, with a warm smile, "Thank you...be right back."

Jude looked directly at Griffin and asked quickly, "Have you resigned yet?"

"There's been talk of it. Nothing's happened yet. Before I jump in, I want to at least know how deep the water is," Alex said as he puffed on his cigarette.

He doesn't mince words, Jude thought. Jude decided a judicious directness was in order. "I've heard a lot about you, Alex. You're quite a cop. You have impressed some people in high places. They tell me you know how to get things done efficiently. I'm here to offer you an opportunity to make some real money, and make some good things happen. However, we will be making some omelets with the eggs."

"I can do a lot of things, like break a lot of eggs. But cleaning up broken eggs is the hard part. I may need industrial strength cleaner. That means I need some industrial-strength money," commented Griffin, seemingly unmoved. "What kind of figures are you talking about?"

"We'll discuss the money later, but I think you will be pleased," Jude said. "The friend that contacted you was Attorney General Mitchell, right?"

The barmaid returned putting the drinks on the bar. Griffin's eyes lit up when he saw the size of his drink. He picked up the Manhattan, put it to his lips, and closed his eyes for a moment.

"Yeah, the Attorney General and I go way back; long before he was the powerbroker," Griffin said sarcastically.

"Mr. Mitchell and I are working on a most delicate operation involving the presidency. And we need help from a person like yourself...someone whose loyalty is, shall we say, undying," Jude said quietly. Griffin looked at Jude, and in a tough New York accent said, "I don't kill people for money. And to mention the presidency...well that's out of my league."

Jude was somewhat startled. "Nobody's asking you to kill anyone. We need outside help concerning a presidential project that will be interesting and delicate."

"Well, I just want you to know I don't kill for money, or do anything illegal. And, well...it has to be worth the money. Do you understand? If I'm going to gamble, I want the high stakes." Griffin was talking like a street hood, but he could do the job.

"I'll accept that, Alex. You'll work directly for me. I expect loyalty and my identity will be kept secret," Jude said.

"All right then," Griffin said seemingly mollified. "Tell me more about the project. How do I fit in and how much do I make?"

"As I was saying, Mr. Mitchell and I, among others, have a very delicate and ambitious project underway. For your help you'll be rewarded quite generously. As soon as you resign from the police force, you will head up a small security company. I will finance it; there will be plenty of money. You'll receive a handsome salary; taxes and benefits will be taken out. You don't mind paying taxes; do you Alex? When we complete our project you will receive a large bonus, a very large bonus. You'll be wealthy enough to retire for life and live well. There will be nothing wrong with the money, or your method of acquiring it. It will be just as if you'd made wise investments, say the last ten years in the stock market and hitting a big one.

"All the records Mitchell has will be destroyed at my request. No one will have any information about your overzealous past, as a special undercover cop. You will be completely free and clear to enjoy life in whatever way you see fit. Am I making myself clear?"

"So what do you want done, and why did you choose me?" Griffin said.

"You've worked well in the past in coordination with the FBI and CIA operatives. You're highly regarded in those quarters, and that's saying something. There are a few favors they still owe you. We expect that to be useful for our program. We also considered your character. What I have learned about Alex Griffin is that you place a great deal of value on loyalty. So do I. You have an outstanding military record, having served in the one hundred and seventy-third Airborne Brigade, where you were awarded a Silver Star, among other medals, for bravery. And you had a hell of a reputation on long-range patrols. In general, you're a good man who can do the difficult and dangerous, calmly. We need that. Incidentally, the salary is seventy-five thousand per year, plus expenses. The project will take a few years; then you'll receive our bonus."

Jude sat looking at Griffin, and then said, "Before I say more, I must have your commitment. Are you on the team, Officer Griffin?"

"Don't call me officer," he said with a smile. "As of now, I am no longer a cop, or at least as soon as I sign the paperwork."

"I trust you are one of us now?" Jude asked.

"Sure am, as long as I don't have to kill nobody."

"I can assure you...nothing like that," Jude said. The repetition was beginning to annoy him. "You are going to be offered a job at the Committee to Re-elect the President, or CRP, as a security supervisor. CRP will also pay you a salary. You'll work under John Mitchell officially, and report to me directly. Is that okay with you?"

"Sure. But, who are you...if you don't mind me asking?"

"My name is Jude Thaddeus." Jude passed him a business card.

"You sound like a Saint," Griffin said in a humorous way.

"It's a name that was given to me in the orphanage. To Catholics, Jude Thaddeus is the Patron Saint of The Impossible. So what I am doing may seem impossible, but in the spirit world, all things are possible."

Jude then pointed to the card. "The number written in pen is a secure line. To call me, add one to the first and last numbers written. That way, if you were to misplace the card, the number won't be compromised. Mitchell is aware that you'll be my man in his organization. However, he doesn't know what I'll be asking you to do. That will be our little secret; your bonus depends on it."

"Keeping a little secret should be easy, since I don't know anything yet." Griffin was starting to relax, as he drew in another breath of smoke, and took a sip of his drink.

"You'll know when the time is right, and I will let you know when." Jude was beginning to take to him.

"I'm going in to resign. What's next?" Alex asked.

"You'll be hearing from Mitchell in a few days. He will offer you the position," Jude said, looking over at the traffic starting to backup. "You'll have to live in Washington for a while. When you're settled in, call that number, and be ready for deployment. I will arrange another meeting. At that time I will fill you in on what we are doing."

"For the next meeting," Griffin stared at the many whiskey bottles on display behind the bar, "maybe we could make the location a little more convenient, with less driving. My car is on its last legs."

"We'll take care of that, and anything else you need," Jude said.

Griffin chewed at his lip, made some mumbled comment about the weather, then with a clearer voice said, "'Scuse me for saying so, but I haven't heard the numbers about the industrial-strength money. Now when you're talking some kind of mischief in presidential politics, I suspect it's a large tab."

"It's industrial grade all right. You will receive five hundred thousand dollars for your efforts. It will be paid to you in installments. I've been acting as your investment counselor; you have been doing very well, although you weren't aware of it. It will take some time to set up the necessary bank accounts and documentation. But far less than the two years the project will probably require."

"Well, this should be a quite interesting tour of double dealings," Griffin said as he got up from the bar. "I have a long drive back." He pulled out another cigarette as he turned to walk out.

"Aren't you going to have something to eat? This is one of the best eating establishments in south Jersey." Jude seemed surprised with Griffin's apparent departure.

"I've already eaten. I grabbed a sandwich on the way down...at the most popular eating establishment in all of New Jersey: McDonalds." Griffin chuckled to himself. "Is there anything else you wanted to talk about?"

"Yes there is," Jude said to him with a smile. "Get a newer car. No one would believe a detective would drive an old battered car, and dress in worn-out London Fog."

Griffin waved and walked toward the door, then yelled over his shoulder, "Maybe now I can buy some expensive shoes, like yours."

For October, it was a clear, crisp, warm afternoon, classic day for a Homecoming football game. The trees were painted a radiant orange and red by the skillful brush of Jack Frost. As Jude surveyed the crowd, it was easy enough to spot Gala, in spite of the excited crowds of students and alumni after the conclusion of the game. All he had to do was look for the Secret Service men. Gala's guest for the game was Tricia Nixon.

Jude found the Secret Service men sober in three-piece suits and conspicuous as elephants among the yelling, celebrating college students. Considering the Secret Service detachment was guarding Tricia, they didn't notice Jude when he approached Gala. With a motion of the hand, Jude pointed to a parking lot near the stadium. Gala made an excuse to Tricia and joined Jude at the entrance.

"Nice wheels." Gala showed him how an elegant woman could slide into a low-slung sports car, as if she were still in college. "I love the color: British Racing Green. It's a new Austin Healy isn't it?"

"Yes it is," Jude said with pride. "It's an Austin Healey Mark IIIBJ8, and there aren't many in this country."

They looked like two prosperous Ivy Leaguers as they slowly drove out the driveway. Gala was patting the dashboard, while looking over at the airplane type gauges. "What a magnificent black leather interior!" She then put on a scarf as speed picked up. "Where are we off to, a little mountain chalet, with a fireside dinner for two?"

"No, I could only get away for the day."

"Don't tell me...we're going parking on a dirt road in the hills," she said with a laugh. He didn't think it was quite that humorous.

"The on-ramp should be along here somewhere..." Jude said as he was studying the road trying to figure out where he was. Gala tapped him on the shoulder and pointed to the sign for the Connecticut Turnpike, overhung with brilliant fall leaves. It was a beautiful day to drive through New England in a British sports car. Top down, wind blowing in your face, with hardly a care in the world, except...

"Is your guest enjoying herself?" Jude yelled above the noise of the wind.

"We both are," Gala called back. "Sometimes I think it would be nice to be that young again. She really is a nice girl. Rather shy, but I guess I might be too if my father were the President of the United States."

"You? Shy?" Jude laughed. "You wouldn't be shy if the Pope were your father!"

He looked for a response. It was a cold glance. He decided to change the subject back to Tricia. "Did you have any trouble finding her a suitable date?"

"I had one of my college friend's younger sister arrange it. Of course, the Secret Service had to be told who he was and where we were all going. The blind date had to be informed and checked out. He was more impressed than annoyed. You know, they arranged for the two Secret Service men to have dates so that they could watch without being so conspicuous, so Tricia should enjoy herself. Only a few people here know who she is and they're all sensible enough not to make a childishly big deal out of it. I've seen to that."

"I'm sure you have."

"Are we eloping to Massachusetts, or have you something else on your mind?" inquired Gala, grabbing the mirror to check how her scarf was holding out.

"It's about the election and your role afterward." Jude eased up on the pedal, so he wouldn't have to shout. "You need to become more than just a family friend and personal confidante."

"I'm already something more than that now," Gala said demurely.

"I mean more useful to him. Let him know you can be very helpful in coordinating the staff for the re-election committee. You can be the liaison between him and the committee, the unofficial voice of the President. You could handle the more personal side of it, including confidential correspondence, and staff coordination. Emphasize the conflicts between New York and the California contingents, and volunteer to smooth the feathers, keeping everyone happy. The running of the country, and the Democrats are enough for him to cope with without trying to settle petty feuds within his own campaign organization. That sort of thing."

"That's not much different from what I'm doing now," Gala said quickly. "The President finds a behind-the-scenes secretary very useful. Rosemary Woods has the title of his personal secretary, but it's just a title these days. She's just a glorified typist, but she's been so loyal. Dick thinks the world of her. But she can't handle anything other than office duties, strictly office duties. So you want me to get a little closer to the re-election committee? One other thing: the Pentagon Papers has everyone upset, first the New York Times and then the Washington Post. No one knows where the next article will appear. The President isn't as upset as Doctor Kissinger. Rumor has it he's furious, saying that it's hurting our war effort. Something has to be done."

"By the way, how do you get along with Mrs. Woods?"

Gala gave him a look, with eyebrows raised. "Why jus' fine, sugar. What kind of a fool do you think I am? Secretaries don't always have the power to say yes, but they are masters at getting negative action. So, I keep Mrs. Woods as happy as a schoolteacher before summer break."

Jude nodded, reassured. "You must keep a low profile dealing with the committee. I know how jealous the California group can be about their prerogatives. Keep yourself out of direct, visible conflict with everyone. We're entering deeper waters now, so we must be careful. Don't write anything down. Memorize key things: who does what and how, and to whom. With the big money donations remember when it comes in, who keeps it, and where it goes. Most important of all though, stay close to the President. When things get tough, and they will, I want him to confide in you alone. He'll be seeing people all around him crumble, but you'll remain confident, unworried, and strong, strong enough for him to lean on. Encourage that."

Gala nodded. "I guess that this is when the game gets interesting."

Jude remarked, "Do you remember Bob Woodward?"

"Yale man and a self-righteous egotist," said Gala as she thought more on the topic. "I believe he's in the navy. Stationed at the Pentagon, I think. He had some big connections somewhere along the line."

"That's the man," Jude said with pride. "I want to make use of that gigantic ego. I just had him transferred from a small suburb shopper sheet he was working, to the Washington Post. He really thinks he's a big fish now. Bob should be our most valuable unknowing player when the time comes. This is where you start earning that handsome salary."

"I knew it was coming," commented Gala, with a sly smile. "What do I do, seduce him?"

"Too risky. No. Woodward in his new position at the Post will be looking for anything to get his name or byline in lights. The next time you meet him at some social event, gently let him know exactly what you do...or what the outside world thinks you do. Keep it very low-key. But make it clear that you're potentially the most inside of inside sources into the Administration. If I've judged Woodward correctly, he'll make the next move, hunting any story. And that's exactly what we want. When the time comes, he'll get his story. String him along with sweet but interesting nothings until I tell you otherwise. Oh, and I've arranged for a new apartment for you in Washington. I think you'll like it."

Gala, who'd been looking off at the colorful trees as if daydreaming, came suddenly alert. "I like my apartment in Alexandria."

"You'll like this one better. The address is 1840F Street. It's brand new with a pool, sauna, and private parking, plus close to fine restaurants, near everything downtown. But what is very important is the excellent security system. It should be ready for you to move in on Saturday. The manager, Richard James, will expect you midday. If you want, I can take the afternoon off and I'll even try to make it down to show it to you personally." Jude laughed slightly, saying,

"It's been a little project I've been working on for some time, so you'd better like it...and my interior designing taste."

Gala laughed. "If it's big enough for a guided tour, and you did the interior design, well, it must be something. And for you to take a whole afternoon off, I should be so grateful. Jude, sometimes you do surprise me. It usually happens when you start talking."

"I best get you back to your hotel," Jude yelled as they drove.

"Are you going to join us for dinner tonight? It should be a lot of fun. Who knows...you may see some of your friends. That is, if you had any."

"Sounds like a great time to be had by all, but I must get back to the city by ten tonight," Jude said looking over at Gala, admiring how pretty she looked. Things were moving smoothly.

CHAPTER 14

Gala walked through the apartment while the manager looked on anxiously, as if worried that she'd find something she disliked and decide not to move in after all. The kitchen had all the modern conveniences: dishwasher, trash compactor, and a Sub Zero refrigerator in addition to the expected sink and stove. All the appliances were top of the line quality. The countertops were custom-made, with glass-paneled cabinets above.

Mr. James demonstrated for her an air purifying system to defeat the sometimes miasmic Washington smog. He explained the air conditioner equipment and the fire and burglar alarm systems. In the other rooms, the fabrics and carpets were as luxurious as she could have imagined. She resisted the impulse to slip off her shoes to feel the deep carpet. She contented herself with just touching pleasantly knobby or silky surfaces. There were lots of closets, a bathroom with shower and bath, nearly wall-to-wall mirrors, and terrazzo floor tile in a pleasant peach shade.

As she walked through the apartment, Gala said little, except to moon a little at the luxuries. As they returned to the living room, Mr. James excused himself, saying, "Please, Miss Dufante, take a good look around. Get the feel of the place; take a look at the nice view. I'll leave the key here on the mantel. You can drop it off when you're ready."

"That's fine. I won't be long." Gala looked around the apartment in silence; she thought Jude spent a lot of money and time to have this place so lavishly decorated. She pulled up the louvered blinds to inspect the "nice view," and found herself surveying the distant Washington Memorial across an intervening haze of trees. Nice indeed. Then she thought she heard a sudden noise and turned to see if Mr. James had come back. But the outer door was still shut. The sound had come from the other direction: the master bedroom. She walked quickly over and flung open the door. There was a man standing there! She was drawing a breath to scream when he turned. It was Jude.

"My God! You almost scared me to death! Where were you hiding? Behind the door? In the closet? No, because we looked in every closet. I don't believe it. You were hiding under the bed."

"I told you you'd like the place, and I didn't mention the furnishings. Was I right?" Jude asked in a nonchalant way, waving about the room.

"It will do very nicely, but I'm not going to accept an evasion. Where were you hiding and why?" She was quite interested in the answer.

"The building's an old brownstone, you no doubt noticed. But the interior's modern and completely gutted. The interior was completely rearranged for your comfort and convenience." Jude spoke like a real estate agent, pushing the apartment.

"Let me guess: you own it," Gala said with a cocked head.

"As a matter of fact, I do, although not officially. One of my companies owns it. But I designed most of it. Particularly this apartment, with its view of the Potomac, and its private entrance."

"What private entrance?" Gala was now even more interested.

Jude took a pen from his jacket and pushed it into an undetectable slot in the side of the closet molding. The back closet's wall slid back, exposing an identical closet on the other side. Jude walked through both closets, sliding the opposite closet door leading into a mirror image of the other bedroom. "Will you join me in here," he said looking quite proud of his work.

As Gala walked through the closets, she said, "I can't wait to hear the explanation about these lodgings."

"I said you'd be surprised," Jude said. "Take a look around. If you liked the first one, you should like this one. I have a call to make. I'll meet you back at the other apartment."

It was the same layout, fabrics, and appliances. "Twice the closet space, but what kind of a person lives in a place like this?" muttered Gala, giving the place a backward glance as she went into the closet for her return trip. When she joined Jude in the living room, with an upbeat voice, she said, "I'm double peppermint impressed." Then added seriously, "Now the sixty-four thousand dollar question, what's it all for?"

"Have you talked to the President about expanding your duties?" Jude asked as if he were her teacher and she, his student.

"We had a very interesting conversation. He thinks I have a lot to offer. You are now addressing the personal administrative assistant and close confidante of the President. In fact, I began getting into some rather sensitive correspondence just yesterday: one opinion versus another and it seems he's already worrying about friction and jockeying for power between the California and New York camps."

"There probably is just enough in-fighting to give you some way to demonstrate your comforting talents. We want Nixon to be nervous, but not in a position to over-react. We need to have a gradually increasing influence on him. Keep your low profile so no one is suspicious. Oh yes; what about our local Walter Winchell, known as Bob Woodward?"

"I've been cautiously checking him out. I found out where he lives and which parties he's likely to attend. I should be able to make contact in a natural way within the next week," Gala said coolly.

"Good. I've been thinking; don't be specific with him about what you do. Give him the impression that you're something along the lines of a member of the secretarial pool. A source, but not a crucial source, not yet. We want to play him like a cheap fiddle. If he's persistent, be vague and ambiguous. Let him get a taste of something. Newspaper people deal in stench. And we will lead him to the cesspool."

"I can be quite vague, but I resent the cesspool crack," Gala said with mock solemnity.

"I have some news for you," Jude said as if offering a toy or piece of candy to a child. "In a few weeks, there'll be a break-in at the national Democratic headquarters at the Watergate Complex. The culprits will be caught in the act. I don't expect much news coverage at first. The Republicans will downplay it, and the Democrats are always complaining about political sabotage. So, it will be just another incident. And that, my dear, is where you come in with our ace reporter, Mr. Woodward."

"Well, I was right about the explanation, although I don't quite know my role in this adventure," Gala said.

"After the break-in is reported, and is making a little news, then is the time to initiate contact with Woodward. Let him know that you have some meager news gossip that could be interesting information. I will give you the material we want dispersed. It will be just enough to stimulate his imagination and start his visualizing the news awards, the fame, and fortune your information can win for him. This apartment will play a part in this enthralling project."

"I know I'm going to like what's coming next," Gala said laughing; realizing how crazy this plan of Jude's was developing.

"I'll get to the two apartments in a minute, Gala," Jude said as he tried to lay out the plan. "At times, it may seem you have a split personality because you are going to play the part of two people." Jude began to chuckle,

"Before you ask, no, you don't get paid twice as much. That's why you will use the A side as your apartment. For convenience we will call the duplicate apartment side B. When you get home for the evening, there will be times when you go into apartment B, change clothes, put on a wig, and go out through the main entrance downstairs. The fictitious woman who rents apartment B is an airline stewardess, so her comings and goings aren't regular. Her name, or your stewardess name, is Susan Cane. She works for TWA. You'll establish and maintain the second identity, starting right away. I have all the documentation you need: airline ID, Social Security number, etc. You have a bank account with a moderate amount of money in it now."

"Why, or shouldn't I ask?" Gala said, with slightly more concern in her voice.

"You'll need freedom to move. This apartment is designed to help you maintain your secrecy. This building is secure; I commissioned the consummate security contractor in the country to do this job. It was expensive, but worth the investment."

Jude paused for a moment, gathering his thoughts, and then said, "After the break-in at the Watergate, don't count on anything. Be very careful. You may be under constant surveillance within the month." Jude went to a cabinet and pulled a device out about the size and shape of a small transistor radio. Displaying it to Gala, he said, "This little toy will be very valuable. See, there's a small light on the side. It's off now, but when the light is on, it will mean that you're being monitored or bugged. Keep this with you always when you're away from the White House; check it inconspicuously, from time to time. Push this button and it will scramble phones or personal recording machines. Don't use it in front of, or with the President. Don't even take it to the White House. Keep it in apartment B: we don't want them to know you have this. I'm giving it to you for working with Woodward. He'll try every trick in the book to compromise you, force you to give information. Don't let him. Any information he gets, he gets from me through you. This little toy will be valuable here in your apartment because when the White House staff and the re-election committee find out how close you are to the President, they will start their own spying on you."

"This is getting confusing, and exciting," Gala said taking it all in.

Jude handed her the gadget and showed her how to operate and test it. He then went on talking about how she was to handle Woodward. "With him it will be like fencing, which consists of two things: to give and to not receive. When it gets to the point where he realizes that you have valuable information, let him know you have more, but impress on him it's dangerous and difficult. Don't ever talk on the phone with him, and don't trust the mail or couriers.

You'll have to work out a simple but undetectable code to meet secretly. When you do meet, you must control everything: when, where, and under what circumstances. You can't take the risk of being identified as the source. We want to control the flow of material. It would be dangerous if you give out too much at one time. You have to convince him that these procedures are in his best interest. We will spoon feed and ration the substance. If he gets the story slowly, he'll have to be patient. Let him know this will be a bigger story than the Pentagon Papers. This would be the same premise: stories coming out a little at a time to keep the headlines in the papers, slowly winning, and then keeping, the attention of the public. It will be like a Chinese torture chamber: one drop at a time. The overall effect is just part of our strategy; it will be a catalyst for future developments."

Gala smiled and said, "Future developments? I'm not going to ask."

"Speaking of the future," Jude said getting a card from his wallet. He wrote on it and said, "Here's a new toll-free number for you. Memorize it while we're here. I'll be in contact with you as things develop, but if you need me, call that number...always from a pay phone, and not anywhere near this apartment. An airline terminal or bus station would be best. Never use the same phone twice." He put his wallet back into his pocket. "Now, any questions?"

"I think," Gala said, looking into a walled mirror, "I'm going to like this apartment."

"Good. I knew I chose the right girl for this job," Jude said, realizing that she didn't blink an eyelash as he discussed the clandestine life she was about to embark upon. "Remember now, we're on the twenty-yard line. So keep cool, keep up the good work, and enjoy yourself. I'll leave through Susan Cane's apartment," Jude said, and then added with a touch of humor in his voice, "You know, she has a boyfriend, but I think he's married. Hardly anybody ever sees him come or go."

"Superman has to change in a phone booth," Gala called after him. "At least I have two apartments to change in."

Jude turned back as he was opening the apartment door and said to Gala, like a ham actor, "In the works of Victor Hugo, perseverance is the secret of all triumphs."

~~~~~~

Jude sat at a small table in The Café Lombardy, drinking a Schweppes tonic with a twist of lime. The Hotel Lombardy was a nice, quiet place to meet. Not too far from the White House, it was a few blocks away on Pennsylvania Avenue. Jude smiled as Alex Griffin walked into the bar area. He still looked disheveled, but it appeared that he had made, some progress with his appearance. He had a decent haircut and his clothes were of a finer cut.

"Welcome to Washington. It seems to be having a positive influence on you, Alex," Jude said as they shook hands.

"It's a little difficult to learn all the streets and to remember the rush hour traffic, but all and all, it's quite a place," Griffin said as he sat down, taking notice of Jude's drink.

The waiter was there, quickly taking a drink order. Alex looked at the bar and fumbled for his cigarettes. With his head bowed somewhat, he said quietly, "I'll just have a Coke."

Jude sensed that Griffin had given up drinking, or was trying to impress him that he didn't drink much, although Jude already knew Griffin was a borderline alcoholic. And he was now showing some of the classic signs. "You are having an interesting transition from cop in the Big Apple to living the good life in Washington. How are things going?" Jude asked.

"The night life is great, the women are plentiful, and the cost of living is about the same. But I'm getting in the swing of things," Griffin said as he started to drink the Coke that was just set on the table.

"I understand that you met with some security people over at CREEP: Liddy, Hunt, and David Young. Alex, are you familiar with the Alpha group in New York?" Jude asked as he picked up his drink.

"Those crazies? They're a fanatical group of former Cubans trying to raise money to build an army to liberate Cuba from the communist Castro. I know them. Basically, they're good people with a useless cause, who sometime have problems with the law," Griffin said as he lit up his cigarette.

"It sounds as though you have had some experience with the group. Are you on good terms with them and do you have contacts with substance within the organization?" Jude asked.

"I know some of the kingpins, and they know me. I've always been fair with them, although it meant sending a few to the Iron Room Hotel for a short time."

"Good," Jude said looking directly into Griffin's eyes. "They will do a lot to fight Castro's communism, including some illegal operations. Am I right?" Jude asked quietly.

"They sure will! They'll break the law and more if necessary. They consider themselves as soldiers against communism." Griffin spoke in a disturbing tone as if he had a great concern about this group.

"I want you to inform your new colleagues at CREEP Security, Hunt, Liddy, and Young, that you've come by information from your connections at Alpha that the McGovern campaign is getting large amounts of money from the Communists through Cuba. Tell them the money is being laundered in Mexico, then double-cleaned in Texas. From there it goes directly to the national Democratic headquarters here in Washington. Let them know you have information from a source who works at the Watergate Complex and has heard certain things, which confirm what you've received from Alpha. But it's nothing solid yet."

With a confused voice Griffin asked, "So... what's the punch line?"

"Just think about it for a moment," Jude said gathering his thoughts. "Wouldn't it be interesting if all the left-wing liberals, and all their peacenik friends, got caught being financed by the Commies? And that's just what we want certain people at CREEP to think."

"Yeah, that'd be one hell of a story. Is there anything to it?" Griffin asked.

"The evidence is there, in the Watergate. And if I know your colleagues, especially Young, they'll be hacking out a plan to get the goods and whatever material they can. They can't get much from the banks, but if they bug the place, they can get more material than just the money on the Commies." Jude picked up his drink and continued. "Now, after you give them this information, I want to know of their plans: when and how. They will have all the money they need to carry off this operation. McCord is their electronics expert; he can get the surveillance equipment. I want you to suggest getting some of the Alphas to do the actual break-in and bugging. You have four agents who will do the job for a reasonable fee. This is preferable. In case anyone is caught, they're not American citizens...no ties to the CREEP."

"So you want to bug the Democratic national headquarters?" Griffin said in a whispered voice.

"I want the Democratic headquarters broken into and the equipment installed," Jude said in a very low voice. "I want to know 24 hours in advance of this operation, and the identity of the people carrying it out. Part of your job is to supply the four Cuban exiles, one of whom is an electronic whiz. They will install this equipment, but it will fail to work properly. You'll see to that. The break-in will be repeated a second time. The reason for the second break-in is to install the bugging apparatus in the office. This will leave no doubt as to who did what, and why. On the second break-in, your Cuban electronics expert will not be available at the last minute. So McCord will have to go in his place. He's an American with CIA connections and fingerprints on file at the FBI. When they are caught, he will be easily identified."

"We're setting up an illegal bugging operation at the Democratic headquarters, and we're setting it up to be caught?" Griffin's voice was even lower than before.

"If you do your job properly, that's exactly what will happen. I want you to contact some of your local police friends and coordinate the arrests. We want it to be low-key, but effective," Jude said in a whisper.

"What about the information about the commie backing of McGovern? Does that get out?"

"It will depend on circumstances," evaded Jude.

"Is this with Mitchell's approval, or is this one of your own crazy ideas?" Griffin seemed to be cooler now.

"Mitchell understands that there will be operations like this one going on. John is aware of my authority in this, and other areas. He's also aware of a much larger plan. No need to go into that now. I'm sure he will verify his approval," Jude said coolly.

"That's good enough for me. If John Mitchell is okay with it, I'm okay with it. But if heads have to roll, there's a lot higher than me going on the block. I'll try to keep mine at a distance," Griffin said drinking his Coke, wishing it were laced with rum.

"When the heads roll, and they will," Jude said quickly, "I'll protect you. You have my word on it."

"Yeah," said Griffin in an utterly flat voice. "That's reassuring. I just hope you're around when the rolling stops."

Jude was glad the meeting was over. He had a large attaché case full of hundred dollar bills to deliver to John Mitchell. He had mixed emotions about Griffin; he genuinely liked Alex and had empathy for the tricky position Jude had put him in. As he was paying the check he thought to himself of Bertrand Russell's quote, "The degree of one's emotion varies inversely with one's knowledge of the facts - the less you know, the hotter you get."

The nightlife in Washington was a bachelor's dream. Lots of young and beautiful women were found everywhere. Griffin fit right in; he liked the bars of Georgetown. One in particular was Blackies Bar and Restaurant. It was a typical local chic-type establishment: low-lighting and loud, mild jazz music. He called his old contact with the Washington Police Department, Wes Dunn, and asked him to join him at Blackies for a drink. After a few drinks, both men were loosened up and talking about old arrests, and about those that got away. Griffin told Wes that he was now a private security advisor; his big client was a prominent political figure, and that he worked on special projects outside the normal security arena. "And that's why I asked you to meet me for a drink, Wes," Griffin said as he gulped down his third beer.

"What can I do for you Alex?" Wes asked leaning on the bar.

"My client is fairly important, and he's okay. But there are some real weirdoes working in a related group. Commie hunters; think there's spies under every bed. One of them has this cockamamie idea…" Griffin paused as if deciding whether to go any further. "I don't like telling tales outta school, Wes. But this guy, he says he's going to break into the Democratic Party's headquarters and bug the place."

"Sounds like a nut to me, but that sort of thing has happened before in this town," Dunn said jokingly.

"Now bear in mind: this guy has no approval from anybody, and he has a few crazies to go along with him. They think they'll get evidence and will become heroes and save the free world. And they expect to make a lot of money in the process. I tried to talk them out of this, but they won't listen. If I go to my boss, and anything goes out of control, my boss could be drawn into a mess that I'm paid to prevent. I would like to have this guy arrested now, but he hasn't done anything illegal yet." Griffin glanced expectantly, looking for a hopeful sign.

"How serious are these folks and what do they expect to find?" Dunn asked as he sipped on his beer.

"They're as serious as a heart attack," Griffin said without humor. "And what they are looking for is not there anyway. The Democrats have already moved personnel and files to Miami for the convention."

"I could arrest a few of them and bring them in for questioning, rough them up a little. That could scare them enough to call off the heist," Wes said, as if thinking aloud.

"The guy is ex-CIA, and his buddy is ex-FBI. They are real, not your barroom spooks. They worked for the Agency and the Bureau. So, when a flatfoot from NYPD has any suggestions, well... you've been here long enough to know how the white shirts work. They are the brains, and we former uniforms are here to offer our services with a smile and 'Thank you, sir.'"

"Sounds like you're in a tough spot, Alex," Wes said slowly, then ordered another round of drinks.

"Astute observation, Doctor Watson," Griffin said, as he pounded a new pack of cigarettes on the table. This was his nervous energy. It compacted the tobacco for a better smoke. It gave him time to set up his prey. "Like I was saying, Wes, this is serious business. If they get caught, this thing could go sky high, and the media would have a field day. It could cost Nixon the election. I have friends still in Vietnam. I can't stomach the idea of McGovern and his band of peaceniks controlling the White House."

"All right," Dunn paused for a moment. "You brought me down here and pumped me with booze," Wes said, as he picked up his refreshed drink. "Now, how can I help?"

Alex knew Wes Dunn was a smart cop with an abundance of street smarts. There was no need to try to push him in any direction. Dunn would make up his own mind as to what to do, and make it right. Both police officers knew how to flow through the sewer when necessary. Police work was sometimes like politics: not everything was as it appeared.

"What I want is a nice, quiet bust. Our ex-spooks get caught in the act, nobody gets hurt, no arguments. There'll be no ties to my organization. They get busted, get off light because it's their first offense, and are out of sight till the election is over. They are out of my hair, and politics. The news reports it as a dirty trick; in a few weeks it's old news on the back page. Everybody forgets and goes about life as before. The election goes ahead uninterrupted, and our spooks go back to writing their spy books."

"Okay. I can arrange a team to set up in the Watergate. When they come in, we bust them. Clean and simple." Wes was confident in his plan.

"You're joking! I said these guys are crazy not stupid. They've done this before. They'll case the joint in advance; they have their own freaking alarm system. Even if you catch them on the way in, it would do no good; they'd figure you were tipped off. They would be back again."

"Then how do you want to handle it, Officer Griffin?" Dunn asked quickly.

"I will find out exactly what night they're going to pull this off. I will keep you informed. You will be in the neighborhood. I will supply you with a radio, so I can communicate directly with you. Are you with me so far?" Griffin asked. Wes nodded his head. "When they are inside, I'll let you know. I will make sure the rent-a-cops, at the Watergate, report a burglary in progress. The night watchman is in the bag half the time. But don't worry... the call to the dispatcher will be placed. Even if he's pasted, he'll want credit for the call in. Maybe there'll be a bonus for him. Anyway, you will be in the area so you can respond quickly. You lead your team to the office in question, arrest the culprits and off to jail they go. You keep them away from reporters. Such a petty crime in the wee hours of the morning shouldn't attract many reporters anyway. Just another burglary in the Nation's Capitol."

"I think I can handle it okay. After all, it's not entrapment: nobody asked them to go break into the Democratic headquarters. And, responding to a radio dispatch, it should be clean. Just one other question: do any of them carry hardware?" Wes asked soberly.

"The only hardware they'll be carrying is bugging equipment. No guns," Alex said smiling.

"One other thing, Wes, there's a thousand dollars in it for your help."

"I don't need money to help you out, Alex," Dunn said, then added jokingly, "you picking up this bar tab is enough...and so rare."

"I'll proudly take care of both items, Wes." Griffin picked up his glass, and made a toast, "Friendship is one mind in two bodies."

The next meeting for Jude was in the office of the new Chairman of the Committee to Re-elect the President, John Mitchell. Jude handed the attaché case over the desk before he sat down. He noticed Mitchell's guise...as if he had a lot on his mind. He appeared tired, although he smiled as he greeted Jude.

"There'll be more," Jude commented. "There's two hundred thousand there. You may want to put it in a safe under the watchful eyes of your trusted staff."

"I'll see to it," John said, taking the case and putting it next to his desk as if a salesman had given him a product sample.

"Our plan is starting to take shape," Jude said, as he sat back in the leather wing chair. *Hmmm. Sturgis leather, fine furnishings; they're sparing no expense*, Jude thought. "In a short time your super security group, or as they call themselves "The Plumbers," will be talking to you about bugging the Democratic headquarters at the Watergate."

"That doesn't surprise me," Mitchell said in an offensive tone. "The Plumbers," as they call themselves, got their nickname over those damned Pentagon Papers. It seems information was leaking out, and these guys tried to stop the leaks. Thus, they call themselves The Plumbers. They have already done some crazy things, so this is right up their alley."

"They will tell you that they hope to get evidence that the McGovern Campaign is getting money from the Communists through Cuba, laundered in Mexico and Texas. I want you to approve their scheme reluctantly. But, under no circumstances is Griffin to be involved; I have made other commitments for him. Remind The Plumbers that, as Attorney General, you are authorizing them to perform similar bugging for national security reasons. They should use the same successful methods that have worked so far. Let them know they will get the money needed for the operation, and you want state-of-the art equipment installed. Tell them you cannot officially approve of such a plan, but you would give it a 'wink-of-the-eye' approval." Jude paused then and looked at Mitchell. "The reason you can't give official approval is in case they get caught. And, John...they will be caught."

Mitchell's head bolted forward, as he reacted incredulously, "What?"

Jude responded unemotionally. "They're going to get caught in the act of breaking into, and electronically bugging the Democratic national headquarters at the Watergate Complex."

Mitchell sat staring like a gloomy statue. Then he said suddenly, "If your master plan calls for the President not to get re-elected, I think you're going about it the right way. But, why not just openly support McGovern, and save this money." He pointed to the attaché case next to his desk. "I know we're way ahead in all the polls, but there's no way the President can get re-elected after breaking into the other candidate's campaign headquarters. When it comes out..."

"Ah, but it won't come out," Jude interrupted flatly. "Not right away. It will not be a big news story for some time; we will build and control the information. We have to painstakingly place each tile into the mosaic to make the final design. Don't worry; Nixon will be re-elected. I wouldn't think of sabotaging his election. No, I have scheduled a greater purpose."

"And I said The Plumbers were bizarre! Their screwy schemes seem logical next to this one," Mitchell said frowning heavily.

"Now don't get ahead of me, John," Jude said in a lighter voice. "After they get caught, I want you to get in touch with John Dean. Tell him that a couple of your boys were a little bit overzealous. Say that they were in some trouble and you want to meet with him. The fact that he was counsel to the President necessitates that we need to find a way to handle this problem before it gets out of hand. Dean will jump at the chance to out-maneuver Nixon's guard dogs Erlichman and Haldeman. This will be John Dean's power play, his portal to the power of the Oval Office. He's the trophy fish. All you need to do is feed him the bait."

"He's more like a carp than a trophy fish," Mitchell said.

"Yes, I agree with you. But remember... carps have a place in nature, too," Jude said as he moved up in his chair. "Now, I want you to arrange a payoff to the people who are caught: money, lawyer's fees, bail, the whole works. They must remain silent, whatever the cost, until after the election. Tell them it's a matter of national security - whatever it will take to keep them quiet. Promise them they'll be taken care of....after the election."

"And will they be?" Mitchell asked.

"They will be taken care of, all in different ways. It will be a life-changing experience for everyone. Some will do better than others - but that's life."

"It looks as if we're entering some difficult weather ahead, and I can't see through all the rain and clouds. I hope you know what you're doing, for my sake as well as the others."

"You will be well taken care of," Jude assured him. "You know how the governor values loyalty, and how he rewards his trusted subordinates."

"Yes, I am quite comfortable he'll take care of us all," John said meekly.

"One other thing," Jude said quickly getting back to the topic. "Contact the President, calm his nerves. Let him know that you're on top of everything; it's nothing to concern himself about. You'll get to the bottom of this mess. Tell him the same as you told Dean that an overzealous team believed there was communist money going into the McGovern campaign, and these guys went off the reservation looking for evidence. Assure him that as soon as the truth is disclosed and documented, those under arrest will become national heroes. Stay on close terms with him. Remind him that their past operations were under Doctor Kissinger's direction. These people were chosen because they could be trusted under any circumstance."

Mitchell folded his hands on top of the desk. "And when do the winds of this storm begin to blow?"

Jude was pleased that Mitchell apparently had accepted the agenda. Perhaps not in a positive manner, but he was a good soldier doing his duty. "Oh, I guess mid-June should be as good a time as any." Great generals always consider the timing before they act.

CHAPTER 15

J ude's trips to Washington were becoming more
frequent as the timetable ticked down toward
the Watergate break-in. He had unimpeachable
business reasons, but his real reasons were to get
first-hand development reports from his chief
lieutenants, Gala and Griffin. In this instance,
he decided to meet near Philadelphia, halfway
between Washington and New York.

He wanted to meet Griffin outside of
Philadelphia. Jude chose a restaurant called the
Ship Inn, located on the historic Lancaster Pike in
Downingtown. This establishment pre-dated the
Revolutionary War. The sign in front had 13 mus-
ket holes shot through it for bad luck. It happened
after the battle of Brandywine in 1777, which took
place a few miles down the road. Some Patriot
soldiers had stopped there and received poor

service from the Tory owner of the Inn, so they shot 13 bullets into the sign.

Jude arrived first, waiting in the small horse-shoe-shaped bar. The bar was filled with regulars, all talking local politics. He was comfortable in such a small room. Any other stranger would stand out. Griffin entered the restaurant and spotted Jude at the bar with his tonic and lime. He joined him at the bar and ordered a draft beer. Jude was untroubled seeing him order a draft beer; at least he was drinking in the open.

Jude spoke first, "Well, how are things going at the CREEP?"

Griffin was a little startled by the quick question. "Hunt and Liddy are hot to go. I wish you could have been there when I told them about the money being laundered to the Democrats. It was like attending a John Birch gathering. Hunt and Liddy were both on the warpath. The idea that Commies were backing that pinko Democrat McGovern was too much. I remember Hunt complaining that here we are fighting a war in Vietnam against communism and, everyday, our people are getting killed, wounded, and tortured, plus the Commies have their own candidate here in America running for President. I mean, he was furious! Liddy was just as bad, talking 'bout 'treachery from within' being more dangerous than the enemies we are fighting. You know, stuff like that. They'll do the break-in anytime, anywhere we say."

Griffin took a gulp of his beer and glanced around to be sure no one could hear his conversation. "I told them about the people at Alpha in New York. If Castro's financing the McGovern campaign, they said they would like to take him out permanently. That's when Hunt says, 'We got our own loyal Cubans. We have already worked with them. They'll do whatever we want; and they are skilled in what needs to be done. We've done Ellsberg...we can do this one.' Then Liddy went off. In his day at the FBI, he helped prosecute some of those foreign communist agents. 'They are like giant whales; they must be harpooned on the surface.' Hunt agrees. He said that when he was with the CIA, he fought the KGB. And the one thing they can't stand is to be found out. And if we could find the link outside the country, with the Commies inside the country, including the newspapers, teachers, politicians or anyone else, then we could purge this country of all communist control."

"Let's get to a table for lunch," Jude said with a twinge of excitement in his voice. He wanted to carry on with this conversation in a more private space. Without any hesitation, they went to the dining area. It was furnished in Early American décor, with wide dark plank floors, and the walls lit with various paintings of the American Revolution. There was a small anteroom which had room for only one table. The locals call it the "cheaters" eating area. It was perfect for Jude's use.

The waitress was waiting for them when they sat down. Jude ordered tonic with a twist, and Griffin ordered another draft. The waitress handed each of them a wooden menu. Jude told Griffin, "The specialty here is the soft shell crab and the tartar sauce is great. Should I order two?" Griffin nodded. His whole life was changing, and perhaps his diet should, too. "You'll like these crabs. They're caught in the Chesapeake just prior to molting, put in tanks, and held until they shed their hard outer shell. While in this soft state, they're delicious." After the waitress departed, Jude bent over the table to be closer to Griffin, and asked, "Have they pitched their plan to bug the headquarters to Mitchell yet?"

"Yeah, they pitched it to him, okay. He wasn't too enthused, but he did go along with it and said he would get us some cash to handle the project." Griffin thought for a moment and added, "When they put the idea to Mitchell, there was another guy at the meeting. He was a slick looking dude, Ivy League type, by the name of Dean. He said he worked directly for the President. I guess it was okay. Mitchell had him there. Just thought I'd let you know."

"That's fine that Dean was there, he's in our script for later use," Jude said quietly.

"Speaking of later, did you know O'Brien, the head of the Democratic Party, has moved everyone of importance, and their files, to Florida for the convention? We won't find much without the key players," Griffin said.

"I am aware of what's happening," Jude responded quickly. "The break-in will go on as planned. Your mission is to sabotage the bugging equipment, so after it's installed it won't work. Thus forcing a second break-in to repair the defective equipment. Make sure on the second break-in that McCord is in the office when the bust comes down."

"I have it all set up. Just about everything is taken care of already," Griffin said coolly.

"McCord has to be in the office when they're arrested. That's crucial," Jude said in a low, determined voice. "Because the Cubans' 'Nom de guerre,' have alias names. Can't be traced; no criminal records. They won't be intimidated, and they won't talk. That's partly good, but it's very important to have the conduit in our plan. And McCord is our conduit."

"It's okay. Really. I understand the importance of key players. In fact, I have given a fair amount of money to McCord. His daughter needs help. He's going to keep me informed play-by-play. Now about getting caught. I made contact with an old DC cop friend of mine, as you suggested. His name is Wes Dunn. He's a seasoned cop working undercover mostly. We worked together with the Secret Service on security for foreign dignitaries, and some terrorist undercover work. We tipped a few drinks, told old stories, and he's willing to help... as long as it's clean."

"How did you work it out with him?" Jude asked.

"He'll be in the area when we want him. We have to make sure the night watchman is sober enough to make the phone call. If he isn't, I have a way to call in the break-in so it can't be traced or recorded. I told Dunn it's a low-key operation. We just don't want anyone hurt. He will be in the area, in plain clothes. This way it won't arouse too much attention. He will take the '10-31' call. In police lingo, that's 'a crime in progress.' He will be there before any black and white can respond. This way, there won't be a lot of flashing lights or excitement. He'll make a quick arrest and they'll be off to the station with as little press coverage as possible," Griffin said while leaning back.

"Excellent. I was certain you'd locate someone suitable. Now, after the arrest, you know what you're to do."

"Yeah, sure. The Cubans know me by sight. They've seen me at the CREEP's headquarters. They don't know much about me, but they will know me when I come to talk to them. I have an 'in' with the local cops, and they'll let me see them anytime...cop-to-cop courtesy, better than lawyer courtesy. And, I tell the Cubans I can see that each man gets a million bucks if he can keep his mouth shut no matter what. I promise them the very best lawyers. I tell them they're heroic soldiers who are doing a great deed for their country and we're not going to forget it, so long as they stay soldiers and don't give anything but name, rank, and serial number, so to speak. I let them know that even at the worst, they won't pull much time. I'll tell them it's national security and that they must keep quiet; and pretty soon things will come out. Then everybody will know what heroes they've been. Right?"

"Very good," Jude said pleasantly. "Everything seems to be going very well."

"Yeah. Very good," Griffin said as he looked at the plate of food delivered. It consisted of two soft shell crabs, fries, and tartar sauce. "Now, how do you eat these things?" he said as if he wished he had ordered something else.

Jude looked at his platter with a different appreciation. To him it took timing and patience: catching the crabs at the right time; waiting for the shedding of the hard shell; exposing the entire crab as soft edible meat; and finally, the chef's making it a scrumptious meal.

Gala was casually dressed in a halter-top and shorts as she was cleaning her new apartment. She was dusting a silver statue of an Irish setter she had purchased in Paris. As she dusted the statue, it brought back memories of her first trip with Nixon, and then her phone rang. She looked at it suspiciously. No one knew her unlisted number except the White House, and she didn't expect any call from there on a Saturday morning. The President and the rest of the staff were in California. She had plans for an enjoyable afternoon, and an even more enjoyable evening. Lifting the receiver, she said coldly, "Yes?"

"Get out the wrong side of the bed this morning?" Jude inquired. "Or were you in the wrong bed?" Without waiting for a comment on this witticism, he went on, "Just kidding. I need to discuss a few things with you."

"That's fine. When and where?" Gala responded sharply.

"Well, the when is now, and the where is behind your closet," Jude said with a chuckle in his voice.

Pausing before a mirror for a moment to brush her hair and check her makeup for smudges, she thought to herself that she hadn't heard a thing. Gala went through the closet and into the opposite apartment and found Jude sitting at the desk, which was cluttered with papers. His jacket was hung on the back of the chair, and he looked as though he'd been working there for some time before making his presence known.

"Good morning, Jude. Looks like you've been working."

"Yes, I have been for some time," Jude said as he raised his head and turned to look directly at Gala. "Our game is starting to pick up speed. Tonight, a team of men will break into the Watergate Complex. They'll be caught bugging the Democratic headquarters." Jude held up his hand to forestall Gala's questions. "No. Before you ask, that's all I will say about the break-in. That is enough to know for now. It's going to be a big surprise to you when you find out, understand?"

"All right," agreed Gala. She was still startled by the blunt news, and slightly annoyed at his secrecy.

"Now, when the news breaks, I want you to contact our man Woodward at the Post. Arrange a very private meeting and tell him you know something about the break-in. Don't give him any details, just that you know something and you're not happy about it. Hint that you think higher-ups are involved; it's not just a bunch of right-wing self-appointed commandos, but higher-ups where you work at the White House. Tell him that if he keeps looking, he'll find something, but you don't want to be involved in any way. You're afraid you'll lose your job. You're afraid to get mixed up in anything so serious, and so on. Convince him there's something to find. Something important enough to scare you into not wanting to be the one who could be fingered as the source."

"I can have him eating our diet of dribbled information, and begging for more," Gala said with confidence.

"We want him digging up whatever he can; keep him starving for whatever we feed him. We want him eating slowly - and keep him as hungry as a wolf in winter. Hint that it's not over, things are still happening, and that you're hearing inside rumors, day-by-day. Especially after the break-in report hits the papers. And the story will remain in the headlines." Jude paused thinking out loud.

"It won't be the break-in that will accomplish our aims. It will be the cover-up afterward. The news coverage will make that a crime."

"I'll have to be careful with Bobby, he is an aggressive character, if memory serves me right. He'd run over me like a big truck running down a hill," Gala said quietly.

"Take our bugging detector with you to every meeting. In fact, keep it in your purse at all times, except when you're at the White House."

"I'm still thinking about what you said about a cover-up," Gala said in a questioning voice. "What is there to cover up? Nixon doesn't even know anything about it. He can separate himself quickly by firing those responsible. Hell, I'm just hearing about it myself."

"The President," said Jude, "doesn't necessarily tell you everything."

Gala cut him off. "You don't either."

"Look at it this way," Jude said. "The break-in is relatively unimportant by itself. Democrats won't even bitch too much because McGovern's headquarters is separate from the national Democratic headquarters in the Watergate. They realize that all the important stuff is at the convention in Miami now, anyway."

"So, what is the purpose of it, then?" Gala asked, always trying to find out more about this mysterious plan.

"Look at it this way, Gala," Jude said calmly. "The Watergate story is similar to hunting for whales. Pretend we're old-time whalers. The break-in story is the harpoon. It has to strike fast and deep enough to hold the whale until it's dead on the surface. It's not the strike of the harpoon that kills the whale. If the whale were to die quickly, the carcass is too large and would sink to the bottom of the ocean. No value. The whale must be harpooned first, and then killed on the surface in controlled conditions so it can be harvested. It's only valuable when on the surface. The skill comes after harpooning the whale, in controlling the rope. Too much rope and the whale will pull away and free itself. Too little, and the boat itself may be in danger from the power of the whale. With just the proper amount of control, the whale will lose its energy and focus and come to the surface exhausted and vulnerable.

"Your role, Gala, is to keep the right amount of tension on our rope and rope the newspaper media. Woodward is our thread. He and his paper must be constantly tugging on our whale. You must maintain control to give and take rope as needed. For instance: sometime after this break-in, call his attention to the fact that one member of the burglary crew is on the payroll of the Committee to Re-elect the President. That should be enough to establish our control of the rope. Some things Woodward will find out for himself if he's any kind of reporter at all. But the important things he finds out will be only as we let him, and when we let him. Clear?"

"More smoke than fire. But smoke all the time," commented Gala. "I can manage that, I think. But you keep talking about the White House. What are we really after?"

Jude smiled. "Short term or long term?"

"Long term. You've spent a lot of time and a lot of somebody's money. So, what is the bottom line?" Gala asked, hoping that this time, perhaps she would get an answer.

"The bottom line is the Oval Office. The presidency itself."

Gala stared at him. "You want to be president?"

Jude laughed out loud. "Not me. I don't think I'd like the hours. And the pay's below acceptable level. I don't think so...not in this century."

"Then who are you going to put into the Oval Office? That's the big secret plan, isn't it?" she asked, eyes wide open.

"I've told you too much already, Gala. Keep this information most confidential, and you will see things unfold as we go along. It's better for now to just enjoy the ride."

Jude was now on the social A-list in Washington. He enjoyed attending some of the more interesting parties. No one took notice of him, he was considered a stockbroker type with some money, but was not considered too rich and too powerful. He decided to attend an extravagant party on Embassy Row, honoring a visiting foreign dignitary. It was a typical embassy cocktail party, with many of the power players of Washington in attendance. Jude chose this party because his invitation was from Dr. Henry Kissinger.

He enjoyed being the rising young stockbroker. He thought he was getting rather good at the economic jargon and discussed Adam Smith indepth. He was particularly interested in any mention of oil and impressed those he wanted to. He was engrossed in conversation with a couple of different young women at the party. They were both special friends of a couple of power makers. Eventually, after several abortive attempts to talk to Jude privately, Kissinger all but dragged him away into an adjoining room.

"Jude," Kissinger said frowning, "how is your project progressing? Those Pentagon Papers have dominated the news as you wanted." He glanced around to ensure they were alone. "I was talking to the Governor the other day and he said things were rather quiet; no new developments. Not since the Amendment went into effect some time ago. Not that it's any of my concern."

So, Rocky is getting nervous. Well, my plan is right on schedule, Jude thought irreverently. Instead of answering, Jude proceeded to offer his congratulations. "I understand from a private source that you are to be nominated for the Nobel Peace Prize." Jude smiled and toasted his drink to Dr. Kissinger. "It cost plenty, but money doesn't buy everything. In fact, we had to compromise and have you share it with the North Vietnamese negotiator, Le Duc Tho. With that accomplished,

you will have no problem becoming our first foreign-born Secretary of State."

Kissinger was startled. He looked puzzled
and excited. "I remember you once said something about the Nobel Prize, but I had no idea you
could rise to this point of influence. I am constantly amazed with your achievements," Kissinger
said in his most animated response, which meant
rubbing his hands together.

"It's not a done deal yet," Jude said. "However,
I was confident that your efforts to end the war
would be recognized in a suitable way. Now the
trick is to have the Nobel awarded at the right
time to fit into our schedule of events." Jude
looked directly into the eyes of Kissinger and said,
"There will be a time when your unquestionable
stature, that of Secretary of State and Nobel Peace
Laureate, will be of great importance."

Kissinger looked thoughtful, as if he were still
trying to figure out what Jude had just told him.
The Nobel Peace Prize and Secretary of State?
Subjects unheard of until now.

Before Kissinger could say anything, Jude
spoke. "I was delighted to have a chance to speak
with you, given your busy schedule. Lately,
you've been out of the country and unavailable
to an ordinary stockbroker like myself. Now that
the Vietnam situation has stabilized, have you
given much thought to the Middle East?" Now
Jude was playing the part of the college professor, to his student, Dr. Kissinger. "It appears that
that part of the world is of great importance to

the United States, with our growing dependence on oil imports. We must be concerned about the fragility of the relationship of Israel to its neighbors, for instance. And, of course, those neighbors are important to our country in their role as oil-producers. I am sure the Governor has a keen interest in the region. I strongly suspect that there will be significant developments in the region very shortly."

Kissinger's face lost all expression, and his eyes were very still. "I gather this is more than just idle conversation?"

"You're very perceptive, Doctor," Jude said with a whim. "Do you know a man by the name of Dennis Porkenhime?"

"I am aware of many behind the scene characters," Henry said in his low, German accent.

"The Governor thinks quite highly of him, and has given him a great deal of authority. He considers him to be in a very high level of power. With the Governor's approval, I have met with Dennis, and he has agreed to persuade the Arab oil-producing states to organize into one body. The purpose of this group is to set a uniform price, and control production. This price will be considerably higher than the present price per barrel. This price increase will cause some havoc in this country. However, in the long run, America will be better off, less dependent on foreign energy sources. But when the tap runs dry, at a time of our choosing, America will be in shock. We are hooked on oil, and won't be able to get a fix. People will be frustrated and angry. That's when we will have the need for a skilled negotiator to deal with the Arabs. One the Arabs can respect. One who can handle such a crisis realizes that it had to come sooner or later, and has been wise enough to act to solve the problem, not oppose it, and can make the necessary connections. Keep the oil flowing even at a higher price. I have reason to believe the Governor would be very pleased at such a development."

"The Governor is prepared for a scarcity of oil, and a rapid increase in the cost of oil, at the same time?" demanded Kissinger sternly.

"He should be aware of what is about to happen. His people have had plenty of time to prepare, and so should make out quite well, if he played the right cards," Jude said calmly.

"I don't know, Jude. Oil is the lubricant of civilization. Interfering with oil production is dangerous. It could destabilize the entire economy." Kissinger looked around with a scowle and whispered, "I don't see the connection to the other matter of importance."

Jude knew that the 'other matter of importance' was Rockefeller's presidential ambitions. "To make our strategy work, we must have a diversion from what we are doing in the open. A sudden oil shortage will help provide that. It will cause unrest and confusion and divert attention. When people can't get gas for their cars, and perhaps have to endure gas rationing, they won't notice what musical chairs are being played in

Washington." Jude looked at Kissinger to see his reaction, and then continued. "It's all part of our plan. In the long run, the Governor will make a lot of money from his oil holdings, and our country will find ways to be more efficient in use of energy. And, we'll have the cover we need to make the difficult changes without too much scrutiny."

"Each time I speak to you, this plan seems to get deeper," Kissinger said quietly.

"Yes, it does, Herr Doctor," Jude said in a mock German accent. "It gets deeper, and you will play an important role when this oil program starts to develop. There's going to be an oil embargo for a short time against America. This will cause a lot of trouble. As Secretary of State, you will recognize a new organization that will be a new controlling force in the oil industry. They'll be known as the Oil Producing Exporting Countries, or as OPEC. You will work with them to set the price America will pay for oil. That will standardize the price for the rest of the world. And, at the right time, oil will flow again at a controlled rate and increased price."

"I must give this matter serious consideration," Kissinger said in his heavy German accent.

"I am sure you will. And one other thing, when you talk to the Governor next, you might advise him to get everything in order...from his personal life to business and political practices, so as to be prepared for close scrutiny from the Senate. There will be a Senate investigation very shortly."

"What are you talking about, a Senate investigation? What have you done?" Kissinger demanded sharply, in a suspicious tone.

"The Senate will be obligated to investigate him before they vote and confirm him as the Vice President of the United States."

"But Agnew is still Vice President. You're not..." Kissinger stopped short, and waved a hand to fend off any possible reply. He thought to himself, *This plan was so convoluted and far-reaching, anything seemed possible.*

"Nothing that obvious," Jude said with a voice of ridicule. "Not yet anyway."

~~~

Saturday afternoon, Griffin sat with the burglars on the final planning session for the return visit to the Watergate Complex. All in attendance felt confident, although they were irritated that they had to give up a Saturday night to go back into the Watergate to fix faulty equipment. McCord seemed to be making excuses for the state-of-the-art equipment not having been installed correctly. The equipment wasn't working, so there was no other way. They had to go back in and fix it. And considering that it had already been installed when they were caught, there would be no excuses or doubts as to who was doing what.

The group of burglars decided to meet later that evening and have a celebration dinner before revisiting Democratic headquarters at the Watergate.

When the meeting broke up, Griffin said he'd be going to New York that night. But he went to the airport, rented a car, and drove back to the Howard Johnson Motor Inn. From there he could clearly see the offices in the Watergate Complex. He'd changed clothes at the airport and added padding that made him look thirty pounds heavier. Since the burglary team was staying at the same motel, he didn't want to risk their spotting him. He had to know exactly when they left for the Watergate, and make sure they were in the office when the cops caught them.

He spent a few hours flipping from one TV show to another. At 9:30 P.M., he walked down to the parking area carrying an attaché case. He walked over to the corner where a large dumpster was located, and waited until a dark, four-door, Ford sedan pulled up.

The car stopped, the door slowly opened, and Wes Dunn got out of the car. Jude walked slowly toward him and handed Dunn a walkie-talkie.

"What's this for?" asked Dunn.

"We need to keep in close contact. I'm Rover Two, and you're Rover One. I'll let you know the developments as they unfold. You'll have a heads-up when you hear the dispatcher radio the 10-31 about a robbery in progress. You'll be the first to respond and make the big collar. And make double sure you clear it with the uniforms on patrol.

We don't want a black and white with red lights and sirens blaring to be first on the scene."

Dunn looked at the walkie-talkie. "I have it all covered with them. Do you want the radio back?"

"Consider it a gift, but get rid of it after tonight. We don't want any loose ends to complicate things," Griffin said calmly.

"Okay," Dunn said in an odd voice. "Today is my birthday and I should be home with my family. I hope you appreciate what I'm doing for you."

Griffin spoke into his walkie-talkie. "I hear you loud and clear, Rover One. I'll make it up to you."

"Ten-four," responded Wes.

They waved to each other as Dunn drove away. Griffin went back to his room on the fourteenth floor to get ready to monitor the gang of burglars as they made their way to the office in the Watergate. From his room, with the help of his high-powered binoculars, he watched as the burglars entered the offices. He searched the sixth floor across the street until he saw the low light beams of hand-held flashlights. They were in the offices. Griffin clicked the speak button. "Rover One, this is Rover Two. Do you copy? Over."

"You're coming in ten-by-ten, good buddy," Dunn responded.

"Stand by. Operation in progress. I'll sign off now. Talk to you later," Griffin radioed.

"Ten Roger. Standing by. Catch ya later. Ten-four." Dunn sat back and waited for the dispatch.

Griffin laid aside the walkie-talkie and reached for the phone. He made a call to the Washington Police, to make sure they were aware of the break-in. He clicked on his scrambler, so the 911 operators could not record the conversation. The first police car on the scene was a dull unmarked Ford. Out jumped plainclothes detectives, unnoticed except by the smiling coordinator viewing from across the street. The detectives went directly to the top floor near the Democratic headquarters. All seemed to go just like clockwork. Pretty soon he saw other police cars arriving.

C H A P T E R **16**

At five o'clock Sunday morning, Gala woke to the sound of the ringing phone. Her eyes blinked, trying to focus on what she was reaching for. She groped for the receiver and answered on perhaps the tenth ring. Searching her mind, trying to imagine who would be calling so early, she whispered into the phone in a scratchy, raspy voice, "Hello."

"Good morning. I told you I'd keep in touch," Jude said in an irritable greeting. "Check the black toy."

Dutifully, still no more than half-awake, Gala operated the anti-bugging gadget on her bedside stand. The little red light stayed off. "Good morning to you. All is clear on this line." She shook her head briskly to clear out the cobwebs. "So nice of you to call...and so convenient, too. Did you just wake up and think of me?"

"Now, now Gala. Have my calls ever bored you?" Jude said quickly.

"Your calls don't bore me, but this lifestyle you have me in is so restrictive. I sit here like a hermit in my twin apartments. I'm running out of books to read. Since I last saw you, moss is growing on my toenails. I know _my_ life is a bore, but as for the stewardess, Susan Cane: she is a disgrace to her profession. She has no social life at all. I don't..."

"I understand what you're saying Gala, but you are about to alter your lifestyle," Jude interrupted. "It is time to chum the water for our hungry Mr. Shark; our new friend, Bob Woodward. The big news story we want covered is breaking now. There are four men in jail for breaking into the Watergate Complex with the intent of bugging national Democratic headquarters. Tell Woodward the real story isn't the break-in itself, but who the team members are. You're uneasy about it. You..."

"I know the scenario," Gala yawned and squinted at her watch. "Jude, for heaven's sake, it's five in the morning!"

"That's why you have to get moving now," Jude said in a hurried manner. "At the top of your closet, under your white hatbox, there's an envelope. It has all pertinent details about the men who were arrested. Memorize it, then burn it, and put the ashes in the trash compactor. Now, at the time you'd normally be getting up, call Woodward as if you'd just heard the news. Dangle the bait; let him know this story is going to heat up. That's all for now. No meeting, just a hint of skullduggery lurking. That should start him running. Within a few days, he'll be after you for more. But you'll be at the Florida White House by that time, unavailable. We want to leave him hungry and thirsty."

"What makes you think I'm going to Key Biscayne?" Gala asked.

"Pack what you need, they'll be calling you soon. You have to contact Woodward first. Enjoy your trip, I will be back with you soon," Jude said as if giving orders.

Gala put the receiver down, smiled, and chuckled to herself. "'He who mounts a wild elephant goes where the wild elephant goes.'"

Bob Haldeman, his chief of staff, informed the President of the break-in just before breakfast. Nixon was furious that such a thing could happen before the presidential election. He predicted, heatedly, that the national TV news media were going to have a field day on this idiotic operation, and they would try to link him to it.

With a bathrobe over his pajamas, Nixon stalked around the bedroom, flinging his hands in the air and shouting, "I want to know who's responsible for this! I want to find out who's to blame and feed him to the wolves. If the media wants someone to hang for this, I'll give them somebody to hang. We're not responsible for this screwball idea and we're not going to get blamed for it either."

After about 20 minutes of listening to Nixon's tirade, Haldeman thought it was safe to voice a comment. "Mr. President, this whole thing looks suspicious to me. Hell, there's nothing of value in the national headquarters...theirs or ours. It seems more like a college prank, like stealing the other team's mascot before a big game. But it does make us look bad. I can see a possible way for us to salvage the situation and use it to our benefit."

Nixon wheeled around, narrow-eyed, and asked in one word, "How?"

Haldeman was trying to contain his jubilation. This was just the incident he wanted to hang on John Mitchell, the big New York money lawyer, with all his connections. The one Nixon chose to head up the largest funded campaign in American history. Mitchell was chosen without consultation of Nixon's inner circle. Rumor had it that Kissinger's influence clinched the position for the Attorney General. It wouldn't do, of course, to move against Mitchell directly. Haldeman had tried to oust him before, but Mitchell had always come out of the confrontation with more influence over the President than before. But, if Haldeman could secure his own power base over this incident, and make sure Mitchell took the heat over this hare-brained scheme, all the better. In the process he would help protect the presidential election and squeeze his rival out of power. Haldeman knew Mitchell would not have any real involvement in such a plan; he was too shrewd a campaigner for that. But those crazies who worked at CREEP, that's another story. And they all reported to Mitchell.

"Mr. President," Haldeman began, "this just shows how thin John Mitchell is spread out over at the re-election committee. I would bet a dime to a dollar he's delegated too much, rather than admit things were getting beyond his control. We must distance ourselves from any hint of being involved. I suggest we set up an investigation and..."

The President's phone rang and Nixon picked it up. "I'll speak to him." Holding his hand over the receiver, Nixon rolled his eyes and shook his head and said, "It's Henry." A moment later he said, "Good morning, Henry. Yes, I heard about it. All right, we'll discuss it right after breakfast here in my room." Hanging up, he snarled, "Even Kissinger knows it's a disaster. What does that tell you?"

"I was saying," responded Haldeman patiently, "I can set up an investigation. We can get to the bottom of this and let those who are responsible pay the price for what they did."

"Yes, well let me think about it, Bob. I'll talk to you later. Right now I have to get ready for a meeting with Henry. He'll start lecturing again," Nixon said as he kept pacing the room.

When Kissinger arrived, Nixon was still in his bathrobe, sitting at the dining table with papers covering the top. He was drinking coffee and reading accounts of the break-in. When Kissinger was escorted into the room, despite the hour, he was dressed in his thousand-dollar, tailored, gray, pinstriped suit and perfectly Windsor-knotted tie. The ensemble was completed by an expensive, secure attaché case. He looked as if he were on his way to the UN. Nixon noticed the manner as Kissinger entered the room. He thought to himself, sourly, that Kissinger was there to rebuke and berate his administration. Now Henry would have to put on the diplomatic face and be above any political skirmish. As a Harvard college professor, it was below his dignity to try to explain embarrassing episodes like this one.

He stood up to greet Kissinger. "Hello, Henry," Nixon said in a flat mood. "Would you like some coffee? Let's sit over here." He decided to try to be upbeat. Nixon pointed to the couch and wing chair on the side of the large room.

"Good morning, Mr. President. No, thank you," Kissinger said in a solemn voice. "I know you are aware of the burglary at the Democratic headquarters."

"Yes, I am aware if it," Nixon said, obviously irritated. "And we're working on a plan to distance ourselves from those idiots who did that stupid break-in. McGovern is so behind in the polls, this kind of stunt is the only hope they have to get elected. In fact, I wouldn't be surprised if they put these clowns up to it just to get caught, like they did before with their dirty tricks. This time, Henry, we will find out who is responsible, cut them loose, and let them face the music."

"Mr. President, I'm sure the political situation is grave. However, my concern is with the integrity of our national security agencies." He paused for a moment, clearing his voice. "I have learned that some of the people arrested were members of a special group over at CREEP. This man, Hunt, is former CIA, and Liddy is a former FBI agent. They were also the ones who did some of the covert work involving the Pentagon Papers, which included breaking into medical offices, spying on private citizens, and private companies. If the news gets out that the same people are involved, it would have disastrous effects on our foreign policy and image. We must not be seen acting like the Soviets or the Red Chinese who spy on their own people. We must, at all costs, prevent a public trial of these men. Our national security and many covert operations could be put in jeopardy if the media indulges its penchant for 'spy bashing'."

"These are the same guys that broke into Doctor Field's office. We're in a hell of a spot, Henry," Nixon said pacing around the room. "I was set to hang anyone involved in that Watergate fiasco. Now you're telling me because of those damned Pentagon Papers that you insist it be kept secret? And, that some of the same people who were involved in stopping the Pentagon Papers leak, are involved in the Watergate? Yes Henry, we are in a hell of a spot."

"Mr. President," Kissinger said with his slow voice, "I agree with you that these prior actions were entirely justified in context to their time. We were at war, with over 500,000 men in Vietnam, and were sustaining casualties of 500 killed a week. The North Vietnamese were getting better information than our own field commanders. Information was getting out and causing American deaths. We had to do something to identify who was responsible for leaking secret information. Something drastic had to be done. What we did was a counter espionage."

"You're damned right it was justified," Nixon flared. "The American people won't care a bit about spying on a few peaceniks who are disloyal to their own country, and giving aid and comfort to the enemy."

"Of course, it was justified, Mr. President," Kissinger said. He then added, "But spying on someone who is breaking the law by disclosing classified information in a time of war is a far cry from spying on the Democratic Party. Now, two of the very men who did these covert actions, on your behalf and the nation's, are now under arrest for similar actions committed against your political opponents, without your authorization. This is very awkward, Mr. President."

Nixon sat down and poured himself a cup of coffee. As he stared at the coffee steaming in the cup, he said, "I see what you mean. The press is going to hint that this is just another instance of my being paranoid. Out to get anyone who ever crosses me."

"Hinting may well be an understatement, Mr. President. We must consider the wider implications. Exposure of Liddy and Hunt's past activities would almost certainly lead to investigation into domestic spying. This could have consequential damage to ongoing intelligence gathering operations. It could cripple those agencies. It can do you immeasurable political damage and would have a cold effect on our international image. We are getting out of Vietnam; we must maintain our international political reputation. So, Mr. President, you must find a way to keep the lid on this without public trial."

Nixon was sipping his coffee; he put it down on the table and stood up. He became excited and animated. "You're absolutely right, Henry. We cannot let this incident be blown out of proportion. I want you, as a former national security adviser to contact the top people at the CIA and FBI. Inform them you had used these men in the past on sensitive operations and advise them to keep quiet about this matter. Find out if they have any suggestions on how best to prevent this covert nightmare from getting into the spotlight of the press." Nixon was now pacing around the room again. With his head bowed and his hands clasped, he said, "I'll have Mitchell handle it on the political side. As chairman of the re-election committee, he should be able to get us a little room to maneuver."

"Mr. President, I would suggest you distance yourself from this affair. You don't want to get tangled in that web. I believe it would be in your best interest to have a personal lawyer handle it. He can answer directly to you, and in that way you can always have the privilege of lawyer-client confidentiality. He should be discreet about what becomes public knowledge." He paused for a moment, looking at Nixon's reaction, then continued. "There's a young and savvy lawyer by the name of John Dean whom Mitchell has promoted. Perhaps he could be of use in this matter."

"Dean. Yes, I have met him once." He thought for a few moments, then said, "I believe he has some political clout. That's how he got the position in the first place. Of course...that could be helpful in getting this thing swept under the carpet. I'll have Dean handle this for me. We must keep this thing quiet for the sake of the country, Henry."

"Yes, Mr. President. We don't want to hang our dirty laundry in public," Kissinger said.

Nixon nodded his head, thinking to himself how lucky he was to have Kissinger on his team, even though, at first, he felt Kissinger's loyalty was to Rockefeller. "Henry, I do appreciate all you have done for this administration. I know you were reluctant to join us at first. I had a suspicion Governor Rockefeller helped influence you to leave the life of academia for the fast world of government service."

"I appreciate the opportunity to serve, Mr. President," Kissinger said in a deep sincere voice.

"We'll keep making history together, Henry," Nixon said in an upbeat remark. "And someday, I hope to show publicly my appreciation for what Governor Rockefeller has done for me and our country."

Kissinger cleared his throat to indicate delicate embarrassment. "Mr. President, we've accomplished a great deal so far, and I am quite optimistic about our future endeavors. As for Governor Rockefeller, I am sure that someday his public service will receive the reward it deserves." He then paused, and looking out the window, he said, "Governor Rockefeller once quoted to me the words of Confucius: 'Worry not that no one knows of you; seek to be worth knowing'."

The arrest of the four burglars was not considered a great accomplishment of police skill or talent. In fact, the whole incident had made the Washington Police Department a little wary. They suspected it might even have been a setup to embarrass the Republican Party. The burglars were real professionals on some kind of mission; they weren't interested in stealing electric typewriters. There were four Cuban nationals, not even American citizens and it quickly developed they were known to have worked for the U.S. government in ultra-secret operations in the past.

The other man was a CIA agent. It looked like another awkward arrest. There'd been instances in the past when FBI and CIA agents had been arrested, leading to later reprimands to the police officers who made the arrests.

The police department would have preferred to be cautious and check with the agencies first, but it was Sunday morning. No top agency officials with either the FBI or the CIA could be contacted quickly enough. The arrests had been made; the news was out. The Watergate burglars would have to be charged like any other criminals and everything would just have to be sorted out later and apologies offered if apologies proved to be necessary.

After all, it wasn't the crime of the century. Multiple murders were common in this precinct; burglaries were considered one step above parking tickets, and ticket offenders were more apt to be caught. On the surface, it seemed to be merely political dirty tricks, and that was nothing new in the nation's Capitol. Its major interest was the timing. They broke in before the election. No one would have even noticed if they broke in after the election. And the fact that the burglars were caught in the office with the equipment already installed raised additional curiosity. Even so, most people thought it was another political stunt.

Both party leaders took advantage of the initial news coverage. The McGovern camp claimed it was the worst political scandal in American history and proclaimed that Democrats would never stoop to such illegal, unethical, or immoral activity (no mention of the reliable way the dead vote in Chicago or how Nixon's make-up was sabotaged during his debates with Jack Kennedy.) Republicans also deplored the break-in; they would get to the bottom of this situation. They put out a rumor that one of the burglars worked for the political consulting firm contracted by the Republican election committee, and that this independent consultant did work for both parties. Perhaps that same firm could have hired Democratic operatives who set out to be caught, thus blackening the name of the innocent Republican Party. There was a lot of smoke, but little heat. Everyone thought the story was like a spring storm: a lot of wind and rain, but no real damage.

Cries of mutual outrage sold papers briskly that week in June. But it was not a national blockbuster. Not yet.

When Gala arrived at work on Monday morning after the break-in, it was rather later than usual. As she entered, Gala was informed the President was looking for her. That meant everyone was looking for her. She went directly to the Oval Office.

As she approached the Oval Office, a Secret Service agent seemed aware of her presence, smiled, and opened the door briskly. When Gala entered the room, she noticed Nixon sitting at his desk, his face buried in reading the newspaper accounts of the break-in. He raised his head when he heard her walk in. "Where have you been? I've been worried about you," Nixon demanded, glaring at her. Gala sincerely hoped he'd never learn that she'd been in a private conference with a certain Bob Woodward. She delicately adjusted a lock of hair. She had to be cool.

"I'm sorry Mr. President," Gala said. "When I got into my car this morning, I had a flat tire. I called Triple A and they'll have it fixed. Then I took a cab, and it was driven by the slowest driver in the city."

Nixon didn't pay much attention to Gala. He was concentrating on what was on his desk, shifting through the papers. "Things are going crazy around here," he said quickly, as if he were talking to himself. His intercom buzzed. He pushed the switch and said harshly, "No calls. No interruptions, except for a national emergency." Turning towards Gala, he said, "Did you see what happened over at the Watergate Complex? I can't believe anyone would be so stupid."

"While I was waiting for the cab I heard something about a burglary on the radio," Gala said as she gained her self-confidence. She was familiar with Washington politics, and what one hears or reads is not always the real story. She attended enough cocktail parties to see the true face of major league politics. Many of the same politicians who fight face-to-face on Sunday morning news shows are backslapping each other on the golf course that very afternoon. She had seen how deceitful members of the same party could be. They would destroy reputations of colleagues in order to get on a powerful newsworthy committee. To Gala, a second rate burglary was all in a day's work.

"If the Democrats don't smear my name, my own staff will do it for them," Nixon interrupted heatedly. "This has been a terrible morning. The five Stooges break into the Democratic headquarters and they get caught red-handed in the act. Now some of my advisors think if Mitchell's responsible, he should be left to hang and twist in the wind. If we're not careful, this whole thing could cost us the election." Nixon started walking around the room. He started shaking his head and waving his hands all about. "I've talked to Mitchell this morning. He says he had nothing to do with it, and that it could be the Democrats themselves who arranged it. He'll get back to me later when he finds out more."

The president paused as he walked around. "Now who in hell would believe such a bullshit story? The Democrats?" The more he talked the more upset he became. "And there's Kissinger, our jet-set diplomat. He informs me that he had these same people working on secret bugging and spying operations for the Defense Department, the CIA, or the FBI, or a combination of all of them. Hired them to find out who was leaking the Pentagon Papers. He had them doing covert spy operations directly out of the White House."

He went behind his desk and sat down staring at the papers on his desk. "I'm caught in the middle, Gala. If I say too little, it looks as if I'm trying to cover up. And that will give the Democrats all the ammunition they need. If I cut Mitchell loose, he and the gang of fools could go to jail. But that would be after their other escapades were made public and could hurt our national reputation and national security."

Nixon shoved away a pile of newspapers, adding glumly, "I remember the election of '48 when Dewey had it won. At least he and everyone else thought he did. But he lost. I know we're high in the polls, but we can't afford to become clumsy and blow this election."

Gala sat in one of the comfortable leather chairs. "Now be calm, settle down. You must keep the voters informed as to your intentions," Gala said reassuringly. "You didn't have anything to do with this ridiculous break-in; let the people know that, and also that you will let the cards lay where they fall. I don't believe the average voter in the street cares who did it anyway. Many Americans believe McGovern's a little on the pink side, and that Cuban anti-Communists were caught trying to get evidence about the Commie money being pumped into the election. A lot of people remember the tricks that were used against you. You must let the public know that you are above petty, second-rate political burglaries. The truth will come out and you will be elected again, with a mandate of the people."

"I think you're right, Gala. But then again, you usually are." Nixon seemed calmer now. "I think we can sell the public on the truth: that I had no idea of what was happening, and as soon as I found out, I did something about it. I'll fire those responsible, and let the courts handle the rest. We can help a little, behind the scenes." He then stopped and thought out loud. "But what about the criminal trial? That could be a public nightmare, bad publicity at the worst possible time, just before the election."

"Put it off, then," Gala said. "Quietly delay things until after the election. It would only be to ensure fairness, after all. It shouldn't be too hard to persuade a judge to go slow on this one. If not, there are many legitimate ways to delay any trial with various legal motions. And, you have the Federal government with a whole lot of lawyers to do your bidding."

"Yes, now we've got to clean up that re-election committee. I want anyone who had anything to do with the burglary, out. We can't stand another debacle like the other night." He was up walking around, picking up his energy.

"Mr. President," Gala said with a slight bit of humor in her voice. There were times when no one was around that she called him by his first name. In the presence of others she displayed absolute decorum, and always addressed him as Mr. President. However, when alone with the President at times, she would whisper, "Mr. President" if she were angry or in a playful mood.

This time she was in a playful mood. "There are two factions over at CREEP. The administration people on loan for the election, and there are the professional election "hired guns." Their job is to get their candidate elected - no matter who it is. At times, they are at each other's throats. I believe that's how the break-in slipped under detection. Now, I don't have the diplomatic skills of Doctor Kissinger, but I think I can help in solving some of the communication difficulties. And that seems to be a big problem."

"You have more skill than Henry, but don't let him know it," Nixon said with a little sarcasm. "We wouldn't want to tarnish his halo. But, I don't want you to get mixed up in this re-election mess. You have enough to do here; and you won't make friends there if either group thinks you're there to spy on them."

"I'm not interested in them. I'm interested in keeping them from causing additional problems. Plus, they're more concerned about whose turf someone is stepping on. Their action, or lack of it, could cause damage to the election." Gala clasped both hands together, squeezing them tightly. "I was so angry when I first heard the news about Watergate; so frightened that it might jeopardize your administration. Please let me help; it's important to me, Richard. I'd really like to try." Gala contrived to look as though she were controlling tears.

Nixon stopped his pacing, held both arms together, and then glanced at the ceiling, a habit of his when he was weighing odds. When he looked at her again, Gala could tell from his expression that she'd won. "All right. But if anyone gets nasty with you, just let me know. I won't have you harassed. You weren't even elected to take that sort of thing."

"Neither were you," Gala said primly. "These are supposedly your friends. And you know the saying: 'With friends like these who needs...'"

"...enemies.' Yes, I know the saying," Nixon interrupted Gala. "And nobody knows better than I about enemies." Nixon paused, thinking while looking out the window. "John Mitchell is in charge of the overall election apparatus, and I have dispatched John Dean to be my eyes and ears over there. I'll have them brief you in an informal way, about what's happening and what they are doing. I think you'll like Dean; he's young and ambitious. I'll be going to the Western White House, as the press calls it, for some campaigning. When I get back we'll see how things are going. Gala, I do appreciate the extra effort you're putting in."

"I'm not worried about making enemies," Gala said in a joking, uplifting voice. "As President Lincoln used to say, 'Am I not destroying my enemies when I make friends of them'?"

"Well, you'll have your hands full making friends with Mitchell and Dean. I've known John Mitchell a long time; he's a Rockefeller man. He was a big New York City Bond lawyer; he helped Rockefeller finance the Marble capital in Albany, and he put together the money needed so Governor Rockefeller and his banker brother David could build their twin towers in Manhattan. Now John Dean's another story. I'm told he is real sharp and ambitious, and quite a womanizer. But, for some reason, Mitchell thinks the world of him. He was adamant about having Dean as Consul to the President. So he must have special talents."

"I will do the best I can to smooth feathers and keep you informed. Thank you, Mr. President. I'll do a good job. It means a great deal to me," Gala said as they met midway at the side of his desk and kissed.

CHAPTER 17

Griffin had been in some nasty jails before, but this was by far the worst. It was old, dirty and dark, the paint was peeling off the walls, there was a strong smell of urine, and the bothersome yelling of the many prisoners was unnerving. Wes Dunn pulled a few strings so Griffin could get access to the prisoners first. As he entered the holding block, he turned to the corner cell. The nearest Cuban looked at Griffin suspiciously through the bars. "What you doin' here, man?" It was a rough voice with a thoroughly Cuban accent.

"Listen up guys. Your lawyer's coming in a few minutes," Griffin said in a loud whisper. "I need to talk to you first. Get those other guys over here."

The Cuban took a long look, as if he didn't trust any member of CREEP security who was free, then motioned to the other three and said something in Spanish that brought them closer. They all looked at him with suspicion.

Griffin, being a New York cop, had picked up a little Spanish, but it was Puerto Rican Spanish, and much different than the Cuban Spanish dialect. He didn't know exactly what they were saying, but none of it was romantic.

Griffin began; he wanted them to do this right. "Now listen fast. Do what the lawyer tells you, and keep your mouth shut. That's what you do. You'll be going up in front of a judge for arraignment. Keep your cool; give your name only."

The shortest Cuban said, "We don' like no trial. We wan to get outta here."

Another chimed in, "We din' do nothing wrong. We were working for the man." Then other voices started up in Spanish and broken English, protesting and pleading.

Griffin's voice was louder now. "Hold on - let me talk for a minute." He waited for the rumbling to die down. "I'll give it to you straight - you're going to have to bite the bullet until after the election, or till we get the evidence on how Castro and the Communists are getting money to the Democrats. You may be here for a while, but you won't be tortured and you won't be shipped back to Cuba."

"Mister," said the first Cuban stiffly, "we ain't little children."

"And I ain't treating you like little children. I'm talking to you as soldiers." The Cubans nodded solemnly to one another. They seemed to gleam when they heard the word "soldier." Griffin went on. "Castro will know that you took part in this operation, so his people will keep a low profile till after the election. But, we have other ways to catch them at their games. For now you have to hang tough. We will find the evidence to clear you, or we can arrange for clemency from the White House. But we will only get clemency if President Nixon gets re-elected."

"Clemency," said the tallest Cuban dubiously. "That's like a pardon, isn't it?"

Griffin popped his head up, saying confidently, "Yes - a pardon. In this case it's called Executive clemency... from the top...the President." The attitude within the cell went to joyous pride. To think the President of the United States would take interest in these lowly Cuban patriots. Griffin went on. "Now, for the practical side: after this is cleared up, one way or another, each one of you will receive $1000 for each day spent in jail. We will pay your lawyers, and make sure your families have money to live on until you get home." Griffin looked over his shoulder to make sure no guards were listening. "After things settle down, there is a $500,000 bonus for you to divide up."

There was a respectful silence. Then the tallest Cuban said, "Hey man, we din' do it for the money - we are soldiers. This is not the first time we put our lives on the line. We all have family and friends in Cuba. We fight the Communists because we want a free Cuba."

Griffin looked directly to the man speaking. "I appreciate that. I have worked with the Alpha Group in New York City. I know how dedicated you all are. The people I work for appreciate what you are doing. That's why there's money to help." He paused and looked at the faces of the four Cubans, then went on. "But remember this may take some time to unravel. We know the news people will try to make Nixon look bad and sway the election. And the Democrats will be bellyaching about dirty politics, but we can't give in. We must remain silent. Are you with me?"

"However long it takes, man. I'm here; my family has fought Castro for over 15 years," the tallest Cuban said earnestly. The rest nodded, speaking in affirmative Spanish.

"If everything goes the way I think it will," Griffin added, "there may be a presidential appreciation-type medal for each one of you for all the secret work you did for both our countries in the fight against Communism." Griffin waited for a response...there wasn't any. "I've already talked to your lawyer. If you need anything, have him get in touch with me, okay?"

"Is he any good, this lawyer?" Everyone broke out in laughter.

"What can I say, he's a Gringo," Griffin said laughing. "I'll keep in touch." He then turned and started down the dreary hall. There was silence as he moved farther down through the jail. He heard a voice call after him. "As long as it takes, man."

Griffin thought as he walked, *"For a $1,000 a day, I'd say the same thing."*

⁓

Bob Woodward was at his typewriter, trying to patch a story together with a combination of facts, rumors, hints, and deductions into a printable expose. He had a problem bringing stories from concept to print. To help him, his boss assigned a good street-smart writer by the name of Carl Bernstein. They would bring their combined talents together to work on the story. He had received some interesting information from an aide to an influential senator. The aide was in his late twenties, married, with dreams of being another John Kennedy. It cost Woodward an evening on the town, a huge bar bill, and he had to make available an attractive woman and a nice hotel room. In Washington, D.C., booze was the most expensive item. When the phone rang, he tucked the receiver under his chin and went on typing. "Woodward."

"Bob," said a soft, feminine voice, "this is Gala. I've missed you. How have you been?"

Hastily, Woodward steadied the phone, his mind put in focus on Gala. "I've been fine, and I missed you too. Haven't seen you around in a while. Were you out of town?" He was an old pro at fencing with single women. He considered himself a great catch for the 'husband hunters' of Washington.

"Bob," Gala said in an odd tone of voice, not wanting to sound desperate, or that she was too interested, "I was wondering if we could get together for a drink? Say, 10 tonight? I'll meet you at the hotel bar of the St. Gregory on M Street."

Woodward's first thought was that she picked an expensive place to drink, and the cost of rooms there were out of his price range. Well, if I say I forgot my wallet, I could just pay for the drinks and let her put the room on her credit card. "Yeah, I can make it. I'm working on something I have to finish, but I'll hustle over there by 10. So, I'll see you then."

Hanging up the phone, he thought it would be too late to buy dinner. Should only cost a few drinks, if I'm lucky. He then thought of the phone call...there was traffic noise in the background. She had called from a street pay phone. It was past lunchtime. He'd expect her to be at work... hmmm. Maybe she was out running errands. Probably just his reporter's mind at work. He began typing again, at first tentatively, and then with more concentration. He liked the rapid sound of fast typing. He had to get some work done before Bernstein came back and complained.

At 10:25 P.M., there was still no sign of Gala. Woodward, sitting in a dimly lit booth, checked his watch with annoyance. Why did she pick such a small, intimate bar? He estimated it would not hold over 60 people. But, it did have a few nice-looking hookers. He had counted four in the last 30 minutes. He could spot them much more easily now than when he'd first come to Washington, but that was as a young Naval officer working at the Pentagon. He expected to go on to law school but the lure of Washington power and intrigue was stronger, so he stayed. He thought to himself, *there are more young women, per capita, in Washington, than anywhere else in the world. Being a hooker here is like being a penguin in Antarctica: nothing rare about it.*

He was just about finished with his drink. Looking around once more he saw another hooker come in. No, she was different. She had the look of class: sandy red hair, wearing Christian Dior gold-rimmed eyeglasses. She was quite a striking figure.

She walked straight across the room as if looking for someone at the far end. The cut of her clothes was conservative and expensive. Her handbag was 'Cote Seine' of Paris. Shoes were 'Artioli', from Italy. He had keen eyes with years of experience to spot Washington's women of power and influence. As she passed by Woodward's table, she suddenly swung around and asked in a modulated, amused voice, "What's a nice guy like you doing in a place like this?"

Woodward almost dropped the drink from his hand. He could identify the voice, but still couldn't recognize the person. He rose in an instant and almost upset the table. He was certainly taken off-guard, and for a woman stalker like Bob, it was shocking. "Gala, is that you? Why the disguise, or shouldn't I ask?" Now his quick mind was thinking, *Kind of kinky*.

"Oh, I knew that a top investigative reporter would spot me right away...or was I mistaken?" Gala said jokingly. "Now, do I get the drink?"

"Of course. Sit down. Uh...what would you like to drink?" Woodward was still off pace. He now was trying to regain his composure.

Gala gracefully sat in the chair, put her hand to her chin, thinking. "I don't quite know...something smooth, I think." Her eyes focused as she thought. "Campari and soda."

Woodward gestured to the waiter to order Gala's drink and another for himself. He was still confused with excited alertness. When the waiter moved away, Gala remarked quietly, "I suppose you're wondering what the occasion is."

Woodward was nervous, as if doing his first interview and Gala had taken control of it so far. He smiled and replied, "I think I'm going to find out."

"You may find out a great deal if you play your cards right. From your vantage point, it could be a story of a lifetime; one that careers are built on. Now, I trust you are interested," Gala said in a business-like voice.

"You can bet I am," Woodward responded quickly. Though he had no idea where she was coming from, she had class, intelligence, and guts. There must be a story there. "Tell me more."

"What I'm talking about could be the biggest story in the history of presidential politics. To you it's a news story; to me it's a nightmare." Gala paused, gathering her thoughts. "You see I work directly for the Nixon's. I was with him even before they came to the White House. I'm not considered staff because I'm kind of a social secretary for both the President and Mrs. Nixon. However, I spend more private time with the President than any of the rest of the staff, including his Cabinet and some of his more visible aides. And I don't like what's happening over there. It's not good for Nixon or the country."

"I'm more than interested," Woodward said. He couldn't believe his ears. She was a conduit to the White House... hell, to the President. And she's right, a once-in-a- lifetime opportunity. "Now, can you lose the glasses? I like to see a person's eyes when they talk; it's an old reporter thing," he said thinking he would gain control of the situation.

"I'd rather not. I enjoy wearing them. I can say things while wearing these glasses that I'd never dream of saying otherwise," Gala said. As an afterthought, she added, "Touché...don't you think?"

"Like wearing a mask or speaking from behind a curtain?" Bob remarked quickly.

"Something like that. It gives me a certain 'something' while in public." She sat back and smiled, as the waiter set the drinks on the table.

Gala seemed absorbed in sipping her fresh drink. Woodward picked up his drink, tasting it. In spite of his professed eagerness, it seemed bizarre that this meeting was going the way it was.

He wasn't in the habit of getting tips about the White House from secretaries disguised as high-level hookers. Gala had arranged this meeting; she brought him to her to tell him something. All he had to do was wait for it. Besides, he enjoyed the way she handled herself. She was shrewd and wanted him to write the story.

The awkward silence was broken when Gala suddenly said, in a low strong voice, "There is a lot more to the Watergate break-in than what's being reported in the papers." She looked at Woodward, as he put down his drink.

"Lots of smoke, but no fire. And so far...no heat," said Woodward as he was positioning the subject to his control. "And, I only print stories that produce heat."

"I'll give you enough heat to melt a glacier," Gala remarked quickly.

"I have my asbestos-coated pen ready," Bob commented.

"Not here," Gala said in a determined voice. "There's a hotel down the street - an out-of-the-way place; the kind of hotel where a man may take a last minute date. And no one will notice... and I already have a room."

"Last minute date," Woodward interrupted. "I like that. It's like mixing business and pleasure."

Gala said quietly, "Pay the bar tab, and let's get out of here."

The hotel was a short walk from the St. Gregory. On the way, Woodward had wondered more than once if this 'last minute date' would turn out to be just that - a novel approach to the basic one-night stand. It wouldn't be the first time he had been seduced. But this was quite different. However novel, this gambit was also plainly quite deliberate. There was a purpose. Woodward was at least sure of that much. One way or the other, it should be entertaining.

When they entered the room, Gala immediately sat down in the desk chair as if romance was the furthest thing from her mind. She laid down her glasses and started to take off her wig. Woodward settled on the bed, lying down, head on the pillow, as if to watch TV - getting comfortable, but prepared for something more interesting. He was still attentive and hopeful of whatever might be the outcome.

Gala sat at the desk, looking into the mirror. She took a deep breath, turned, and looked directly at the eyes of Woodward, lying on the bed. "Bob, I've decided to take a chance on you. What I'm about to say can change both of our lives. I could have taken this information to a number of qualified reporters who would kill for this story. But I have chosen you for a couple of reasons. I want you to understand that if I'm going to do this, it must be my way. I've known you for a long time. I must have complete trust in the person I will be dealing with, and I believe that you can handle this story the way it should be handled."

Woodward sat up in the bed, realizing that this was not the casual encounter he had suspected. "All right Gala, tell me what we're getting into."

"There's a lot going on over at the White House, starting with the President. He's involved in the Watergate affair up to his chin, and is doing everything legal and illegal to hush it all up as quickly as possible. And that's wrong," Gala said, as if greatly relieved.

Woodward was startled for a moment, and then said, "This is very serious. You're talking an impeachable offense here."

"Yes, I'm quite aware of that. I know it's hard to believe," Gala burst out.

"Look...the President is so removed from most everyday things, no one believes he knew anything about this thing at the Watergate. Even the Democrats think it was some screwballs in the re-election committee who did it. And there's no proof that 'higher-ups' had anything to do with such a hare-brained idea. The White House is major league politics; they don't go around breaking into opponent's offices. They didn't need to. Nixon would have beaten McGovern even if he didn't campaign."

"Look...I work at the White House, and I know what is going on," Gala said in a rough, determined voice.

"Well, Gala, I'll need more than your opinion. I need proof," Woodward shot right back. He regained his composure. "Understand I just want to make sure there's something to this, not some broad who is mad at her boss and is trying to get even. If I stick out my neck and reputation, it's got to be real. I'm as eager for a Pulitzer as the next guy, believe me." He paused for a moment looking into Gala's eyes and said calmly, "Now tell me about it...kind of fill me in. Who's doing what? Who's been involved?"

Gala sat erectly, gathering her thoughts, then began. "The Watergate break-in is like a surface tumor. To the ignorant it looks harmless...just a lump on the skin. But, to the eye of a surgeon, the lump can be a tumor. So, when he cuts into it and discovers that it goes very deep, the cancer has to be cut out slowly and methodically. That's the way I see this story progressing. Once you cut into this story, you will find that it runs very deep. You must follow the tumor to wherever it leads. It will take time and a lot of hard work. I can get you the key information you need. From that you will have to build the story. This will not be a one-time headline; it will be a big story, drawn out over a period of time, slowly and methodically. It will take time to unveil the whole story and the truth about the players involved. We must keep the story in the public's eye, so it all can be exposed."

"Well, I'll start looking into the break-in, and I'll have to confirm everything you tell me, with as many sources as possible - company policy. Just give me the end of the thread and I'll follow it to wherever it leads," Woodward said.

"As far as the Watergate break-in goes, it will be difficult to get much information right now; everyone's on high alert until the election is over. After that, they'll let down their guard a little. As I find out more, you'll know more. I can direct you to others who have information. I expect you to have double, or triple confirmation to what I give you. I have to be very careful. I can't give you anything that can be traced back to me. Once this story heats up, they'll be looking at, and spying on everyone - phones, electronic surveillance - everything. It'll be worse than the Pentagon Papers. I promise - I'll nourish you with enough scoop that the Pulitzer will be a minor compliment. But, you must navigate the story correctly. The key is in molding the story and playing by my rules."

"What rules?" Woodward asked sharply. "I make the rules, Gala. I've been in this business long enough to know how to play the game."

"Bob, don't flatter yourself. You don't know how to play in the big leagues...not yet anyway," Gala said with a smile. "It wasn't by chance that the 'Washington Post' brought you back from your promising career in the burb's at the 'Suburban Sentinel' where you'd still be reporting on kids' soccer games. And it took some cajoling to team you with Carl," Gala said focusing her eyes on him. "You see, Bob, you really don't know how the game is played, or how really tough it's going to get. This is a big story, with big players. This story could change history. You have a career at stake. I have my life at stake. We play by my rules or the game is called off, here and now."

Woodward didn't like the way Gala handled herself. She was holding a lot of strong cards, only showing what she wanted. Gala wanted control, and that frustrated him as much as anything. Like a young boy being scolded, he answered sheepishly, "All right, Gala. What are the rules?"

"My rules are simple, Bob," Gala said calmly. "My name - you must never use it again in this context. When we speak or communicate, you are never to use it. For any arranged meetings or on the phone, the name to use is Judy. To the outside world, I will remain your distant friend Gala. You will never try to contact me. I will contact you. If you need to contact me, put a flowerpot on your balcony so I can see it when I drive by. Do you get the 'Washington Star'?"

"Every morning," he said sheepishly.

"Look in the classifieds, under Used Volkswagen Parts. When you see an ad for 'engine parts - used once,' the selling price will be the time to meet, all in the P.M. So, if the part is for sale at four hundred and fifty dollars that would mean to meet at four fifty P.M. There will be a phone number. Call it one hour in advance of the meeting, and I'll give the location at that time. Understand?"

"Yes, I understand. It seems pretty cryptic to me, but I can handle it." Bob said quietly.

"One last thing," Gala said as she reached for her purse. "I know you will keep me out of the picture, and I appreciate that. However, there's more involved for me than I have confidence in your ability to keep silent. I am at total risk with nothing to gain; so, I need insurance of your commitment to silence. As long as I live, you won't reveal my identity."

"I have always protected my sources. But, if my word isn't enough, what type of insurance do you want?" Woodward said confidently.

"I want a simple letter, written and signed by you," Gala said without emotion.

"Sure, what do you want me to write?" Bob said as he glanced around the room for something to write on.

"That you are responsible for the pregnancy of Mary Ann D'Angelo, and that you convinced her to have an illicit abortion from which both she and the baby died."

Woodward dropped the pen he was holding. When he bent over to pick it up, there was an instant in which he thought he might faint. He started to breathe deeply.

"How the hell do you know about that?" Bob said, shaking.

"As I said, Bob, you don't know the game that well, or how big this game is. I want the letter," Gala said.

"It wasn't a crime. It was more of an accident that happened years ago. She was over 18." Bob was getting angry. "You don't need a letter from me. If my word isn't good enough, we'll just forget the whole thing."

"If that's the way you're going to play it Bob, okay. But, when you walk out that door, I can assure you that Mr. D'Angelo will be informed. After all she was his only daughter; his pride and joy. And her two brothers have never gotten over it. I believe Mr. D'Angelo was considered to be a loving father, but a rather tough Rhode Island mobster, with a nasty reputation." She paused for a moment. "I'm sorry, Bob. I wouldn't require it if I weren't convinced that it was absolutely necessary."

Woodward gnawed on the pen top for a moment. Then he hastily scrawled the note and shoved the paper to the edge of the bed where Gala could reach it. She picked it up slowly and scanned it, remarking idly, "Why is it, that writers have such miserable handwriting?" and tucked it into her purse, snapping the clasp.

Gala stood up, gathering her items on the table, then said, "By the way...the tape recorder that you always carry? Why don't you see if it picked up our conversation?"

Woodward, startled again, slapped a pocket almost guiltily. "Oh, this one? It's not running."

"Fine. Just try it anyway, to please me. Speak into it and let's see if it's working properly," Gala said in a light, playful voice.

Woodward pushed the red bottom down and began counting to fifteen. He then rewound it and listened. The recorder played a high-pitched humming sound. Woodward looked at her purse; it seemed too small to carry a scrambler, or some other electronic device. His eyes then started searching the walls for anything noticeable.

Gala saw his eyes grow larger as he began to realize what he was getting into. She walked over to him, patted him on his chin and said, "Yes, Bob, we're in the major leagues now, and I am not taking any chances. I must be on my way now. I'll be in touch."

Woodward tried to gather his masculine image to salvage what he could. "We have the room for the night. I can get some drinks and we could talk some more."

Gala put on her glasses and said, "Despite the disguise, I'm not in the mood just now."

"How about a rain check, then?" was all Woodward could think to say.

"After the election, there will be lots of rain checks; enough to flood the nation's Capitol. I'm leaving now. Wait at least 15 minutes before you leave. I wouldn't want my reputation soiled."

As the door clicked shut behind her, Woodward reflected on the meeting that just took place. It was so new, and she's so powerful...no wonder she has the run of the White House. He sat on the bed, contemplating what had just happened and what was going to happen, and he thought of a comment made by the new governor of California, Ronald Reagan. 'Politics is supposed to be the second-oldest profession. I have come to realize that it bears a very close resemblance to the first.'

Chapter 18

The election rolled on with a few further dirty tricks on both sides. The Democratic Party had visibly tilted to the left. The traditional moderate Democratic base of Big Labor refused to support McGovern, the peace candidate, with America still involved in waging a war in Vietnam. If anything, they confirmed what had been the President's policy for the past four years. The election results were no great surprise to anyone. Nixon was re-elected, almost by acclamation.

During these months the news coverage of the Watergate break-in was confined to the occasional headline in the Washington Post. It was enough to keep the topic fresh, and give Democrats something else to criticize.

Not all of Nixon's supporters celebrated on election night. Five were still in jail, awaiting trial.

But they were confident that their day in court, when it came, would prove them heroes; or like many other spies, they would have to be silently rewarded with a handsome bonus for their valiant actions, and, their valiant silence.

The inauguration went off smoothly one cold, brisk January morning. Nixon spoke, in this second address, of the mandate of the people and of how the next four years would be even greater than those just past. He would remember, and work for the silent majority, complete Vietnamazation, and end the mandatory draft of young men.

Nixon had a new confidence. For the first time in his long political life, he wasn't looking toward the next election. This victory was his own personal high-water mark. He'd accomplished what no other president in history had ever done, or will likely do again - carry 49 of the 50 states to win the presidency. And he did it his way, with his people. He was the most popular president in American history.

The people around him shared that confidence, a settled kind of jubilation and a conviction that, in the eyes of the American people, they could do no wrong. They had the power.

⁓

Griffin's visits to the Watergate burglars had become so routine an occurrence that they had a regular room available for their meetings. When guards escorted the men in, Griffin was already sitting at the table, looking glum. They took their seats, exchanging uncertain glances, grumbling in Spanish.

McCord spoke as soon as he sat down. "Well, the election's over. I hope everyone had a good time at the inauguration. Now we ought to be getting out of here, right?"

"And the bonus," chimed in one of the Cubans, winning grins and chi chi's from his companions. The grins faded when Griffin didn't say anything.

"Sometimes this world is a rotten place," remarked Griffin eventually. "I'm sick at what I have to tell you. I was the one who told you to wait, keep the faith. They kept telling me that when things quieted down, you'd be taken care of. Well, it's not going to happen. This morning, they told me there's not going to be any help. You're on your own."

"This is a joke, Grif, right?" demanded McCord. "It better be a joke."

"No joke. CRP's cutting you lose. Now, they figure you can't do them any harm. You're going to go to trial and be convicted and do whatever time the judge says."

"And the bonus?" demanded the tallest Cuban, "that we were promised?"

"No bonus," Griffin said flatly. "Not a cent. You take your chances. The Committee to Re-elect the President has decided to forget they ever knew you. Like I said, it makes me sick. And there's nothing I can do. It makes me sick."

There was a long silence. Then McCord burst out, "They knew what we were doing! They told us to go ahead! They knew what chances we were taking. It was just another national security job. We have to be taken care of, just like we would have been if the job had been in California or New York. They can't call this just a burglary and forget it - we worked for the President of the United States!"

"The President!" repeated the tallest Cuban emphatically. And several of the other Cubans shouted in Spanish. McCord was beating his fist on the table, hollering, "They can't do this to us! Those bastards!"

"Keep it down," ordered Griffin, scowling at the door, realizing the guards were on the other side. After a few minutes, the five sat frigidly attentive. Griffin went on. "It's not the President. It's those rotten, spineless cowards at the re-election committee, the glory seekers, the election professionals. I've tried to get through to the President, but I'm not high enough on the ladder. And Mitchell's put out the word that I'm *persona non grata*. Nobody will listen to me or talk to me anymore. I'm out of a job too, not that that's anything like the screwing they're giving you guys. If there was some way to get around the committee, I'd do it, but…" He paused, looking around soberly. "Look, it's up to you. All bets are off. You're free to say anything to anybody you think will do you any good, no matter what your lawyer tells you. That's what I say."

McCord stood up, and with a raised, determined voice said, "Go public, you mean."

"I'm not telling you what to do. You can make your own deals now," Griffin said quickly.

The Cubans were rapidly trading remarks in Spanish. One turned to Griffin, saying, "No, we will not. We did this for Cuba. The other break-ins we also did for Cuba...for el Presidente and against los Communistos. We are soldiers. We will go to jail if we must. We will not speak." The other Cubans nodded firmly.

"Look," said McCord to the man who'd just spoken. "We don't owe them any loyalty, the way we're being treated. Maybe the whole thing was a set-up, and not for national security at all. Just plain election politics. Maybe it was just a way to get the dirt on some Democrats. You want to go to prison for that? I say we go public. I say we tell who hired us, and for what. The President trusts those over at CREEP, and he ought to know they're backstabbing bastards. We owe it to him. Look, if Grif can't get to him, then we sure can't. But the newspapers can."

"McCord's right," Griffin said. "If you just keep away from the real national security stuff, just talk about the Watergate, CREEP will be the only ones under the gun. Then, maybe the President will see that you were used without his knowledge, that you acted in good faith, and that you're owed a square deal. Then he can step in and get rid of those CREEP bastards and maybe use his influence to help you. That may not seem as good as a bonus, but an American President is a good friend to have."

The Cubans consulted among themselves. There was intense Spanish vocabulary and hand gesturing, with frequent use of the word 'Presidente.'

"You've been straight as an arrow in flight, you have a good reputation, after all, you worked for the agency," Griffin told McCord. "They'll listen to you." Griffin pointed to the Cubans sitting at the table "And you guys, just keep to the Watergate stuff and you're still soldiers - soldiers betrayed by the high command. The election commandos. You can't let them get away with that, for the President's sake."

After more discussion, the Cubans agreed there was honor in revenge, if one is betrayed. Especially to protect the 'Presidente.' It was agreed McCord would break silence first and talk about the role of Hunt and Liddy. The others would back up the parts of the story that they knew firsthand. A united front, a united story. Nothing but the truth.

When Griffin left the jail, he stopped at a public phone and dialed the 800 number he'd memorized. When the connection was made, Griffin said tersely, "They're going public."

"Good," Jude said, and hung up. "Now for one of my favorite chess moves: The Smothered mate," he laughed.

Jude immediately put in another call - this one an overseas call to Dennis Porkenhime. It took some time to track him down, but eventually Jude was able to make contact. The line was not very clear and had a lot of static. The phone line was in reality a radio connection.

Finally, Jude could hear a raspy British voice yelling, "Hello! Hello! Can you hear me? Hello?"

"I hear you. Do you hear me? Over," Jude also yelled in his phone.

"I hear you now. Go ahead," Dennis said loudly.

"Do you remember the timetable we agreed upon?" Jude yelled.

"Certainly. Over."

"We go to Step B now. And I want you to make travel arrangements for a certain sausage. Do you understand? Over," Jude yelled again.

"Sausage perishable, is it? When do you want to send it? Over," Dennis replied.

"As soon as possible, okay?" Jude yelled.

"The sausage sent to where? Over." Dennis's voice was getting tired.

"Your general territory. It'll need an official invitation, of course. I trust you can handle it. Okay?" Jude yelled again.

"I'll take care of all arrangements on this end... will initiate program here. Have I got it straight so far? Over."

"From the highest perch. Yes, go ahead," confirmed Jude. Then he added, "I'll be in touch with additional info...over."

"Well, I hear what you say...we need to talk soon. It's getting tough to keep the lid on our little nest over here," Dennis yelled through the unrelenting static.

"Okay, that's all from this end. I will be in contact soon...over," Jude said, hoping for the end of this conversation.

"Cheerio, dear boy. Will see you soon. Over and out." Final words and the line went dead.

Jude hung up his phone and rang his secretary, asking her to put a call through to Henry Kissinger's office. A meeting was arranged for later that afternoon at Kissinger's New York apartment.

After a minimum of small talk, Jude got down to business. "You'll soon be receiving a special invitation to visit the Middle East. It will come through official channels within a few weeks. Of course you accept. You will meet with representatives of the Organization of the Petroleum Exporting Countries. They call themselves "OPEC.""

Kissinger broke in. "They're a bunch of Bedouin oil bandits. They don't represent anybody."

"They will after you meet with them because they're our new oil partners in the Middle East," Jude responded quickly. "I'll touch on that later. Now where was I? Oh, yes.

"While you're away, there'll be uproar in this country about the Watergate matter. Certain information will become public, implicating Nixon's re-election committee. I trust you've spoken to the directors of the CIA and FBI."

Kissinger nodded. "They agreed to do what they can to help the President, without jeopardizing their own position. However, I believe both have done enough to bring criticism rather heavily upon themselves...if their activities were to become public."

"When you meet with the President, tell him of your meeting with the members of OPEC. Let him know that they have organized to effectively control the production and pricing of crude oil, and are going to rapidly raise the price of oil to the industrialized world. They are threatening an oil embargo against America. You must convince the President that the danger of being cut off from Arab oil is immediate, and that the solution is the long-term development of our own oil resources. Although it may take years to implement a plan to achieve full domestic production, we must start now to conserve until we are oil independent." Jude paused for his showmanship to surface. His voice went up nearly an octave. "As President, it will be his responsibility to start this difficult process. The short term may be tough - perhaps even gas-rationing, but it's a challenge of modern democracy." Jude paused, smiled, and said, "He'll like the last part. By the way, the petroleum industry will be happy to help sell the idea."

"There are plenty of petroleum lobbyists on the Hill. They already have a convincing argument about our dependency on imported oil. Of course, they want to drill more on U.S. soil to offset the flow," Kissinger said as he was lecturing.

He then added, "I assume our friends have been sufficiently forewarned about this opportune development?"

"Needless to say, Herr Doctor, this plan would not be initiated without the approval of this nation's single largest importer of oil, and the single largest purchaser of Persian Gulf oil, our dearly beloved Standard Oil," Jude said lightly.

Kissinger again nodded, apparently satisfied. "I confess that I fail to see the relationship of this coming oil crisis with our other agenda."

"Well, Doctor Kissinger, food, water, electricity, and oil are the basic essentials of American life. Food is much too plentiful. Any attempt on control is out of the question. Water and electricity are controlled as utilities. That leaves oil - an essential ingredient of our lifestyle, not regulated or controlled by the government. And it's almost as vital as the other three. So, when an oil shortage occurs, we'll see an amazing reaction. It's the reaction I'm interested in, not the oil, per se. I want the American public to be so concerned about oil and gasoline that politics will get only secondary interest. When we make our move, the American public will be in lines waiting for gas, and furious about it. It will be a new experience, causing a lot of confusion and fear," Jude said with enthusiasm.

"Rather drastic as a diversion, don't you think?" Kissinger commented.

"In the long run, the nation will be better off. A small crisis now rather than a severe one later. Besides, those in control can be prepared and set up, so that national security is never severely jeopardized. Incidentally, some of the right people are going to make an absolute killing on this scarce commodity. We need to create an appropriate level of diversion for the installation of the first appointed President of the United States."

Kissinger was startled again. It seemed at each meeting Jude scared him with another revelation. "I concede the point, Jude," Kissinger said mildly. "I will get my affairs in readiness for an extended foreign trip."

The two men parted cordially.

The Watergate story seemed to take on a life of its own, and no one at the White House could understand why the story wasn't dying. It was old news, minor news, and yet every day the Washington Post had an article by its new star reporter, Bob Woodward, dredging up some new fact or rumor about the affair. It was becoming a political soap opera - each day a new epiphany. Each morning's paper arrived like a ticking bomb, and there were muffled explosions in the offices throughout the White House at each fresh story.

Clearly, there was someone in the know who was divulging critical information. Efforts were made to locate the source, or sources, of the leaks, but the only practical result was shorter tempers and ambient suspicion drifting like a greasy cloud. Who was trustworthy seemed to become a

very important question. The President was more
incensed than anyone else. After the daily brief-
ing, he would retire to his own office and try to
figure out how to solve this dilemma.

He felt as if he were being betrayed, he alone
against the press and other political enemies. He
believed they still resented the fact that he had
won re-election with a mandate. His family was
not aware of the strain these newspaper articles
were causing. His daughters were now married,
and the First Lady seemed overwhelmed with a
full schedule of official social obligations to handle. Nixon's own personal staff were all jockeying
for power, all more eager to show up somebody
else's faults than accomplish anything construc-
tive. The President felt that many had lost their
personal loyalty to him, which should have bound
them together as a team. Instead, they seemed to
be more concerned with the perks, power, and
prestige of his office.

The one person the President felt comfortable
with, who understood his public, as well as his
private life, was Gala. Their close relationship
was growing stronger; he was depending on her
more and more. At the end of the day he would
often go to her office or summon her to the Oval
Office, and he could vent his anger and frustra-
tion. He could trust her. She was a good listener,
nothing shocked her, and she had good political
sense. And she helped to uplift his spirits from his
ever-increasing dark moods.

In one of these evening Oval Office conferences, as Gala handed the President a drink, he looked into the glass as if he were looking for an answer, then suddenly remarked, "Things are a lot rougher than even I thought. The North Vietnamese are planning to attack again soon; they're building up their forces with Russian help. And this damn Watergate thing is getting more and more press every day, eroding our strength in Congress. Now, with that jerk Woodward beating the drum, I can't seem to get to the bottom of it. Everybody's looking out for his own skin. They're all...afraid. Nobody's trying to stop this cancer. I alone have to do the fighting. And today I talked to Kissinger in the Middle East, and he's talking about an oil problem of some sort. I've known for years that the Arabs could be a problem if they ever decided to curtail production, but I don't know how bad it's apt to be. He's handling that problem; it's about oil, so I'm sure Henry has received direction from the Rockefellers."

"I'm sure Doctor Kissinger will be able to handle things over there. You can get a more realistic view when he returns," Gala said in a soothing way.

"Sometimes I wish I were with Henry over there instead of banging around this 'fish bowl' as Truman used to call the White House. It's more like a funhouse, or house of mirrors, with cameras and reporters. And all of them trying to dig up whatever sludge they can find."

"Not much fun," commented Gala wanly, tucking her legs under her and adjusting a couch pillow. "Everybody's tense and worried now. Me too, although I try not to let it show."

"You're the only serene person left," Nixon assured her with a fond glance. "You're a wonderful companion and comfort to me; not like so many others - trying to make a ladder out of daggers in somebody's back. Then if anything goes off color, it was someone else's fault. Sometimes I think you're the only person with real loyalty left."

"I'm sure that's not true. It's just that when people get tense and suspicious, they're not on their best game. You mentioned that Doctor Kissinger has concerns about Arab oil production. I was thinking... an oil shortage could be a useful thing right now, if it doesn't get too out of hand. Who's going to be interested in stale news about Watergate when there's talk of gasoline rationing like during the Second World War? Not that we'd want to manufacture a crisis, of course. But if it happened, it could bring the attention of the media and the public back to real concerns of life - things that are really important to this country." Gala took a sip of her drink and waited for a response.

"That's a thought - drag the Arabs into the mix." Nixon's spirit revived, thinking it a great idea. "An international crisis always pulls attention away from the domestic front. The people rally behind their leader. That's been a fact for political life since the Babylonians. There could be a need for rationing stamps for gasoline - we could have them printed even if they're never used. It's a good headline grabber. And that's what we need now. We need to get the spotlight off that Watergate."

"Most of America would be more anxious about having gasoline for their car than worrying about who did what at the Watergate," Gala said with a smile as she sipped her drink.

"Yes, you're right Gala," Nixon said as he shook his head, and then continued. "They have already indicted some people from my re-election committee. I've told John Dean to make a thorough report so I know where we stand. We can't get drawn into that mess."

"When is Doctor Kissinger due back?" Gala asked idly.

"I believe he's scheduled in Friday night. Why do you ask?"

"It might be pleasant for him to get a personal reception at the airport...the sort he got during the Vietnam negotiations. That would emphasize the importance of his Middle East trip and put a presidential spotlight on this pending oil crisis in our near future. We wouldn't want the American people kept in the dark. The President and his prestigious statesmen are now working to solve the oil conundrum," Gala smiled and seemed quite pleased with herself.

Nixon grinned, his first cheerful expression that day. He was getting excited. "Yes, Gala, in the 1960 election, Kennedy kept harping on a non-existent missile crisis. Now we have our own crisis: with oil. But I remember Jack Kennedy saying, 'When written in Chinese, the word "crisis" is composed of two characters. One represents danger and the other represents opportunity.' With this oil situation we have both. Oh yes, I'll personally go to the airport to greet Henry. Not with a brass band - no, that would be in poor taste. No I'll greet him with the press corps. He may miss the sound of the trumpet, but he'll like the flashbulbs more."

They both enjoyed the rest of the evening together. Many years before, Nixon read a book by Napoleon Hill. He remembered a quote, which he thought of this night. "Do not wait; the time will never be 'just right.' Start where you stand, and work with whatever tools you may have at your command, and better tools will be found as you go along."

Kissinger showed no outward surprise at the official reception at Washington's National Airport. The press corps was out in force with TV cameras and a blaze of flashbulbs, and reporters shouting questions. A short press conference was held on the tarmac. He was pleased with the personal presidential greeting. Both men gave short speeches emphasizing the crucial importance of Middle East stability for world peace, and the significant influence oil plays in the modern day western lifestyle. When they were safely settled in the presidential limousine, the motorcade was off to a quick exit of the airport, with sirens blaring and red lights flashing. Kissinger sat back, took off his heavy glasses and began polishing them, looking slightly bemused or perhaps amused. It was often hard, with him, to tell the difference.

President Nixon and Henry Kissinger were now alone in the speeding limousine. There was some small talk about the flight and the reception. But once they hit the main highway, Nixon said abruptly, "I expect you're wondering what all this hoopla was for."

Kissinger studied his glasses, and then put them back on again without haste. "It will do very well for my image in the press. However, this has put a crimp in my cocktail conversations. I tell beautiful women that I work well behind the scenes. Some of them go behind the scenes with me." He chuckled to himself. Nixon didn't. "Yes, Mr. President, I was pleasantly surprised that you took the time to welcome me home."

"Well, Henry, I didn't come out here so that you could have an improved repertoire with your cocktail lady friends. It's not your image at stake here; it's mine. The press won't let go of this Watergate business. You'd think they caught me in that damn place! I want to give them something else to think about. I hope this oil cartel situation you referred to isn't just a flash in the pan. If there's something substantial to it, the media might run with it, and take some of the heat from our present Watergate headlines."

Nixon paused for a moment getting his thoughts in order. "We'll need a new public oil policy. It will have a substantial effect on the oil and gasoline industry. We must do something newsworthy to get the media's attention. That could take the heat off this wretched Watergate business until I can get to the bottom of it, and get it settled once and for all. You know, Henry, the New York news media is always excited about the Middle East, even when it doesn't affect Israel. This oil contingency could spark their interest. So maybe we can give them a story they'll like: gasoline shortages and rich Arabs."

"Oh, the news coverage will be substantial, Mr. President," Kissinger said solemnly. "I wish it were not so. But we are in for some difficult times. I still have hopes of defusing it, but I am not too hopeful. I believe it will make a lot of news, Mr. President, whether we wish it so or not."

"Then it's definite what you said on the phone about raising the price of crude oil," Nixon said quietly, considering the ramifications.

"From $3 a barrel to approximately $13. It hardly seems adequate to call that a mere price increase. They're also going to cut production, so that even the black market sources will dry up. It will only be a matter of months before their decision takes effect. They have also hinted at the possibility of cutting off our oil supply altogether, if we refuse to decrease our support of Israel.

That should win the hearts and typewriters of the New York media, I would think." This comment was offered in a caustic tone. Nixon glanced at Kissinger sharply, unsure whether it was sarcastic or not.

They sat looking out their windows in silence for a few moments. Then Nixon asked, "What kind of impact do you expect this to have?"

"Politically or economically?" Kissinger replied slowly.

"Leave the political out of it now. We can handle that later. What will be the effect on the economy? That's what's important." Nixon's concern seemed to be growing.

"The economy is where we will feel it the most." Kissinger cleared his throat, raised his head and began. "Right now, gasoline is approximately 30 to 35 cents per gallon. With this increase you're looking at gasoline prices of at least a $1.20 per gallon. And that comes right out of the pockets of your silent majority. The first winter will be an enormous hardship for the industrial northeast. Heating oil will go up by 300 percent. Many homeowners and many businesses will suffer considerably. And we're one of the lucky nations because we import only 60 percent of our oil. Japan and some other countries import 100 percent, so we could see some international pressures developing. We have a large domestic supply, and many of the large oil companies would, with the right financial incentives, be encouraged to undertake massive exploration for new domestic oil fields. We could help develop alternative sources of energy. The greater use of coal and perhaps atomic power will help, eventually. But, to the homeowner in the coming winter, that will be of little solace."

"Will gasoline rationing be feasible?" Nixon asked.

"Feasible? Perhaps it is wise to look into such a contingency. We must conserve our reserves. At this time I don't know if that will be necessary."

"Rationing gasoline would put the problem right on Main Street, in the face of the American people," remarked Nixon. "Foreign oil has seeped into our industrial veins and we're hooked on it. So far, it's been an abstract thing to most people. They don't understand or care about it. We'll let the American people know firsthand - at the gas pumps - that we've got an oil crisis! And this time we'll let the news media do the work for us."

"Yes, the media, Mr. President," echoed Kissinger. "The media will be doing a lot of work all right. But I cannot emphasize too strongly that this will be an international crisis of the greatest gravity. We must consider this a major shift in political power because oil now is power. This action taken by these Arab countries is an attempt at economic blackmail, unprecedented in history. If oil can be arbitrarily manipulated to reward friends and punish enemies, the industrialized world will, in a very immediate and practical way, be at the mercy of the Arab oil-producing nations. Such a state of affairs must be avoided at all costs, short of war, because the potential of war is there, Mr. President. For nations like Japan it could become a matter of economic, and therefore national, survival. And desperate situations not infrequently result in desperate measures. Any equation involving the neighbors of Israel is always volatile in the extreme, even discounting other factors. I am gravely afraid that this situation, mishandled or ignored, could precipitate a hot war."

"Henry, we will not mishandle or ignore this problem," declared Nixon forcefully. "We'll have to see that our allies aren't put in the kind of desperate situation that you have outlined here. We have to take the initiative to set a new policy on world oil production, availability, and allocation. We'll be ready when the Arabs make their move. We'll set up our own oil administration, and we'll demonstrate to the world that in a time of crisis, America will take the lead."

"That will make a fine speech Mr. President," Kissinger said. "We are facing a serious situation, and this must be brought to the attention of the American people. For the Administration, it will be a high wire act. Dealing with the American public, who will be clamoring about the cost of oil, and balancing that against the interests of the large oil industry, won't be an easy problem to solve. The leaders of the oil industry are very sensitive to the potential of nationalizing their business. I know from personal experience that they have a lot of political power. They must be managed very carefully."

"Very good point, Doctor Kissinger," Nixon said. Addressing him as Doctor was Nixon's sentimental way of passing a compliment. Noting Kissinger's affection to the oil interests of his mentor, Governor Rockefeller, Nixon added, "They won't be pleased if the profits in their industry are determined by government edict. They have a right to make a fair profit. We'll have to balance the good of the people with the rights of the oil companies. You're absolutely right. We may need to establish a new Cabinet level department to deal with oil and energy. The new Energy Department would coordinate the major oil producers, get their cooperation, and ensure the flow of oil at reasonable profits. In this way, they won't spend valuable time and effort fighting us. Yes, this sounds like a good approach, Henry."

Nixon relaxed, drinking in the moment. Another point of history to be made. He sat back, smiled and said, "And Watergate will become yesterday's news. A footnote to history, listed under dirty tricks. Of course, the Democrats will have a whole page of their deeds, and we will have but a footnote." Both men chuckled lightly.

"How is this Watergate thing coming along, Mr. President?" Kissinger asked. "It is becoming international news and a somewhat embarrassing subject," he added.

"John Dean tells me that he has it under control. He's right on top of it. And, he assures me that no one of importance was involved except those at the re-election committee."

Nixon made one more comment, softly, a Latin proverb - "Fiat justitia; ruat coelum - Let justice be done; though heaven fall."

Both men sat back in their seats and began to relax and enjoy the ride.

CHAPTER **19**

Six months after the Watergate break-in, Jude set up a luncheon meeting at New York's Jockey Club with John Mitchell. After a few drinks and small talk, the conversation led to the real purpose of the luncheon.

"Well, Jude, how's your plan going now that the Watergate people are on trial? I understand that your man Dean is acting as the President's legman. Or, the way I hear it, he's acting as if he were the President," Mitchell said.

Jude smiled perfunctorily. "Dean is playing his part as if assigned from Central Casting. He's out planting a lot of land mines and without a map. So when everyone runs for cover, there will be a lot of explosions."

"And a lot of casualties, as well," Mitchell said with a scowl.

"There will be sacrifices and rewards," Jude snapped back. He then took a sip of his tonic and lime and continued the conversation calmly. "Now, can you tell me about our friend, Mr. Jack Fehan? What has the I.R.S. learned about him?"

"Agnew's Maryland associate? Quite a lot, actually. Jack Fehan is President of Ever Green Development Company. He has underworld connections, and many of the deals he has worked went south. He's willing to testify that he gave Spiro Agnew a sizable bribe. And he has witnesses."

Jude smiled as if he knew. Nodding his head, he asked, "Enough to indict?"

"Oh, easily enough. Even if he were an average citizen," said Mitchell uncomfortably. "But he is the Vice President of the United States. I've checked it from a legal standpoint - he is considered a common citizen. If he were president, well... indicting a sitting president would be something else."

"John, I want you, as former Attorney General, to contact someone with authority at the Justice Department, and, as friend of the court, arrange a deal for the Vice President. He'll plead 'nolo contendre.' In return, he will resign as Vice President, serve no jail time, and pay a moderate fine."

"You think it'll be that easy? He's pretty popular, and he's no slouch. He's been a real fighter. He may not just roll over," Mitchell said.

Jude passed Mitchell an envelope. "Here is a list of people to contact. They will give all the information and statements you need. He will have two options: either resign, or go to jail. Either way he is no longer Vice President. That's our objective. Our timing is important. So, four weeks from now, arrange a meeting with the Vice President. At that time, we will present his options clearly to him. I'm sure that when he sees the evidence, and the big picture, he'll roll right over indeed. By then, everything should be in order."

Mitchell replied calmly, "I understand." He put the envelope away in his inside jacket pocket with as much nonchalance as though it had been a bribe. Then he added, "To quote Andrew Carnegie: "'As I grow older, I pay less attention to what men say. I just watch what they do.'"

The oil crisis had developed as predicted by Dr. Kissinger. It was in all the papers. The Department of Energy was established and heavily funded. Its first order of business was to regulate the allocation of existing oil supplies to ensure that there would be no shortage of heating oil and gasoline.

The attention of the news media was duly focused on the crisis, showing cars waiting in long lines for gasoline. There were hardships in the northeastern states due to the unseasonably cold weather and the high cost of heating oil. There were regional resentments as well. Recent restrictions put on the oil industry resulted in hard feelings in the southwest, where some bumper stickers read LET THE YANKEES FREEZE IN THE DARK. And the Arabs were under the media spotlight, as subjects of stories showing rich Arabs making big money just because they roamed the desert above the pools of oil. The American oil companies, or "big oil," came under the close scrutiny of the press. The phrase "windfall profits" began to appear on the nightly news. However, the oil companies and of course the man that owned the biggest oil interest of all, made out quite well.

Gala made frequent but irregular reports to Woodward, to maintain the tight reign. Certain items were bound to win headlines, so she'd wait for the next slow news day to unveil a new bombshell. In spite of the oil crisis, the newspapers maintained a certain level of interest in Watergate because the gradually uncoiling details were leading to a major cover-up story. It wasn't hard to gather interest, since a seemingly unending flow of witnesses continued to unveil new insight of a growing conspiracy. The news stories seemed uncanny in depth and scope, and would pop up at the most opportune times.

For a time, the public, for its part, didn't seem to know what to make of the whole Watergate business. After years of James Bond and Mission Impossible, it was considered an acceptable fate for the Watergate burglars to go to jail, since they'd been caught - and that should be the end of it. Only it never was. Defenders of the President claimed, in print and in private, that the coverage was just a malicious witch-hunt. Anything to get Nixon. Then the gas shortage began, requiring such inherently un-American activities as waiting in long lines and paying over a dollar per gallon, only on alternate days, providing one could find a gas station with gas to sell. The final, ugly stages of the Vietnam War were still an open wound. The mood of the public was full of angry confusion, divisions, and frustrations.

The one person not tainted by any of the Watergate fallout had been the Vice President, the administration's chief media-basher. Even his critics had respect for him. He was considered above any hint of political corruption. Then news stories started to appear, indicating that the Vice President of the United States was rumored to have taken bribes and was currently under investigation. Within the White House, there were some with solemn indignation and great private glee that Agnew's halo was about to come off.

The public opinion was mixed and disoriented; some thought it was an additional indication of the corruption in the administration. Others felt that this was just another personal attack on Nixon. Agnew had shown himself a strong, clear, and tough verbal combatant in all previous confrontations. Everybody expected a similar performance on Agnew's part, given the current accusations; it looked like just another political attack against the administration. Agnew could take on all comers. He wasn't afraid to combat the educated elite of the eastern establishment, the biased news media, or the spineless politicians.

Whenever it seemed things were quieting down, or an effective counterattack had been launched and was successful, out of nowhere some new bombshell would explode and everyone at the executive branch would go into their fire drill frenzy.

These bombshells kept Nixon in a state of constant rage; his nerves were becoming more fragile. He'd never been a favorite of the press, and returned their enmity heartily, but this constant barrage of negative headlines seemed even more than normal. Finding himself the target of almost continual media attack, he further demoralized his already-divided staff. The pressure was on to locate the inside source of the damaging news leaks. But, with so much press scrutiny, everyone was limited to legal and practical methods of surveillance, and no single source could be identified. The atmosphere at the White House was stifling. The days of any banter were gone; it was morally depressing and the grueling days were unpleasant. The day-by-day Chinese water torture was taking its toll.

"You ought to take a working vacation," Gala suggested to Nixon during one of their customary evening conferences. "To Florida or the California White House. And this time, take off your business suit when you walk the beach. You need to get out of Washington for a while." She was quite well aware of the ill-feeling most Americans had toward these expensive estates, which the President managed to acquire while in office. Most Americans were waiting in gas lines while their President flew overhead in Air Force One to a beautiful estate on the beach - not the type of home one expected from a "man of the people." The public resented it, but the media liked it because the stories sold newspapers.

"Yes, well, getting out of Washington is difficult now. That damn Watergate! The only ones they can really get are Hunt and Liddy," reflected Nixon, "and both of them are former special agents. They're tough...they won't talk. John Dean said he took care of them. They'll stand pat. And if they don't...well, they'll just go to jail. They're the ones who set up the break-in, let them pay for their own mistakes."

But Nixon was still preoccupied with the perfidy of the Watergate burglars; he was told everything had been taken care of. Now, the burglars were talking after they'd promised to keep quiet. It seemed nobody was to be trusted anymore; even the burglars were sinking to the ranks of the politicians - looking out for number one.

"I sometimes wonder..." Gala said thoughtfully.

"About what, Gala?" Nixon's ears perked up. He knew that Gala didn't just babble.

"Well, I sometimes wonder if Mr. Dean is that reliable. He's had little political experience. I wonder if it's wise to delegate so much authority to someone like that - someone so young. You asked me to keep you informed, and I heard some things that are a little unsettling. There's talk that Mr. Dean is just an errand boy, but he uses your name to get whatever he wants. He is beginning to scare some people. He's not a real investigator and everyone knows that. Rumor has it that you knew in advance the results of his 'investigation.' There have even been claims that Dean's chief job is to cover up for you. Now," she added, forestalling interruptions with a lifted hand, "we both know that's not true. But public perception seems to mean so much. I wonder...would you be better off having a credible outside investigator step in, whose findings would be believed, and put an end to this Watergate nightmare?"

"I don't know, Gala." Nixon took a gulp of his freshly poured scotch. "We've had a bunch of investigations so far, by the Washington police, FBI, the House and Senate, and more. What makes you think an independent would make any difference?"

"Because," Gala remarked quickly, "all of those agencies you mentioned indirectly answer to you as President. So the public is led to believe by the media that you have control over them. It's like a police chief investigating himself."

"I don't know," Nixon, said, head bowed as he was now pacing around the room.

"Suppose," Gala raised her voice, "you were to appoint an outsider. A registered Democrat, maybe. A law professor, egghead-type with no political axe to grind. He would be an independent investigator who would end the claims of cover-up. He could work directly for the White House, but as an outsider he would be able to settle things once and for all, and he would have to be listened to."

Nixon turned and looked at Gala. "I don't like the idea of bringing in a political enemy."

"Would you prefer one of your political friends to handle it?" Gala inquired with a laugh. Nixon was not amused. Gala went on. "There's political, and then there's political. All Democrats aren't your sworn enemies. There are a few academic ones with open minds. I was thinking of one man in particular. He's a friend of Doctor Kissinger's, from the Harvard Law School. No politician - quirky kind of fellow - insists on wearing a bowtie for heaven's sake. He may be just what the doctor ordered, no pun intended," Gala said with a chuckle. "He's a perfect egg-head law professor who couldn't make it out of the academic world: impractical, utterly incorruptible, and therefore altogether blind to political realities. He'd be made to order for this job, 'Special Watergate Investigator.' I believe his name is Archibald Cox."

Nixon, eternally restless, wandered to his desk and began poking at papers. "Might be harmless," he admitted after a minute. "Might be useful. And Harvard Law School, that would be good, I mean, sounds good. I'll ask Kissinger about him. After this thing is over he might want to be a federal judge."

"And it doesn't bind you to anything," Gala mentioned. "Since he's an outside investigator, he's considered an outside consultant. If you don't like what he's doing, you can just fire him."

"Dean won't like this: he claims to be on top of everything. But it's getting worse," reflected Nixon, as he tossed down a file on his desk. "But if those rumors you mentioned prove to be true, and if he's misleading me, well then he will be cut loose to answer questions to the new investigators. Then maybe we can end this mess."

Some days later, in a meeting in the Oval Office with John Dean, Nixon put matters more tactfully, praising Dean's efforts and citing the advantages of bringing in someone visibly unbiased, an outsider. Nixon's trust in Dean had eroded, and Dean's duplicity, incompetence, and misleading behavior was surfacing and becoming apparent to those in the inner circle. Dean himself knew he was over his head in deep water and didn't know how to swim.

John Dean had been to the Oval Office many times, but today the atmosphere was different. Dean sat tensely, looking as nervous as a hooker at a church revival. He spoke in a high tense voice. "But what happens if this outside investigator gets sidetracked and finds out information that I couldn't? What if he finds something to suggest higher-ups had something to do with the break-in, beyond Hunt and Liddy? This could lead to territory where we don't want to go." Dean was concerned that his own activities would be uncovered.

"They won't because I have already spoken with John Mitchell, off the record. We're clean and there's no one else involved. I have his personal assurance. And if Cox finds out otherwise, well, Mitchell understands that in a political war, as in any war, there are bound to be casualties. I am determined to get to the bottom of this so we can put this thing behind us, and go back to governing." Nixon sat quietly with a poker face.

Somehow, John Dean didn't seem to find the expendability of the President's nearest associates very reassuring. If Mitchell could be sacrificed, and be thrown overboard, then there were no sacred cows left. Dean put up no further objections and faded back into the White House routine as the special counsel to the President. He felt his political barometer falling. A change was coming and he had best hoist his sails to catch the best wind. He decided his best chance for survival was to get a good lawyer, have a good story, and make new friends in high places.

As Jacques Benigne Bossuet once said, 'The greatest weakness of all is the great fear of appearing weak.'

With the appointment of the special prosecutor, the situation went from bad to worse. When Archibald Cox met with John Dean, he saw through him with X-ray vision. It didn't take the wisdom of Charlie Chan to realize what Dean was doing. They started looking into the past investigation, and not much shaking was required before things started shaking loose. And as it shook, more information fell directly into the headlines. The media clamored for more information, and the more they got, the more the story grew. The Washington Post was on a zealous mission; its entire energy was focused on the Watergate. They did whatever they could to chip away at the administration, the President, and his staff. No one was exempt, other than the popular Secretary of State.

Dean clearly wasn't a professional actor, so to speak, but he played his part so well that he deserved an Oscar nomination. He up-staged everyone who testified in front of Senator Sam Ervin's committee. It was grand theater - like something from a Frank Capra movie in the 1940s. Sam Ervin, the North Carolina Senator/statesman, was overweight, round-shouldered, with white hair, and he spoke with a slow southern drawl. It was hard for him to believe, as he asked his basic country lawyer questions. "Are you saying that the President used the influence of his office?" Dean sat attentively, listening to each question like a repentant choirboy. He had a new story and a new image: his short hairstyle, new tortoise-shell glasses, with his beautiful adoring wife just a few feet behind, within camera view. He sang like a lark on a spring morning. His words didn't make much sense, but the tune he sang was music to the ears of those on the warpath in Washington. He turned State's evidence to set his record straight, in return for immunity and a book deal. He had prepared himself well for his grand performance before the Ervin Committee, and his performance culminated his importance to the entire Watergate investigation. He portrayed the image many Americans felt. He came to Washington with a clear mind and a poor heart, only to be corrupted by Richard Nixon.

As time passed, many of Nixon's friends and aides were under indictment. They had joined him in the '68 campaign with their New York backgrounds. With the feeding frenzy going on, the media finally had in its sights the prized target they had so long awaited. The President became more and more reclusive, depending more and more on Gala for emotional support. For public and political support, Nixon came to rely on another Harvard professor: his new Secretary of State, Henry Kissinger.

It was late in the evening when the Secretary of State arrived in the Oval Office. He was escorted in directly. The President had his chair swiveled toward the window. It was hard to make out who was sitting there. Kissinger stood quietly, waiting.

Eventually, Nixon swung around and waved Kissinger to a seat. "Thank you for coming at such a late hour, Henry. I hope I didn't cut your cocktail party short." His slurred words indicated he had been drinking.

"Mr. President, I serve this office at all times," Kissinger said in his monotone German accent. "I am happy to be here. How might I help, sir?"

"We certainly have had a lot of changes around here. Haldeman and Erlichman are gone," Nixon was clearly acting strangely, "and I need a Chief of Staff; a top notch administrator; someone who will be smart, and loyal to me, no matter what happens. You know what I mean, Henry. He's got to be as clean as a hound's tooth, and as pure as Ivory Soap, and as loyal as a St. Bernard...without the whiskey."

Kissinger was concerned about the President. However, he stood erect while responding. "Well, Mr. President, since you asked, General Alexander Haig is a member of my staff; a very able and disciplined man. I recommended him to his present rank over 250 other candidates. If you recall Chief of Staff George Marshall chose a young colonel by the name of Eisenhower over hundreds of other candidates to become a general. It seemed to work out well on that occasion. Haig's done a great deal of staff duty at the Pentagon. He's had experience in international diplomacy. I consider him fit to meet all the requirements you've mentioned. I would highly recommend him for consideration."

Nixon sat up straight in his chair, looking directly at Kissinger. "Okay, Henry. Talk to him about it. Make sure he understands that he will work directly for me, and only for me. Understood?"

Kissinger couldn't wait to get out of there. "I'll talk to him first thing in the morning, Mr. President." Kissinger departed, concerned about Nixon's condition. He hoped nothing out of the ordinary would happen that night.

Kissinger arranged a meeting with General Haig. In that meeting, Kissinger assigned the job to Haig, along with Kissinger's own guidelines. Although he would be officially the President's Chief of Staff, Haig would report everything directly to Kissinger. In practice, as the President's Chief of Staff, Haig served as liaison to Kissinger, who was increasingly controlling foreign affairs. Kissinger was taking a high road and distancing himself from Nixon. He was now unavailable for sudden conferences that were becoming general reassurance and handholding, or just good old "bull sessions" he once had with Nixon. Kissinger was now a super Secretary of State whose image was towering over Nixon's. But Haig himself was brisk and businesslike, not inviting confidences, even if Nixon had been inclined to share any. So Nixon was left without a continual confidant other than Gala.

Every television in the free world was saturated with John Dean's image. He was considered by many who knew him as a spineless character whose stories were fabricated to shield the real truth, and to feed red meat stories to the wolves in the media. He was turning into a political hero. The press cheered him on as he recounted every personal, private conversation with clarity, without doubt or interpretation. Everything he said was considered as gospel, as the ultimate truth - no matter how self-serving.

"I can't believe he is getting away with that line of bullshit. To listen to him, he was kidnapped, drugged, and dragged into the White House," Nixon complained to Gala one night as they were having a few drinks. "You'd think he'd memorized every word anybody ever said to him for the last several years. He talks in-depth, and remembers the smallest details of all of our meetings. You can always tell a habitual liar; they always remember little details - things that most people wouldn't even notice. I know he's a flat-out liar. There has to be some way to discredit him!"

"Calm down, Mr. President," Gala said quietly. "Your turn will come. After all, it's your word against his... and you're the President. Dean's a whining nobody, and deep down inside, everybody knows that...even the press. When your turn comes..."

"My turn?" Nixon interrupted her. "I'm not sure anyone will believe me now. That's a hell of thing for a President to have to say, but it's true. If I say one thing, Dean will give one of his famous detailed 'interpretations,' and he'll be listened to, with teary eyes and sympathetic ears. He's perched behind those microphones, looking so innocent, and singing the song they want to hear. I'm sure they won't listen to me."

Gala got up to make Nixon a fresh drink. The only sound was clinking ice and glass. Then she turned, biting a lower lip thoughtfully. "Your word against Dean's supposedly infallible memory. That's the problem, isn't it? Is there any way you could discredit his verbal memory, if there were a record, or a witness to these meetings? Didn't you keep notes of your meetings with him? That would help refresh your memory. I once heard President Johnson had a taping system in the Oval Office. What became of it?"

Nixon was sitting with his face buried in his hands. His voice was muffled as he replied. "I had it taken out before I took office." Then he looked up, his eyes widening. "But I had another system put in to replace it. Mitchell took care of it for me. There might be tapes of those same conversations that Dean is lying about."

"And if they contradict Dean, this thing could blow up in his face, and we'll have Mr. John Dean's scalp," Gala said with malicious satisfaction.

Nixon was clearly excited. "Those tapes! I forgot all about that taping system. I have to check with Butterfield, I think he's the one who handles them. The press will have to believe the tapes, no holds barred. I should have thought of this sooner. Those tapes will cook Dean in his own juicy lies. Then the truth will come out. Actually, I should end up looking pretty good." Nixon paused to gather his thoughts. "I had Dean investigate the Watergate break-in to see who was involved. He turned out to be incompetent and screwed it all up. Ike used to say, 'You can't depend on the man who made the mess to clean it up.' So I appointed

Archibald Cox to get the truthful answers. Dean tried to make himself look good by lying, and thus made me look bad. Cox nails him for lying and other things, and I'm walking in tall cotton. And that should be it for John Dean and the Watergate Affair."

"Then you'll finally be vindicated, and you can get back to being the President, and serve the people who elected you," Gala said, handing Nixon a fresh drink. She clinked his glass with hers, making a toast. "To Mr. John Dean: an eye for an eye before we all go blind."

Nixon smiled and took a large gulp. "To a bright tomorrow. He who controls the past commands the future. He who commands the future conquers the past'."

CHAPTER **20**

At one in the morning, a long black limousine drove up the driveway of the Maryland home of the Vice President. The car stopped at the side entrance, inconspicuously. Jude got out of the car first, followed by Mitchell. Both men carried attaché cases and looked bent on serious business, as indeed they were.

The Vice President opened the door and greeted them in a courteous manner. The Vice President was completely dressed, including a suit jacket, despite the hour. He escorted them to a large paneled recreation room in the basement. It was a room that exuded a warm family atmosphere, complete with pictures of the children in their various sporting events. At the far end of the room was a fireplace where a fire crackled cheerfully.

Both Mitchell and Jude declined Agnew's offer of a drink, and the Vice President settled on the couch opposite them, as though not quite knowing what else to do with himself. Like Mitchell, Agnew was a big, broad-faced man. In action, he looked decisive, powerful; on television he gave the image of a statesman. Now, he looked confused and uncertain.

The Vice President decided to forego the small talk and get right to the subject at hand. He opened the conversation by saying, "I believe I know why you're here tonight. I appreciate the President's concern, but I'm going to beat this allegation. It's a private matter regarding something that happened before I became Vice President. It has nothing to do with either the President or the administration. I have a good lawyer. Both of us are confident we'll beat this thing. I know the President has a lot on his own plate now, so tell him I'm very confident and will take care of it myself."

Mitchell sat glum-faced and looked directly at the Vice President. "That's not quite why we're here, Spiro." Mitchell deliberately didn't address him as Mr. Vice President.

"But you said..." Spiro broke into Mitchell's words.

"Mr. Thaddeus and I have another perspective to bring to bear. I don't believe you know Mr. Thaddeus very well." Mitchell forced a smile in the direction of Jude. "He's a trusted and special kind of political consultant to a mutual friend of ours, Governor Rockefeller."

"What's Governor Rockefeller's concern in this? He's been a good friend - I know he's the one who pressured Nixon to give me the job as Vice President. But I don't see..."

"Hear us out, Spiro," interrupted Mitchell. "You're quite right. You owe your position to Rockefeller's influence. And the Governor has been rather good to you over the years. You've been loyal - a good political worker during the Governor's last presidential campaign. You and the Governor have shared many professional and personal good times. With that in mind, the Governor requests, with personal regret, that you resign as Vice President of the United States."

Agnew's look grew harder and far less friend-ly. "After that first term, I've made it my own way. What you're suggesting is ridiculous. Just because some joker's trying to beat a tax rap by incriminating me, that's not going to bring me down. And you don't know me very well. If you think I'm going to roll over and play dead just because an old political supporter asks me to...no, absolutely no is my reply. And if that's the reason you came out here tonight, I'm sorry, but I have nothing more to say."

Jude sat quietly through the meeting until now. He picked up his briefcase and put it on the coffee table as Mitchell and Agnew watched. He opened the case with two loud snaps and removed a fold-er. "The Governor isn't merely asking, Mr. Vice

President, he's telling you. It can be easy, or it can be difficult. But either way, you're resigning." He passed the folder to Agnew. As Agnew began to look at the papers, Jude went on. "You'll find notarized affidavits from a total of five individuals to the effect that they gave you bribes during your tenure as Vice President. They're all business associates of yours who have been dealing with you for many years. There is also a statement from a part-time waiter - a student. He will be an unimpeachable and unshakable witness, willing to testify against you. His deposition states that he personally gave you a very large check in public view. You may remember him; he's the one who knew where the term 'golf' came from. I believe there was a $50 tip involved. The documentation alone will hang you. And there's the testimony of other witnesses and your appointment calendar proving that you were with these men on the dates they specify."

Agnew threw the folder aside, shouting, "This is a pack of lies! Just lies! I didn't take this money as a bribe. I remember the large check; it was for $50,000. But it was belated proceeds of a legitimate business deal. They all knew that. I'll sue every one of them. They can't get way with this."

"You can't effectively sue for slander from a jail cell," Jude said with a composed and quiet voice. "Mr. Vice President, you have no support from within the administration. Considering the Watergate witch-hunt going on, nobody's going to make any waves to defend you. You're a lawyer

- you practiced law. Be realistic. You know what all these witnesses can do in an open court. We have the statements and the cancelled checks."

Before Agnew could speak, Mitchell broke in saying, "As former Attorney General and friend of the Court, I've worked out a deal with the Justice Department. If you plead quietly to one count of tax evasion and resign as Vice President, you'll pay a small fine, and no further legal action will be taken against you."

"I never imagined you'd turn into Rockefeller's hatchet man," snarled Agnew, as he got up and paced around the large room, glancing at the family pictures.

"The Governor is a good friend, and still considers you as one. He's willing to help during this difficult situation. But you must cooperate," Mitchell said in a soft voice, trying to be conciliatory. "Upon your resignation from the Vice Presidency, you will become an influential and wealthy representative to Arabian royal families. You are aware that the Governor has connections to make your future quite comfortable. The Arabs would value you highly, both due to your own achievements and the Governor's strong recommendation. Further, you will receive the amount of $1,000,000 to start your own consulting firm, which is to be involved in all oil construction projects in the Persian Gulf. This is a golden opportunity...for you and your family." Mitchell pointed at the kids' pictures and commented, "They look just about college age, and it costs a lot of money for good schools. Spiro, this is a good exit deal for you. Plead 'nolo contendre', resign, and walk out the door a rich man. And the Governor and friend, to whom you have been so close, and whom you served so well in the past, will be eternally grateful."

Agnew looked at Mitchell and then at Jude with contempt. He felt like saying something, but he knew it would do no good. He was in a terrible position. The political flames were raging about Watergate. One more scandal would only add fuel to an uncontrollable fire. No matter how he'd plead for his innocence, the media would muffle his voice. Perhaps this is the best way out of a political life that was becoming less attractive with each passing day.

Jude closed his briefcase - two sharp snaps. "Mr. Vice President, the decision is yours. You can go to court, spend whatever money you have on legal defense, lose, and then be impeached and jailed. A long trial could put intolerable pressures on you and your family, including heavy personal, legal, and financial burdens. Or you can resign on a simple count of tax evasion and enjoy the rest of your private life as a wealthy international businessman. It's a simple decision; go to the bank with a million dollars and with the Governor's continuing blessings, or go to jail alone. I don't believe you're a stupid man, Mr. Agnew."

"I appreciate your fine opinion, Mr. Thaddeus," Agnew said with a rigid expression, akin to a smile. "I find myself thinking that I would not be the first Vice President to resign. Aaron Burr did, and lived long enough to shoot Alexander Hamilton. I wonder if I will live long enough to shoot one of my enemies."

"It's true Burr did kill Alexander Hamilton in a duel," Jude said with a cool smile. "But dueling with pistols is now illegal. Today's weapon of choice is ink. And you don't want to duel with anyone that buys ink by the drum. Besides, as a wealthy jet-setting business executive, you'll have other things to occupy your talents. It will be a big change in your life, and in the long run it may be a good move."

Agnew sat staring at the carpet, and then said quietly, "Confucius said, Only the wisest and stupidest of men never change."

"Everything is arranged. All you have to do is show up at the court house tomorrow morning at nine, plead no contest, sign a few papers, and walk out the door a private citizen, and a rich man, with an outstanding business opportunity in the Middle East."

John Mitchell was in lower spirits than usual as he and Jude drove away from the Vice President's home. "It's going to be tough on him and his family," Mitchell said quietly.

"It will be for a short time, but the money he'll make on the construction contracts will make his life a lot more pleasant for a lot longer," Jude said calmly. "That reminds me, I'd better call our Secretary of State and tell him who our new Vice President is going to be."

John Mitchell looked at Jude with squinting eyes and said, "Let me guess. The next Vice President of the United States will be the Governor of New York, Nelson Rockefeller."

"Mr. Attorney General, you mustn't be too quick to move the king. Let the bishop move in to ensure a clear path," Jude said as if lecturing a student on the game of chess. "No, Governor Rockefeller would cause too much interest at this time. We must let someone else lead the way. We don't want any political surprises or legal battles on the validity of the Twenty-fifth Amendment. So we submit a candidate of our choosing that is liked and respected by both parties, so that he will fly through confirmation hearings without any conflict or delay. Then afterwards, he will follow our direction on important matters."

"Then you have a candidate already chosen?" Mitchell asked.

"Oh yes," Jude said softly. "He's a candidate chosen for the part. He knows how to block and lead; he was an all-star football center and linebacker on a National Championship team."

Agnew's sudden resignation seemed to take the whole country by surprise. Those in the know thought it would be a long drawn-out legal battle. He was known as a political gladiator and would not back down from any partisan enemies, cliques, social elite or the media. Agnew's resignation made the headlines, along with the current Watergate news, and some stories on the gas shortage.

Nixon was as startled and shocked as anyone. He had just met with Agnew a week before. Both men were committed to see this thing through, no matter what. Both believed that it was a set-up, and that Agnew would be cleared. But now, Agnew's capitulation stunned Nixon as much as the rest of the country. He hoped Agnew would bull his way through the adverse publicity, while pulling the headlines from Watergate and Nixon – at least long enough for Nixon to get his own troubles under control. All of Nixon's close official aides were now gone, except for Kissinger, to whom he immediately turned for advice.

Nixon was not only surprised at Agnew's resignation, but he was furious, as well. He summoned Kissinger to the Oval Office for a strategy session. When Kissinger arrived, the President was pacing around the Oval Office, waving a crumpled letter. As soon as the door was shut, Nixon started in. He shouted, "Spiro admits to one minor criminal offense, writes a one line letter of resignation, walks out of the courtroom and into the sunset. And this makes the evening news one time, and that's that. Not another peep from the press. But me...if I were to die, the damn reporters would follow me through an autopsy, into the grave, and report on what St. Peter says when I get to the Pearly Gates."

After making empathetic and incensed comments for a while, Kissinger then tried to point out the matter at hand. "Mr. President, what the Vice President did was shocking and unexplainable - but it's history. The office of the vice presidency is now vacant. What is needed now is a clear and untarnished appointee to fill that vacancy, as is provided for in the Twenty-fifth Amendment."

"Do you want the job, Henry?" Nixon suggested, in a savagely sardonic voice.

Startled, Kissinger was caught off-guard. He searched for words and said, "No, no, quite inappropriate, Mr. President. After all, I am foreign-born, and the Constitution clearly states that no person, except a natural born citizen can be eligible to be President."

"Who then? Who's willing to be seen with me these days?" Nixon was feeling sorry for himself. "Hell, I have a hard time finding anyone willing to come over for dinner or watch a football game. Teaming up with me now isn't any way to improve a political career." Nixon paused, went behind his desk and sat down. He tried to calm down. He was tired, and was trying to focus his mind. "I'm sorry Henry, I know this is serious business. Your political instincts are probably better than mine right now. Do you have anyone in mind?"

"Mr. President, I suggest you consider the Minority Leader in the House of Representatives, Congressman Gerald Ford."

"Gerry Ford," Nixon said quietly. "Lyndon Johnson said he'd been hit too many times in the head playing football."

"He did play on two championship teams while at the University of Michigan. In fact, Green Bay and the Chicago Bears recruited him. And he was voted 'Most Valuable Player' on the 1934 team."

"All right Henry, he played football. But he's from Michigan, not one of your Ivy Leaguers," Nixon bantered.

"Well, he did go to Yale Law School, so he does qualify," Kissinger chuckled at his humorous interjection.

"Okay, Henry. He's got an Ivy League class ring. But he's a lightweight. He has no executive experience, no understanding of foreign policy. He's been content as Minority Leader. He doesn't appear to have any real *drive*," Nixon said, as he became more interested in the topic.

"As you pointed out, you must take your allies where you find them. Gerald Ford is well liked by both Houses of Congress. His reputation is impeccable, and Gerry is popular with the American people. He could be assured of a quick and relatively painless confirmation. I agree that he does lack experience and ambition. But at this time, do you really want a heavyweight as vice president with your own position under siege?" Kissinger remained quiet for a moment, and then continued. "I would suggest a candidate without political ambition. In fact, this is one of the reasons

I recommend Ford. Last month he announced his retirement. He has no political ambition to clutter this already chaotic White House. Did you know that his real father, Leslie King, was rather wealthy, and that during the Depression, young Gerry turned down a fortune and stayed with his stepfather? That's the type of fellow we need now as vice president."

"Agnew's resignation came up so suddenly, I haven't checked into the legalities yet. How does this Twenty-fifth Amendment process work?" Nixon asked Henry.

"I had it researched. It's a simple process, Mr. President," Kissinger said, his voice stern now. "Mr. Agnew has tendered his resignation, which has been accepted by you. Now, Mr. President, you have the unique pleasure of submitting your nomination for Vice President to me as Secretary of State. I will then turn it over to the Senate for debate, and I would hope, speedy confirmation."

"I dread the thought of submitting anyone's name to the Senate for another confirmation. They just use the confirmation process to get in front of the cameras to pontificate about how honorable they are," Nixon said, apparently thinking of some of the recent explosive encounters he'd had over other appointees.

"The confirmation needs to go smoothly and nominating Gerald Ford, Mr. President, would be a wise choice. Though a loyal Republican, he's considered an independent thinker. He was on the Warren Commission, has not been closely tied to you in the past, and as Minority Leader he has many friends on both sides of the aisle in Congress. I believe he could be confirmed with a minimum of unpleasantness."

"You're right, Henry," Nixon said, shaking his head. "It's got to go smoothly. The nation and the world are watching how we are handling this mess. But Ford's not the only possibility. What about John Connolly, the ex-Governor of Texas? He might be a good choice. He's as clean as a surgeon's hands, he's highly respected, and he and I get along quite well."

"Connolly," responded Kissinger patiently, "is a fine man. But he would be a disaster as a candidate. The fact that he changed political parties would alienate both Democrats and Republicans. The first appointed vice president should be perceived as an unambitious man, non-threatening to the normal political process. The right candidate will help garner support for you in Congress. We need someone who will sympathize with your difficult position, and in no way challenge your authority."

"It sounds as though you've thought this through pretty thoroughly, Henry," commented Nixon, not wanting to argue further. He felt alone, about to depend only upon his two remaining confidantes: Henry Kissinger and Gala.

"Mr. President, my job is to think things through," Kissinger said with pride. "And I can assure you that I have given a great deal of consideration in looking for the right person. My staff and I went through a large reservoir of candidates, and weighed the virtues of many. All things considered, Ford's name kept rising to the top of the list. I did a lot of soul searching before making such a strong recommendation."

"Henry, I know you are doing the best for the country," Nixon said, in a defeated, demoralized manner. "I don't have anything against Gerry myself. He's always been a good party man. And you're right in that he's never been after the presidency." Nixon paused for a moment and looked at Kissinger. "You know, Rockefeller hated Ford. It goes back to the 1964 campaign. The race was close between Rockefeller and Goldwater for the nomination, and Gerry could have been a kingmaker and endorsed Rockefeller. But he chose to endorse Michigan's 'Favorite Son,' George Romney. That cost Rockefeller the nomination. Rocky vowed to get even with him, but that was a long time ago."

"Yes, it was a long time ago, Mr. President," said Kissinger without emotion.

"I rely on your judgment, Henry," Nixon said. "If you say Ford, then Ford it is. You'll get my official nomination just as soon as I can get it drawn up."

"I believe that will be the wisest choice, Mr. President."

As predicted, Ford's nomination and confirmation to the office of vice president made less stir than had Agnew's leaving of it. Everything went smoothly, almost cordially, a rarity those days in the Capitol, when anything involving the White House was criticized and brought under unrelenting scrutiny. Everyone seemed pleased that the unassuming Minority Leader from the House had become the first appointed Vice President of the United States. The initiation of the Twenty-fifth Amendment went smoothly, as designed.

CHAPTER **21**

On the overnight flight to Rio de Janeiro, Jude read an account of Ford's swearing-in ceremony with great satisfaction. He was pleased as he read how graciously the ceremony went. All in attendance were relieved, and confident about the new Vice President. Even the press seemed to approve of the proceedings. In Washington, things seemed to be calming down...for now. As the plane approached the International Airport, Jude's thought pattern was broken by the voice on the intercom.

The stewardess announced, *"Those sitting on the left side of the aircraft, if you look out your window, you can see the magnificent Mt. Caracovado, rising 2,500 feet, almost straight up from the sea, and the world famous statue of 'Christ the Redeemer,' overlooking the Bay of Guanabara. Ladies and gentlemen, good morning...and welcome to Brazil."* Jude joined the rest of the passengers in looking at the striking landscape. As a boy in the orphanage, he had seen pictures of the 90-foot high statue of Christ. Now he would see it up close.

But that was not the purpose for his visit to South America. Officially, this journey was for business investment considerations. The real purpose, however, was to meet one man. His code name: Lancehead. Although the plan was a completely secret operation, a unique part of the plan had to be hypersensitive. Jude went to the Zebra Group, to help in recruiting the right contacts for this dangerous and critical stage. This phase was so sensitive that a stealthy personal meeting had to be arranged. Jude would have to handle this part of the plan very delicately. He had to deal with a deep-secret, international organization. Their rules were simple: "There are no rules."

During the Second World War, President Roosevelt appointed Nelson Rockefeller to be in charge of "Inter-American Affairs" - a front for the OSS; which meant he headed up all spy and espionage operations in Central and South America. He had made many powerful contacts, both public and covert. There were key operatives, many of whom were still active, on retainers for special programs. In the international oil industry, dealing with dictators was normal business. One must have access to the right cadre to deal with this caliber of colloquial person. Jude traveled to Brazil to meet with this enigmatic representative.

Clearing Customs, he hired a car to take him to the Hotel Gloria. As he walked to the car, it became apparent it was mid-summer in tropical Brazil - and Jude was dressed in his finest New York winter attire. He rode from the airport along the beautiful beaches of Copacabana and Ipanema, and observed the spectacular view of the twin peaks of Sugar Loaf.

The Hotel Gloria was one of the grand hotels built during the Roaring Twenties - large bright white exterior, the interior dark Spanish décor, with very high ceilings. The walls were arrayed with classic Portuguese Art. The service was old country continental, with bellmen and staff all moving throughout, determined to make their guests feel regal and comfortable.

Jude was unpacking his suitcase, looking forward to getting into something lightweight, when he heard a knock at the door. When he opened it, there stood an elderly bellman with a few white towels, folded neatly. He handed them to Jude, smiled, bowed his head, and disappeared. Nothing seemed out of the ordinary as Jude walked to the bathroom. But, as he put down the towels and unfolded them, one contained a neatly typewritten note that read: "*Go directly out front of the main entrance and cross the street. Carry a newspaper under your right arm. A blue taxi will approach you and ask if you like ice cream. He will take care of you. Destroy this note.*"

Having burned the note, Jude followed the directions and soon was heading into the mountains in a rattling, blue taxi, driven by a man who offered no conversation, and glanced at him furtively in a cracked rearview mirror. After about an hour, the taxi wheezed to a stop in front of an old Portuguese mansion.

There was no one to be seen. Jude looked at the large three-story manor house, set in the midst of well placed, very tall Jabuticabeira trees. The sunlight broke through exposing the moss hanging on the limbs and vines. The grounds were well maintained; the scene looked like a southern antebellum plantation. This was a comforting setting for this unusual meeting.

Jude left the taxi and, when he offered to pay, the cabbie simply said, "I'll wait here." So Jude walked up to the huge front door. He experimentally pushed opened the heavy straphanger door and went through into a large, windowless, musty-smelling room. He was still waiting for his eyes to adjust from the sunlight outside when another door opened at the far end of the room. He walked through, finding a smaller room, which had a long, impressive Spanish-style table in the center, and two chairs, one at the end nearest him, the other chair placed at the head of the table. Behind him two doors slammed, almost simultaneously. From the dimness, a harsh voice ordered, "Senor, please sit down."

Brushing some dust off the chair, Jude did as he was directed. An elderly man in a faded white shirt and drab trousers moved out of the darkness into view and sat at the head of the table. He was small in stature, with unkempt hair. Jude immediately noticed his black, sharp eyes.

"Welcome to Brazil, senor," said his host, in a rather formal Portuguese accent. "I understand you have traveled a long distance. Why is it you want to talk with me?"

"I have traveled a long distance to talk with Lancehead," Jude said flatly. "Are you Lancehead?"

The mysterious man replied with a question, "Who wishes to know?"

"Gemstone...or let me say that I am representing him," Jude said and waited. "I believe he assigned you the distinguished code name, after Brazil's deadly viper snake, the Golden Lancehead."

"I am Lancehead. It has been many years since I have talked to my friend Gemstone. He was quite the leader during the Second World War. Together we fought the Japanese and the Germans. And he fought with Hoover of the FBI, and Wild Bill Donovan of the OSS. But he had a lot of money and influence, thus he became head spymaster of secret wartime operations for all of South America. He was the one who secretly connived the sinking of the German cruiser The Graf Spee in Montevideo. Oh yes, those were the days."

"I bring greetings from your old friend, Gemstone. I have been told of your comradeship during the war, of your working together on special operations. He said you could be trusted

implicitly with any mission, however dangerous," Jude said.

"I was contacted, and I am here. The pact
made long ago is still a pact. The alliance formed
many years ago is still an alliance. Gemstone and
I worked together even after the war in various
countries throughout the world. But you must
know that."

Then the old man asked, "So why, senor, are
you here?"

"On behalf of Gemstone, I came to ask you to
perform a difficult and dangerous mission; perhaps more difficult and dangerous than anything
you have ever done before. You are under no obligation to attempt it. If you choose not to go ahead,
I will understand, and we will depart as friends.
Shall I continue?" Jude asked.

"Senor, throughout my career, nearly all of my
contracts were difficult and dangerous missions
- some more difficult than others - but all dangerous." He sat back and looked Jude in the eyes as
if his manhood was being challenged. "Our operation in Chile resulted in the deposing and ex-
ecuting of El Presidia Salvador Allenda. And, for
the first time since 1917, a Communist country
reverted to democracy. And in Bolivia, I helped to
track down, capture, and dispose of the Marxist
Cuban 'Hero of the Revolution,' Che Guevara.
The Lancehead may look like a garter snake, but
it has venom more deadly than a cobra's. So tell
me of this mission."

"The mission," Jude said as he moistened his lips and sat erect, "is to assassinate the President of the United States." Jude couldn't believe he said it, but he did.

Lancehead sat motionless. Then, in a very business-like manner, he responded, "Kill the President of the United States. I see Gemstone still has respect for me. Why not just wait until Senor Nixon is dismissed from office. Then there will be fewer guards. Then he'd be easier to target."

"Nixon is not the target," Jude said hastily. "The target is President Ford, who will become President after Nixon resigns. We'll need time to set everything up properly. This has to be a perfectly executed operation."

"This is strange, even for me. And believe me, senor, I have done many strange things in my life...but this is something else." He paused to think, and then asked softly, "Of what advantage is it that he be killed?"

"When President Ford is eliminated, then Gemstone will become President," Jude said.

"Ah...clearly this will be a great undertaking. It will be very difficult. I think it can be done, senor... but very difficult," Lancehead said as he rocked his head.

"Gemstone doesn't expect you to carry out this mission in person," Jude said. He was getting nervous even talking about such a thing. "He relies on you to direct the operation. We don't want any political repercussions - no Russians, Cubans, even Latin Americans. No hint of any conspiracy.

"You have a reputation for knowing everything legal and illegal that's going on all over the Americas. There are some countries supplying America with a lot of drugs - cocaine being the biggest seller - but you can throw amphetamines, heroin, and LSD into the mix. There's a whole new underground drug culture." Jude paused for a moment to gather his thoughts. "There are a lot of weirdos addicted to these drugs. Many of them have their minds all screwed up. And these addicts will do anything to support their habits: sell their bodies, rob, steal, and even kill. From this culture of misfits, drug addicts and mindless robots, we want to recruit a few amateur assassins."

"This is common knowledge. I agree that those of whom you speak will do anything to support their habits," the old man commented. "But they are irrational and make poor shooters. Not the type I'd work with."

"Nevertheless, the shooters must be drug addicts. The Governor of New York has highlighted this epidemic, passing new laws to crack down on this social scourge of drug addiction." Jude accented the latter part for humor. "So you can see that a drug addict taking a shot at the President... well, these actions can be explained away as the madness of drug influence. And to make it more plausible, there should be more than one assassination attempt. There should be three separate attempts - all in California, where drugs and addicts are plentiful, and if the shooters are a little insane, so much the better. The first two only have to try to make a clear assassination attempt. Shoot in the air or at him. If Ford is wounded, it won't matter. So long as he isn't killed."

"No danger of that, if the shooter is an addict," commented Lancehead, in a cool, disapproving voice.

"The third shooter: he or she is the one who must be carefully chosen, carefully guided. The third shooter must be successful. This one, too, must be an amateur. But an amateur of your choosing."

"It is possible," Lancehead said with a reserved attitude. "In so great a task, it will take time to choose the right people. Even though the right people will, for the first two, be the wrong people." The old man showed a smile which revealed his bright white teeth. "Now, for the fatal hit, as Colonel Krivisky of the KGB would often say, 'any fool can commit a murder, but it takes an artist to commit a good natural death.' I would suggest a subtle method: one that is not quite as shocking, but just as deadly. This will take some planning and highly skilled operatives. I may suggest a clean medical way. A simple handshake is all we need, like we used on Ho Chi Minh - he died quickly of a massive heart attack. Of course he was small and the dose was non-detectable. But, we didn't use enough when we went after Vladimiroovich Amdropov, the Soviet KGB leader. It resulted in a non-lethal heart attack. But we have learned since then. You might say 'a better world through chemistry'."

"I guess I came to the right place. I had no idea you were so experienced dealing in these international disposal matters," Jude said with some amazement.

"Yes, senor, you are in good company. Did you think that Governor Rockefeller was appointed to the Advisory Board to oversee CIA activities by chance? Now, when do we need to carry out this operation?" Lancehead asked, as if he were concluding any normal business meeting.

"President Ford will nominate Governor Rockefeller as Vice President. However, he has to be confirmed by the Senate to make it legal. This confirmation process will take some time. So we must wait until Gemstone takes the oath of office as Vice President before we strike," Jude spoke in a confident voice.

"It will take some arranging. We must be very careful, but so far we have slipped by the North Vietnamese, the KGB, and even escaped the wrath of Castro. I am confident we can accomplish this for Gemstone," Lancehead spoke with aged confidence.

"If I need to contact you for any reason, I'll need a system," Jude added.

The old man took a piece of paper from his pocket and wrote something on it. He folded it and handed it to Jude. "There is a phone number of a Swiss bank. You can call and ask for Snowball Four. They will contact me." The old man stood up. "Is there anything else? I have my work cut out for me. Good-bye, Senor Thaddeus."

Jude rose out of respect, saying, "Payment for your services will be handled in the traditional fashion, whatever the cost. Gracias, Senor."

Upon returning from his South American excursion, Jude moved into a suite at the Watergate to more easily monitor the activities taking place in Washington. He was very pleased with how everything was going.

Nixon had been goaded into one mistake after another. He allowed an aide to his new Chief of Staff to testify before the Watergate Committee. In his testimony, the aide let it be known that there was a secret taping device in the Oval Office, and that the President had been searching for information to refute the testimony of John Dean. This revelation was like a bombshell of the first magnitude. The President was secretly taping conversations! The world was aghast.

The President went into an unprecedented rage at the disclosure. The system was voice-activated. There were intensely private conversations on the tapes, which had been routinely replaced without being reviewed or transcribed. There were sensitive conversations with senators, congressmen, and foreign heads of state. The tapes were stored to be used later as historical reference in the Nixon Presidential Library. Nixon had intended to use selected written transcripts as a basis for refuting Dean. Gala was not able to persuade Nixon to use the tapes themselves. Not even the knowledge of their existence spread beyond a select chosen few. So Dr. Kissinger's influence was used to select the right person to appear in front of the Senate's Ervin Committee, and to make an almost inadvertent disclosure, which would reveal the use of a secret taping system in the White House. The committee and the national press went ballistic.

Of course, Cox, the Special Prosecutor, immediately subpoenaed the tapes, causing a national uproar. And, of course, Nixon refused categorically, citing national security concerns, and separation of powers. The battle was now fully joined. The President was no longer a bystander. He had now become the main event. In addition to the ongoing Senate investigation there was another Grand Jury, which was considering additional legal means of exposing other criminal activities involved in the Watergate break-in. The entire news media was on top of what was now almost universally considered to be a full-scale cover-up mounted by the Nixon administration - and perhaps even the President himself.

Leaders of the Republican higherarchy knew the President was becoming a severe liability to the party. He could not run again, and his new Vice President didn't instill much confidence. Many of the most powerful players began putting slow, but steady pressure on Nixon's remaining friends and supporters. The strategy was simple: the politically astute would watch the smoke to see which way the wind was blowing, and keep themselves clear, and keep themselves out of any political jeopardy. Nixon was on his own.

Nixon's political compass was completely off. He was seeking advice from a shrinking, incompetent staff. He'd always trusted Gala, and he again turned to her for guidance. Gala's advice was simple: things were coming apart, turning into a calamity, and elaborate machinations were no longer prudent. She advised the President to demonstrate his strength in defending the authority of the Executive Branch. After all, the Executive Branch was equal to both the Legislative (Congressional) and Judicial Branches. The President appointed Cox as Special Prosecutor, and if Cox overstepped his legal boundaries, then the President had the right to dismiss him. If Cox wouldn't cooperate, then Nixon could simply replace him with a more professional, less blindly idealistic prosecutor. The President should appoint a person who would take into consideration national security, and the responsibility entailed being the Chief of State. After all, the President had sensitive conversations which were of both political and national security importance. Nixon believed he should have the authority to carefully edit written excerpts from the tapes, and then supply the written transcripts to the special prosecutor. Gala's advice seemed logical and made sense, so again, he followed her counsel. Cox demanded the original tapes; Nixon refused and fired him, and closed the Office of Special Prosecutor.

The firing of Cox was politically a seismic eruption, a political screw-up and a public relations nightmare. The Attorney General resigned in protest, and so did his second-in-command. That left the job up to Robert Bork, acting Attorney General, to carry out Nixon's orders. The news media had a field day, calling the firing of the Special Prosecutor, "The Saturday Night Massacre." This event caused a widespread public outrage. For many in Congress, it was the last straw. A Constitutional confrontation was in motion. Nevertheless, a new prosecutor was appointed with a clear mandate to bring the Watergate investigation to a speedy close. And the new prosecutor agreed to accept the written transcripts of the by-now almost mythical White House tapes.

Evidently, the House of Representatives believed the Senate had hogged the TV cameras long enough. To ensure equal coverage, the House empanelled the Judiciary Committee, under the direction of Peter Rodino, to investigate and if need be, submit charges for the impeachment of Richard M. Nixon, President of the United States.

The members of the House committee were well aware of the publicity they were receiving nationally and, more importantly, how it played in their own districts. Many of the Republicans on the committee didn't like the position they were in: many had campaigned with the President. But they were all aware of the criminal convictions being handed down almost daily on one or another of the Watergate defendants. The President's highest staff members were being sentenced to jail terms, and the people back home were looking at their Representatives to see what justice they would deal. Other political futures were on the line, other than just Nixon's. And every member on the House Judiciary Committee knew it. Many old politicians feared even the Republican Party itself might not survive the Watergate scandal – and that it might disappear forever from the political landscape.

Nixon began releasing transcripts of taped conversations to the new Special Prosecutor. There was no advance notice to Congress, friends, or foes. Only the Washington Post seemed to know what was on the tapes. Congressmen were furious to read in the newspaper of conversations they'd thought were shared with the President in absolute confidence. Congressmen professed to be outraged, and the public was equally shocked by the unabashed profanity and obscenity disclosed as a routine feature of conversations in the Oval Office. Lyndon Johnson, everybody knew, had employed such language and worse: but Johnson had been careful to maintain the utmost civil usage in public, and his tapes were not yet in the public domain. The Nixon tapes opened a window into private conversations from the leader of the United States and free world. What was being reported in the headlines was not popular and, each day, a new transcript was released. It was always worse than the one the day before.

The administration was effectively punch-drunk. Each time some obstacle was overcome, some challenge met, a new bombshell would detonate, sending politicians and reporters scrambling for a different news slant. Each of these conundrums made headlines. Everything the White House did appeared to alienate more and more of the populace.

To make things even worse, the new Special Prosecutor, Leon Jaworski, was now suing for 64 taped conversations. This time, there were no transcripts, only the actual tapes themselves. He would not accept edited transcripts. He felt they were adjusted to suit the President. Jaworski contended only the original, unaltered tapes would show the truth.

The judge handling the special grand jury ruled the President had to accede to the Special Prosecutor's demand and turn over the tapes. Nixon, in a white hot rage, contended the authority of the Executive Branch exceeded the jurisdiction of a mere federal judge. The President's attorney appealed the judge's ruling to the Supreme Court.

That promised blessed relief, due to the normal caseload before the court. Nixon felt it would take a few years for a case to be heard by the full Supreme Court. And even then, there was the possibility that the Supreme Court might not hear the case. However, moved by the special circumstances, and perhaps by certain pressure funneled through the legal community emanating from New York, the Supreme Court moved with unprecedented speed, and scheduled the case to proceed at once. The case was heard quickly, and the Court decided against the President on a 9 to 0 ruling. He would have to turn over the original tapes in their entirety.

The prospect of full, unedited disclosure set off a panic in the Oval Office. To make matters even more onerous, during the process of typing the transcripts, a substantial chunk of a critical tape was erased - 18 minutes in all. Nobody admitted to knowing just how this could have happened. Rosemary Woods, the President's secretary, was greatly upset, wept a lot, and seemed in danger of major hysterics. Certainly, she could not have erased the tapes. There was no question in Gala's mind; she knew the essential section of the tapes and knew how to record and erase. But, what was done was done, and the gap was there. It didn't seem possible things could get more nefarious, gap or no gap.

The Special Prosecutor immediately raised questions as to whether the President had tampered with the evidence. That, in itself would be a federal criminal act, and a potentially impeachable offense.

Nixon was very despondent. While walking down the hall with Gala he made a comment. "I wonder - how can the Special Prosecutor know what is on specific tapes? He hasn't heard them yet. We have not turned over any tapes to his office or any investigating committees. I don't know what's on them! There must be thousands of hours of conversations. Yet he went to court for specific tapes."

Gala was caught off-guard. She couldn't think of anything rational to say that would make any sense. She quickly changed the subject to Mrs. Nixon's health, which distracted Nixon for a time.

The momentum for impeachment now seemed all but irresistible. The House of Representatives were drawing up the documents. The Judiciary Committee, headed up by Peter Rodino, was hell-bent on impeachment. The legal staff consisted of energetic young political esurient Democrat lawyers. They worked feverishly, searching historical documents for the evidence necessary to begin impeachment procedures. One notable, relentless young attorney was Hillary Rodham. She would later face impeachment charges against her husband, President Bill Clinton.

It was generally known the White House was in utter disarray, with General Haig and Dr. Kissinger overseeing daily operations - in effect, running the White House. They paid lip service to Nixon being President, and titular Chief of State, but they handled the calls of importance and made the decisions, and Nixon took no action to oppose them. The President was concentrating on fighting to keep his office. He was distracted by the daily siege mentality of the news media, and he seemed to be tormented with nowhere to turn.

In the House of Representatives, the Judiciary Committee voted on the Articles of Impeachment against President Richard M. Nixon. The vote was a decisive 27 to 11 vote, whose charges included obstructing justice, abuse of power, and defiance of subpoenas. It was becoming clear if Nixon could not be persuaded to resign for the good of the country, and of the Republican Party, he would almost certainly be the first President of the United States to be successfully impeached and removed from office. Then he would have to face criminal legal battles. The overall effect was beyond comprehension.

Somehow Nixon, like Spiro Agnew before him, had to be persuaded to resign. Somebody had to tell him to "go softly into the night."

CHAPTER 22

E arly one evening, a delegation of the Republican leadership from both Houses of Congress was escorted into the Oval Office. Sunset was breaking through the windows, casting long shadows in the room, as if a sign of the day end and a harbinger of the twilight soon arriving. Nixon rose to greet the delegation, wearing his usual dark blue suit. He forced a smile and inquired lightly about pending legislation and thanked them for taking time from their busy schedules. Several members of the delegation realized, with some shock, how the President had aged. He seemed to have lost any of the social graces he once possessed. His posture was rigid, as if he were carrying the world on his shoulders.

They all took seats and there was a moment of awkward silence. It wasn't going to be easy to ask a man to commit political suicide, rather than be executed by Congress. Before attending this twilight meeting, Senator Barry Goldwater of Arizona and two other members of the delegation, were secretly given excerpts of some of the taped conversations. The intent this meeting was to discuss openly and frankly the terrible situation facing the President.

Senator Goldwater was senior statesmen and spokesman of the group. He was respected and feared for his no-nonsense politics. He looked the part: square-jawed, with distinguished wavy gray hair; his large eyeglasses completed the look of maturity and intelligence. It was he who broke the silence. "Mr. President, we are here on a most regrettable and difficult mission. We are all aware of the many good things you have done as President. It has been through perilous seas that you have guided the Ship of State. And we appreciate all the help you have given us in past elections. But we are here this evening because we feel we must bring to your attention the situation as we see it." He paused, clearing his throat, and then resumed. "First, Mr. President, the country can't take much more. Our party can't take much more. Vietnam, gas lines, the Vice President's resignation, and this cancer of Watergate is causing unimaginable domestic and international trauma. Not a day goes by without a new revelation about a new crime committed by this administration. At this time in our history, we need a President who is above reproach; one who can lead this country in a full-time, unobstructed march out of these troubled, perplexing times."

The President sat, not moving a muscle. The others were listening, as if hoping they wouldn't be required to speak.

"Mr. President," Senator Goldwater went on, "speaking for this group and members of your own party, in and out of office, I must inform you that you have no political base whatsoever in either House. The Supreme Court has ruled unanimously against you; the House of Representatives is drafting impeachment proceedings. I believe you will be impeached under Article One: Abuse of Power, and Article Two: Obstruction of Justice. In the Senate, there are only 12 members who will support you. In order to avoid such a forewarned calamity, we are asking you to resign as President. In doing so, you will help to preserve the Executive Branch and save the American people from a long and terrible ordeal."

Senator Goldwater and the President stared at each other like opposing statues for a few moments, neither saying a word.

Finally, Goldwater, spoke in a soft low voice, asking, "Mr. President, do you have any questions of me, or anyone else here?"

Nixon suddenly sat erect, as if just waking from a nap, looked directly at Senator Goldwater, and in a low voice, said, "No, I have no questions, Barry. But let me explain something to you. A strong Executive Branch is essential to our Republic. That's why our founding forefathers made three separate and equal branches of government. As President, I am the Executive Branch. As the steward of the Executive Branch, I will take the action necessary to maintain this separate and independent branch and keep it intact. I do have the interest of the American people in my mind and heart. I also have to consider the future men who will hold this sacred office. I must see to it that the authority of this office is not eroded by a news media feeding frenzy. I have to assess what I do now, and best judge how it will affect the actions of future Presidents. I will consider what was said here tonight, but I can assure you, I'll do what I think is right, for the American people and the Executive branch of this government."

Senator Goldwater glanced to check the faces of his group. They were motionless. He then said, "Thank you for your time, Mr. President. We needn't keep you any longer."

The President paused, his face impassive. Standing up, Nixon said, "I realize how difficult these times are for all of us. I appreciate the burden you men carried in here this evening. I will consider everything you had to say. Thank you for coming in."

Nixon escorted the men to the door. He had to force a smile. He shook each man's hand and spoke a few kind words of departure. As the small gathering left the White House, they all had the uneasy conviction, that in spite of everything, Nixon meant to fight on to the bitter end.

Nixon went back to his desk and touched the intercom. "Gala, they're gone. Could you please come in here?"

"Mr. President," Gala replied, "could you possibly come down to my office? No one is around."

Too numb to even wonder at the request, Nixon agreed, adding, "Have a drink ready for me...I need one."

A few moments later, Gala could hear him slowly walking down the hall. Nixon entered Gala's office with his head bowed. He walked as if he had a lot on his mind, and was surprised to realize that two other men were present: Jude and Henry Kissinger. Nixon frowned as he looked at them, trying to understand the reason for their presence, while accepting the drink Gala handed to him. He stared at Gala, but couldn't hide his look of surprise. He said nervously, "Gala, I thought you said..."

"Gentlemen," Gala said firmly, "please be seated," as though convening a meeting.

"I've just seen one happy delegation," remarked Nixon, dropping into a chair. "I didn't expect to have another one...not tonight anyway." He thought he was being humorous but nobody smiled.

"Mr. President," Gala said, in the same flat businesslike voice, "we are here to discuss your future. You can speak freely in front of Jude. And of course Doctor Kissinger has been your confidant for many years."

Nixon didn't like the tone of Gala's words. He couldn't recall having heard that particular pitch in her voice or having seen her conduct herself in quite this manner. She seemed foreign and distant. He finished half his drink in one swallow. "I don't know what you think you're playing at. My future is in my own hands, and I am the President. I intend to be President for the next three years. If I need any advice, I'll ask for it. And I haven't asked. I am sick to death with advice, and advisors. It was bad advice that got me into this mess in the first place."

"We're here to help you out of this mess, Mr. President," Jude said calmly.

"I don't remember appointing you to anything," Nixon said his words slurring. "You're way out of line."

"On the contrary, Mr. President," Jude responded quickly. "This is exactly my line. I'm here to help you comprehend the options of either resigning to a more tranquil way of life or impeachment, which means personal disgrace, loss of office, financial ruin, and going to jail."

"You don't know what you're talking about! You have a lot of gall coming here. I'm the President of the United States. I have full power of the Executive Branch." He took another large gulp of his drink. "I am the Commander-in-Chief of all the armed forces. The FBI and CIA and the rest of the government...they are all under my control."

"You're not quite in control as much as you think, Mr. President. For some time now, the Secretary of State has been running the whole show. In fact, the Secret Service has you monitored on a suicide watch," Jude said calmly. "The directors of the CIA and FBI have orders not to respond to any request you make. And, none of them will jeopardize their careers for a short-term, constricted President. The military is under the control of your chief of staff, General Haig. Doctor Kissinger, and General Haig, have been operating a caretaker government in the interim. You have no administrative support, no congressional support, and no judicial support. You, Mr. President, are completely cut off with no moves of your own. We are your only hope."

Nixon lashed a quick glance at Kissinger, then at Gala. "It's the tapes. They can't do anything without the tapes. And as President, the tapes belong to me. All I have to do is burn them. Then let them try getting evidence. I can say that for national security, I'll destroy all of them. And that will be that. They can bitch all they want, but, no evidence no impeachment." Nixon smiled as if he found a way out himself. *Why didn't I think of this earlier? Just burn the damn tapes.*

Nixon again glanced over to Gala. There was something about her tonight...and it was Gala who had first made him remember the tapes existence. He began to have the dreadful suspicion that this might not have been a coincidence. His mind threw up the almost-forgotten information that Jude and Gala were old acquaintances. And Kissinger...he never quite trusted him.

Jude spoke again. "As far as the tapes go, yes Mr. President, you can destroy your set. But our set has no gaps and is quite clear. All your conversations are on them. What you said officially and unofficially, what you said about your friends, enemies, and some interesting things about your own family. Oh, the vocabulary why that alone would offend most of the minorities, and your silent majority. And don't forget the most embarrassing tapes: the ones made on your private line, they are by far the most embarrassing ones...and they'd require an X-rated earphone." Jude looked over at Gala, and remarked, "I'd hate to see Gala's reputation tarnished."

Nixon looked from Gala to Jude and back to Gala again. He was sweating and losing color in his face. He stood up as if aroused to fight. "You're bluffing. I have all the tapes in the White House vault. They have been there under lock and key. No one can get at them."

Jude replied coolly, "If you remember, when you had the state-of-the-art taping system installed, Attorney General Mitchell arranged the installation. Well, it happens that the company, being paid by private funds, put in two systems. So we arranged to have a complete set of duplicate tapes. We have all our tapes stored a distance from the White House in a very secure location. I have listened to many of the tapes; they are powerful and quite damaging. What is said on those tapes is shocking. They would not only finish you as President, but also as a husband and father-in law, and they would horrify the American people."

It suddenly had become more than Nixon could bear. His eyes filled with tears. He sat down on the couch, lowered his head, and sobbed openly.

"Mr. President," Jude said in the same deadly voice, "We know if those tapes are released, you will be impeached and subsequently tried, convicted, and jailed - an unprecedented disgrace. You will live in a world of enemies...no friends or family. Your private fortune will be exhausted. The Secret Service has orders to monitor your activities, so you will not even be allowed to commit suicide."

Kissinger spoke for the first time, with quiet emphasis - a familiar voice, one Nixon was accustomed to rely on. Kissinger said in his low accent, "The alternative, though harsh, is at least better than that, Mr. President. If you resign the presidency, you will be pardoned, so there will be no need of the tapes. The duplicate set will be destroyed; you can do with your set whatever you wish. You can leave the presidency with some kind of dignity. You can resign without destroying the office you held and served with such distinction. Many will say that you avoided a Constitutional crisis."

He paused. No one said a word.

Kissinger continued. "Mr. President, by re-signing, you will save yourself and the American people a tragic chapter in American history. And if you resign, you will be afforded the comforts, benefits, and security accorded any former President. You can live a life without financial worries. Your political friends and family, along with many other Americans, will rally to your support, once this unpleasant time is past. Mr. President, you can demonstrate that you chose the best for the American people over your own personal interests." Kissinger's faintly oratorical voice fell silent, letting the vision of peace and respect hang tangibly in the air.

Jude paced back and forth, waiting for his 'coup de grace'. He closed in for his kill. "Mr. President, you have a choice to make. If you fight, you will have no support. Everything you have worked and stood for will be destroyed. You will be impeached with the loss of everything - including your freedom. If you resign, a comfortable and interesting life lies ahead for you, Mr. President. You're reputed to be a fine poker player. I understand that you made a small fortune that way in your younger days as a naval officer. In the world of politics, you played your cards quite well, and your accomplishments show that."

Jude walked over to the couch, and sat next to Nixon, seeming to comfort him. Jude said quietly, but deliberately, "But, Mr. President...I must tell you. You've been playing with a marked deck ever since your job at Pepsi Cola. You were given certain cards and you played them well. But the cards were marked, the game was rigged, and the game is over now. It's time to take your remaining chips and leave gracefully, or lose what chips you have left and be carried out and disgraced in public."

Jude waited a few moments and continued. "The explanation you can leave with is that you were unjustly persecuted and hounded by the news media, and they took unfair advantage of you. It will be difficult for a year or two, but gradually your image and reputation will improve. Gala has arranged to have that charming young blond, Diane Sawyer, to remain with you, to help in writing your memoirs. She's very smart, a Wellesley graduate, and law student. She'll help polish up your image. The American people will gradually take notice with a more balanced view. Your achievements in foreign policy will be appreciated at their true value and, in ten years or so you will be considered a virtuous senior statesman, respected throughout the world. But that can happen only if you resign."

Nixon was staring at Gala. "I can't believe it. You were against me from the beginning?"

"I was never against you, but I was hired to do a difficult job. Part of it I enjoyed a great deal and overall, it was a wonderful experience. As President, you often ordered men into battle, putting many lives in jeopardy. I know it was difficult for you, and you did it time after time. This assignment was difficult for me, and I did it. But, my part is finished. And now, I suggest that we both leave with as little pain as possible," Gala said, almost reaching toward him and controlling the gesture.

"And loyalties...at least I thought you were, ah... never mind," Nixon said harshly, looking from one to the other.

"No, Mr. President," Kissinger said with heavy conviction. "Our true loyalties are unchanged. But as Miss Dufante said, the present situation is finished. We enjoyed working in this administration. These are regrettable circumstances we find ourselves in, but it is time to move on. We need a decision from you."

"Then it was you. You were the card-dealer who set this thing up," Nixon said, turning toward Jude. "But why? What have I ever done to you?"

"You have given me the most entertaining game in the world. But, the game is over - you might say, checkmate. Do you resign or do I release the duplicate tapes in the morning?"

Nixon looked at Gala, then Kissinger, hoping against hope, looking for a spark of loyalty. Gala nodded her head slowly, and Kissinger said, "It's time, Mr. President."

Slowly Nixon nodded, choked, and began again to sob. Brokenly, he said, "Henry, please make the arrangements. I'll resign tomorrow. I must go upstairs and tell my family of my decision."

The nation, and the world, watched the President give a teary-eyed final farewell to the White House staff. For the first time in American history, a President had resigned. The office was not vacant for a minute, when on August 9, 1974 Richard M. Nixon's resignation took effect at 12 P.M. While flying on Air Force One to California. At the same time, in the east room of the White House, Gerald Ford took the oath of office as President of the United States. Chief Justice Warren Burger administrated the oath. Continuity had been maintained, even in this most difficult of Constitutional crises. This was the first time in American history, a sitting President resigned his office, and for the first time in American history, the new President was not even elected as President or Vice President, but appointed through the implementation of the Twenty-fifth amendment. This President was appointed to the office, and so would be the next Vice President. Jude was quite pleased with this classic chess move, '*Capablanca-Tartakower*'.

In Washington and the rest of the world, there was a collective sigh of relief. The American public had had enough of what some people called "interesting times." They were ready for a harmless, slightly oafish, domestic President who, in the morning, made his own toast and coffee. He carried his own luggage and, now and again, might stumble and fall. But he was likeable and trustworthy, and that's what the country wanted - and needed.

CHAPTER 23

Opinions about how Nixon should be treated were mixed and intense. Not all Americans were pleased to accept Nixon's resignation and let it go at that. Some people wanted the former President imprisoned, while some felt he had been punished enough. Everyone was confused as to how he should be regarded. He was the only living former President.

The two unofficial caretakers, and the new President, met privately, shortly after Ford's swearing-in ceremony in the Oval Office. Kissinger and General Haig had a great deal of influence with the new President. Gerald Ford, like everyone else, had mixed attitudes toward Nixon, and was also concerned with his own image as President. The meeting seemed uncomfortable at first, for all three men. Ford sat behind the desk

- Nixon's old desk. Things happened so quickly that Ford's personal desk had not yet arrived.

The new President immediately took command. "Gentlemen," Ford said, "I asked you here to discuss the overall, current, situation we face from an international and domestic standpoint. I need your input. So feel free to speak openly."

Kissinger spoke first. "Mr. President, from an international viewpoint, it is of utmost importance we have a Chief Executive who is above reproach - strong but not too harsh. The State Department has everything under control. We can meet later and discuss the situation country by country. The international community is looking to see what kind of President you will be. The international community is watching how you'll handle the Nixon situation, and whom you will appoint as Vice President. These two items will be high profile and will be criticized no matter what you do. But I suggest you come out of the gate strong, clean, and fast to establish your image as a decision maker - a true, unmistakable leader."

"I agree, Doctor Kissinger, please continue," said President Ford.

"I believe that, as quickly as possible, we should vaporize this lingering cloud of Watergate from the White House. I believe this government will not really start attending to its present business until that painful chapter of our history is shut. Therefore, I believe a presidential pardon should be given to former President Nixon. His resignation has rendered the impeachment proceedings moot. However, a prolonged criminal investigation and courtroom trauma could be a terrible distraction to the American public and devastating to our international image. Not to mention all the information disclosed at an open trial." Kissinger paused, frowning, and continued. "There are enough people already prosecuted and in jail. Old wounds should be allowed to heal, and all matters relating to Watergate, the resignation, and the whole sordid affair should be put behind us. Mr. President, the most plausible means of getting back to some kind of a normal operating government is quick decisive action on this matter."

Ford looked at General Haig, and asked, "General Haig, what do you think?"

"Mr. President, I'm a soldier, not a politician, so my viewpoint may differ in substance, but in reality, it is similar to Doctor Kissinger's. I look at President Nixon as a defeated soldier. Even in Roman times, defeated enemy commanders were treated with dignity and allowed to keep their honor and state. As a military officer, we treat captured enemy officers with respect. We must keep in mind; after all, that Richard Nixon is a former President. For your own dignity, sir, I believe it would demonstrate your high character as President to issue a pardon. This would avoid prolonged unfavorable press, and would help to restore prestige to the office of the presidency."

"Thank you, gentlemen, for your opinions," President Ford said, as he digested the suggestions.

"Very well put - a persuasive argument. But I believe there would be a public outcry. You've seen the nightly news. Those folks want jail time for Nixon, not a pardon." He paused, thinking. No one said a word for a few moments, and then Ford continued. "I believe as you do: I can't see prolonging this ordeal any longer than necessary. But, if I pardon him, there will be hell to pay."

"Mr. President, may I point out," Kissinger said quietly, "that you are within your rights as President to pardon anyone. You can do it with the stroke of a pen, and the cloud of mystery would dissipate quickly. Some may object, but no one could challenge it. I'm sure it may be unpopular for some time, and there are those who will never forget. But I believe that now we have to concern ourselves with governing the future of this great country."

Ford barked a short, laugh. "You're both right. We have to start thinking of what's good for the country. I'll tell you right now that I am more concerned with getting this administration back on track and doing what we are paid to do, than about how we stand in the popularity polls. I think it's necessary. So, unless there are some powerful reasons against it, that haven't yet been voiced, I'll grant the pardon."

With a voice of authority, President Ford said, "I'll have the Attorney General get to work on granting the pardon. Now, about filling the vacancy of the vice presidency, what are your thoughts?"

"Mr. President, the choice must be yours, of course," Kissinger started. "So many politicians are associated with these scandals just by being part of the establishment that it brings its own aroma of suspicion. However, I would suggest you nominate someone who is outside the Washington political arena - someone with no taint of Watergate. I do believe you should appoint a person who has an outstanding reputation, and who is well-known internationally."

General Haig piped in. "Mr. President, I find myself in full agreement with Doctor Kissinger's assessment. I would only add that your vice president should be an able administrator, considering the current disarray in the Executive Branch. Given the fact that, however prominent you've been in the Congress, you've not been much in the public limelight, from an international standpoint. I'd suggest someone with an outstanding international reputation. This would help to strengthen the image of the administration, and would impress our allies and enemies as well."

"I begin to think that you gentlemen are way ahead of me. Do you have someone in particular in mind?" the President asked.

"As I said earlier, Mr. President, the choice is yours," Kissinger said, then paused. "However, we must consider the image we wish to establish. It was inevitable that the General and I should have discussed the matter. And, my personal preferences aside, I would seriously recommend for your consideration, Governor Rockefeller of

New York. He's certainly well known, viewed as a strong leader, and has international experience. He's a capable businessman, which should endear him to the Republicans. He's not associated with the Washington political establishment, once considered a handicap, now a virtue. He's been a popular Governor - elected four times in turbulent New York. And last year, he retired from public office. So he would not have competing political goals. I think he's the best available choice for this unique situation."

Ford sat thinking for a moment, then asked, "Doctor Kissinger, you know him as well as anyone. Do you think he'd take the job as Vice President? I know he's refused it before."

"Mr. President," Kissinger replied, "the governor understands the meaning of public service, and the country needs him now. I believe he would accept. Certainly, I would do everything in my power to convince him to accept. And now that the twin towers are complete, he and his brother David will have spare time on their hands." Kissinger chuckled, "It's officially called the World Trade Center, but the joke around New York is that the towers are called David and Nelson."

"General Haig?" the President asked quietly.

"All things considered, Mr. President, I believe Governor Rockefeller is the best choice," Haig answered.

"All right." Ford thought for a moment. "Then Doctor Kissinger, consider yourself a committee of one. Talk to him and report back to me as quickly as possible."

"Yes, Mr. President. I'll call him shortly and let you know."

There were a few insignificant items discussed before the meeting broke up.

For over a year, the Rockefeller staff polished and enhanced the Governor's image. Since he retired as Governor of New York, his sole attention was to make certain his background would meet the scrutiny of a critical Senate confirmation committee. He wanted to be as clean as a Papal candidate. He was prepared for a grueling Congressional examination on his nomination for the vice presidency. It had often been said, in public and in private, that he had an abrasive personality; many people on the confirmation panel were no friends of his. But after three days of questions and cross-questions on the minutest aspects of his life - public, political, and private - the only focus committee members could seem to find to fume about was that he apparently enjoyed giving away money. Rockefeller testified he was the one who had convinced the Harvard University professor, Dr. Kissinger, to join the Nixon administration. It was brought to light that even the Secretary of State had been the beneficiary of some of Rockefeller's many monetary grants.

But no ulterior motive could be suggested or documented.

The fact that one of the richest men in the world enjoyed giving away a relatively modest sum of money was no impediment to his becoming vice president of the United States. Still, the committee subjected Governor Rockefeller to three days of testimony before granting his appointment as vice president. It was the right game plan to have happy-faced Gerry Ford run the nomination gauntlet first. There were no legal challenges.

President Ford made good on his promise to pardon former President Nixon. Although the action caused an immediate outcry, relief, and a kind of exhaustion, it quickly smothered the flame. It seemed the people had had enough of scandals. All the Watergate criminals were either in jail, out of jail having served their time, or, like ex-President Nixon, pardoned. The long tribulation was over. Americans hated to admit they voted for "a crook" as President.

Some people's faith in politicians had changed forever. There were still problems - Vietnam, and the gasoline shortages, but the soap opera of Watergate no longer dominated the news media.

A kind of weariness continued to permeate the nation, up until the time of an assassination attempt on President Ford in California. Although three shots were fired, none hit the President. The news was reported with an odd calm. The would-be assassin was a loner, like the man who'd shot George Wallace. The one difference was the fact that the women's movement was making progress; this was the first attempt to assassinate a President by a woman - Lynette "Squeaky" Fromme, a follower of Charles Manson. She had a history of mental illness, and drugs were a large part of her life. There was no appearance of conspiracy, just an isolated nutcase. Since Ford had escaped unharmed, the matter was quickly shuffled through the criminal legal system.

The second assassination attempt was 17 days later: practically a replay of the first. Again it was a young woman. Her name was Sara Jane Moore. She was the picture of mental instability with a drug-induced personality. She fired three shots at President Ford as he left the St. Francis Hotel in San Francisco. One bullet ricocheted off a wall and wounded a bystander before the shooter was subdued. There was no great show of public or media concern. The culprit, quickly seized, was mentally unbalanced, on drugs, and without political associations. There was no mystery, just another one of California's plentiful supply of violence-prone peaceniks.

The third attempt would be the charm.

Jude sat at his desk in New York late one afternoon, half listening to the radio while filling in the zeroes of a doodled figure - $10,000,000. He expected to have fully earned it within a matter of days. Now it was only a matter of one last move

- checkmate, and the game was over. Everything was taken care of; he had paid off all the key players. He was reminiscing on how each was chosen to execute his or her role, and how well they had all succeeded. There were many heart-throbbing episodes not recorded here. He had years of planning coming into fruition. History would be changed, and Jude would be free to disappear and go wherever he wanted and do whatever he wanted. He smiled, and drew an arrow on the dollar sign.

The secure line rang, interrupting these pleasant musings. He knew the raspy voice at once: the Vice President of the United States, Nelson Rockefeller.

"Hello Jude, this is Nelson." There was a pause for a moment. "Can you hear me all right?"

Jude replied quickly, "Yes, Mr. Vice President. I can hear you fine."

"Good, Jude. I've sent a message to our snake friend, calling off our deal. I wanted you to know and understand. Of course I will pay you the figure we agreed to, as if it were a completed deal."

Jude mumbled something incoherent.

Rockefeller said cheerfully, "Good, that's settled. Now, I'll be in my New York office at Rockefeller Center tomorrow. I'd like to talk to you then. We have a few things to settle, like signing a check. Can I expect you to be there about noontime?"

Jude, still in shock, managed to reply something vaguely positive. "Yes, I'll be there at noon tomorrow." He found himself holding a dead receiver.

His mind raced. Rockefeller was going to renege. Why would he change his mind, after years of setting this up? Maybe he hadn't called Lancehead at all. Once Rockefeller became President, Jude would know too much. This development caused some unrest for Jude. This was the one contingency he hadn't planned against. Was Rocky going to get rid of Jude and save $10,000,000? Jude thought it over for a moment. No, it wasn't Rocky's style. One thing Jude understood, given Rockefeller's international reach and power, you could run but you couldn't hide from the long arm of his organization. A face-to-face meeting was just as safe as any other thing Jude could think of. All things considered, Rocky did take care of those who worked for him - Kissinger, Mitchell, and others, including some caught up in Watergate. Well, no matter what, he had to make the meeting - to be paid if nothing else.

The following day, the limousine rolled up in front of Rockefeller Center. When Jude stepped out he took a few moments to take in the sights, and to contemplate his upcoming meeting. Rockefeller Center was an impressive complex, consisting of 19 commercial buildings, covering 11 acres. The buildings were constructed during the Roaring Twenties, and were in the Art Deco style. Jude had a lot on his mind as he looked around at the essence of wealth and power.

Jude put away the whirl of conjecture. He had plans and counter plans which had bedeviled him through a long and largely sleepless night. Entering the office complex, he reflected on what he had once said to Nixon: "It had been an interesting game."

Security passed him through and he went up the private elevator to the seventieth floor. It would be only the second time he'd meet Rockefeller in person. If anything, he was more nervous now than when, as Henry Kissinger's protégé, he'd first blurted out his idea. He was pleased with his reward of crisp hundred dollar bills. He had changed the world, and few would know of his input.

An attractive and professional-looking woman met him as the elevator doors opened. She smiled and said, "This way, please, Mr. Thaddeus. My name is Judy Taft. Have you been here before?"

"As a matter of fact, no. This is my first visit. Quite impressive." Although he felt uncomfortable, he was standing on very thick and comfortable carpet. The reception area was a large, lightly paneled room with two reception desks. Throughout the sanctum artwork was precisely placed on the walls, furniture, and on the floor. Jude was impressed by what he saw.

"We usually give a little tour for the VIP visitors, but the Vice President is waiting for you in his inner office. After your meeting, if you'd like, I'll be happy to give you a tour. The vista is very nice, and we have a nice view of the new World Trade Center."

She was leading him through corridors of offices: closed doors with brass numbers, some with nameplates. One section had a glass partition. Loud voices were heard, speaking in different languages, and motion beyond, reminding Jude that this was, after all, a working office. It was an atmosphere of continual bustling, with deals being made at virtually every point on the earth. The sound of typewriters and telexes faded when they reached the far end of the floor. Miss Taft tapped lightly on a large oak door. It opened on the second knock - either electrically or by magic. Whichever, it was impressive.

Jude entered the room not knowing what to expect. Rockefeller was behind his desk doing some paperwork. He was alone, signing papers with a determined, mechanical scribble. Shoving aside the last, he looked up and greeted Jude with a broad smile.

Rocky walked around from behind his desk and extended his hand, with his signature ear-to-ear smile. "Jude, I'm glad to see you. May I get you anything? A drink...or perhaps fine cigar?" He pointed to the large couch at the far end of the office. "Sit down and let's visit for a few minutes."

Jude settled in on the leather couch, hands tightly clasped between his knees. "We were so close, Mr. Vice President." He said no more - he wanted to hear an explanation.

Rockefeller sat in a leather chair next to Jude. He now had a look of determination on his face. "Jude, I'm glad to see you and I expect you're looking for a clarification of my call yesterday."

Jude listened without moving a muscle.

"Well, I had thought about just ending it and letting it go at that. Maybe just sending you a note," remarked Rockefeller, leaning back in his large chair. "But you put a lot into this project and you've done a good job...a remarkable job! Until the swearing-in ceremony, I never really believed it was possible. Though it was fun to watch how you got rid of that bastard Nixon - something for which a grateful nation should decorate us both." Again, Rockefeller grinned, apparently as completely relaxed and cheerful as a well-fed shark. "But I've got to hand it to you...you delivered. Henry was right; I was wrong. And now I have within my reach what I always wanted: the presidency. And who knows? Maybe something of a divine nature could happen and I still may become president. But I will leave that to fate."

Jude was nervous, but broke his silence. "After all the planning and expense, not to mention the hardship put on some of your own people, this is a little hard to understand." He had to catch himself. He didn't want to criticize his paymaster before the check was written.

"Let me try to explain, Jude." Nelson paused thoughtfully, and proceeded calmly. "I began to wonder: is it worth it? It's one thing to unseat a man like Nixon, or to keep a nut like McGovern from being elected. That's a civic duty. But taking out Gerald Ford, who's a decent enough person...Well that had me losing sleep. And I am at a time of life when sleep is important. Doctors tell me my heart isn't in the best condition and that I don't have a lot of time left. That leads me to another consideration; the presidency wears men out. We both know it is a very strenuous job. As far as power and the prestige goes...as you have witnessed yourself, I have a lot more power and influence than anyone ever could imagine and I don't have to answer to Congress. Anyway, I have so much in life to enjoy, and too little time to enjoy it."

Rockefeller paused, got up, and walked to his phone. "Please bring in the bottles of champagne." He turned to Jude. "I took the liberty of ordering a few drinks to celebrate our accomplishments."

Nelson returned to his chair and began to speak again. "Now, the game of chess, is your passion of life isn't it Jude? After all, it is with the strategy of a master chess player that you designed the overall plan, right? When the board is cleared, and there are no defenders left, the king is there for the taking...or checkmate. That's the end of the game. It may be difficult for you to understand, but..."

In walked a tall redhead with a perfectly shaped figure - beautifully attired, quietly self-controlled, and graceful as a cat. She carried a tray with glasses and two bottles of spirits. Saying nothing, she laid a hand softly on Rockefeller's shoulder as she put the tray on the coffee table. "Will there be anything else, gentlemen?" she asked, while glancing over towards Jude with her turquoise eyes.

"Thank you, Megan, dear, that's all for now. I'll be with you in a little while." Rockefeller smiled as he spoke to her, and then turned to Jude with a more serious look.

"I hope you like champagne. This is Louis Roederer, Crystal 1913 . A champagne which is very rare, with quite a unique taste. This was the last vintage before the First World War. I hope you enjoy it." Rockefeller then poured two glasses of the pure, white, bubbly drink.

"To success," Jude toasted.

"To success, indeed!" Rockefeller responded. Both men drank the champagne. Rockefeller spoke again. "Jude, you may be interested in this other bottle on the table. It is a Napoleon Reserva Cognac, 1802. It is the finest bottle in my extensive wine collection. It belonged to my father. It was the pride of his collection. It remains a very valuable bottle because it has not been opened. Once it has been opened, in time the air will ruin its flavor and it will become worthless. I have had this bottle my entire adult life. I have been waiting for the right occasion to open it. This may sound odd, but the presidency is, in a symbolic way, similar to this bottle of cognac. Once it is opened it starts to deteriorate in flavor and value. I believe there's more importance in life by not getting everything we want. If I became president, almost my all of my whims of life would have been satisfied. If we are granted everything in life, somehow we lose appreciation of life, and then we begin to deteriorate. If I became president I'd have nothing more in life to strive for in life. So I decided to keep life interesting and challenging, so you might say, I'd like to keep the cork in the bottle and see what happens. So I have decided not to open this bottle of cognac, nor to make the final move to attain my lifetime goal to be President."

Jude sat quietly, he seemed to be baffled. "I somewhat understand, although it is a little confusing."

"Well, look at it this way," Rocky responded, in his raspy voice, "if I achieve every goal in life, then my life becomes less interesting - because it means I control everything. I know I don't control everything; I know I'm not going to live forever. So I'm letting fate be my master. If I were really meant to be president, I will be president. It means that life will remain a mystery to me. The bottle will remain unopened. I have had everything in life I've ever wanted. After being in Washington, and working with Gerry Ford, I began to see that the office of president isn't such a glamorous job after all. I see the President bowing to politicians, Congress, the State Department, and the news media. He has to live in the spotlight - every move evaluated and criticized. It's not my way. I informed President Ford yesterday that I am retiring from public life and I will not be his running mate in November. Me not being on the ticket and the Nixon pardon may cost him the election, but I guess it doesn't matter now."

Rocky got up and walked a few steps, turned toward Jude, and spoke again. "This may sound strange, but let me put it this way. It's as if I purchased a racecar for the Indianapolis five hundred. The biggest thrill of race day is the very beginning - when the engines come alive in a thunderous roar. Well Jude, you arranged for me to be in the second row. I can hear the race track announcer yell, *Gentlemen - start your engines!* - But I don't want to race. I would rather drive to the pits and party.

"Let me freshen up your champagne, Jude," Rocky said, as if he were still thinking of what to say.

"You're the boss," Jude said in a troubled voice. "Mr. Vice President, I serve at your pleasure. You might say you're in the driver's seat... and it seems my services are no longer required."

"You're right, Jude," Rockefeller said sadly. "Now, about our deal. I believe ten million was the figure we agreed upon. Because I'm bowing out, that's no fault of yours. You did a superb job. So I decided to give you an additional ten million dollars as a bonus. The profit on your oil program more than paid for the whole deal. And you can keep the Wall Street brokerage company to play with anyway you want. You know, it's worth twenty million just to know I'm only a heartbeat away from being president of the United States. Not many people can ever say that."

"No sir, that's true. It was a remarkable chain of events that made it all possible." Jude took a large sip of his champagne, and then added, "I appreciate your explaining to me your feelings about stepping aside to see what happens. I mean I hope you really know what you're doing...I mean about passing..."

Before Jude could finish his statement the redhead reappeared. "How are you gentlemen doing?" she asked as she entered the room. Both men followed her with their eyes as she walked slowly toward them. "Would you like some more champagne?"

"Megan, dear, will you pour Jude a little more champagne? We have another toast," Rocky said, turning to Jude. "By the end of business hours today, the money we discussed will be wire-transferred to your checking account at the brokerage firm."

The redhead picked up Jude's glass and started pouring gracefully. As Jude watched, he noticed that she was not interested in the champagne... rather odd, he thought. She looked like the type to fight over golden bubbly. He suddenly had a chilling thought – *I do know a lot, maybe too much? Pre-administered antidotes and poisons unknown to science, was this one of the tricks of Lancehead? No everything is fine, the game is now over.*

Jude lifted his glass to make a toast with a voice of confidence saying, "Mr. Vice President, to your long and enjoyable life."

"Thank you, Jude. I expect to enjoy all the time I have. And I trust you'll enjoy your new lifestyle. I trust you understand this relationship we've had is now over. From now on, you will run your business independently and distantly from ours." Rocky smiled at Megan, and took her hand. "Now I must get to work - enjoying my art collection and some of the finer and 'funner' things in life."

"Goodbye, Mr. Vice President," Jude said as he got up to leave. "It was a pleasure working with you and your organization. We did make some history, and played quite a game of chess."

"Yes we did, Jude," Rocky said. Then, almost as an afterthought, said, "And thank you for all you have done. It was a great game. It was re-markable...but no one would believe it."

Jude shook his hand and departed. He was down the elevator in a few minutes. It was a beautiful day, so he decided to walk back to his office. He was in high spirits. He was pleased with his morning so far, twenty million to be deposited in his bank account. He had his brokerage firm with some very interesting contacts, nationally and internationally, which would bear future cultivation, in the ordinary way of doing business.

Jude started walking briskly toward 5th Ave. He was very happy and a little cocky, smiling at people as they passed by, and thinking pleasantly, "I've done it, oh how I love the game of chess. Using the right strategy, I was able to pull off the greatest chess maneuvers and changed history;

it was so well crafted no one even realizes what happened. Ah, Frank Marshall must be smiling down at me now. Yes Frank, I enjoyed your book and it was quite a swindle wasn't it, right to the very end? He wondered if Gala would be free for a late afternoon lunch."

Suddenly, he was starting to feel fuzzy. The champagne was stronger than any he had ever had...or was there something in it? His eyes became blurry, his head started to pound. His fear swelled as he thought of the sweet champagne: what was in it? A quote from the chess master Tartakower screamed in Jude's brain. "Victory goes to the player who makes the next-to-last mistake."

He's head started to spin as he began to stagger and stumble.

A policeman standing on Rockefeller Plaza yelled out, "Stand back... he looks like he's on drugs or he could be crazy."

Jude's vision became blurred and the last thing he remembered was the sidewalk rushing toward his face.

The End
Of Jude's Sanity

63111866R00235